SUPAPODIA

SUPAPODIA

DARKNESS AND LIGHT

JOHN AUBIN

© John Aubin 2020

Published by John Aubin Books

A CIP catalogue record for this book is available from the British Library.

ISBN 978-0-9933425-2-3 (Paperback)
ISBN 978-0-9933425-8-5 (ePub)
ISBN 978-0-9933425-9-2 (Mobi)

Book layout and design by Clare Brayshaw

Cover design: Black Swan Book Promotion (blackswanbookpromotion.co.uk)

Prepared and printed by:

York Publishing Services Ltd
64 Hallfield Road
Layerthorpe
York
YO31 7ZQ

Tel: 01904 431213

Website: www.yps-publishing.co.uk

'Still falls the Rain
At the feet of the Starved Man hung upon the Cross,
Christ that each day, each night, nails there,
          have mercy on us…'

                              Edith Sitwell, *Still Falls the Rain*

'The time is out of joint – O cursèd spite,
That ever I was born to set it right!'

                    William Shakespeare, *Hamlet Act.1 Scene 5*

CONTENTS

1

Dead rain sleeting, the wind driving the ice, the grey fields bare, empty of life save for one ploughman bent double behind his steaming, stumbling horse.

Julian wiped at the misted glass. A broken bridge flashed by, a branch line leading to nowhere choked with growth; a tumbled shed, its red, rusted corrugated sides burst open; a row of houses, one without a roof, the stubby tower of a church with its pointed windows boarded up....

He turned away from the window. The bullet train flashed on unstoppable, the streaming silver flanks gleaming wetly, the small round portholes flaring light.

Too late now to change his mind. He was hurtling towards SupaPodia.

SupaPodia represented the future, of which at last he would be a part. No more stagnation in the crumbling past, where nothing worked any more and life was simply a struggle for survival; now he would be involved with modernity, in a place where the world was moving on and would take him with it.

"Julian?" a woman's voice said.

The voice held a ripple, like the music of a sunlit stream flowing over pebbles. Her short hair was black, her eyes dark and deep, her parted mouth two gashes of painted red. He didn't like the red. It had been a long time since he had seen a woman with a painted face.

"It is, Julian?"

"Yes." He struggled to his feet, extending an arm. "You know my name?"

She took his hand briefly. Her fingers felt like a trapped butterfly trying to escape.

"Of course. I've been expecting you."

"Oh, really. I didn't know. I haven't been told anything. Only that I was to get on this train." He laughed squeakily, his nerves taut.

He really knew so little. Just that he had won a competition against 10,000 others to join the staff of SupaPodia His few personal possessions had been forwarded ahead – to the address on the label he had been sent: 'SupaPod No. 16. Goodwins Bar. Ramsgate. Level 19 – 87/379. Julian F. Foster, Educator 2nd Grade."

"I'm Marion. I work in Education. I'm to be your Inculcator."

"My Inculcator? What is that?"

She smiled. "I'm going to show you what your job involves. I'm going to *inculcate* you into the life of SupaPodia. It's bound to be a culture shock for you at first, coming so late from the OuterWorld, but I'll help you all the way. You see, I'm to be your boss – yet, I very much hope, your friend as well."

In scarcely more than a generation, like some great swelling, voracious leech, SupaPodia had expanded to predominate in society, sucking wealth into itself so that very little remained Outside. Most people worked today – if they worked at all – to keep the SupaPodia monster satiated: that at least was what the cynics believed; as, indeed, had Julian before the sudden chance of working for SupaPodia had come to him.

"They pack 'em in there," one old man had told him in the White Horse – a rundown pub in his equally rundown home town. "Like peas in a pod, they are. That's why they call 'em pods".

"They does nothin' all day but lie there," said another. "Everythin' given 'em. Everythin' done for 'em. Even someone to wipe their arses for 'em."

"Makes you sick, don't it?" This from a younger man, wearing a ragged, torn coat and stained, shapeless trousers. "Never mind wiping their arses, I work mine off for virtually nothing that I can keep. Most of my bloody money goes to keep that lot going

"We're left in the shit!" a couple of voices shouted out, one supporting the other. "Everything's gone. No money for us now. No power, no communications, no transport. It's like the bleedin'…the bleedin'…."

"Dark ages!" That's what it is. "Civilisation has ended."

"But it's a way of looking after all those who don't have enough to live on and can't fend for themselves." The comment was made by a bespectacled man seated in a corner reading an old-fashioned book.

"What by making the rest of us poor and starving. What sort of crazy idea is that?"

"We should do something about it."

"Like what?"

"Rise up and take back what's ours: I mean our way of life, what we were, what's still there, just about, before the last of it goes down the pan."

"Perhaps the practice of SupaPodia is not yet perfect," admitted the man with the book. "But its ideals can't be disputed. A good fulfilling life for everyone – with security, shelter, and enjoyment. That has to be the way forward, surely. It's what all of us would wish for ourselves."

And, despite the hostile comments, the type of populist chatter you will always get amongst the poor and ignorant, most people left in the OuterWorld seemed to agree with him. They clamoured to be taken into the SupaPods. SupaPodia was popular. The SupaPods were now so full, available places were very limited, normally only filled as lottery prizes. The vicious circle turned. The SupaPods consumed everything, making those outside poorer and poorer. As life grew increasingly harsh, the only hope, the only escape, seemed to be a SupaPod. The wheel turned, and turned again. If you opted out of that circle, then life was grim and relentless, cold and hungry, but you kept your independence – for whatever that was worth. You could still die free if you insisted on it, but SupaPodia was the future now that most people wished. SupaPodia had become a dream world – a utopia – for those still stuck Outside.

On the SupaPodia Express, Marion was telling Julian about SupaPodia. Coming from her sweet lips, the SupaPods were as honey. And Julian, casting aside all the old, stale, ignorant stories he had heard, was prepared to suck at the honey and believe everything she said. The doubts he had felt before taking up his appointment at the Ramsgate SupaPod (the largest of the eighty or so SupaPods now in full service throughout Britain) were being dispelled as the beams of a rising sun penetrate the mists of long night.

"What you have to understand, Jules…" (this was the form of his name Marion began to use now: no one else had ever done so)… "and you must take this to heart right from the start, is that once you're part of SupaPodia, it's your home and no where else. You'll be allowed to go back to the OW – the OuterWorld, that is – from time to time, to see family and friends, and suchlike, who're still stuck there, or if you're sent on a refresher course about the OW, such as I've just been on, but that's about it. Oh – I nearly forgot – there's also the occasional trip out to an OW holiday camp for the deserving and long-serving, if that's your sort of thing. They can be rather boisterous, I've been told. Generally, though, SupaPodia is your new world now – your physical world and your inner world too; you should give it your very soul, not that I believe in souls as such, of course, at least not as those bygone religious nuts used to preach."

She broke off to nibble at a chocolate bar a train steward had brought her, nipping at it with perfect white teeth while looking at him full in the eyes. She offered the bar to him. He took a bite. The chocolate tasted sweet and sickly. He could not remember when he had last eaten chocolate.

"How long have you been with SupaPodia?" Julian asked.

"Oh, all my life. I was born into it. My parents were entrants when it first started up, way back in the '50s. I was brought up more by SupaPodia than by them."

"But that's terrible!" he exclaimed without thinking.

She gave him a sharp look. "Why do you say that? Of course it wasn't terrible. It's the way things happen now. For the best, too. Though, I admit I've been lucky. I've had the chance of seeing both worlds – the old and the new – and I tell you…." She placed her face close to his, so he felt intimidated by the closeness of her red lips. "….I very much prefer the life of SupaPodia, in particular as a staff member".

He felt he should not say any more, but something compelled him to ask, "Would you want to be one of the residents, one of the ordinary folk?"

"Residents? Folk? Oh, you mean Podders." She sounded a bit snappy now, leaning away from him, crossing her legs under the shiny, lilac-coloured uniform dress she wore. Pinned to her left breast was a badge reading 'Marion. Educator. Ask me anything'.

"Of course, I would," she added. "Anyone who's not shackled to the past longs to get into a SupaPod. Everything you might reasonably require – and much more beside – is catered for: there are no worries, no stresses…free food, free entertainment, free medical care. Life should be a pleasure, not an ordeal – and that's what we at SupaPodia aim to achieve. Who but an idiot would wish for any other life?"

"Do the residents – the Podders – do no work then?" Again he felt the need to ask, although he sensed the question might be controversial.

"Work? Of course, not. What is work but the need – the quest – for money? And what is money but a useless exchange? In SupaPodia you don't need it. There are some necessary chores, of course, for the Podders' own welfare, but little else. Most Podders, though, volunteer for extra activities – sports, games, singing, dancing, drama, any number of clubs and groups – discussion groups, welfare groups, keep fit groups, health groups, sex encounter groups, personal grooming classes, art classes, all that sort of stuff, some of it necessary, some perhaps more frivolous and tedious...." Her voice tailed off.

"Excuse me, Jules" she said "I'm going to have a rest now. One or two late nights, you know." And she took the seat next to his, leaning her dark head against his shoulder. Soon, from the tiny snores she was making, he knew she was asleep.

Like this, not daring to move unless he disturbed her, he spent the next ten minutes while the SupaPodia Express gobbled up the remaining miles through Kent into the Ramsgate Terminus (all change for SupaPod No.16).

2

"Greetings, Erich."

SupaPodia Commisioner Zara de Guinchy extended one long tanned arm towards Erich Hertzog and he dabbed his thick lips upon her fingers in the approved manner.

"Do you keep well, Erich?"

"Indeed, my dear, I do." He puffed out his white-fronted chest and led her towards the vast plate-glass picture window. From here on the 412th Floor of SupaPodia Tower No.3, high above the River Thames, there could be made out a glittering landscape of other tall buildings thrusting at the sky; they stretched away to the far horizon – glass-sided shapes of stars and crosses, crescents, pyramids, and slanting cylinders (the latter set with vast fins like space rockets about to streak skywards). SupaPodia had chosen London for the headquarters of the British division within its international empire.

They drank in the scene for a while, from time to time sipping at glasses of a delicate pink concoction brought to them by waitresses, who moved with their trays amongst the hundreds of other Eliti delegates of SupaPodia International (SPI). With their spouses, partners, secretaries and assistants, they filled the vast open floor. A hubbub of conversation rose to the high vaulted ceiling, lit by huge chandeliers cascading floorwards in streams of brilliant glass.

"And how fares SupaPodia in Germany?"

"We do well, Zara. Germany has sixty-three now, with a new *SupaHülse* opened just last month at Bremerhaven. It will become our largest. There are over a million of our people seeking a place, but it will take little more than a tenth of that figure at present. However, we have other *SupaHülse* well advanced. We are clearing our cities first, but after that some large tracts of countryside as well, so I can expect some fine hunting grounds before long."

"Ever the great hunter, Erich. Your Teuton blood, no doubt."

"Ja, mein Frau." He clicked his heels together, and raised his glass. "I will drink to it – the blast of the *Jagdhorn* and the cry of the hounds. And you, Zara, will you not come exploring my new forests with me this year?"

She laughed. "No, I thank you, Erich. My husband would not like it."

"He is not a hunting man?"

"He is a she, and we are much more concerned with preserving wildlife than killing it. We own estates in Northumberland close to one of our SupaPods at Speeton. There, we spend much time watching the seabirds and the sharks and dolphins too. The SupaPod's tidal generators affected them badly at first, but, I'm pleased to say, their numbers are recovering."

"That is *gut* indeed."

With a smile, Zara de Guinchy moved on to greet a lady in one of the high-waisted 'Jane Austen' gowns that were just coming back into fashion.

"Pamela. How lovely you're here."

"Why, Zara. How are you keeping? And Roberta?"

"Very well, thank you."

"And the Theatre?"

"It is now open on the cliffs above Eastbourne."

"Rupert and I must come. Is it difficult to find?"

"Our audiences usually come by air. The roads are so bad, don't you know. We have a landing place at Birling and it's only a short journey from there. The Romanian Commissioner, with his whole family, came by helidrone for our performance of 'A Mid Summer Night's Dream' last month. We were packed out."

"Such a lovely hobby for you, so much better than those dreadful – what do they call them? – 'live events', others are putting on. All Podder sex and violence, I'm told. And from where does your performing company come?"

"From the nearby SupaPod at Cuckmere Haven. There is a drama group there. They are really very good. A number of Podder performers have roots back to the old London theatres before they were forced to shut down. Talent survives in the genes, it seems."

"Talking about live events, you know Arnold Schellestein's parcelled up much of Somerset. He's taking over that Glastonbury Festival that was once so big and noisy and letting Podders out to attend."

"My God, there could be mayhem. Why can't they just stream it to the SupaPods the usual way?"

"Arnold's very much a Greenie. He talks of the benefits of real light and air for Podders."

"Well, be it on his own head if they end up running all over the landscape fighting with the locals."

"I don't think they'll be allowed out of the special trucks that'll take them there."

"Little point in the fresh air then!"

"Yes, you're probably right. But a few eccentrics like Arnold help us to seem to be doing the right thing for Podders."

"Mmm, perhaps. At least it's not football."

"No, all that's now streamed straight into the SupaPods. Many Podders, though, want to play and, I'm told, they make up some of the best teams these days. There's a new SupaPodia Premier League, I understand."

"Is there, indeed? Proves there's still active life in the SupaPods then!"

"Well, I must go, Zara. Keep up the good work. Shall we see you and Roberta in the Cape this summer? We're flying there for the next SPI Southern-Hemisphere convention. The High Director will be making one of his rare appearances, so we can expect a lot of toadying from some of the delegates. There should be plenty of playtime, though, as well."

"We'll be there for sure. Chow for now."

"Chow."

3

The scene at the terminus station looked to Julian like one of those archive films he had viewed at college as part of his history module of the last century, showing displaced people uprooted and made homeless by war, with their few pathetic belongings about them. The new entry Podders – the lucky ones – were pouring from the rear of the train, holding cases and bundles, some with babes in arms and children scrambling about their feet. A babble of noise – shouts and shrill calls and the wailing of infants – filled the domed roof of the station.

Julian closed his eyes, shaking his head, and suddenly the press was gone. He did not quite know where to, but it seemed to have been funnelled into a large entrance way beyond the platform, with walkways that moved endlessly downwards, as he dimly remembered from the underground stations of London before they had been closed.

He was standing now beside Marion, together with some others in the lilac uniforms of SupaPodia. A train, of one glass-sided cabin – the word SUPAPODIA, accompanied by a smiling face, etched repeatedly along the glass – had slid in silently on the far side of the platform, and this they now boarded. The cabin jolted forward, so suddenly that people grabbed for the straps hanging from the roof. Looking through the wide windows, between the bobbing heads and clutching hands, Julian saw a sudden view of the sea – just a fleeting glimpse of grey sky and rolling, white-flecked waters – before they plunged into a lighted tunnel which seemed to go on for ever.

Marion, who had been talking with a youngish man in a lilac blazer (his breast pocket embroidered with 'Head Educator' in a stylish flowing script) turned to Julian. "Jules. Meet Stanley. My boss, and yours too. After me, that is." She giggled. Julian did not quite know why.

He shook hands with Stanley, who had a slack, damp palm like a dead fish. When he spoke, his delivery was so quiet that Julian had to bend his head forward to hear. The words, though, poured out smoothly, like thick liquid from a jug.

"Welcome. I'm placing you, to start with, in Re-Education. Re-Education, as well as Ongoing Education, will be explained to you by Marion, who is responsible for your own education. Is that clear?"

Julian did not think it was, but he mumbled assent. Stanley continued, "Re-Education is a valued post here because it will place you between our two worlds – of the Inner (that is, of course SupaPodia) and the Outer (everything outside SupaPodia). It is a post much sought after by SupaPodia staff. You are fortunate, therefore, that there is a current vacancy to be filled from the OuterWorld. It does not…"

He halted in mid-sentence, and Julian stood looking at him. Stanley's eyes seemed far away as if he was in deepest thought. Beyond him, Julian could see the tunnel walls, brilliantly lit, flashing by.

"…does not happen very often." Marion supplied the missing words.

"No, it doesn't." Stanley was back. "So you're lucky, er-Julian. Very lucky." His head fell forward. "Hell, I'm tired".

"Have a rest," Marion said. "Here, lean against me."

The cabin raced on down the interminable tunnel while, to Julian's astonishment, Stanley stood against Marion, his head held by her between her breasts. No one else of the lilac-wearing company seemed to pay them any attention.

Marion looked across at Julian. "Poor dear, he's been working so hard. We all go through patches like this."

Oh God, thought Julian, calling upon a deity he did not believe in. What on earth – this earth, or some other – am I coming into?

When the cabin at last stopped and its two doors fluttered open, Julian saw that they were positioned on a vast concrete platform open to the air, framed at its far side by the wrinkled grey-green of the sea, and, behind, by a line of high white cliffs curving away until veiled by billowing grey mist. Crowds of seabirds wheeled above them, some gulls swooping to flutter against the cabin and peck at the glass.

"Keep your arms over your head when you get out," Marion hissed in his ear. "And watch your eyes. It's only a short walk." She had released Stanley, who seemed able now to stand by himself and was giving Julian a weak smile. "Sorry. I felt ill for a moment. Much better now."

Marion's breast therapy must work then, thought Julian, his brain in a whirl.

No bird pecked at Julian's head as he stepped behind Marion the few paces to the sliding doors of a flat-fronted building with a sign above its entrance, SUPAPOD 16 STAFF PORTAL. As he entered, another sign caught his eye. It was a large framed poster fixed to a pillar: in the foreground, a land in darkness, with tall smoking chimneys and huddled houses upon which bright rays labelled SUPAPODIA shone, lighting up distant green spaces filled with ecstatic, dancing people, and underneath in a violent red, HERE SUPAPODIA BEGINS. MAKE SURE YOU LEAVE THE OUTERWORLD BEHIND.

* * *

Julian had changed out of his old clothes – he had thought as he took them off they looked really shabby and were a bit smelly – for a fresh, scented lilac shirt, lilac slacks and a lilac blazer (a slighter deeper lilac) just like Stanley's. The clothes had been ready for him on a peg in a large square room. The peg had his name above it in black letters. The SupaPod must have received the measurements he had forwarded to SupaPodia Staff Recruitment because the clothes fitted perfectly. Two other staff entrants opposite – he had not seen them earlier but they were obviously new too – were also getting changed, one a rather tubby youngish man and the other a slim girl with sort-cut blonde hair. They seemed to know each other. There was no provision for privacy. The man was red in the face, whether with effort or embarrassment was not clear. He surrendered his grey flannel shirt and baggy trousers to a vacuum hatch that sucked them away in a flash while pulling a one-piece lilac tunic over his head.

"Say, how is it you get to wear trousers while I have this bloody skirt?" he called out to Julian.

"What are you in?" Julian asked.

"In? I'm a doctor. So Medicine, I guess. And you?"

"Education."

"Ah, same as Tina then."

He indicated the girl beside him, who had her back to the room at that moment and was wriggling into a narrow lilac-coloured dress with a high neckline and long sleeves. Her skin was nicely tanned, Julian noticed, cut by the briefest of white underwear. She seemed entirely unselfconscious.

She turned and held out a small hand to Julian. "Tina. Short for Christine. You're in Education then. What grade?"

"Two."

"I'm only a Three. Perhaps I'll be under you?"

The unintentional double-meaning distracted him. It had been some time since he had known a woman.

"I'm Julian."

"And I'm Peter," the other man said. They all shook hands formally, which seemed rather strange to Julian under these new, bizarre circumstances.

"Do you know anyone else here?" asked Peter, "Tina and I met up coming in."

"No, no one," answered Julian, who was glad he had now made a couple of contacts.

Marion came into the room. She looked pert and alert; that nap on the train had evidently done her good.

"All ready? Good. All old clothes down the shoots, please. Make sure there's nothing in the pockets as they go straight to the incinerator."

Julian hurriedly collected a pen and wallet from his jacket, before allowing the suction of the shoot nearest to him to take it away.

"Shit!" Peter cried out. "I forgot my money belt was in my trousers."

"You won't need money here."

"It had my phone too."

"Outside phones aren't allowed either. Weren't you told that?"

"No!."

"So, you've lost nothing. Remember the OuterWorld ends here. Now, the three of you, come with me."

An elevator, the size of a squash court, took them deep down into the Cretaceous Chalk beneath the Goodwin Sands The SupaPod was like a gigantic ants' nest, with Level after Level (148 in total, to be precise), each with its Sub-Floors of accommodation stacks, recreation courts, kitchens and sustenance halls, education rooms and medical wards, connected by a network of corridors, passages, tunnels, shafts, and pipes, in a sunken silo a half mile in diameter and bored to a depth almost as great, following a pattern of construction now approved worldwide by SupaPodia International.

The lift gave out no feeling of movement. However, buttons were flashing brightly on a console beside Marion's arm. Julian tried to adopt an air of nonchalance. Peter looked tense and a little ridiculous, with his bare hairy legs projecting from the tunic (fortunately the temperature stayed a constant warmth), but Tina, in her figure-hugging dress seemed perfectly relaxed. He decided to emulate her, and bit back the questions he wished to direct at Marion.

The flicker of lights in the console suddenly stilled, and there was a loud pinging noise as the doors slid open. They came out into an open hallway, lit brightly by overhead lights, and then passed through large wooden doors at one end into what – to Julian's sudden surprise – was an auditorium with curving rows of plush, purple seats, many of which were already filled with lilac-clad individuals. As they entered, music sounded out – some bars of a strident trumpet fanfare, followed immediately by a soothing melody that, to Julian, seemed to flow like the sea waters that were presumably scores, if not hundreds, of yards above their heads.

Clapping broke out around the auditorium, and Julian saw that Marion was clapping too, then Tina and Peter as well, and he realised he must do the same, so all four of them were clapping as Marion led them to seats at the very front before the stage. Here was another surprise, for with legs astride on the boards above stood Stanley, he whose weariness had so recently been soothed between Marion's soft breasts.

Stanley, however, was now greatly changed, fully charged it seemed, with flashing white teeth and glistening hair, his arms raised high. "Welcome! Welcome! To the three new staff of our beloved SupaPod 16. Gentlemen and lady, meet some of your SupaPodia family. To you, Peter, Julian, and Christine, we fellow Lilacs say a very big Hi."

"Hi, Hi, Hi…" sounded around the room, while, at a nudge from Marion, the three of them stood smiling, circling their bodies and clapping their hands above their heads, all the time calling back "Hi" – not an expression, Julian thought, he had ever used before.

At last, with a wave of his hand, Stanley silenced the audience. Julian found himself pushed back into the soft comfort of his seat by Marion, who sat herself beside him. "Stanley's going to give his talk," she whispered into his ear. "He's a whizz at it. He gives it once a week to pep up his staff. It's great for you newees; just what you need."

The darkness behind Stanley resolved itself into a great curving Screen upon which words began to leap and flow – SUPAPODIA. IN CASE YOU SHOULD FORGET WHY WE'RE HERE, LET US REMIND YOU WHAT HUMANITY USED TO ENDURE…. The huge words, flaring fire, trailed off into blackness. They were replaced by a series of images of the OuterWorld that had been, and, to a degree, still was, beyond the reach of the SupaPods. Stanley spoke, his treacly voice amplified by a microphone.

"Remember…Remember…perhaps some of you don't because you've never lived Outside. You're the lucky ones. See…" [a picture of a bombed city somewhere from some long past war] "…devastation, destruction, disease, death…" [pictures of dead bodies, of the emaciated and injured, of crying children, a dead baby stuck with a bayonet] "… such things as these represent the very worst of the old OuterWorld, but look at more ordinary, common things too…" [more pictures, of smoking, stalled traffic, of a train crash, of crowded shopping malls, of people squabbling over boxes of goods, of fighting youths, of prostitutes in short dresses, smoking – the last brought a ripple of laughter from the audience] "…and these too…" [shots inside an old peoples' home, of elderly people sitting alone in rags, of staring, mad people with tattooed skin and coloured hair, of long queues for milk, water, and loaves of bread, of patients sprawled out in hospital corridors while men punched each other above them, of storm and poisonous air and dead animals in rubbish-choked fields] "… Such an awful life inevitably made the OuterWorlders want to try and escape it, resulting in this, and this, and this…" [images of naked gatherings on a beach, people having sex openly on a street while crowds watched, children vandalising a church while the priest looked on, his arms raised in shock, brawls in drinking halls, crowds of youngsters smoking and injecting drugs while frenzied music blared: the pictures had become clips of moving images now complete with sound, masking the gasps of shock from the audience].

Flapping his well-manicured hands, Stanley continued, "Probably those people had to be inebriated, or to be on drugs – often prescribed by their doctors, you understand – to survive the tedium, the stress, the horror of their lives, many with no money to pay their way and no pity from their rulers – those who were once your rulers too, all our rulers, before SupaPodia was founded and our own enlightened times began. SupaPodia has freed us from want and need, from sick, anti-social behaviour, from hatred, racism, inequality and bigotry, and most of all from the false hope of religion and the irrational believes which accompany that. Now, there are no inequalities between any of us in SupaPodia. The only differences that remain are between the world of SupaPodia and that OuterWorld which still continues beyond our borders. We are all equal here, but not OUT THERE. If only we could bring many more inside with us, very many more. More SupaPods are being built and opened world wide, but, of necessity, the process takes time. There are far more applications than can be filled at present…." He flung his arms out wide. "So you are the LUCKY ONES, my Lilacs and all those many Podders who have already gained a place in SupaPodia. Our hope is a final triumph, when one day, not so distant, perhaps within the lifetimes of many here, the WHOLE WORLD WILL BE SUPAPODIA! Yet, you know, unbelievable as it may sound, there are still some who do not want this and follow the bad old ways. SHAME ON THEM!"

"SHAME! SHAME!" yelled Stanley's audience. "OUT! OUT! Out with the OuterWorld. OUT!" – shouts in which Julian felt he should join. Peter, on the far side of him, was on his feet, shouting too and waving his fists in the air. He couldn't see Tina in the half light beyond him. He imagined

14

she was sitting demurely, self-possessed, not carried away like the others. He remembered the silky material of her dress that he had watched sliding over her tanned back and buttocks, and he felt in that moment a great desire for her which he knew he must suppress – he, who from his lofty fifty or so years, could be her father; he doubted if she was older than her early twenties. In any event, he thought it unlikely SupaPodia would approve of sexual contact between staff. So how then did its staff – the Lilacs – live and have relationships, sexual or otherwise….?

He realised there was very much he didn't know about SupaPodia and what might be expected from his new life here. His head seemed to swell as if to accommodate all the knowledge he must fill it with, so that it felt his brain would burst out through his eye sockets. To cover his feelings, he rose to his feet too, outdoing Peter in his shouts of "OUT! OUT!" He hoped Marion would notice and approve of his enthusiasm, but he saw she was intent on checking some notes on a glittering small Screen held against her thighs, her tight lips a silent, red 'O'.

Stanley's place on the platform was now taken by a dark-skinned, bearded man, with thick-framed glasses, wearing a loose lilac-coloured suit without buttons or markings of any sort, cut high around the neck so that there was nothing between the blackness of his beard and the lilac top. Why on earth was that awful colour chosen for the SupaPodia brand, thought Julian? Perhaps this man will tell us, for, after announcing himself as Professor Debinski, he began to declaim the history of SupaPodia, with much waving of his hairy hands to emphasise his points (just like an ape, thought Julian, realising at once to his horror he was guilty of racist profiling). To steady himself, he tried to concentrate on Debinski's words and the pictures that had begun to flash up behind him. The whole auditorium, in fact, had become a Screen because Julian saw the walls and even the ceiling were now filled with flickering images, the audience tilting and rolling their heads in their efforts to follow them.

Debinski intoned, "The idea of SupaPodia arose out of the model of the simple supermarket – some sixty years ago, it must be now. For those of you who understand what part of time a year represents, that's a *long* time!"

"Supermarkets were the way goods used to be sold in the OuterWorld, as some new Lilacs will know: I believe I am right in thinking that they still exist in some more affluent areas of the Outside. As you see here…" [moving film showed shoppers with piled trolleys, kids stumbling and whining at their feet] "…It doesn't look very comfortable or convenient, does it? All those goods to pick out, then unload and *pay for* with what was then called money, which you probably didn't have enough of anyhow – and then to lug somehow or other to where you lived, probably in some dirty back street with thieves to pinch it from you as you went…" [pictures of an indifferent-looking policeman, unshaven, standing over a fallen woman, her legs askew, still clasping a bag, with blood running from her head] "… Such supermarkets were generally divided into aisles, connected by cross passages, each marked with the type of goods being sold – for example 'Meat' (yes, it was the bad old time when raw animal flesh was still available, but very expensive), 'Bread', 'Vegetables', 'Hardware', 'Entertainment', and so on."

"It was while SupaPodia's great founder and first High Director, Sir Dickie Randsom (Lord Rand, as he was to become – the name by which you will all know him: to his friends he was simply Randy)…" [pause for some uncertain laughter] "… was visiting such a supermarket, his goods spilling out of the torn bags he carried them in – as he liked to tell the story – and having to wait to pay for them (that is give over some of his money while others openly stole about him), that he had the brainwave that was to result in the first SupaPod (the one, as many will know, built at Marazion in Cornwall: it's known as St. Michael's and is currently being greatly expanded and refurbished). In a nutshell, his idea was: Why do all these people have to struggle from their homes to these supermarkets, fighting and jostling, many unable to pay for what they want or having to use credit that would put them in perpetual debt to the detriment of their lives, when they could live under one roof – as it were – and have everything they need in life provided for them, immediately on hand, without having to go through that dreadful circle – that dreadful spiral really – of finding a job, working for peanuts (what Randy used to term 'paynuts'), which was never enough, and then having to travel at further cost to the supermarkets and other great halls where the necessities of life were sold, and then struggle back to their homes once more, only to have to do the same thing over and over again? Wouldn't it be more practical, and far more moral and humane, for some great organisation – but not the old governments that were so self-serving, being run by inner cliques of ignorant numbskulls known as politicians…" [laughter] – "…to provide everything people required in one great central place, where they could find not only the necessities but also everything they needed for the enhancement of their lives – for their pleasure, entertainment and relaxation – with nothing to pay, totally free at the point of use, no bills to have to remember to pay, no debt to get into?"

"So, from that initial idea, the first SupaPod was born, and SupaPods have grown and multiplied ever since and spread to others of the old nations of the world, to become the vast organisation of SupaPodia International that we know now."

He paused. The images, and moving film, of those earlier primitive societies, with the coiling queues of desperate-looking people, had continued behind and around him all the time he was speaking.

"It's amazing how much progress has been made so relatively quickly. I was born at a time when the SupaPods were still very basic by modern standards. You won't believe that the first one I entered still had floors and corridors marked like the old supermarket aisles – 'Dining', 'Sleeping', 'Playing', and such like. These were the names given to individual SupaPod areas. You might be at Level 12 'Dining', for instance. It's amazing how tradition can still linger on despite the incredible social advances that are made."

Laughter and applause sounded out, filling the auditorium in waves. Even Marion beside him was clapping, having made the last of her entries into the small, shiny machine she carried in her hand.

Debinski had not finished, though – not quite yet. "What are the benefits to society of SupaPodia? Believe it or not, that question is still being asked in the OuterWorld, as if there can be any doubt!" [Contemptuous laughter] "There are so many advantages it would take me a large amount of time to describe them, and then I would have missed some out! I know there are many practical things all of you wish to get on with rather than listen to me." [More laughter] "However, if I were to summarise the main benefits, they are these…" – he beat with one hand on the lectern before him, making it wobble with the force of his blows – "…"SupaPodia means the end of petty individualism bred by the cult of liberalism, the end of the nation state also, and the end of the exclusive bigotry of superstitions and religion. We extol instead an overarching creed of rational atheism that is wedded to SupaPodia's general doctrine, so that no one can claim a superiority of belief or purpose. This means we can live in the SupaPods as 'collective human beings' – that is the term I like to use – for the common good and the universal *comfort* of mankind, for all men and women, whatever their origins, whatever their diversity of race and origin, advantage and disadvantage. We have also controlled the exploitation of our planet's resources which were threatening the globe through emissions affecting its climate and stability. We have greatly limited certain technologies that were threatening humankind's ability to think and act and enjoy its own destiny, in particular I am thinking of the development of artificial intelligence which SupaPodia has quite rightly decreed to be a danger to the earth rather than an asset."

Debinski gathered himself for his final flourish, "So I say to you: SUPAPODIA, LIVE ON! You are the NEW DAWN OF THE EARTH!"

Cheers broke out and everyone rose to their feet. Marion turned to Julian, beaming. "Splendid, isn't he?"

Julian tried to smile too, although he felt uneasy, perhaps because he had still so much to learn about the practicalities of the new life that was awaiting him. What happened when the cheering and the laughter ceased and the routines of this new existence began?

As the applause began to die away, Professor Debinski, hands raised, called out, "Are there any questions? Perhaps from our new entrants whom I see in the front row here."

It was if his eyes were drilling directly into Julian, who had slumped back into his chair. Under their scrutiny, and aware of silence from Tina and Peter beside him, he jumped to his feet again. He was desperate to ask a question, so as to appear positive and to the purpose before this great man, and before this audience of his fellows too. He blurted out that query which had come into his head a while back.

"Why does SupaPodia use the colour lilac? I mean of all colours? Does it have a particular significance?"

He realised it was not a good question as he heard the audience go deadly quiet and Debinski appear to draw in his breath, before forcing his dark, bearded face into the semblance of a smile.

"My good man, you have come recently, I think, from the OuterWorld, which remains obsessed with small-minded things. You have yet to learn. It is not your fault, for you will soon gain far greater knowledge. We are not concerned with trivialities here, but with deeper matters of human behaviour and common good. What does the colour of our clothing matter? But, since you do ask, I believe it was Lord Rand's favourite colour and, being largely gender-neutral, it was adopted by him for the staff of the first SupaPod. No one's had the petty thought or energy to alter that since."

Julian felt his face crimsoning in the darkness, hoping others around him did not notice his discomfiture. Oh God, he thought – forced by his embarrassment into naming the deity a disbeliever should set to one side – why did I have to ask such an idiot question? Yet, at some level of his reasoning, remained the thought: but some one – a whole department probably – must be designing SupaPodia's clothing with all its different styles, purposes, badges and buttons. Surely, therefore, the types of material to be used, and their colour, will be an important matter for SupaPodia – and not a triviality. But, he understood – or at least thought he understood – that such reasoning should be dispensed with if he hoped to grow to be a true servant of SupaPodia.

Filing out of the auditorium after the main audience had dispersed, he found Tina and Peter at his side. Tina's face was tilted up at him, her brow furrowed.

"Lilac," she said. "I'd call it purple, really. I think it's rather nice."

"Oh yes, it is," he agreed eagerly, pleased to receive some normal comment to disperse his sense of foolishness. "Don't you think so, Peter?"

"No, I bloody well don't," he grumbled.

Peter, Julian thought, is going to be hard to please. He may not like it here. The thought was strangely unsettling. Another thing he did not know. Could you get out of SupaPodia once you had come in?

Marion came up to them. She looked displeased. The red lips were set tightly together. "Jules, do ask *me* the bread and butter questions. The high ups here only want to talk about the philosophy and ethos of SupaPodia. But don't worry, we all make mistakes at first."

She stroked him lightly on the arm and he was pleased to see her smiling once more. For some reason that only made him blush again.

Come," Marion said. "I'll take the three of you to your quarters next, and we'll have a look at a couple of SupaPod floors."

4

Sub-Floor 87, Level 19 of SupaPod 16 was an astonishing revelation to Julian. Corridor after corridor, hall after hall, room after room, filled his gaze, and, most prominent of all in the accommodation areas, Pod after Pod, raised up ceiling high, Stack after Stack, row after row, all lit with the soft lilac glow that predominated here. Julian thought the use of this coloured lighting was intended both to be restful but also to complement the general lilac and purple colour scheme of SupaPodia – not only the uniforms of the staff but of the many wall fittings, floor coverings, and soft furnishings that he had noticed as well. Clearly a great deal of thought had gone into this, whatever the dismissive answer of that professor to his question. He still felt a little raw about that.

Marion had left Peter and Tina in a rest room, telling them she would be returning to them, and had first escorted Julian to his own accommodation Pod. He had thought as he left the other two that he might never see them again: he had not been too over-concerned about leaving Peter but he very much hoped he would meet up with Tina later. At least he knew she would be in Education with him.

Julian's Pod was at the very top of a Stack and was referenced L19/87/379/224B. Marion had given him a plastic key on which this reference was printed. There had followed an initial briefing about living "in your own sweet little Pod" (her words), but also about other aspects of life in the "collective SupaPod" (again, her term). Then, rather abruptly, she had left him there. He should familiarise himself with the Pod as far as he could, she had told him, and then perhaps have a rest, because when she returned (after dealing with Tina and Peter, Julian imagined) she would take him to a place where his 'instruction and induction' would continue. His spirit had shrunk a little at that. He was indeed tired and very much overwhelmed.

The Pod was oval in shape, its curving, bulbous sides of a dull grey colour, but the domed roof, a shiny black. It was filled mainly by a broad couch, with a side panel curved to fit the shape of the Pod wall, raised at the head and foot (there were levers that could control the heights). The couch itself, covered in a lilac fabric, felt pneumatic to his touch, as if pumped up with air, as it probably was. The side panel contained a small inbuilt cupboard and a shelf which pulled out, the latter clearly intended for 'personal care' as set against its back was a small ceramic bowl and two small taps. He tried both: one gushed out warm water, the other a trickle of liquid soap. At the foot of the couch, set within a gleaming steel lavatory pan, was a shoot for body waste. He inspected this cautiously, pressing the button that made the cover slide open, pleased to find there was no smell but only a pleasing perfumed scent. Set into the far Pod wall was a viewing Screen, unlit (he could not find any instructions as to how to switch it on). Beneath it, extending to the other curving side wall of the Pod, were a number of other shoots, closed by sliding metal hatches, each lettered and numbered in a way he did not understand: he did not investigate them further, thinking Marion will explain these to me later.

On the floor, awaiting him, he found the suitcase he had been allowed to send ahead of him: its required measurements had been carefully stated. He opened it, and placed his few personal items in the cupboard, sliding the case into a slot beneath the couch, as a label that had been stuck to its outside instructed him to do.

He sat on the couch, feeling a mingled set of wonder and fear. Was this really the place where he was to spend the rest of his life? Would he never see broad spaces again and birds and trees and sunlight, and feel fresh air and rain on his face? The reality of SupaPodia was crashing in on him like a sea breaker on the shores of the OuterWorld he had now left behind. What then had he been expecting, he wondered? Of course, it was just the strangeness, the newness, the confusion of everything that was affecting him. It was a new world. He would soon find his feet here, he was sure. Everything was going to prove far superior to his recent life in the OW. As had so recently been said, he was one of the 'lucky ones'. He must not then view anything as wrong or disillusioning, just perhaps strange. Coming into SupaPodia was like travelling to a distant, exotic land where the customs were different. He only had to absorb them, and grow accustomed to them, making the necessary mental changes, and then everything in and about SupaPodia would be very fine indeed. He was going to be happy too in the work that would be given to him. He was really looking forward to it, to having a role – albeit a small one – in the administration of this grand new world he had entered. He was so glad he had achieved a place on the staff and was not just a resident – a Podder. He would be able to make use of the teaching skills he had learnt in the OW, but had been unable to practise there for several years.

He wondered who occupied the Pods immediately around him, alongside and below. There was no way he could see into them: each Pod had its own entrance way, depending on its height in a Stack – through a lift, or an open ladder (the higher ones likely for fit and able occupants only) or a mesh-enclosed flight of stairs. Leading down as well from each Pod were curving steel shoots which could be used as an alternative method of exit. The large hatch for his own shoot he could see situated beside the door opposite the head of the couch. A flourish of the key Marion had given him caused the door itself to slide back soundlessly into a recess in the Pod wall. Very neat, he thought. What genius, he wondered, had designed all this? What engineers had built it? He had never come close to any SupaPodia site under construction, and information about them had always been hard to gain in the OW, in particular when the communication systems available to OuterWorlders (he used this SupaPodia term for the first time) had largely collapsed, as they had done in recent years.

Marion had brought him into his Pod. Because of its height at the very top of a Stack, his was one that had a lift. It rose in a narrow, glass-sided shaft set against the Stack. The cabin was only a tiny space, a miniature form of his Pod, in fact, shaped like an elongated bubble. There was really only room for one, and then with the body doubled up. Marion, however, had squeezed in with him, their heads bent low under the ceiling, his groin pressed hard against her buttock. He had felt embarrassed by the contact, but Marion simply laughed, singing out, "Getting to know you, getting to know all about you...." with a girly giggle. And she is my boss, thought Julian, rather scandalised.

Before they had gone up to the Pod, Marion had told him about the shoot which looped down in a steel tube close to the lift shaft, reaching the ground in a gentle curve, like the helter-skelter (he remembered that name!) he had seen once when very young. It had been at a seaside fairground his parents had taken him to, when such attractions were still in business: soon afterwards, as the age of austerity bit deeper, they must all have been taken down, their materials sold off for scrap.

If the lift failed, or simply to make a quick exit, Marion had said, you could slide down the tube. However, climbing up it was much more difficult: it could only be done by pulling yourself up on your back, making use of handles that could be flicked out from its upper surface. "Push those handles back," Marion had warned him, "or you'll scrape your goolies off the next time you slide down." That comment had rather shocked him too.

The Pods here were all Lilacs' Pods, he had learnt, but they differed very little from the individual Pods used by the Podders themselves. There were, of course, some much bigger Pods for Podder couples, and indeed whole families, but these were uncommon for staff use as almost all Lilacs were single. The Lilacs and the Podders – the terms still sounded strange to Julian. No matter. He would soon get used to them.

He wondered about the Lilacs; how, for example, you met a fellow Lilac for ordinary social contact, let alone....His mind could not yet consider anything more intimate, but surely that must exist here as well, otherwise it would be against nature. There must be birth in a SupaPod. And death too, of course. These were matters that strangely he had not considered yet, and on which he had no information at all. No SupaPodia literature he had read, or publicity film he had seen, had shown the very young, or indeed, for that matter, the very old. The thought worried him, but he brushed it aside. He had only just arrived. Everything would become clear.

He thought suddenly of Tina. Perhaps their work would bring them together. But what would a spring-fresh girl like her see in a dusty fifty year old like him, with his thinning grey hair, his skinny body, and long-blunted intellect? He thought of himself as a boring man, an ageing man lost in his past, hoping against hope that SupaPodia might take him to a brighter future; hardly a man to gain the attention of any woman, let alone an attractive one probably young enough to be his daughter He would like to get to know her, though. He had no idea where her Pod was. He had passed through such a maze of passages and chambers and halls on his journey with Marion to his own Pod, just here on this one area of one Level, that he knew he would get totally lost if he set out anywhere by himself. Many things were very strange, some radically different from the OuterWorld.

One such was the system for measuring time. Marion had given him a hurried introduction to this subject during her earlier briefing, telling him he would need to understand straightaway how SupaPodia time was gauged, since exact time-keeping was not only a virtue but very much a necessity in a SupaPod. Time here did not conform to the standard 24 hour clock of the OW, although the same broad distinctions of night (the twelve hours of 'sleeping time') and day (the twelve hours of 'fulfilment time') were largely adhered to. Without regular access to the open air, knowledge of day (as light) and night (as darkness) were soon lost by both Lilacs and Podders alike.

A SupaPod, therefore, maintained its own time system, measured by a particular instrument that was based on the dial of an old-fashioned clock: these instruments, in various sizes, were displayed widely in fixed positions throughout the SupaPod – in rooms and halls and corridors, in lifts and kitchens and shower rooms – and transmitted as well onto the Screens that were everywhere.

Portable versions of the time instrument were available for Lilacs. Marion had handed him one so he could familiarise himself with it. The circular dial, some three inches in diameter, was not divided up by hours and minutes (these measurements were unknown in the SupaPod) but by five coloured segments representing time periods, in sequence – Green, Orange, Red, Yellow, and Blue. Each of these in turn was divided equally by four black lines, forming five sub-segments within each colour. A thin black bar shaped like an arrow pointed to the time position on the dial, at the centre of which the relevant letter and number were also displayed. Julian saw that it currently read 'O5', meaning the fifth segment of Orange. He had been told by Marion to descend from his Pod to meet her at its ground floor entrance at 'R3' (Red Three). By consulting the dial, he saw that was rather less than three time units away.

He watched the small display window intently as the letters and numbers clicked up and the black arrow hand jerked periodically across the coloured segments; first, a large 'R' appeared, then immediately below it the number 1 – 'R1'. There followed a lengthy wait (perhaps ten of the OW's minutes, he thought) until 'R2' came, and then another long wait (surely it was longer than the first) until suddenly there it was, 'R3' staring out starkly at him. His mouth was dry. He wished he had thought to find out how to get a drink in his Pod, but there was no time now.

He flourished his key, sliding open the Pod door, and entered his tiny lift. It descended automatically, without the need for a command, emerging in the hallway to his Pod Stack, which, to his surprise, was now full of other Lilacs; it had been empty when Marion had brought him here. He was greatly relieved to spot her straightaway. She was talking to a tall thickset man in a tunic garment, such as doctor Peter had been given to wear. 'Servicing' was written on a badge pinned to his chest.

"Julian." Marion said, after he had weaved between groups of Lilacs to come up to her, "Meet Oscar. His Pod is near yours."

"Oh, really. I was wondering who my neighbours might be." Julian thought this sounded breezy and out-going. He reached forward and offered Oscar his hand, which the other took in a clammy paw. "And what do you do here, Oscar?"

"Servicing," Oscar mumbled in a way that seemed out of character with his strong build.

"Yes, I see that on your badge. What's does it mean exactly?"

"All sorts of work," said Marion breaking in. "Oscar works for the Maintenance Department. He's the man to get your Pod fixed if anything goes wrong. Aren't you Oscar?"

"Yes, ma'am." Oscar's eyes were cast down, and Julian wondered why. He thought, I won't have much confidence in him. The introduction depressed him. Were all his colleagues going to be like this? He remembered the soppy Stanley with his expressions of exhaustion and his head buried on Marion's chest, then bursting forth later on stage like a firework. Was he perhaps on drugs?

Julian was struggling to accept the incredible reality of SupaPodia. He wanted people he was to work with to appear and act normally, otherwise he feared being dragged under by this new world entirely, and being unable to cope. What he needed was for everything to become much clearer so he could hope to understand. He had expected bright, brisk efficiency, but that was not the impression he had received so far. Still, he reasoned, he had only just arrived. He must give himself time to learn and grow, and not allow himself to be despondent. Cheerfulness and optimism must remain his order of the day. But there is no such thing as a day here, he thought, only a sequence of colours played out endlessly.

Marion was exchanging greetings with other Lilacs issuing from their Pods or coming into the hallway to return to theirs, but she did not introduce Julian to any of them. Instead, with a curt "Follow me" she led him down a long, brightly-lit passageway (no discrete mauve light here) to an elevator, then a short descent of one or more Sub-Floors, and an emergence into another passage that ended at double white doors above which was a glowing green cross and the words 'MEDICAL STATION – IMPLANTATION'.

Passing through the doors, to his sudden surprise Julian saw Peter come out of a side passage and turn to walk ahead of them. Peter's lilac tunic was now supplemented by a long shiny apron of a deeper purple colour. Before Julian could catch Peter up and greet him, the latter had turned into another doorway. Marion led Julian into this same room, where he was surprised to find not Peter, who had disappeared, but Tina seated on a chair by the wall with the right sleeve of her dress pulled up. Above her elbow was a large stick-on bandage. Her face was very pale.

"Hello, Tina," Julian said, delighted to see her again. "How are you getting on?"

"Alright, I suppose. But I didn't like the chipping."

"Chipping?!" He turned to find Marion, but she had gone over to a woman at a desk. "What's chipping?"

"They put an implant into your arm – a microchip. Didn't you know? It's punched by a machine into the bone. I've just had it done. That's why I'm feeling a bit sick."

"No, I had no idea. No one's told me anything." Julian was horrified. He didn't like the idea of what was probably an identity chip (he had heard about such things) being inserted into his body, presumably so he could be tracked wherever he went.

Marion came over from the desk. "Am I going to be chipped?" he asked her, thoroughly alarmed now. "I was not told about this as a condition of working for SupaPodia."

"Don't be so silly," Marion said. "Everyone here is chipped, Podders and Lilacs alike. It's not so much for your location to be known centrally – believe me, we're not *that* interested in you – but to help *you* not to get lost and for you to receive information. Most people steer by their chip as they go through the SupaPod. You'll get used to the pings that sound when you stray from your preset courses: there're different sounds, for instance, for left and right and up and down."

"Good God!"

"You shouldn't use that expression here."

"I'm sorry. Why wasn't I told about this before I made the decision to take up my appointment with SupaPodia?"

"I don't know, but are you seriously saying a little matter like that would have meant you stayed in the OW?"

"I don't know anymore what I think."

"Come on now. Look at this young lady here. She can take it."

"I'm a bit sore, but it'll be worth it," Tina told Julian, unconvincingly. She then added. "You've got no choice now, anyhow. It has to be done."

"Good girl, quite right." Marion looked approvingly at Tina. "Come on," she said to Julian. "How can you gain the respect of your colleagues, or the Podders for that matter, if you drag your feet over such a little thing? Everyone has the implant, even babies."

Before Julian had time to think any more about his objections, his name was called out by an elderly woman enveloped in a long lilac tunic, and wearing a lilac cap with a green cross on it, who had come into the room from a far door.

"Julian Foster!"

He rose to his feet, his heart beating fast. He followed the nurse – if that's what she was – back through the door from which she had just come. He was told to remove his blazer and to lie on a flat couch, his head nestled into a pillow. He was aware out of the corner of his eye of a lilac uniform and a silver tray approaching. He raised his head, and saw the uniform and tray were carried by fellow new entrant, Peter. "Hello," he croaked.

"Why, good day again. The other new boy, and my first for a chip. You see they've got me started right away. Lucky it's something I'd practised on animals in the great Outside." He guffawed. "But don't worry; I do know what I'm doing, even if I don't quite know where I am. You must feel like that too."

Julian made an attempt to nod his head against the pillow. His throat seemed to have closed up and he didn't know what words he might get out.

"Now lie still. This implant won't hurt – only a jolt really. Nurse, get his sleeve right up."

Julian felt the woman pulling at his right arm, and, raising his head, saw her wrinkled fingers with chipped, reddened nails sliding across his skin. Involuntarily, he shuddered.

"Now then, now then, this will soon be over," Peter said. He saw a shining flat disk aimed at his upper arm, with a long black handle extending from it. "Very still".

The disk was attached to his arm and pressed hard against the bone above the elbow. He saw Peter's fingers move to a switch on the handle, and immediately felt a shock that seemed to jar his whole body: he sensed his flesh trembling like the smooth surface of a pool that has just been splashed by a stone. A low pain filled his arm, growing steadily in intensity so that he felt he must cry out, but then suddenly dropping away. The nurse wiped his brow while Peter removed the disk and swabbed his arm. Then he pressed down a large pink bandage over the punctured area of skin.

"All over, my mate! Congratulations. I haven't even received my own yet. Better get away while I can, eh!"

Peter's attempt at humour dismayed Julian. What had been done to him? His arm felt heavy and sore. The elderly nurse was bending over him to help him up. He could see her sagging breasts beneath the loose folds of her tunic top. He retched.

"There. There. You may feel a little sick at first. Pick up your jacket and go into recovery. You'll soon be fine." He was helped outside by the nurse, his right arm dangling uselessly at his side.

Marion greeted him. She made him sit down beside her. There was no sign of Tina.

"You'll soon get the strength back in your arm. Poor boy." She ran her fingers through his thinning hair. Boy! he thought. I was that when she was still in nappies.

But he leant against her shoulder, feeling his head dipping and wheeling. He closed his eyes. When he opened them again, it was to find his senses had steadied. He felt much better. He tried out his arm. It was still sore, but at least he could raise it now. He moved his fingers experimentally. They all worked.

Marion looked up from a magazine she was reading. "How are you?"

"I'm alright, I think." He hoped he had not made too much of a fool of himself.

"How long have I been here?" he asked.

"Oh, only a little while."

"And I haven't done or said anything silly?"

"No, of course not. You looked so peaceful lying in my lap."

"What!"

"Don't worry. Some can walk out almost straightaway – like Tina before you – but others take a little longer. It's my job to ensure you've recovered."

"Yes, but…"

"But nothing. We must go now. The next part of your induction is due soon, and we should have something to eat first.

Julian realised how hungry he was – and thirsty too. It had been a long time since anything had passed his lips. For everything now he was dependent on SupaPodia. He had to know their systems even to feed himself. This sudden realisation was discomfiting; but he calmed himself by telling himself yet again, it was only a question of learning.

* * *

The Lilacs' canteen for Level 19 was situated a lengthy distance from the elevator by which they had returned from the Sub-Floor of the Medical Station; or at least that seemed to be the case, for the journey on foot involved many passages and side-passages, some hung with pictures showing abstract designs in which lilac and purple predominated, others with bare white walls, festooned in places with steel tubing and bunches of black cabling. They went up stairs, and down stairs, and travelled at one point on a moving floor. People passed them at times, all staff, it seemed, from their different types of lilac uniforms, some greeting Marion with a wave of the hand, others clearly indifferent to her. There must be hundreds of Lilacs in just one small area of one Level, thought Julian. How on earth was it all organised and paid for? Then he realised that, of course, pay did not come into it. The staff were paid nothing. He would be paid nothing. For Podders and Lilacs, all services in the SupaPod were free. Their security was their pay; their work, their purpose and reward.

"How will I ever find my way through this maze?" he asked Marion, as she slowed down for him to catch up. She had put on a brisk pace which he found difficult to match, she being much younger than he. But, of course, years, as with days, wouldn't be counted here. How were people's ages measured then in a SupaPod, he wondered?

"That's what your implanted chip is for," Marion answered. "It'll help guide you around. If you go off course on any set route, it'll bleep at you and set you straight again. Go anywhere you shouldn't, then the noise is continuous and becomes unendurable."

"But surely," he said, "you can turn it off if you make a mistake and it becomes a nuisance."

"I'm afraid not. Only a medico can do that, and then only for part of its Guidance functions. But a medico can also supply the necessary cancellation data to a senior Lilac, so he or she can amend the Guidance control programme of their staff for special purposes. All this is for a very good reason, you see, to stop people straying into areas where they shouldn't be, and not bucking the system." She smiled at her last words. "I did say *bucking*, didn't I?"

"I think so." He was surprised by the implied crudity. Perhaps he had thought SupaPodia would be free of the obscenities of the OW. His academic life had sheltered him from much of it; that was until, like so many others, he had been forced out into the wilderness of the unemployed.

"I'll tell you more later," said Marion, adopting a brisker tone.

They set off again. He admired her trim figure in the shiny dress ahead of him, the wiggle of her hips and the undulating motion of her slim bottom. He shouldn't, of course, be having such sexual thoughts about a SupaPodia superior. Julian's experience with women had been very limited the past ten years or so, ever since his wife had gone off with another man – a steward to a rich Eliti estate in Hertfordshire, who could promise her a more secure way of life. There had been just the occasional fevered grope since, usually with street women who asked for payment for anything further – money he did not have. Once, while prone with a much more yielding woman, one desirous of him too, a gang of ragged boys, spotting them ill-concealed on a patch of waste land beside a disused petrol station, had driven her off with their crude jeering; a pity as she had been quite a classy lady too, fallen on hard times. She had fled, leaving her coat behind. He had felt particularly sorry about that because new clothes were hard to find and expensive. He had exchanged the coat later for a new jacket for himself.

Pacing behind Marion, Julian dismissed these crude memories, realising how irrelevant they were to his current situation. His thoughts concentrated instead on the chip now sitting snugly within his arm bone. What were the implications of its tracking function that would create sounds to guide him? What else could it do?

They had paused at a short flight of steps going up. "So, is my chip working yet, or not?" He spoke the words from behind Marion, touching her shoulder to gain her attention. He thought he was entitled to an answer now, not later.

He had expected her to be short with him, but she wasn't. "No, it needs to be activated first."

"But when will that happen?"

"In a short while. By the next Orange, probably. That's less than a full Sweep," she added.

"You mean less than twenty-four hours?"

"I mean *less than a full Sweep*," she emphasised. "You have to learn! Always think New, not Old."

God! was, in fact, what Julian was thinking. The word still came easily to his mind, despite long ago having dismissed religion from his life.

"Once it's activated, you'll need to get used to the various sounds in your head."

"What! In my head? You mean, the sounds come straight into my brain, not through some device I'll be carrying?"

"That's right, Jules. I'll be honest – how exactly that's done, I don't know. I don't have too much knowledge of technology, or physiology for that matter. But, the point is, it works, and it works brilliantly when you've got used to it. Mine's working now as I walk with you. It doesn't trouble me a bit."

"Is it never quiet in your head then?"

"Yes, of course it is. If you're not off course, or when you've arrived in the place where you should be, then there'll be no sound. And, of course, there won't be any sounds either back in your own Pod. There, everything shuts off – otherwise, silly, you'd never sleep. And that would never do."

She saw the dismay on his face. "It's only the Guidance that comes direct into your head. You will get a Control Pad that you have to carry (we call them CPs) for most of the other stuff coming via your chip – instructions from me for instance, teaching schedules, assignments, timings, temperatures, general SupaPod and wider SupaPodia, information, news from the OW – all that sort of stuff. It means you don't need to be by a Screen. It's a more refined, superior version of the old mobile phones people carried in the OW and still try to bring into a SupaPod. They wouldn't work here, anyhow."

Julian remembered Dr. Peter's device going down a disposal shoot.

"Jules, you do get used to it all very quickly," she said, trying to sound reassuring. "Now, don't become a worrier. If you do, you won't learn half as fast as simply accepting things are different here."

Marion's words were easier said than done, Julian thought. He felt himself so heavy with worry, about this and so much else, that he seemed to be literally bending at the knees. And he had only just arrived! As they started their journey again, Julian was thinking, What have I done? What have I come into? SupaPodia could become SupaMania, if I'm not careful. He realised that They – SupaPodia – would be able to monitor and control his every move. And not only movements on SupaPodia business, but in his personal affairs too – that's if he would be allowed any time to himself. He felt a sense of growing panic.

He made an effort to calm himself. He hoped that as time passed, and he knew better and understood better, he would come to see how silly his fears were – silly, irrational, and inconsequential.

They came at last into a large, open hall with a high ceiling inset with many lamps shining like bright stars. Here, tables stood in random patterns about the floor, some of them long with bench seats against them, occupied by several Lilacs, others round and smaller, with chairs where only two sat. A shelf on one side of the hall was lined with high stools on which some sat alone. Screens set at points into the walls seemed all to be showing different programmes. There was no sound, the figures flickering across the Screens, or standing still and talking, doing so in apparent silence.

Seeing Julian looking at a Screen, Marion anticipated his question, "Yes, there's no sound coming out. The sound for each Screen comes through the Lilacs' CPs depending on which one they are closest to, relayed by a tiny amplifier in the ear: you'll get one of these with your own CP. It's used as well for other communal activities where separate sound is generated. It makes the sound seem to be coming directly into your head, much like the Guidance System (or GS, as we know it), only that, as I've told you, *is* in your head, but this is different altogether – an old technology really, due for updating, I think. You can't see anyone troubled by it, though, can you?"

She was right. Everything – for once – seemed very normal here, like any staff canteen, Julian thought, although the only one he had known in the OW had been a grim place with a few shabby trestle tables, a counter covered by cracked and broken tiles, and a woman behind it in a dirty apron, who handed out chipped mugs of a weak tea poured from a battered metal urn. That had been the last job he had done before the SupaPodia competition, when he had worked as a clerk for his Area Council – an organisation weighed under by all the tasks it should perform but could not do so now; no supplies, no food, no machinery that worked, few staff, little pay, little of anything, in fact, civilisation collapsing into anarchy as the former great cities and towns were emptied of their best people into the SupaPods, leaving mainly the sick, the elderly, the disabled, the insane, and the inherently idle to linger on. The only people who flourished were the construction workers building the SupaPods, for whom special camps were laid out: they were usually paid with tokens that they accumulated to be exchanged one day, if they still lived (their accident death rate was enormous) for a place in a SupaPod they had helped build. Criminal gangs did well also; they ran black markets and took bribes for the promise of gaining a SupaPod place, a promise seldom fulfilled. There were never enough SupaPod places to clear the streets entirely, and some good people, worthy of SupaPodia, starved (literally) to death before their chance came. Their bodies would be found in the streets and on the pavements in the mornings, and gathered up by horse-drawn carts.

"Do the Podders have these CPs too?" Julian asked, forcing his mind back from the horrible past he had known to this uncertain present.

Marion laughed. "No, not that lot. No way. They'd only lose them straightaway. They have to get used to any confusion of sound in their communal places."

It was the first time he had heard Marion talk disparagingly about the Podders. He thought, I am learning, I am learning. And I'm not sure I like what I hear.

Food and drink in the canteen were dispensed at a long, stainless-steel-topped servery by a series of hatches beneath which you placed your plate. There was no menu and no indication of which food was going to tumble out of which covering.

"You get to learn what's in each hatch," Marion said, "since it seldom changes. Sometimes there's a surprise." She helped herself to a doughy mixture of what seemed to be pie with some pieces of meat at its centre. Julian selected this as well. The filling of the pie gushed out onto his plate, and he was just in time to cut it off by pulling the plate away before it overflowed. Following Marion's example, from other hatches he added mashed potato and a round green vegetable that he was told were sprouts (he had never come across these in the OW). Across all, a flexible hand-held tube spread a thick gravy. Other tubes also dispensed drinks, and he found a tea that was to his taste.

He followed Marion to a table where some others were seated, a man dressed in a tunic like Peter, so perhaps he was a medico, and three girls who wore smart lilac jackets and skirts, like the uniforms of the stewardesses he had known on aeroplanes as a child, before the whole air transport system of the OW had crashed – literally and metaphorically.

"This is Julian," Marion said. "Just started here. Just implanted."

"Oh, you poor thing," said one of the girls. "I know how you'll be feeling. Sore and confused probably." She giggled. "It doesn't last long, though. You'll soon get into the swing of it."

They all seem to say the same thing, Julian thought.

"Which Pod living area are you in?" asked the medico.

"Hell, I can't remember," Julian stuttered.

They all laughed. "Neither could I at first," said another girl, pretty with long, dark-brown hair curling to her shoulders. "When's your chip activated?"

Julian looked helplessly at Marion, who had begun tapping something into the bright instrument (a CP presumably) she carried. Seeing her occupied, he replied, "Tomorrow, I think."

"Tomorrow?" said the medico sternly. "You couldn't have been told that. We don't think in days and nights here."

"No, of course not," Julian gabbled, realising his mistake. "Sorry, I know time here is not like Outside."

The medico looked at him intently. "*Of course* it's the same. It's just that we quantify it differently. You'll have been told that, I'm sure."

"Yes, yes," said Julian, feeling foolish. He looked again at Marion, but she was still busy with her CP and did not appear to have overheard the conversation. He glanced towards a large timepiece on the wall; it showed they were in Yellow now and said lamely, "I think it's after two or so of those coloured segments, perhaps after the Blue. I can't remember exactly."

The medico seemed unimpressed. How am I expected to take in all these things so soon? Julian thought. I'm never going to get used to them. I'll lose my mind first. He suddenly had a very real fear that he was indeed going mad and that all this was not the promised land he had so much hoped for, but part of a long drift into insanity.

Seeing the confused expression on his face, and obviously sympathetic to his inner struggle, the third of the uniformed girls, who was blonde and buxom, said, "Why don't we have a party to welcome Julian?" She looked at her own timepiece carried on her wrist. "How about we collect you from your Pod at Green Three?"

Marion had now put away her CP. "Why not?" she said to Julian. "It'll be a good way for you to meet some of your fellow Lilacs. Tell you what, I'll be free too, if that's alright?" Did Julian detect a lack of enthusiasm in the nods and assents about the table? "Don't worry," Marion said to the others, "you don't have to come and fetch him. I'll bring him with me. Staff Lounge, is it? SF11/80?" More nods. "Well, that's agreed then. We'll see you later."

* * *

"I'm taking you into a lower Podder area now," said Marion as they left the canteen. "It's one where Podder facilities are at their fullest. On our Level 19, there is less infrastructure, as we have there mainly single working Podders who will often be sent Outside on freight or maintenance work, and their main sustenance is provided there."

"There are usually twelve Podder Sub-Floors to each Level," she continued, speaking in a monotone as if reading from a manual. "There are exceptions to that, of course, but for the moment keep it as a general ratio. Each Lilac has on average a thousand Podders he or she might be directly responsible for, depending of course, on their actual job. SupaPodia is trying to raise its staff levels, but the high standards required are keeping out all but the very best recruits." She turned to him with a smile. "As you well know, Jules."

"How many Podders are there in this SupaPod?" Julian asked.

"I'm not entirely sure. Our Statistics Unit will have the exact figures. Their offices are deep down in the SupaPod – on Level 140, I think. They balance up births and deaths and new entrants on a daily basis."

"I thought there was no concept of day here," Julian said rather smugly, feeling he had caught Marion out.

Her reply was sharp. "Don't try to be clever with me, Dr. Foster!" – the first time she had ever referred to him by his formal title from the OuterWorld

– "No, we don't have days here but our method of time reckoning can still make use of the old terminology – a quaintness, an anachronism perhaps, which will eventually, I'm sure, fade away entirely, but for the present it serves an easy conversational purpose, if no more."

Julian was a little startled by her tone. At all costs he mustn't quarrel with her. That would be a very bad start to his SupaPodia career. "Of course," he said. "I'm sorry. I just feel a bit overloaded with everything."

"That why I think a little socialising later on will help you. There's fun here as well as work, you know. In fact, one of our favourite slogans is IT'S YOUR SUPAPOD: ENJOY IT. Don't let it all weigh you down too much. Remember, a SupaPod should be a happy place to live in. Worry and stress and misery belong to the OW which you've left behind you."

They came to an elevator where others were waiting – all in lilac clothing, some in dresses, some trousers and jackets, some tunics, sweaters and skirts, a few in sports gear, most wearing name badges, others with chevrons or numbers sewn on their sleeves. Quietness reigned here. Everyone looked intent on what they were doing, where they were going. A number held CPs such as Marion carried. If any spoke, it seemed to be to themselves, which Julian thought strange.

Marion told him, "That woman there…" – she nodded towards an elegant older lady in a formal blouse and skirt who was saying, then repeating, several things with her head bent towards her right arm – "…is asking her chip for directions and not, I think, getting the answer she wants. It happens occasionally. No system's perfect. I may have to help her."

She went across to the woman and spoke with her: she responded with a bright smile. Marion came back as the elevator arrived. "She wanted Commodity Supplies, which she wasn't programmed for. I've given her the right reference, so she'll travel manually until her chip's upgraded." Julian's head spun. Will I ever know what Marion knows, he thought?

They descended for what seemed a long time, the elevator stopping several times, some people leaving, others getting in. At last, as the doors opened at a level referenced on the lift's flash display as L32/SF46/P005, Marion exited with Julian close behind her. They emerged into a wide hall full of Podders. At least, that is what Julian assumed they were, for here were woman and children, and men, of differing ages, all milling about, or standing or sitting while looking up at flickering, coloured Screens set in the walls. Many, from their faces, looked fleshy and overweight, but it was hard to tell since their dress was uniform – a loose fitting, bright orange-coloured blouse with matching baggy trousers (worn by both men and women), below which white sports shoes with thick rubber soles stuck out like penguins' feet.

A sound of screaming, wailing music, punctuated by much percussion, filled the air, coming from all directions; several different forms of music, it seemed, intermingled and not apparently relating to whatever was showing on the Screens. Filling any gaps in this sound, was the constant sound of people's movement and conversation.

Marion moved across the hall. Julian was surprised to see how the Podders stepped smartly aside to make way for her, with Julian following close behind her. She entered a passageway leading from the far side; it was covered with coloured pictures of smiling faces, whom Julian assumed were entertainers of some sort, or perhaps sports people. They must be of particular importance to the Podders, but he recognised none. More pictures further along were not face portraits but of the body full-length and, to Julian, quite shockingly divest of clothing – some women bare-breasted and one man, flexing his muscles, fully naked, bar a small leaf resting over his genitals.

As in the hall, on-coming Podders swerved away at their approach, passing in the passage with their heads down, all except one small girl who looked up at Marion, reaching her arm out to her, until she was hurriedly pulled away by her mother. At the end of the passage, where another made a T-junction, Marion said. "I'm going to show you next a section of Podders' accommodation Pods, and then their Education Centre where you will be working – well, for some of the time, anyhow."

Julian said nothing. He was overwhelmed by the constant flow and movement of these orange people, their apparent obesity, their sameness in appearance and dress, and the fact that no one spoke other than in a mumble, sometimes with heads pressed close together. There was no loud talk, no laughter, no seeming camaraderie or inquisitiveness, just a kind of dull monotony and acceptance – yet, at the same time, no pain or concern or worry either; so this was the Podders' life flowing on as it did each day, or rather as it did each segment of Green, Orange, Red, Yellow, or Blue time.

It is hellish, was Julian's predominant thought – but how could that be? For everyone looked well, and at some level they seemed content. They had nothing to do, it seemed, but to exist and please themselves. How could there be anything wrong in that? It had to be Julian's own attitude – his still lingering prejudices and bigotry, yes, and even elitism, that was out of tune.

Marion ducked into an opening lower than any Julian had yet seen, and bending double he followed her. Within, the light was darker, the walls nearest the entranceway painted a chocolate brown colour without any further decoration at all. Raising his eyes, Julian could see that they stood now in an enormous open space filled with towers of metal-sided Pods reaching up high overhead. It was as if he were in one of those areas of an OW city where the huge, soaring tower blocks of yesteryear had stood, some indeed still standing, as Julian had seen them last, their sides running with rain water and leaking chemicals, others long since fallen so that the earth was littered with vast heaps of concrete rubble out of which great iron beams, heavy with rust, projected.

As he gazed upwards, he could see nothing was derelict or fallen here, however. Instead, crisscrossing bright steel beams, grouped together in clusters, holding coloured glass and plastic panels, stretched upwards like great cathedral spires, so high Julian could scarcely make out their top, with small lifts moving continuously against them amongst the sparkling lights, taking the Podders to and from their home Pods.

"Wow!" was all Julian could utter.

"Impressive, isn't it?" Marion said. This is just a single area of the accommodation Pods for this one Level: there are many hundreds of other areas within the complete SupaPod. They can seem to go on – and go up – for ever. Some rise through several Sub-Floors and can be accessed by the Podders at other heights, other Floors."

"But how on earth was all this built?" Julian flapped his hands in his incredulity. "How long did it take to get to this degree of…of…?"

"Of excellence? Yes, it's phenomenal, isn't it? It just shows what humankind can achieve when it applies itself properly to good works, and doesn't waste time and energy on the unprofitable – of which history must show the pursuit of warfare as the most wasteful activity of all. Thank SupaPodia; thank Lord Rand especially, that all that is now ended, and humanity can now build for the future and give each individual the sort of life he or she deserves, whatever their background or diversity, whether young or old, of the present generations or those yet to be born."

This was quite a speech, Julian thought. He gazed at her in a new light. Her head was tilted upwards, her red lips parted, her eyes aglow. He could see she truly believed in what she said. There was no pretence from her now. He was unfamiliar with such belief, such emotional commitment. The OuterWorld he had come from had been filled with half-truths, half-beliefs, cynicism and despair. What it was to be part of a society that was going forward with such dedication and energy! All his earlier doubts and worries were dissolving. He knew his decision to come to SupaPodia had been the correct one. Admittedly, he had an enormous amount to learn, but it was so good to be part of this disciplined world that would take him forward within the grand progress of mankind, instead of backwards into chaos.

Marion looked so lovely standing there with her hands clasped before her bosom, her chin raised, her black hair glistening in the low lamp light, that he felt a sudden great urge to hold her and kiss her, yet restrained himself. That would be far too forward; it might even get him sacked. Yet he touched his hand against her arm and said simply. "It's such a privilege to see this. How wonderful is SupaPodia. I'm so glad I was able to come in from the Outside".

And to his very great surprise it was she who turned to him and kissed him on the cheek.

"So am I, Jules" she said.

* * *

Julian followed Marion out of the great courtyard that lay before the Podders' accommodation Stacks. They emerged through one of the low doorways into the approach passage they had used earlier; other doorways he could see busy with the Podders coming and going, like a swirling sea of orange-coloured waters, funnelled through the dark openings to be washed up against the bright Pod towers.

Marion made no comment about the kiss she had bestowed on him, and he did not like to refer to it. He seemed so far from anything he really understood that he thought it might just be the way people behaved here: perhaps they greeted and left you with a kiss, although he did not think he had noticed anything like that earlier. He wasn't sure, though. Certainly, people – the Lilacs, anyhow – were friendly enough. He imagined that a closeness, a bonding, mutual respect and liking, were necessary for survival. He remembered how Stanley's head had been nursed upon her breast by Marion. Probably that did not represent anything salacious, but was simply caring and nurturing. He shouldn't read too much into anything he saw, and queried, until he had had time to assess SupaPod life better, and that would take days, even months. He checked himself. He had forgotten again already. Hours and days were banned here, as were probably months and years. Perhaps – a disturbing thought – cumulative time wasn't measured here at all.

When they arrived back at the main elevator shafts, Marion said, "I'm taking you to this Level's Education Centre now; actually, it's known better as an EEC, that's an Education and Entertainment Centre. In SupaPodia we believe these two facilities for Podders should lie side by side. You learn best when you're being entertained. We don't aim to cram in knowledge to the unwilling simply for the sake of it, but only when the Podder can find it fun. Remember 'Fun', Jules. It's a word we like to keep at the front of everything that happens in SupaPodia.

Surely not, thought Julian rebelliously, while remembering that he should be accepting, not questioning. He couldn't help asking himself, though: How can pain be fun? Defecation? Washing yourself? Laundering your clothes? Walking endless passages? Having bleeps sounding in your ears? Life – at least, his fifty years plus of life so far – had contained little fun. Was that a quality he wished for now then, above all, or rather was it not contentment and peace of mind that he sought? There was fat chance of the latter at the moment.

His reflections were interrupted by Marion. "Jules, you'll need to make your lessons to the Podders fun, in particular the re-education you'll be required to present. Actually, the latter's not so difficult, as it's easy to show how stupid the OW was, and still is, in comparison with SupaPodia. Those of us who have been brought up Outside, like you, and me too to some extent, can see clearly what an Age of Stupidity we have escaped from."

Again, his mind rebelled a little. Certainly, he had found the OW a trial, but was it stupid? Perhaps it had been stupid to allow itself to be bled dry by the new SupaPods, but that was a very contentious thought indeed – treasonable even – and he didn't want to have thoughts like that. He was longing simply to accept and to conform.

They were standing by the elevator. People – both Orange and Lilac – were passing, but it was only they who were waiting for the lift. Marion reached forward and pulled at the collar of his shirt. "You should wear that outside your blazer," she said. "It looks more trendy, more sporty, and will help your image. Will you do that for me? She looked pleading.

"Of course". He helped her adjust his collar.

"That's a good boy." She patted him on the arm, her face close to his. He had half-expected another kiss but it did not come.

"In time, Jules, you'll be going back into the OW to undertake Re-Education. There's a programme to introduce SupaPodia to particularly backward areas. Some there are still living with the old folklore full of prejudices and superstitions. We want to make a start teaching their children the new history so as to make their eventual transference to us easier. Do you understand?"

"I do." Julian thought he must sound comprehending and on the ball, although he didn't really understand what she meant at all. The OW was being eroded away to nothing, its belief system, its knowledge, its history overturned. But that did not mean its past had no value and did not deserve to be recorded fairly in the context of its own time. Did Marion mean that the history of everything Outside had to be rewritten, and damned, in the light of SupaPodia's superior, more progressive ethics? Looking at her, with her face thrust towards him, her lips pouting, he realised that's *exactly what she does think* – or has been told to think. So who is it who controls SupaPodia and determines what shall remain of the OW and what be struck right out, and what it is its Lilac and Orange inhabitants should believe?

He knew the answer to his own question – the Eliti. He had heard about the Eliti (there had been many stories about them in the OW), but he had never met one of this most favoured breed. Would he get the chance now? Did they ever come to inspect the SupaPods? After all, it was they who had been instrumental in setting them up. Lord Rand, whom that professor with the funny name had mentioned in his talk, had only provided the idea. The Eliti had implemented it. Would that be something he had to teach? It was all very perplexing. He had only been with SupaPodia a short time, and he had been alternately lifted up, then cast down again – once, twice, three times; how many more? He must return to his vision of rightness that Marion's earlier declaration had given him. It was unsettling – frightening even – that his perceptions of SupaPodia were so contrasting, swinging from good to bad. What was it he truly believed? He could not teach what he didn't believe in.

The Sub-Floor to which Marion brought Julian next was greatly different in layout from the one with the accommodation Stacks he had seen earlier. There were fewer passageways and much greater open spaces. In one large hall into which they peered through a wide entranceway, Podders were sprawled about the floor, many in groups – family groups probably, thought Julian, as there were children with them, some of whom were running about screaming and mingling with neighbouring groups. Tots in orange romper suits crawled on the floor, while babies were asleep in cradles or held crying against their mothers' breasts.

Many of the Podders looked very fat, Julian noted again; they must feed well. They lay back against piles of cushions, watching the Screens that filled the walls, upon which a film – or rather, several films – were playing. It was hard for Julian to watch the action from Screen to Screen, but one film seemed to be an old-fashioned 'cowboy' from the OuterWorld, with guns firing and men falling, while another was in black and white with a couple of comedians hitting each other over the head. The sound boomed out from each Screen. As Marion had told him earlier, unlike the staff areas, there was no attempt here to isolate the separate sounds, or transfer them directly into the listeners' ears. The result was a cacophony Julian found pretty intolerable.

On one smaller Screen, tucked away in an alcove to his left, he thought he could make out images that were pornographic (there was a large group around this Screen). The more Julian strained to see, the more he made out things he had seldom, if ever, seen on film before, and he was shocked – greatly shocked!

Seeing the direction of his gaze, Marion said casually, "Yes, there's some sex experience material here for the Podders who want it, but they'll mainly look at that sort of stuff on their own head sets in their Pods, beamed directly from their chips. We allow a milder form of it here in the communal areas because it's educational and fun. The older children can learn while playing."

Julian's mouth was dry and he felt a sickness in his throat. Surely not. Surely she realises how harmful this is. If what I can see is considered mild, then what is the strong stuff like? In the OW before the Great Crash of the late '50s, hard pornography had become commonplace, available to all, from the youngest to the oldest, despite the feeble efforts made by a decaying central government to restrict access. Indeed, it was said by some moralists that the Great Crash had been partly caused by the moral decline induced by this evil. He had imagined a SupaPodia that was free of it. The problem in the OW had declined, anyhow, as the technology for viewing pornography, along with everything else, had gradually seized up owing to the collapse in communication infrastructure and the non-availability of viewing devices. It was distressing, therefore, to find it flourishing in the new world of SupaPodia.

He had anticipated a utopia, not a hell. Amongst his see-sawing reactions to SupaPodia, this was perhaps not the most important matter, but it represented his first clear disillusionment, from which collectively in time he would find it hard to recover. Yet there was so much to admire about SupaPodia. Could he not then learn to turn a blind eye to the things he found so personally offensive?

Marion could possibly sense he was upset because she said nothing further, but led him to another adjoining hall, the central part of which was taken up by rows of curving seats with a podium placed before them. The seats were full of Podders, adult men and women as far as Julian could tell from the heads projecting above the lumpy orange suits. The podium was occupied by Stanley – a somewhat different looking Stanley than earlier because he was now wearing a bulging lilac blouse and loose trousers, very similar in style to the orange attire of the Podders.

"These are fairly new entrants, I believe," Marion told Julian. "They are having their first re-education session. This is one of the places where you'll be working, taking over from Stanley who – poor dear – has much else to occupy him. You'll need to mug up on the re-education stuff. It's easy really. 'OuterWorld – Bad: SupaPodia – Good'. Keep that before you. That's all there is to it."

Was she now being cynical, Julian thought? He had thought her absolutely sincere before, but now he was finding it hard to judge what Marion really thought.

Pulling him by the sleeve, Marion drew him closer to the Podders in the back row of the seats – so close, in fact, that some turned to look at them. Such empty eyes, Julian thought, such dumb, unquestioning faces. He found rebellious thoughts entering his head, thoughts he knew were wrong and not really his at all. They did not correspond to his real beliefs, nor to the ideals he had expected of SupaPodia. Yet, still the perverse thoughts came. He did not seem able to switch them off.

Why do these people have to be educated anyhow, his head asked him? Give them a pile of food and put a games panel before them, and they will be happy by the hour (sorry, by the coloured segment) until SupaPodia gives them something else to do; because that is it, isn't it? SupaPodia controls in everything. There is no more freedom here than a kid has with his toys in a nursery. The kid may seem preoccupied and all-happy, but let him try to leave the room and find out for himself about anything else that is going on – or could be going on – and…and…and that won't be allowed.

That last conclusion seemed rather tame. He may not know what the real Marion thought, but by the same token he did not know what the real Julian thought either, that Julian from the OuterWorld who had striven so hard to come inside a SupaPod. The roller-coaster of thought went on and on. He liked, then he didn't like. If 'not liking' was the bottom of the loop, then he was beginning to think that was where he should stay.

For the first time, within these nascent thoughts, fear raised its spiky head. What *did* happen if you disobeyed what SupaPodia told you to do? It was a question as applicable to him as a staff member (a Lilac) as any ordinary Podder resident.

Julian felt suddenly quite shaky. Was this the effect of the implantation he had so recently endured, or was it on account of these surging thoughts in his head? Really, he should find the strength to repress them. Once again, his brain played with the alternative, the view that he really wanted to be able to adopt if only his conscience would let him, that time passing would surely put these matters into a much better perspective.

Stanley's soapy voice began to penetrate his ears. He paid particular attention to what he said, as Marion had told him it would probably not be long before he stood in his place.

"....And you will soon come to realise, now that you are secure here in SupaPodia, that much of what you will have been familiar with in that OuterWorld from which you have been so fortunate to escape is a gross distortion of the truths and values you should have been born into. You have had a life of struggle when it might have been one of ease and fulfilment. Outside, you will have had your rulers telling you they were doing their best for you, whereas in reality they were taking advantage of you, using you for their own gain, creating wealth out of you, then discarding you to the four winds when you were not needed anymore. Look at those who controlled your lives – your bosses at your place of work, whose income was so vastly greater than yours; is it any wonder that they kept you on the lowest wage possible, so as to be able to seize the wealth that you had helped create for themselves, their friends and their fellow class of money men? NOW, here in SupaPodia, you will not NEED money anymore: everything SupaPodia has is shared with you...and you...and you..." [Stanley was pointing around the room] "...EQUALLY. And look again at your former rulers – the kings, queens, dukes, earls, bishops, archbishops, and so on, and so on; what a useless, seedy bunch they were, corrupt, debauched, self-serving, most certainly not interested in YOU. Once, they even made you go though the absurd business of voting for them and their agents, known as politicians; that is what they called your 'democratic right', what an abused term that was and what a burden for the ordinary people confronted by it, for how could they – how could you – possibly have had the knowledge to know what they wanted you to vote for? So often the wrong result was given and the people, through no fault of their own, had to be chastised accordingly through loss of benefits and further taxation: it was all most unfair and the cause of much discontent. Thankfully, all that has gone now, the former politicians being replaced by SupaPodia's own growing numbers of OuterWorld Commissioners. You will certainly owe one of these Commissioners a great debt, for it will have been he or she who has provided the means for getting you here inside our SupaPod."

"You will understand, SupaPodia was first opened as a retreat from the decaying OuterWorld – an alternative life in a controlled environment, one that is organised entirely in its residents' own interests – but now we are reaching out again to the OuterWorld, not to exploit it, not to drain it of resources – it has done pretty well in those areas itself! – but to RE-EDUCATE IT. Re-Education is our No.1 priority, and you will hear many more talks from me and my Lilac colleagues based around this all-important requisite – RE-EDUCATION. We will soon set you some little tests, and the very smartest of you will earn rewards – for we do believe in rewards for those who do their personal best for SupaPodia, as well as enjoying its benefits. All of us like a little competition for which we can win prizes. And what are our prizes? No, not a trip back into the OuterWorld! Who wants that?" [Stanley laughed, and there was a titter about him]. "But a transfer – temporary or permanent, as you may wish – to another of the now global-wide chain of SupaPods. How do you fancy moving to Hong Kong, or Sydney, or Honolulu, or Rio de Janeiro, or Beijing, or Shanghai, or Dar es Salaam – different people to mix with, different foods to eat, different entertainments to enjoy? How exciting will that be? Why, I think I'll enter one of those competitions myself!" [more laughter].

Stanley's face was so flushed, Julian felt concern for him. His wild gaze swung over the rows of seats before him, then suddenly lighted on Marion and Julian standing at the back. "And if I, myself, should disappear out to Moscow or Helsinki or Papua New Guinea, or more likely when you get tired of my voice, or more likely still when it gives out [more titters], I will have a new protégé – a new Lilac – to entertain you and inculcate you with the wisdom of SupaPodia – my new colleague here, DR. JULIAN FOSTER." [Stanley was waving his arms towards Julian, and he saw all the heads turning to look at him]. "That's not a medical doctor, folks, you understand; not the Dr. Foster who went to Gloucester. Ha! Ha!" [he laughed uproariously at his own joke] "But it's what you're called for studying at one of those posh colleges in the OuterWorld. Still, we can't all be perfect! Ha! Ha! Julian has only just come in from the OW to join us as a Lilac. He'll soon be working here with you."

For an awful moment Julian thought Stanley was going to summon him up to stand beside him on the podium, but fortunately he didn't. As Marion tugged at his sleeve to leave, he heard Stanley begin again:

"Now, where was I? Ah, yes. Next, I'm going to tell you about all the wars that were forced upon the people Outside, some of them relatively recently, although it seems hard to believe. Thank SupaPodia, we don't have such things now, not here in SupaPodia – but all those generals and other army men who used to proliferate in the OuterWorld very nearly destroyed it, and what for? Yes, you have it: for the pursuit of money; the things which create money, for example oil or those other commodities found in the ground – uranium, titanium, gold, diamonds, the list is a long one....Ridiculous, isn't it? Whole populations were slaughtered in the quest for more land where you could dig that stuff up. Unbelievable, isn't it? And it's not as if those generals, and the like, were any good at the killing and destruction they were meant to do: many were the spawn of their rulers, effete and ignorant. They couldn't plough a field, as some of you have done, or put a tap on a pipe, or clean a chimney, or do the laundry – and they couldn't command an army either. Their incompetence in war after war led to hundreds of thousands of deaths, deaths that were totally unnecessary. Well, I tell you, there's no more of that in the world of SupaPodia. Here we have no armies, no policeman either with truncheons knocking you about – a lot of that used to go on in the OW, and it still does, I am sure...."

Stanley's voice grew fainter as Marion at last succeeded in prising Julian away – he had been fascinated by Stanley's rant, thinking will I be expected to spout such stuff too? – and then it was shut out entirely as she pushed together the double doors to the Education Hall (as a sign on the doors named it). They stood in a broad passageway that curved away on both sides. Along the walls were many notice boards, looking very OW and old-fashioned here, being festooned with posters and cards and even scruffy scraps of paper. Several passing Podders were stopping to read. The beating, screeching music that seemed to permeate many of the Podder areas was still playing here, but thankfully, for Julian at least, the volume was low.

"Has Stanley ever lived in the OW?" he asked Marion.

"No, I don't think so. He was fast-tracked to us from another SupaPod. He occasionally goes Outside to extend his knowledge, but not for long. As I do too. Why do you ask?" She was peering at some of the notices, frowning.

"Oh, he seems so sure of everything. I thought it might have been from personal experience. So how then does he know what he teaches?"

Marion turned to fix her dark eyes on him. "Now, don't be cynical. There's no place for that in SupaPodia. Or, indeed, for any doubt about the core beliefs of SupaPodia. We have been selected for a purpose, and we must fulfil it to our utmost. If you cannot believe at first, then pretend to believe until belief comes naturally and spontaneously."

"But that's...." He didn't finish. In the old OuterWorld, he would have used the word, 'brain-washing'. But he didn't dare do so to Marion – Marion

45

who had kissed him so gently and with feeling. He didn't want to upset her with his internal turmoil.

Kissing – and sexual contact more generally – were certainly things the Podders seemed interested in, for many of the notes and papers attached to the corridor walls were taken up by these subjects. Marion appeared fascinated by them too, as if she had never looked at these notice boards before.

"See this," she said, indicating a large card scrawled in red and blue inks that she had been reading. 'Single F Podder, born this Pod long time, now fully developed, seeks single M, or with others F and M, for mutual satisfaction. Double Pod. Pod L33/SF21/P279/863Z ref. to find. All welcome."

"She's living dangerously," Marion commented. "That sort of casual encounter would not be allowed in her Pod Stacks."

"But how do Podders meet other Podders, then? – I mean to..to.."

"Have sex? There are official dating groups, where you can pair off. Or there are communal body exploration encounters…"

"What lots of people together?!" Julian was horrified.

"Yes, why not? It serves a purpose. The rooms that are used all have little alcoves where Podders can have some privacy, if they wish." She laughed. The OW, despite its vaunted sexual freedoms where virtually anything went, is, or rather was – I don't know what things are like now – still a pretty puritanical place. People expressed horror – or pretended to do so – at love expressed in public. We don't mind that so much here, just really where exactly it takes place. In a structured society like SupaPodia, there need to be rules. We don't want sexual activity going on, for instance, in the passageways or the main communal halls."

I'm pleased about that, thought Julian.

"But while we're on the subject of sex and procreation" Marion said, walking him further along the passageway away from the notice boards, "SupaPodia tries to keep the birth rate within the accommodation Pods as low as possible, just so that new life can always be present and developing, but with due consideration as well for the limited available space in most SupaPods. Huge as they are, space for new entrants, and that includes new birth, has to be carefully controlled. Of course, babies are an important component of the SupaPodia communities, but we have to be very careful to get the balance of young and old right. It's most unusual for any female Podder to be allowed more than one child. I'm a member of a committee that oversees these matters. We place the greatest emphasis on the use of contraceptives where full M/F sex cannot be avoided, but educate on other forms of recreational sexual expression where procreation is not the desired result – M/M or F/F sex, for instance, or simply self pleasure. Each Podder can call up from his chip any amount of material to help inform and stimulate."

Yet again, Julian's new world was blurring and taking new shape, then blurring again, so that he did not quite know where he was or what he thought. He didn't like some of what he was hearing from Marion, yet on the other hand he had to ask himself what he had really imagined would be the situation in such an artificial environment as a SupaPod, with so very many complex issues of social organisation. There was very much he still did not know. Did Podders come up from the bowels of the SupaPod into the open air, he wondered? And, if so, how often? He certainly hoped he, as a Lilac, would be allowed to. He could not bear the prospect of being cooped up for long periods – or forever? – within concrete walls under artificial light. He had to be able to see daylight and feel fresh air on his face, at least from time to time. Surely, everyone – Podders and Lilacs alike – would share that desire.

The trouble, he realised, was that he had not really thought about life in a SupaPod at all. Having obtained his prized ticket into SupaPodia, away from the mean flat where he had been living, with its fungus covered walls and the platoons of rats that patrolled the landings, and his job that had scarcely brought in enough to feed himself with one small meal a day, there had been only one principal thought in his mind – to actually get into the SupaPod to which he was assigned, where, despite likely downsides, surely security and progress must prevail. He had thought of his immediate future as an adventure and a discovery: the reality had little concerned him – until now!

Marion was looking at him speculatively, "I hope I haven't shocked you at all, Jules. The sex thing here works well enough on the whole. We don't have any real trouble. Just the occasional fight amongst the Podders."

The last comment sparked Julian to ask a further question. "Who deals with that then? Does the SupaPod have a police force?"

She laughed, "No, most certainly not. We don't need one: people in uniform with blue lamps on their heads charging about, exerting their authority. How awful that would be. There is a small monitoring unit of Lilacs on each Level, however, and sometimes on each accommodation Sub-Floor. They are there for everyone's safety. They would intervene, if necessary, and take any recalcitrants away."

"Where would they be taken to?"

"You know, I'm not sure. I've heard a rumour that it's somewhere on the Lower Levels. They'd probably be put to work there for a while, until they're deemed fit to return."

"What work is done there then?"

My, Jules, you are asking such questions now." She aimed a playful punch at his arm, hitting the place where his implant had been made, so he winced. "Oh, so sorry, Jules. Here, let me make it better." And she bent her head to kiss the furry fabric of his blazer over his sore arm. Then she kissed him once more softly on the cheek. "There, better?"

"Quite better," he said, feeling a stirring of excitement in the pit of his stomach. Could he..? Was it conceivably possible...? He liked Marion. Did the kissing mean she liked him? Could he get to know her better? He didn't know. Amongst all his confusion of thought, he quite forgot to follow up on his question about what happened on the Lower Levels of the SupaPod.

5

Julian felt very tired. He had returned to Sub-Floor 87 of Level 19, from where he had begun his tour with Marion, how many hours ago? – oh, of course, hours didn't exist here, so it was simply 'a long time'. Marion had said she felt tired too, and they should both have a rest before the party that had been talked about.

Marion had led him back into the entrance court of the Stack of Lilacs' Pods, which included his own, L19/87/379/224B, as printed on his key, which was as well because he knew he would be unable to memorise this reference, at least not for a long time. Neither would he ever learn all these tortuous, twisting routes with their innumerable locations. Marion presumably did so through the Guidance provided by her chip, and he felt a gulp of nervousness that his would be activated soon: what would happen if he couldn't cope with all the bleeps and sounds emanating from it? Why did the directional signals have to come directly into his sensory system? Why couldn't they be relayed through the Control Pad (CP) Marion had said he would be getting soon, or some sort of headset? The answer was probably that those devices could be separated from the individual. SupaPodia clearly demanded that Lilacs be available at all times and in constant position.

The OuterWorld had by now been left far behind SupaPodia in scientific advance. All the very best scientific brains had long since been recruited by SupaPodia, and lived and worked – or so the rumour had come to Julian – not in the SupaPods themselves but in the exclusive new scientific parks opened by the Eliti on regenerated city land, where their shining laboratories, their deluxe apartments, their parks and gardens with cascading, crystal fountains were a marvel to view. Every advance in technology and medicine, therefore, went not to the OW but to the world of the Eliti, who fed aspects of it into the SupaPodia systems as seemed most appropriate and cost-efficient and controlling: the implanted chips were one of the best and most recent examples of this.

The main beneficiaries of the many medical advances were, of course, the Eliti themselves, who were said to be able to live routinely past 100 years now (years, of course, still being keenly counted in the world of the Eliti, if not in that of the incumbents of their SupaPods). Many a gleaming white smile, an unwrinkled skin, a pert jutting bosom, a bushy head of hair, an everlasting golden tan, a youthful beating heart, and strong regenerating livers and kidneys could be attributed to the medical talent now working directly for the benefit of the Eliti. In the OW that Julian had left behind, you would be lucky to find a doctor at all, and most hospitals now were old rambling places, made up of crumbling rooms with antiquated equipment. Ambulances rusted outside, jacked up on bricks with their wheels removed. The wheels were needed for the hand-pulled carts that took their place.

This is what Julian had seen with his own eyes shortly before leaving for SupaPodia. His own father had died of neglect in such a place, kept on a trolley bed beneath a leaking roof, and visited by a doctor at last only to pronounce him dead. His mother, years earlier, injured by a fall, had thankfully died at home, but only after months of pain with a badly set leg, as there had been no one but the mad woman up the lane with her bag of herbs to tend her.

All these thoughts ran angrily through Julian's mind as he found his way, via his tiny lift, into his Pod once more, relieved to see that it was as he had left it, with his suit case pushed under the couch. He had no idea of who else might have entry to his Pod, key or no key. When was his chip due to be activated? Tomorrow was it? When would tomorrow be? There were no more tomorrows. He seemed to remember Marion had said, by the next Orange. How long then was that? He had already lost all idea of time. All he knew was that he was very tired and he wanted to sleep. So he flung himself down onto his bouncy couch and he slept.

How long he slept, he did not know. Opening his eyes, he found himself enveloped in blackness, a frightening sensation, for it was as if he were cut off from everything he understood and was floating deep in outer space. Then, with a jolt, he remembered where he was – in his Pod, but there was no outline to the Pod at all now, just a long night that drifted before his questing eyes as if he lay within the blackest of swirling mists. He checked the growing impulse of fear that threatened to engulf him, and swung his legs over the edge of the couch. Immediately a light shone out above his head, and grew steadily brighter, so that soon the shape of the Pod became clear to him, with one of the cupboard doors half open and he could see his few possessions there – and he recognised them and himself also.

His head was buzzing, and he shook it to clear it, but the action made no difference. He sensed that something within him was different, and in a flash he realised – the implanted chip had been activated! This was what his life would be like from now on – noises in his head to control him and direct him, just as Marion had said, only she had never really explained anything clearly at all. He felt hungry and thirsty. How was he to obtain food and drink? How was he to find clean clothes? How was he to live and find his way amongst all those monstrous tunnels, galleries, and huge vaults that he had been shown? – yesterday? – only now there was no time here either that he understood. Time was not needed now. To the denizens of a SupaPod, the accumulation of time in relation to the OuterWorld was clearly an irrelevance.

"God," he groaned out loud, forgetting again his determined atheism. "What have I gone and done? What will happen to me next?" If he expected the chip to give him an answer, he was disappointed. There was only silence. Even the buzzing had now died away.

He had a brainwave. In fact, it was more of a sense of compulsion, as if someone or something beyond him was now telling him what to do.

"Food," he called out. And immediately a tray slid out of one of the slots on the far side of his couch. The tray was covered with various foodstuffs sealed in plastic coverings. He selected two packets, and the tray slid away again. He struggled to open the packets, and in exasperation called out "Knife", and immediately another smaller slot delivered to him a cutter with a revolving blade. It was hard to use, but eventually he was able to slice open the packets, finding they contained biscuits and a tube of what seemed to be margarine or liquid cheese: he squeezed this onto the biscuits.

He munched at his meal, then said "Drink", and the tray returned with various small bottles set into slots on its surface. He selected one that was labelled 'Water' and another that contained some indeterminate fruit juice (it had a picture on it of purple berries). Both bottles and food packets were marked with the letters 'S' and 'P', separated by a slanting spearhead, which he assumed was a symbol of SupaPodia.

The door to his Pod slid back suddenly with a swishing sound, and, startled, he turned his head to see Marion standing there – at least he thought it was Marion, for he scarcely recognised her: she was wearing a short purple skirt, a mere pelmet about her plump thighs, and a white woollen top that swelled into two sharp-pointed peaks. Her legs were encased in high polished boots that shone like mirrors. Running across her short black hair from ear to ear was a silver metal band.

"Ah, I see you're activated and making progress," Marion said, sitting beside him on the couch. "Ready for the party?"

"How can I be?" Julian grumbled. "I don't know what I'm doing. I don't know where anything is? The chip – if that's what it is – is bursting my head."

She laughed, laying her hand on his arm. Her thighs, cut by the skirt, swam before his eyes. "I know. I was just like you. All the staff here have gone through the same thing. Believe me, you'll quickly get accustomed to it, and then…" – she swayed her body, pushing out her breasts at him – "… then you can start having some fun."

Julian ignored the breasts inches from him, although he ached to touch them. He knew it would be a great mistake to do so. Probably she was an enticer, set up to judge how he behaved. If he transgressed any code of SupaPodia ethics, he might yet be flung back to the OW, or, worse, be consigned to join the Podders.

"Here," she said. She held out a booklet. "This is a Guide. Everything you need to know about living with the implant is set down here. I should have let you have it before you were activated, but I had to dig out a copy. There're in quite short supply."

He took the booklet, which had on its cover that icon of SupaPodia, an ecstatic face, he had seen before; he could not remember where exactly. The title in silver lettering was, 'Your Implant and You'. He flicked through the pages. There were descriptions of the chip and how it worked, and explanations of its different functions, including a step-by-step guide to 'First Activation'. He was finding it hard to concentrate. The print was jumping up and down before his eyes. He blinked to try and clear them.

Marion laughed. A hard, unkind sound, he thought, but probably not intended as such. "You're in quite a state, aren't you?"

She tugged the booklet out of his hand and threw it behind her onto the couch. "Let me take you through the most important things. You can speak instructions for routine daily needs – food, clothes, washing items, and the like. All the key words are programmed in. There's a list at the back of the booklet. I can see you've worked out some of that already. Well done! Now, how about waste? Let's get rid of the rubbish." She pointed at Julian's empty food and drink packaging. "Say 'Dispose'. You have to do so, not me, as this Pod's zeroed to you."

"Zeroed?"

"Just a term that's used here."

"DISPOSE," Julian said, as loudly as he could.

"You don't have to shout".

"Sorry."

A shoot, similar to the one he had pitched his old clothes into when he had first arrived in the SupaPod, opened in the wall at the foot of the couch. Marion tossed in the empty food containers, and after a pause the shoot disappeared back into the wall.

"What would you like to deal with next?"

"My clothes."

"Ah yes. A bit more complicated, I'm afraid. You can get replacement uniform items just by saying the relevant words via your chip. Someone will actually bring those to you from Stores: there's no delivery tube for them as yet, although I've been told by Stanley one's planned. Underclothing and night attire is brought to you in the same way, but you should have some here already. She leant forward and slid out a tray in the base of the couch. Inside, Julian saw some lilac-coloured clothing in plastic bags. Marion pulled out one item, holding it up; it was a brief – very brief – pair of underpants, more like a loincloth than anything else.

"There you are," she said giggling. "You'll look a wow in those. Hardly get your tackle in. But you can specify new styles and measurements anytime."

"How?" said Julian. He was irritated by Marion's intrusive silliness and her vulgarity.

"Look, it tells you here." She flipped the pages of the Guide and stabbed with her finger at a section, 'How to Order Your Clothes'. Just say 'Clothes' and give the new sizes. It goes through automatically to the Clothes Department."

"Will they know who I am?"

"Of course. You have a unique reference that's transmitted by the chip. All your personal details are on it, including the clothes sizes you will have given when you were recruited."

"Ah, yes." Julian remembered the strings of personal questions he had had to complete after his successful assignment to SupaPodia had come through. "All this seems too incredible to believe. How on earth does it work?"

"How does anything work? It does, that's all you really need to know."

"But, you say, tens of thousands – hundreds of thousands – of people are all linked up by tubes for instant service? Are the – er – Podders served like this too?"

"Yes, of course. Their food is not as good as ours, and they only have one type of clothing, unlike us; but their Pods are connected in the same way.

They take their main meals in their communal halls, though, as we do also – only ours are separate from theirs, as you've already seen."

"Don't these systems ever break down?"

"Oh, sometimes there are snarl ups, yes – blockages, you know – but there're soon cleared."

"Who services it all?" Julian thought his head would burst with a mixture of wonderment and disbelief.

"The Podders themselves in the main. Or the SupaPod's Maintenance Department. We have some top engineers here, the very best brains that SupaPodia has recruited."

Ignoring his still furrowed brow, she stood up, pulling down the hem of her skirt. "Now let's get back to immediate practicalities because time's short." She checked the timepiece on her wrist with its coloured segments. "When it comes to your own casual clothing – I mean non-uniform – you can tell them what you want. They'll send you a catalogue of what they have in stock. You can see it on your Screen. Of course, I haven't told you about that either. The most important thing of all!" She slapped her thigh as if to chastise herself. "You have two Screens. One's here in your Pod…" She pointed at the Screen Julian had already noted in the wall at the end of the couch: he hadn't known how to switch it on. "…and the other's with your portable device, your Control Pad. It'll be the same type as the one you've seen me using. It's kept here, if it's been stored properly… Ah, yes…" She felt within another tray that slid out from the base of the couch and pulled out a CP. "The Screens are synchronised: they have exactly the same information and controls, one to use in your Pod and the other outside. They will be ready programmed for you – for all your personal needs and your work as an Educator."

She pressed a button on the side of the CP and both it and the wall Screen immediately lit up. 'Welcome to SupaPodia, Julian Foster', a message read.

"Simply say, 'Clothes Catalogue'," Marion said.

He did as she said, and illustrations of men's clothing filled the main Screen one after another, responding to his command, "Next…Next."

"Just use the word "Send" for anything you like and it will be delivered to you. There's no restriction on the number of items, or indeed type of garment. You can try out what you like and send it back. If you feel like going transgender, you'll be able to get girlie stuff too."

He looked at her, alarmed to see she wasn't joking. Yet, that disturbing thought apart, he had to admit to being excited at what he could now wear. New clothes had been hard to come by in the OW. Most had been secondhand – mainly from the recently deceased, or so it was said. The jacket he had worn to the SupaPod, and had had to discard, had cost him a month's wages at the Area Council offices, where he had worked after his university lectureship had gone bottoms up, together with the MidWealden University itself.

"What about my clothes for the party?" he asked, remembering the invitation he had been given and very much aware of Marion's own most casual appearance.

"Oh, just go as you are. You can take off your blazer to look a bit more relaxed. And undo a couple of buttons" She picked at the front of his lilac shirt with her red nails. "There, that's much better."

She looked at her timepiece again. Julian could see the arrow hand was well into the green segment, the agreed period. "We should be off. Are you ready? See how you get on with the chip self-guiding system. Say 'Guidance Set', followed by 'L19 SF11/80 Staff Lounge'."

"Guidance Set. L19 SF11/80 Staff Lounge," he called out obediently, immediately aware of a dinging sound in his head like that made by lifts when they reached their destination.

"Let's go," said Marion. They left the Pod, and used the curving tube next to the lift to the landing below – like two whooping, excited children, Julian thought. Scrambling to his feet, momentarily glimpsing Marion's jumbled legs and underwear, he became aware of more buzzes in his head, which lessened as he walked forward into a gallery, but increased in pitch if he veered towards a side passage.

Marion came up beside him. "You see how the chip will guide you. Keep in the right direction and there's no sound, but go the wrong way and it will let you know through a series of rising bleeps. Go too far off course and they can become quite painful."

"So, how do I stop that?"

She laughed. "You can't. I've told you that already. But you can always switch the Guidance off, then reset it."

"How the hell do I do that?" Julian was growing testy with this encumbrance to his natural movement. Before things in the OW had grown as bad as they were now, he had liked to walk in the country, climbing the Downs by steep winding paths, enjoying the views from the hill tops, feeling a sense of freedom in the open air. And now, he couldn't even tread these claustrophobic deep-buried tunnels without having a noise in his head – no freedom at all, not even to turn momentarily to one side. This was progress? Yes, of course, it was! SupaPodia was progress, the way forward for civilisation. He must not allow those central truths to be blunted by a few inconveniences that were only temporary.

"You simply use the commands 'Off' and 'Reset'," Marion said. "Simplicity, isn't it. "It won't reset, though, unless it's off first. I think that's being worked on at the moment, so eventually you'll be able to say just 'Reset' and you'll get the new course straightaway."

Julian shook his head in silent wonderment and continued his progress. The sounds in his head drew him on: a deeper sound, he learnt, meant he had to take an elevator. Now which way – up or down? Marion stood to one side, watching him. It was clear she was not going to intervene. When the lift appeared, it was going downwards with others, and they got in. The buzz in his ears increased to a sharp intensity, plaguing him so much he called out 'Off', and the high-pitched buzz immediately disappeared. No one reacted to his spoken word, but faces did seem to have sympathetic smiles.

When they halted at last and the doors opened, the elevator emptied leaving only himself and Marion inside. She said, "Yes, the wrong way. That happens to most of us early on. You have to be patient. There are only so many elevators."

"But didn't your own chip pain you?"

"My Guidance is not on. I know the way. You have to experiment with elevators – the ups and downs. Sometimes you have to proceed by trial and error. But at least you *won't* get lost. You'll get there in the end, and soon – like me – you'll learn many routes without Guidance. Then it'll be your turn to feel smug, watching others learning."

In response to Julian's renewed command in the elevator, they soared up to Level 18, and exited into a scrum of Lilac medicos, with stethoscopes dangling about their necks, waiting to descend. Julian spotted Peter amongst them and waved a hand at him. They then trod a network of passages until they reached the Lilacs' Lounge, announced by a red glowing sign above the double wooden doors. For the last part of the journey he had not been troubled by any Guidance sounds at all; once he was set on the right path, they died away completely. Oh, it's not so bad after all, he thought.

A corner of the lounge had been decorated with dangling strips of silver and gold foil, fixed to door posts, light-fittings and ceiling vents, and there was an enormous hovering balloon in one corner, upon which two blue eyes, a round nose, and a wide mouth with smiling red lips were painted. Close to it, a lilac-coloured cloth banner, decorated with sparkly stars, had 'WELCOME JULIAN' written across it in large black letters.

As Julian and Marion entered the room, music began playing, a song Julian did not know, but the tune was catchy and he began to flick his fingers to it.

If I knew you were comin' I'd've baked a cake
baked a cake, baked a cake
If I knew you were comin' I'd've baked a cake
Howd-ya do, howd-ya do, howd-ya do

Oh, I don't know where you've come from
'Cause I don't know where you've been
But it really doesn't matter
Grab a chair and fill your platter
And dig, dig, dig right in

Smiling at the asinine lyrics, he saw across the room the three girls whom he had met in the canteen earlier. They were leaning against a counter that served as a bar, each with a drink in her hand. Marion had been immediately engaged in conversation by a bearded man wearing what looked like a white nightgown, so Julian walked over to the girls. The curvaceous blonde who had suggested the party thrust a drink in a tall glass at him. Her breasts pushed out of her pink dress like ripe fruit. His eyes were drawn to them like magnets

"I assume you like lager."

He dragged his gaze to her face. "Yes, I do. Thank you." He took a sip appreciatively. The beer in the OW had been watered to look and taste like river water. This lager was as full and strong as any he remembered from more distant years.

"How are you settling in?" she asked.

At the door, there was a sudden multi-coloured swirl of people entering. Before he could answer, his questioner was swept away by a tall black man wearing skin-tight blue trousers and a white tee shirt. "Ah, Gina, my girl." Then to Julian, "Excuse us, please." And she was gone, towed away, with just a backward glance at Julian that spoke to him, "I'll be back." They disappeared through a side door.

The pretty girl with the long brown hair whom he had particularly liked earlier laughed, "That was Dennis. He's got a pash for Gina. Taken her straight off without even a drink." She giggled with her neighbour. Both wore dark trousers and white blouses. "But then we all have a pash for Gina, don't we Clarrie?"

Clarrie blushed and looked shyly into her drink, while Julian, feeling suddenly awkward, took a great gulp of lager. No, not that; not here. It was the OW surely which was promiscuous, lax and decadent, without sexual morals. What then had he expected in SupaPodia? – Chastity? Restraint? so-called Normality? No, none of these, perhaps. Yet…..He couldn't complete the thought, for he realised he didn't know where it was going.

If I knew you were comin' I'd've baked a cake
Hired a band, goodness sake
If I knew you were comin' I'd've baked a cake
Howd-ya do, howd-ya do, howd-ya do.

Someone put another beer into his hand. It was a brown bottle labelled 'Strong Lager', with the logo beneath of 'SP' separated by an angled spear. He poured the beer into his glass, his head already beginning to swim a little. He peered up at the person who had given him the bottle, seeing that it was Marion.

"How are you doing?"

"Fine, thank you."

"Where's Gina?"

"She's gone off with Dennis." Julian said this glibly, proud that he was learning names.

"Don't get drunk. You'll have to give a speech."

"A speech?! You never told me that."

"Just a few words to say thank you and how pleased you are to be with SupaPodia."

She left. Julian said to the long-haired girl. "How long have you been here?"

She laughed. "What here now?"

"No, in this SupaPod?"

"I don't know. All my life."

"So you don't come from the OW?"

"No. I was born here. My parents were Lilacs."

"Where are they now?"

"They passed on."

"I'm sorry".

"Don't be. I'm not."

Julian stood looking at her, not knowing what to say. "What's your name?"

"Jane."

"It's a business working this place out, Jane."

"Why?"

"It's so confusing compared with the OW."

She laughed. "I have the advantage of you then since I've never been there."

"But how do you understand it then – the OW, I mean?"

"We get masses of films. There is an enormous library here about the OuterWorld. It's easy to pick up what it was like – still is, I suppose."

"It's not all bad, you know. There are some good people there trying to get by."

"Of course, I appreciate that."

"What do you do?"

"I'm a courier. Same as Carrie here. We show visitors about the SupaPod."

"What, visitors from the OW?"

"Sometimes. But mainly Eliti members."

"Really. That must be interesting."

"Yes, it is. They come from all sorts of OW places. We've just had a delegation from the Maldive Islands where their first SupaPod is about to open."

Julian felt a tap on his elbow, and he turned to see Carrie offering him another bottle of lager.

"I shouldn't really." He took it. "But thanks."

"What lovely girls you are," he said, topping up his glass.

"Do you really think so?" It was Carrie who spoke.

"Oh, yes." Julian's head was feeling fuzzy. "If I was a bit younger, I'd be asking you out – I mean both of you." He added the last bit hastily not wishing to offend either of his audience.

"What, at the same time?" They giggled together.

"And why not?" said Julian, feeling suddenly daring.

"Out where?"

"Ah, that's a point. Where does a man take a girl on a date here?"

That brought another bout of giggling, although Julian did not quite know why? It had seemed a reasonable question to ask. The party was growing busier and noisier. Another group, mainly still in their lilac uniforms, swept up to where Julian stood with the girls and engaged him in banter, while plying him with yet more drink – this time a can marked 'OW Export. Scrumpy'. He was so taken up with trying to make sensible answer to the comments flying at him that he poured the can's contents on top of the remaining lager.

"D'you get lots of booze here?" he asked a large man wearing a tunic, who had a black belt around his middle like a kung-fu fighter. He sensed he was slurring his words, and made a mental note that this must be his last drink.

"No. Fuck no. It's all smuggled in from Eliti stocks. A blind eye is turned on the whole. You're new, aren't you?"

"Yes. Only just arrived. I'm Julian." He pointed vaguely towards the banner next to the grinning balloon face.

"Well, Julian. You'll learn. Good luck."

"He was being slowly pushed into the middle of the throng, brushing against men and women, all noisy, turning, swirling, calling out, hanging desperately onto their drinks, almost all young, he dimly realised through the haze about him. Where then were the oldies of his own generation?

Had you dropped me a letter, I'd a-hired a band
And spread the welcome mat for you.
Oh, I don't know where you came from
'cause I don't know where you've been
But it really doesn't matter
Grab a chair and fill your platter
And dig, dig, dig right in.

The music stopped abruptly. A sudden clapping of hands. "Attention everyone. Attention. Silence! Silence!" The hubbub of conversation died away. Julian saw that Gina had returned and was standing up high on a circular red box, her arms raised. Her tanned legs, so wonderfully on show here, seemed to his disordered brain to be glowing. He felt a tremendous urge to have them spread over his groin. How under this eternal artificial light did she get her legs so brown? Her breasts, though, spilling from the pink dress were a snowy white, as were her arms, so perhaps she was wearing stockings. He remembered stockings, in the haze encompassing his mind, long ago before they had disappeared forever from the OW. Only aristocratic Eliti ladies wore such things now, or so the stories had done the rounds amongst OuterWorlders. Julian's thoughts tumbled on….

"It's good to see so many here," Gina was saying. "Any excuse for a party, eh?!" – a ripple of laughter – "But this party is to welcome a new Lilac, a distinguished academic from the OW who is to work in Re-Education. Here he is – Dr. Julian Foster!"

Spotting Julian in the throng, she beckoned to him to come up beside her, and he found himself, with head humming, pushed and pressed up to the red podium. As he reached Gina's enticing legs, clapping broke out around him, interspersed by one or two catcalls and whistles from the rowdier elements present – "Good on yer, Prof." "Welcome to Paradise." "Drink! Drink! Drink!"

He obliged by draining the glass he carried in one long gulp, which was greeted with cheers. Gina climbed down from the podium, and, taking Julian's arm, helped him step up. More cheers and applause. Inebriation can result in either a confused, embarrassing failure for the afflicted or it can provide the freedom for an inspired triumph. For Julian now, it was fortunately the latter.

"I'm so pleased to be here," he declaimed, waving his arms from the box. "I had no idea what to expect, but if it's all like this party it will be *tremendous*." There were cheers at that. "The SupaPodia I've seen so far looks superb. How pleased I am to escape from the tawdriness, the spite, the hatreds, the failure of the OuterWorld. What great comrades you are, my fellow Lilacs. I so much look forward to working with you, and" – he added on an impulse – "*playing* with you."

The last brought cheers and shouts of laughter, amongst which he heard, "As long as you don't play with yourself", which added further shrieks of merriment.

Gina caught hold of him as he stumbled down and nearly fell. They stood for a moment together, her arm about his shoulders and her left breast squashed against his chest. "Thank you for this party," he said to her.

"You're most welcome." She kissed him on the cheek and the applause sounded out again.

Everything became a blur after that. Despite his resolution, he had several more drinks, and he spoke nonsense to many faces that swam before him, which then disappeared as abruptly as they had come. He remembered seeing Gina with Dennis again, his hand cupped over her rounded pink backside as they disappeared from the room once more. He did not like to reflect on what they might be getting up to. Eventually, as the party began to break up, he remembered Marion and looked around for her. A strand of worry pierced his sozzled brain. How do I get back to my Pod without her, he wondered? He remembered he had the Guidance now, but what was the reference to his Pod? Of course, thank the Lord – a guilty correction of himself for invoking a deity – he had the reference on his key, which was still, most thankfully, in his trouser pocket. Carrie and Jane helped him call out the reference to his chip, giggling as they did so. He wanted to kiss both of them, but they were holding each other so tightly, like a pair of Siamese twins, that he didn't feel he could.

"L19/87/379/224B," he intoned against the background noise. There was no answering bell within his head.

"No bell," he said, peering at the girls, distressed. They collapsed forward laughing, then Carrie said, "Shhh! Too much noise. Say it again, Sam." More giggles.

"I'm not Sam, I'm Julian."

Laughter, then "Shhh!" again from both girls. Carrie's hand, he noted blearily, was pressed against Jane's crotch. He shook his head, as if bewildered – which he was. All this was new – too new – for him. He couldn't be sure with his swirling head, but he felt it was not what he wanted. Still for now, do what the devil does. If God was not allowed here, was the devil?

He said the reference again, and this time the bell sounded. "I'm off," he said triumphantly, steering a course through the few remaining party goers to the door. "Good luck," the girls called out. Turning with a departing wave, he saw them collapsed against each other, kissing.

The journey turned out to be far simpler than he had feared. Only once did the bleeps sound in his head, when he mistook a V-shaped junction of passages. He had no problem with the elevator at all, in which he was the only passenger. At last he approached the Pod Stack, which was his home. Standing beside his lift shaft in her short skirt and jutting white top was Marion. Just like a hooker, he thought, feeling no surprise. Somehow he had expected she would return; had perhaps been testing him.

She smiled at him. "Had fun?"

"Oh, yes."

"Good. I have some more inculcation to give you."

He remembered she was his official Inculcator in the ways of SupaPodia. What did she want now? He felt too tired to learn much.

He went first into the lift and she squeezed in behind him, her breasts squashed against his back. His head was still a little furry, but his senses were sharpening. Once inside the Pod, she held him and kissed him. His tiredness fell away. He told his Inculcator how lovely she was.

She took off her top and the purple skirt. "I've wanted you since I first saw you on the train," she said.

"Me too."

After that there was only pleasure, followed far too soon by darkness, then sleep. When he awoke, she had gone.

6

Life began to set into a routine for Julian. He ordered clothes and received them: a smart, tailored suit in a grey cloth, sports shirts and slacks, briefs and a thick woollen jumper (the latter in case he should be allowed to go to the surface to enjoy some fresh air). He asked Marion about fresh air access.

"Oh, yes. You can get as much, or as little, as you want. Up on the Upper Deck is best, although it's not actually open to the air. In your own time, of course."

She did not refer to their sex – one, or was it two or three of his old days past – and he treated her, and she him, as if it had not happened. It all seemed dreamlike now, but then everything in SupaPodia was dreamlike.

"What about the Podders?" he asked.

"*What* about the Podders?

"Can they go up to the surface?"

"Oh, yes. If they have a need. But only a minority want that. The great majority are quite content with their conditions below ground."

"I find that hard to believe. How can they not want to see – and feel – the real world?"

"A Pod *is* the real world," she said severely. "Most Podders recognise that and have no desire to go upstairs to drool over an OW they have either lost contact with or have never known. However, many are encouraged to use the exercise areas on their Levels, as obesity is a problem amongst Podders, and getting worse"

"I had noticed. Some real fatties. Their kids too."

"Yes, Jules. You don't have to be so judgemental. That's an OW attitude; not one for here. Just make sure *you* don't grow fat."

Julian looked suitably abashed. He must rid himself of all those prejudices which still dominated the OW.

Forcing her features into a smile suggesting forgiveness, Marion continued, "There are opportunities to go Outside as well for those who wish it, or need to."

"Need to? What Podders, you mean?"

"Yes, those who work maintaining links with the OW; those who work at the freight portals, for instance, supervising all the goods coming in. And then there are the occasional group trips out – some educational that you, yourself, might lead, to see the OW and visit some well-known places that still survive. For example, a trip went to Stonehenge fairly recently, just before some of the stones were taken down to be moved elsewhere. There are events Outside as well – pop concerts, and the like – that Podders can apply to visit. Oh, and sporting events, of course. There are Podder teams in most events, and they sometimes play OW teams."

"I had no idea of that. I hadn't heard of matches against Podders in the OW."

"They're quite discreet, where they're played; not in OW areas as such, but on the Eliti estates."

"Ah, of course, the Eliti. I was forgetting them."

"Yes, the Eliti," she said, a bit petulantly. "Don't forget the Eliti. Without them, we in the SupaPods would be nothing; indeed, we wouldn't exist."

It was a sombre thought, which he dwelt upon for a while. The Eliti had not been liked by the people still stuck in the OW. The collapse of most things was blamed on them – the OW economy, its government, its transport services, its education, its health care, and much more All resources from the OW were channelled into the SupaPods or to the Eliti themselves. Or so he had been told. He suspected now that the truth was very much different, and probably the OW only had itself to blame.

Marion only stayed with him for limited time periods now, half a Green segment or an Orange, which he thought related to mornings in the OW. Certainly, he had learnt that Blue was sleeping time. His sleeping had been good and deep in his Pod, much better than it had been in the OW, where the sounds of some late night drunken fight, or the noisy sex of his gay neighbour, had tended to penetrate the cardboard walls of his flat.

Julian had a wrist timepiece now. He had ordered this on his Pod Screen, and it had been delivered via a shoot directly to his Pod. It was still a wonder to him how this worked. The system involved in all the necessary shoots to Pods, from stores and kitchens and other places, twisting and turning, rising and falling, throughout the SupaPod, baffled his brain. And yet, he thought, this is only one part of the infrastructure. What about all the pipes, wires and cables that bring water, power and light, to each of us, Lilac and Podder alike, plus pictures and messages on Screens from every corner of the world? What a triumph of technology and engineering it is.

He had experimented with his Screen, ordering more clothes from the catalogue, including a silk dressing gown with a fire-breathing dragon embroidered on it, and a pair of silk pants that he thought Marion might appreciate. He still found it hard to believe the sex they had had, and he hoped it would come again. Disappointingly, Marion had not so far shown any inclination to repeat the experience.

He had glanced through the long list of key words in the Implant Guide that would produce a response from his chip. Most of these related to 'Guidance', 'Food', and 'Clothing', but there were others which intrigued him under 'Entertainment and Sports', including 'Sex Equipment', where he found listed a range of sex toys and sexual health products, as well as contraceptives, that could be ordered. There was nothing then puritanical about SupaPodia, he realised. He had been a little shocked, though, at his glimpse of the pornographic films in the Podder area he had visited with Marion. But, if he were honest, he also experienced a certain frisson. Such products had once been prevalent too in the old OW, but had vanished more recently, as with so many other idle things. There, it had become necessary for people to huddle up simply to keep warm, rather than indulge in sexual titillation. .

He tried out on the Screen certain key words of his own choosing, merely for his amusement to see if there would be any response. He spoke out 'Woman', then 'Tart', then 'Prostitute', then, greatly daring 'Sex', but the response Screen just stared back at him blankly. He stopped doing this when he realised later that such queries might well be recorded, and he might well be asked questions about them. He did not wish to jeopardise his position as a Lilac through any such silliness. Least of all did he want to be regarded as some sort of sexual deviant. However, he did hope for Marion to return to her previous favours, and he did think of Tina whom he had so admired that time when they had both arrived in the SupaPod. He had had no sight of her recently, but he remembered she had told him she would be working in Education, so he had some hope of seeing her again.

He had sorted out his Pod and grown used to its various features – the differing shoots, the small washing table (he had yet to find out where he might take a bath or a shower: he must ask Marion about that), the toilet (which flushed everything away and remained sweetly smelling), the sliding trays, and the small cupboard. The personal items he had brought from the OW, he had taken from the cupboard and arranged on shelves in a small alcove beside the Screen: there was a glass dish his mother had loved, a small box with an ivory lid inherited from his grandfather, a fossilised shell he had once picked up on a walk on the Downs, a key ring with the emblem of his old university on its tag, and a stainless-steel paper knife from the distant days of letters in envelopes, which he had been accustomed to employ in emphasising points to his students. He held it now, enjoying its smooth familiar feel, testing the sharp point against a finger tip. Together with the other items, the knife served as a tangible reminder of his previous life, which, despite all the bad things that had come into it, he had no wish to forget entirely.

He had returned to his Pod from a meal at the canteen (he was gaining for greater confidence in navigating himself to the different locations Marion had shown him), when there came a rattling on the outer door. Sliding it open and expecting to see Marion, he was surprised when a cheery red face topped by a lilac head scarf appeared, followed by a female body in lilac dungarees bearing a tube-like instrument with a long, flexible hose.

"Hello," she said. "I'm glad you're in. I'm Sandra, your cleaner. If you'd like to pop out, I'll pop in and do yer."

Julian laughed at that. "Oh good," he said. "I was wondering how I got the Pod cleaned. Not that it gets very dirty."

"Oh, you're a tidy gen'leman, are you? That's good. I wishes all was like yer."

"Are you a Lilac then?"

"No, dearie, I'm a Podder attached for Lilac duties. They'se gives me this lilac clobber t'wear. I likes the work. I gets Lilac food and drink."

"That's good then. You want me outside, do you?"

"If you doesn't mind, sir. I'll only be a couple of jiffies." Sandra had already started up the tube cleaner and was sweeping it around. She went to his little bathroom area, and he could see jets of some liquid being sprayed onto the stainless steel.

Julian had to squash past her to get to the door. Bent double to leave, he said above the whine of the machine, "I'm new here. I'm still learning. I wonder if you can help. Do you know how I can get a bath or a shower? What the facilites are?"

She turned off her machine. "They should've told yer. You goes to your Screen. 'Hygiene' is the word you'se have to say. Then you'll get some options and locations, and you'se can choose the time sector you'se want." She dug him in the ribs. "If you'se like a massage, dearie, there's some who'd do it, know what I mean?"

She gave him a wink that sent him sliding down the steel tube to the bottom floor. He waited there for her to come out. "All done, sir. I'll give you my name and location if you'se need any extra." And, dropping a plastic card into his hand, she made off to the next Pod Stack. He looked at the card. 'Sandra Goodheart. Cleaner to the Lilacs. Personal Attendant L17/29/185/856J'. Oh well, he thought, at least I'm learning how things happen here. Now why couldn't Marion have told me about that? Where is Marion, anyhow? He hadn't seen her for at least four time segments, and it was now well into Yellow.

Perhaps Marion was in tune with his thoughts, in some mysterious way that Julian did not understand, for it was only one gradation of Yellow later that she took the place of the recently departed Sandra at his door. She came in and squeezed beside him on the couch. "Well, Jules, how are you coming on?" She spoke over his stumbling, "Very well, thank you…" There was so much in his mind that he wanted to ask her that he couldn't get his words out.

"You'll begin work at the next R2. You'll meet up with Stanley at…" She looked at her CP. "I've just sent you his location reference. Speak it into your GS and you'll have no trouble finding him. How are you getting on with the Guidance by the way?"

"Very well. I've actually…."

"What are those? What are they doing there?" She had spotted his personal items set out in the alcove and had leant over and swept them onto the couch beside her. She picked up the paper knife, rubbing it between her fingers. "A knife too. Do you wish to cut your throat then?"

He laughed. "It's not sharp enough for that. It's just one of my things with memories for me. Sentimental things."

She took his head in her arms. "Dear Jules. You don't need them. You don't need anything that reminds you of your previous life in the OW. SupaPodia doesn't like it, and I don't like it. You like these, though, don't you?" She had opened her lilac blouse and fed one of her nipples into his mouth.

Any reply he could have made would have been inadequate. It was B3 before she left, leaving little sleeping time for a man facing the first day of his new job.

7

Julian wore a new pair of trousers, just received through one of his shoots, and his lilac SupaPodia blazer to attend for his first day of work training. He pinned a badge to his left lapel stating 'Julian. Educator: Grade 2'. He had found this, together with another badge in one of his blazer pockets. He must have been given them when he first arrived. He couldn't remember now. The second badge – 'Ask Me Anything' – he pinned to his right lapel.

He spoke the reference that had been transmitted to him by Marion into his GS and, exiting his Pod by the elevator, made his way without undue difficulty – it was wonderful, he thought, how quickly I've grown used to the Guidance bleeps and buzzes, just as Marion said I would – via passages and cross halls, with one elevator descent, to a corridor shut off by a clear panelled door marked 'EEC Offices'. Passing through this, he came to Room 106/A (he remembered this number as the last component of the situation reference) where the GS sounded two long buzzes in his head that signified he had arrived at his destination.

He knocked on the door. "Come in," a man's voice called. He entered, and there was Stanley seated in a swivel chair with his knees raised, making slow revolutions at the centre of the room. He turned some two or three further times, and then held out a hand to his desk to stop himself. His other hand he extended to Julian. Julian shook it; it felt as limp as it had before when he had first been introduced to him. However, there was no sign now of the failing creature who had had to be tended by Marion; nor, for that matter, of the self-satisfied, oozing orator whom he had heard rant on to the Podders. Stanley's cheeks were plump and rosy with apparent good health, and his manner quiet, courteous, and thoroughly professional. Julian had expected one or other of the previous Stanleys, not this new one.

"We're just waiting for my other new entrant," said Stanley. "And then we can make a start. How are you settling in?"

"Very well, thank you, Mr. er…"

"Please just call me Stanley. I've found first names help bond my team."

"Quite. I agree. Thank you, Stanley."

Julian did indeed agree. He had once headed up a working committee of fellow academics at MidWealden. It was after the British Army had been disbanded, and the Department of Environmental Studies, to which his committee reported, was advising Government (the former national government which still functioned then) on population demographics in the South which might make use of abandoned military land and properties. Julian had insisted that, whatever their seniority (and academics had been very sensitive about such things), they all used their first names. The project completed its recommendations on schedule, but the report was shelved. The first three UK SupaPods opened only two years later, one of their principal purposes having been to relieve the effects of overpopulation. Most of the hundreds of thousands of acres of the Defence Estate were to go to the Eliti, and some provided the sites for the next wave of SupaPod building.

As Julian stood smiling down at the seated Stanley, this long train of memory still running in his head, there came a further knock on the outer door, which brought Tina into the room. Julian was so pleased to see her again. She looked lovely in a lilac blouse and purple trousers, slim and graceful, her blonde hair drawn back and tied into a bun at the back. She shook hands with Stanley and smiled at Julian. She wore a large badge dangling from a chain about her neck; it stated: 'Christine. Educator: Grade 3. 'Ask So You May Learn.'

"Good, good," said Stanley, rubbing his hands together and swinging his chair from side to side. He waved Tina and Julian to two armchairs facing him. Behind Stanley was a *trompe l'oeil* window, painted as if the viewer were looking out through open shutters onto a garden, with green trees and blue sky seen in the distant perspective.

"So glad to have you two with me. I have been badly understaffed of late. Julian, I think Marion may have told you, you are going to have a big role in Re-Education. I am afraid that will mean several trips back into the OW – and Tina – you prefer Tina, don't you?..." [she nodded] "...you will partly understudy Julian, but will also work with me as my personal assistant. How will that suit the two of you?"

Both Tina and Julian nodded. "Sounds most interesting, Stanley," Julian said, striving to add a note of enthusiasm, although really his mind was full of confusion as to what his work would actually involve. "I'm always up for a challenge. I'm sure Tina is too." He looked at her, pleased to see she was smiling and nodding as well.

"Good. Good." Stanley rose to his feet and walked to a board covered by coloured markers set upon a black grid. Julian could make out the headings of some of the grid rows: 'Geography', 'Lit/Flick', 'Self-Help', 'Superstition', 'History'. He said, over his shoulder. "Julian, your specialism will be History. Tina, I will need you in Lit/Flick."

"What is Lit/Flick?" Tina asked.

"Oh, all about books and film – culture, you know. Who wrote what, where and when? – that sort of thing. We like the Podders to have the background to what they read and view. If I'm honest, they don't do much book reading, but they ought to know who first wrote what was later turned into film or musical, pop opera or rappersong – or whatever. They particularly like the more sensational details of a writer's life, if you understand me."

"Yes," said Tina, looking down. "I am sure I can give them that."

"Good, good."

"Stanley," Julian said. "I have taught History but my PhD is actually in Geography. Would I not be more useful to you in that subject rather than History?"

"Yes, Julian. I did think long and hard about that." Stanley seated himself again, swinging his chair towards Julian. "But we have a very good, long serving lady professor who is in charge of Geography. She's particularly good on the New Geography, so I must keep her in place, and I'm sure at your Grade you wouldn't wish a junior role under her.

"No, of course, not, Stanley," Julian said hurriedly. He was not sure what was meant by New Geography.

"I will send to your CP the History syllabus, plus that for New History, which forms part of Re-Education. The latter may contain a few tweaks from what you probably learnt at college, but I'll expect you to get *au fait* with it pretty quickly"

"Yes, I'm sure I will."

None of this was what Julian had anticipated. Doubts began to flood into his mind, and he strove hard to suppress them. New Geography? New History? Education in SupaPodia was clearly not like the world of academia he had once inhabited in the OW – not even remotely like it. But he supposed needs and priorities had to alter in this great age of social change, when nations and boundaries had ceased to exist and differing cultures, environments, and what used to be termed civilisations, were mixing and merging. Elitism, with its thread of one group of humans climbing high on the backs of others through power and privilege, had to be exposed, understood for what it was, and banished forever. But then, what about the new elitism – the present Eliti? This dangerous thought rose in his head, to be dispelled immediately. There was no resemblance, no possible parallel, he told himself.

"I'll be sending both of you your first assignments a little later," Stanley said jumping to his feet, sending his chair scooting back to crash against the wall with the painted window. "That's about it for now. Not too bad, was it? Tina, stay on and I'll take you through some of your jobs as my assistant. What do you have on next, Julian?"

"Nothing that I'm aware of, Stanley."

"Well, go back to your Pod and start going through the stuff I'll send you."

"Right ho." He hesitated. "Stanley, do you know about going up to the Upper Deck – I think it's called – just to have a look at the Outside. Are there set times to do that?"

Stanley looked surprised by the question. "No, I don't think so. Most Lilacs don't want to. But I expect you're still not properly acclimatised here." He looked at his timepiece. "I shouldn't go now, though. It'll still be dark in the OW, and I heard a short while ago from someone who's just come in, it's blowing a gale there."

Julian looked at his own wrist timepiece. It showed Green 3. That's useful, he thought, at least I now know more of how SupaPodia time matches up with OW time – well for the present, at least.

"Thanks, Stanley," he said. "I'll do my homework first and take a breather up there later." He looked at Tina. "Would you like to come up too? Since you'll be working with me, we can have a chat. We could meet by the elevators."

She looked at him with that calm, inscrutable look he was becoming used to. It unnerved him a little. He checked his timepiece again. "If you can come, how about Red 2?"

"Perhaps. I don't know yet. I'll see."

"I may be able to release her in time," said Stanley, overhearing the conversation.

And with that he had to be content.

* * *

Back in his Pod, Julian just had time to eat a sandwich, delivered on one of the sliding trays at his order, when, with a series of dings and dongs on both his CP and main Screen, the material Stanley had promised him began arriving. This was much longer and more complex than he had imagined. There was a string of pamphlets with titles such as 'The Educator's Role in SupaPodia', 'Instruction in a SupaPod', or 'Old Education versus Re-Education', each pamphlet adorned with the SupaPodia logo of the tilted ecstatic face, this time presumably a learning face. He skimmed his way through them, and then found a meatier production under the title 'Re-Education: Countering Offensive History.' This work was by a Commander Stanley Gaylord, whom Julian suspected was, in fact, Stanley, his superior. He had had no idea Stanley held the rank of Commander; indeed, until now, he was not aware of any such overall ranking structure within the SupaPod – all Lilacs he had met were just designated by their particular job title and grade.

After the surname, which Julian presumed was inherited and not an indication of Stanley's sexual orientation, were the initials SPMA. He thought this might relate to a Master of Arts degree obtained at SupaPodia (with the increasing collapse of education systems within the OW, he had heard of SupaPodia colleges offering both external and internal degree courses).

Julian browsed through the pages of this booklet on his Screen, leaning back against the soft pillows of his couch, the remains of his cheese and ham sandwich in his hand. Re-Education, he could see, meant to Stanley the rewriting of history, but not in such an extreme form that events were left out entirely, or the results of battles reversed. Yet, there was a constant insinuation that historical events had been created and led in the main by social inadequates – some cruel, others simply stupid, but all acting from positions of privilege. It was only with the rise of Liberal Socialism in the last two centuries that Stanley was able to identify and highlight leaders of clear intelligence who had achieved good for humankind; this, despite their having to struggle against the continuing, if enfeebled, power of the inadequates, who still succeeded in holding up Progress (with a capital 'P').

Stanley's main scorn was reserved for the money men – the capitalists – who had managed to organise society for their own personal gain, his scorn extending to their class as a whole. The eventual collapse of capitalism in the mid years of the present century was, for Stanley, the triumph that had made SupaPodia possible. Then, through SupaPodia, a new Age of Enlightenment had been born, and a world order established that Stanley believed would last for a millennium and longer.

Julian had a certain sympathy with some of Stanley's interpretations, but he felt they went too far. He did not know if he could teach a history that so radically overturned concepts that he had always felt to be at least broadly true. To use selective facts (many grossly misrepresented) in such a contentious way, in order to put over a particular theory (or bigotry more likely, thought Julian) was overturning one reality, albeit flawed, to create another that was more fiction than truth. He would be happy to debate Stanley's theories with him, or indeed within a teaching class, but he could not accept them as established fact or the truth absolute.

And where were the primary sources now for historical research? Those that had survived remained out there in the OW, where they must be at ever-increasing risk: losses through mould, water damage, and fire could never be replaced. The digitisation of historic archives had only ever achieved less than 10% of their total paper content. The fire at the National Archives on its Guildford Parktown site (caused by the arson of individuals seeking fuel to burn for warmth) had meant the loss of over 25% of Government records, some dating back to Saxon charters. The complete Foreign Office and Treasury record holdings had been reduced to water-logged ash.

So what should he – Julian – do faced with this dilemma of professional and personal conscience? He had been a geographer by training, but many of his specialist projects had been involved with the history of landscape. So History – the veracity of History – was very important to him.

He began to look at Stanley's prescribed syllabus for the re-education of adults in British history. He frowned. By the standards of the old OW, this was stuff that veered between the fatuous and the frightening. He looked at one example – a module on the British seizure, rape, and exploitation of Africa, with its encouragement of slavery. Had not Britain been the European power most active in ending slavery? There was no mention of that fact in the course notes.

He thought of the life he had known recently in the OW – the poverty, the collapse of established order, the growth of anarchy, the rise of criminal gangs, the acceptance of illiteracy as the new literacy (so-called 'good English', it was said, was the language of the controlling Toffs). So, which was the worst of the illiteracies, that prevailing in the OW or the new education of SupaPodia?

What he must do, therefore, is what, most fortuitously and thankfully, he had in fact now achieved; enter a SupaPod as a teacher, and stay there where he would be secure, comfortable, and fed. There, inside the SupaPod, surely in time he would be able to reach a position where he could start to change the things he perceived as wrong. He would have had no hope of doing so if he was still Outside. It was only from Inside that change for the better could come. So he would work now to help make SupaPodia run on truth rather than pretence, for without truth SupaPodia would become like all the other false systems and eventually crumble. He could make a start right away by doing the job Stanley had allotted him.

He must be careful, though. He must do whatever he was asked at first. To make any direct challenge straightaway would be futile, even dangerous. He had to be far more intelligent than that – to fully learn the system here, obtain the confidence of Stanley and those others over him, and bide his time. His watchwords must be 'Step by Step'. Slowly, and 'step by step', he would provide an education to the SupaPod that represented Truth – the truth, without bias and falsification, of both the Inner and the OuterWorlds; the truth of the one should be that of the other. Then everything might be possible. Who was that Roman general who had destroyed the enemy, not by direct battle but by slowly wearing them down? Ah yes, Fabius Cunctator – the Delayer. He must be much more like the Cunctator then.

Time should be the determiner that would slowly turn SupaPodia – brilliant, as it was in many ways, yet seriously flawed in others – into something much nearer the true utopia of his ideals.

Julian looked at his timepiece. It was just past R1. He had mentioned R2 to Tina as the time to meet. He had no idea of what the Upper Deck was like. Was it near the staff entrance where he had first come into the SupaPod, or was it a separate place, even a separate higher Floor, altogether? They called it a Deck; he wondered why.

He had suggested to Tina meeting by the elevators. He assumed there would be a top floor, where the elevator rose no higher and they would be able to go out into some open area or other. Still, if he could not find her, it would not matter. She may not have wished to come, anyhow. The most important thing for him was to see the sky again and look out over the OuterWorld he had left behind.

Leaving his Pod, Julian made his way to the main elevator block that served this part of his Level. Here, he spoke 'Upper Deck' into his Guidance, hoping the term would be recognised. There was a satisfying confirming ding in his head. He took the first elevator that came. It was empty, so he pressed the button labelled 'Express' and then a button with a Zero on it which he hoped meant the topmost Level. The lift doors closed. He stood still, not conscious of any movement, while lights on the control board flashed and shimmered. There was no sound from his Guidance at all, so he hoped he had headed in the correct direction and had not ended up in the SupaPod's basement. The doors slid open.

He exited into a large, white-panelled hall, where only a few lilac-clad figures stood talking. In addition to the elevators, three moving stairways came up into the hall from an open mezzanine floor below. These stairways were empty. He looked carefully around, but there was no sign of Tina anywhere. At the far end of the hall were broad, glass doors, which, to his great pleasure, he saw were lit brightly from the outside – not with electric light, but with daylight! He strode towards them, half-frightened that someone would stop him, but no one was paying him any attention. The doors swung open at his approach, and he found himself standing on an open-fronted structure – open, yet roofed and framed with glass, like the long, glazed promenade deck of one of those old-time ocean liners he had seen in films. So this must be the Upper Deck – the name was explained. The Guidance confirmed the fact by two buzzes in his head.

Before him, seen through the glass, was the open sea, the grey-green waters breaking in foaming white on the sands of the Goodwins. Seabirds swept and swooped above the waves, but he could not hear their cries. The OuterWorld was now a silent world, shut off by thick glass. He could not hear it, or go out into it, or feel its air, as he so wished, but he could at least see the line of the white chalk cliffs away to his right, lit by a sun veiled by long trails of cloud. After what already seemed an eternity of artificial light within the buried world of SupaPodia, the life-giving sun shone upon him once more, so bright it seemed he must close his eyes before it. To his left, the great curving Bar, built to drain the Goodwin Sands for the construction of the SupaPod, stretched far out into the ocean. Along its length, for as far as he could see, were the dark square shapes of turrets, which he suspected housed tidal generators supplying the power for the SupaPod.

Julian walked further along the Upper Deck. There were one or two other Lilacs stood there looking out at the water. He came to a kiosk with machines that dispensed drinks and chocolate bars, and he helped himself to a frothy cup of coffee and a gooey stick of chocolate that melted in his hand. How wonderful this is, he thought. I must come here as often as I can, just to refresh my mind and keep myself sane. It helps me at least to see the brim of the OuterWorld, even if I know that what I see is something of a mirage. I admire its light and the changing surface of its waters, but beyond that illusion the OW offers little that is good and much that is evil. I am far better off – am I not? – in SupaPodia; but if only this SupaPod could be open to the sky and not sunk into the earth!

The Upper Deck made a bend, and from here the view was more directly out to sea, away from the sand flats below and the distant sight of the cliffs.

The high silhouette of a ship stood on the horizon and Julian wondered where it was going and from where it had come. Was it bringing in goods for the British SupaPods from SupaPodia International across the ocean? The SupaPods were dependent on the production of the OW for much of the food and other commodities they consumed. And that was surely right, for it provided jobs and income for those left Outside – still by far the majority of the population. Yet the ratio was slowly changing. One day, the SupaPods would be more numerous than the Outside communities, and what would happen then? Would SupaPodia's technology have advanced so far that it could be self-supporting, meaning it could do entirely without the OW? Surely, Julian thought, the two worlds should co-exist, each benefitting the other.

But who would wish to remain in the OW, with all its grinding poverty and hard work for little reward? Only the Eliti flourished there. Ah! The Eliti – now that was the ideal status to achieve. Julian realised he had as much chance of joining the Eliti as flying off to Mars. You were either born into the Eliti, or you gained access to its ranks by some freak activity that was suddenly in demand – like being very good at banging a drum or singing a song, or kicking a football about, or acting in a film, or by being as attractive and sexually active as a Messalina or a Casanova. If, like this, one of the Eliti became your patron, then you might in time just about make the grade – although it was rare and only if you had the money to support yourself in your new status.

The route for advancement to the Eliti was seldom directly from the OW, anyhow, but through the SupaPods. Julian knew he would never achieve such advancement, even if he did something that was dramatically favoured by SupaPodia – and what would that be, he wondered? In any event, at more than fifty, he was far too old and played out. He lacked the ability, the energy, and the self-belief, and he was also very much out of date, being rather more in the old world than the new, however much he proclaimed his belief in SupaPodia. No, the best future he could hope for was some comfort and perhaps a small achievement or two in the cosseted Lilac ranks of a SupaPod.

These thoughts, and many more, ran through Julian's head, gazing out to sea, where the ship he had spotted had crawled slowly over the horizon, so that only its upper works could now be seen, like an insect stuck on the glass. He became aware of someone approaching and stopping by him. He caught a scent of clean skin and perfumed hair, and he knew without turning who it was.

"I couldn't see you by the elevators. So I came out to look for you." She sounded a little piqued.

"Tina, I'm sorry. I was about to go back to find you."

"Well, I'm here now. What have you learnt?"

He laughed. "Everything is so new, so wonderful. It's like a dream."

"I'm getting more used to it."

"You're much younger than I, so you're probably more adaptable. Are you used to the chip Guidance?"

Oh, yes. That's very simple. As a practical tool, it's invaluable. I don't know how they coped here before it was brought in."

He looked at her. Her blonde hair was catching the sunlight that had broken through the chasing cloud. He thought how much the lilac of her dress suited her. Her eyes met his and she smiled – a serene, natural smile that seemed of the very essence of her. In the OW, could he ever have hoped to have gained the company of a young woman like this?

"How do you find Stanley?" he asked. "Are you going to enjoy being his assistant?"

"He seems a nice enough man. I'm sure we'll get on well."

Her face now was expressionless. He couldn't tell what she was really thinking. She can be like an ice maiden, he thought – smiling at times, unemotional at others. She attracted him for those qualities. He had grown used to a blowsy, shouting woman – his wife who had left him, beaten down by life's hopes and fears, struggling to live with him in those days when the OW had begun to deteriorate fast. That was a long time ago. There was Marion now: she could be a demanding woman too. Their coupling had been as sudden and unexpected as anything else that had happened to him in SupaPodia. He doubted if it would continue. He had the feeling Marion had simply had a need, which he had been able to fulfil (just about), but then would pass on to some other new and much younger recruit. She most likely made a practice of such behaviour. The thought left him with little joy.

"Let's see how far this Upper Deck goes," Julian said, placing his hand against Tina's back and steering her forward. They walked side by side along the long promenade. To their left was a white panelled wall, and above them and to their right, the enclosing glass. From time to time they passed pictures attached to the wall. These were mainly seaside posters copied from the old OW – 'Skegness is So Bracing', 'Filey for the Family', 'Barry, The Children's Paradise', 'Ramsgate, Harbour of Happiness', telling of more pleasant times before that world began to disappear into 'grime and crime'.

Ramsgate, of course, was where he was now, or at least close to that town which still stood, with its choked harbour and sewage-running streets, full of helpless inhabitants whose hands were held out to enter their local SupaPod, but who probably never would. He felt a sudden wave of pity for them. Here he was walking down this quiet promenade with a lovely woman at his side, all ordered, all controlled, food and drink available at the touch of a button, the sun shining behind the glass, the breeze not actually on his cheek, as he might have wished, but at least he could see it sweeping the wave tops, and the seabirds swirling in its currents. He stood so close to the actuality of the OW, separated only by a simple sheet of glass, that it was as if he was looking at a screen upon which one film of life was being played out while he viewed it from another. As part of his job involved going back into the OW – or so Stanley had said – he would be able to penetrate that screen and experience the reality once more.

He paused by a pillar supporting a glass panel and turned to Tina. "Tell me about yourself," he said. "How were you selected to be a Lilac? Did you get in by open competition, as I did?"

"No," she answered calmly, but looking away from Julian. "I volunteered."

"You volunteered! How come? I didn't think you could just put yourself forward and get accepted."

"My family are Eliti. They got me in."

The scales fell away from Julian's eyes. Of course, the Eliti could do as they wished. Tina was from a different class of society altogether. But why had she actually entered a SupaPod. She could have had any role in SupaPodia management and still lived Outside – the very best of both worlds, surely.

"Are you just here for the experience then?" he asked.

She met his eyes, and he saw a quick flash of anger in them. "No, nothing like that. I'm not playing at life. I want to make a difference."

"A difference? In what way?"

"I want to give to the people here – the Podders, as they're called…" – she said the word as if she did not like its use – "…knowledge of a belief that has long existed in the OuterWorld, and still does so – a belief they may not have known at all, but which should guide us all, for we are human beings, the same, whatever our position and our place on this earth." She stopped, as if she was uncertain of stating what would come next.

He prompted her, "And what belief is this you speak of?"

"The greatest belief of all," she said, a flush on her cheeks. "Belief in God."

"But all that is banned here."

The words were out before he could stop them. His heart sank. So this lovely girl was one of those people who still practised superstition. He had heard of their continued wild ramblings in the OW, where religion was little approved of, if just about tolerated. He had heard the worst superstitions were taking root again, not just of one god from one religion, but of many. Despair makes people grasp at spells and invocations for support, filling the air with holy smoke and mumbo-jumbo. But surely in a SupaPod, whatever her background, Tina would not be allowed to practise anything like that.

"I will be very discreet," she said. She stood very calm and still, her hands clasped before her, her eyes bright "I will only speak to those who wish to hear."

"But you will be stopped."

"I am not frightened. Truth will overcome fear."

"Which …er…type of religion are you? What do you call yourself?

"I am a Christian."

"You do not share then the beliefs of the other religions? What are they called?" He struggled to remember. "Buddhist? Hebrew? Moslem? – that's a few of them, I think."

"We have much in common, but they must speak for themselves."

"And what do your parents think?"

"Only my father is living. He would not approve. He does not share my beliefs. He will think I am here just to teach for SupaPodia."

"But you could get him into trouble too." Again the words tumbled out of Julian before he could stop them.

"Perhaps, but I don't think so. He would simply disown me."

"Does he have a particular position amongst the Eliti?"

She didn't answer him straightaway but drew herself up against the glass wall, filling her chest with air so that her breasts stood out through the thin lilac cloth.

"My father has a senior role in SupaPodia International," she said at last.

Of course he has, Julian thought. "And you don't think your behaviour here would affect him?" He had to ask that. What she had told him had burrowed into his skin, and was already worrying him. She was so beautiful. He didn't want her to be hurt, or her father either, by her misconceptions. How could someone like her possibly hold such antiquated, foolish views; and be so obsessed by them as to be in danger of making a martyr of herself?

"He is the High Director of SupaPodia International."

Julian's world shelved away from him. He felt a mixture of awe and fear. The High Director (the HD) was the top individual in SupaPodia, the head, the boss, the chief executive, the president, all rolled into one – a fabled figure, the person who commanded everything, of what was, and what was to be, of the new world order. Julian did not even know his name: perhaps he had no name.

He stood looking at her for what seemed a very long time, his jaw fallen, his eyes wide; and then slowly the promenade came back and swum around him – the long promenade deck, the glass walls, the moving, white-crested sea beyond.

"Do they know here who you are?" he asked. "I mean, for instance, does Stanley know?"

"No. Just that I am of the Eliti, which is why, of course, he has made me his assistant. He seeks preferment. I am plain, simple Christine, an Educator Grade 3.

"Why are you telling me then?"

She laughed, a sound that seemed out of place to Julian given the seriousness of what he had heard. "Because I have to tell someone, and because I like you and I think you will help me. And, not least, because we will be working together."

"You presume a lot," Julian said, bitterness rising in him. "I have just begun a new career here and I don't want that blighted in any way. If anything goes wrong for you, you can presumably go home to daddy. I have no where to go."

She took his arm. "I won't compromise you, Julian. But I need a friend. Will you be my friend?"

He was confused. Blood was rushing in his ears. He did not know what to think, but here was this beautiful young woman looking up at him beseechingly. He wanted to hold and to hug her, as he would his own daughter – the daughter he had never had.

"I will be your friend," he said.

They parted on the elevator landing to Level 19. She kissed him lightly on the cheek. "Keep what I've told you to yourself," she said.

"Oh, yes. I will. Don't worry."

"I'll see you around then."

"You will that. First, at training with Stanley, and then you're going to work with me." He brightened. "It should be fun."

"Oh yes, it will," she said, turning down the passage the other way.

"Tina," he called out. She stopped. They were quite alone. "What's your real name?"

"It's Christine."

"I don't mean that. Your surname?

"I can't tell you, I'm afraid. It was a condition of my employment."

"Of course," he said. "I shouldn't have asked."

8

Time passed. Julian did not know how many of the successive Green, Orange, Red, Yellow, and Blue segments had flashed by, but he thought it must be several months of them seen by the time of the OuterWorld, which he would view occasionally from the Upper Deck, looking out at the sea and the distant white cliffs. At the cliff tops, he could make out a glimpse or two of green that told of the grass that grew there at the sea edge, so close to SupaPodia that he wished he could reach out and grasp it, to feel and smell its richness blowing in the salt air. He hankered after the naturalness of the world he had left behind, to walk in the dappled shade of trees, to see a wheat crop shimmering yellow in a valley, to watch birds soaring and hear their song – all this was denied him here in SupaPodia, however clever the virtual reality films that were shown to the Podders in their EECs. There, 3D trees grew and flowers bloomed, and birds winged overhead, making the Podders fling up their arms and point, as if they were spotting something strange they had never seen before, which in many cases was true. It was a million miles though, Julian knew, from the real thing.

With Tina beside him, Julian had trained in Re-education, and had mastered the approved syllabus with its robotic patter that allowed for rapid input and no argument. As his Inculcator, Marion was responsible for much of this training, with Stanley overseeing on occasions. Tina, demure as ever and softly smiling, would often come from whatever work she had been doing for Stanley and join in with Marion's lesson. Before long, Julian had taken his first class of Podders, which had listened to his long harangue about the evils of the OW they had left behind in unquestioning silence. It had been at his second such solo session that a Podder – a middle aged lady wearing glasses, with two hand-embroidered flowers sewn to the breast of her orange blouse – had come up to him and expressed her appreciation of the lesson.

"It was so wonderful to hear such a clear expression of OuterWorld degeneracy and corruption."

"I'm pleased you found it that. I still have much to learn myself."

"You're doing very well. All the ladies of my Pod love you."

"Thank you. That's good to hear. It makes my job much easier."

"My," she said, pressing the coloured flowers on her chest against him, "you do have such a fine way with words."

Tina, who had overheard the conversation, had looked at him with eyebrows raised. "All the ladies love you," she repeated with a giggle.

"Maybe. But it's not them *I* love." And she had blushed and looked away.

Julian, indeed, had come to love Tina in that absurd soppy way that older men often feel for attractive younger women, as a father looking after a daughter rather than anything overtly sexual. He knew Tina had no such feelings for him; he was simply a good friend. As she was the High Director's daughter and a committed Christian, the whole idea was an absurdity anyhow here in the SupaPod. Nevertheless, he could flirt with her occasionally, and this gave him a certain excitement every time he met her, occasions which he looked forward to greatly.

He had seen her with groups gathered about her after the re-education sessions, men, women, and children with their eyes fixed on her face, some with arms raised. It was all very improper in a SupaPod, as it had indeed been in the OW. But no one came to stop Tina, so the powers that be – and he was still very unsure who those powers were within the SupaPod – must know of her background.

It was Peter, in fact – medico Peter with whom he had first entered the SupaPod and who had inserted his implant – who was to tell him about those controlling powers. They had met in one of the long, featureless passages deep on Level 20. While following the bleeps and buzzes in his head on his way to find a particular Training Room, he had seen Peter's unmistakable stocky, bustling figure in his short lilac tunic coming towards him.

"Got time for a chat?" Peter asked, on recognising him. He had led him into a side room that was little bigger than a cell, with a fixed concrete table at its centre and a concrete bench against one short wall. He shut the door behind them, then waved Julian to the bench, seating himself beside him.

Julian thought Peter looked pale and drawn. He seemed to have lost some weight. "How are you doing?" Peter asked him

"Fine. Well enough. And you?"

"Not good. I hate it here."

Julian looked instinctively back at the door to make sure it was closed and they were by themselves. He knew it was bad form – treasonable even – to make adverse comments about SupaPodia. He had learnt to suppress his own earlier doubts.

"What's wrong?" he asked. "Don't you like your work?"

"Not really. Things are a bit primitive. Few drugs, you know."

Julian was surprised. "Surely not. I thought SupaPodia medicine was the best. We have everything here, don't we, compared with the OW?"

"It depends who you are."

"I find that hard to believe. The whole purpose of SupaPodia is surely the equitable society – everything for everyone. That's what I teach."

"You don't know anything." Peter flung out a hand and took Julian's arm. He said tensely, "You go Outside, don't you?"

Julian was alarmed by his manner and voice. "I haven't yet, but I'm programmed to do so."

"When you do, can you let me know, so I can give you a message to take?"

"But you can send that yourself, surely. Lilacs are allowed to message the OW, aren't they?"

"Yes, but you have to know someone with the means to receive a signal. And I don't have that."

"Oh, I see. I don't either, I'm afraid. I've got no family or close friends in the OW now."

"I'll write you out a paper message to take. You can put it in the OW post, that's if it's still working. It'll be worth a try, anyhow."

"To what effect, may I ask?" Julian was suspicious of Peter now. Was he placing him in danger?

"It's best you don't ask."

The answer only increased Julian's worry.

"You have to understand," Peter said, dropping his voice to a hiss. "SupaPodia is not what it seems; not what its propaganda puts out. If you knew what happens on the Lower Levels. I've seen…." He stopped, and placed a hand over his face. Julian could see his fingers were trembling. "No, it's best you don't know."

Thoroughly alarmed by now, Julian rose to his feet. "I'd better go or I'll be late."

"There's a new implant on the way," Peter said, his words stopping Julian short, his hand on the door knob. "Yes, we're doing tests at the moment. The Podders will have it first, then the Lilacs. It won't take long to implement once Medicine's fully equipped and the programme begins."

"What's the implant for?" Julian was both curious and frightened. He had to admit he didn't like his implant, however used to it he had become. He accepted its necessity in the concrete warren of the SupaPod – both for direction finding and access to Food, Clothing, Entertainment and Welfare services – but the whole thing seemed unnatural. He hated the idea of something artificial working away beneath his flesh, transmitting straight into his brain. Surely it was half way down the road to robotics.

"It will transmit your voice to a Central Control," Peter said. He had got to his feet beside Julian, and was whispering now, his mouth close to Julian's ear.

"What do you mean? What Central Control? What here in the SupaPod?"

"No, Outside. It's somewhere above us on the land. It's known as Control Station 15. Everything from the implants in this SupaPod is transmitted there. Soon everything you say will be recorded there as well – your likes, your dislikes, any criticisms of SupaPodia, your moans of pleasure, your groans of pain, everything, in fact, that comes out of your mouth or surrounds your body, including the people you are talking to. It's going to be best to keep your mouth shut and keep your thoughts and feelings in your head."

"You're exaggerating, Peter. Aren't you? Why would they do that? Who would monitor it, anyhow?"

"To identify and wipe out any dissent, that's why. And yes, they have the means. If you're going into the OW as part of your training, ask to see Control Station 15. They're proud of their data. They'll probably show you some of it – but they won't tell you what I've just told you."

"How do *you* know then?"

"Because of my job. Because I have to do the implants. All the medicos know."

Julian felt a surge of anger. "Why are you telling me this? I've got nothing to worry about. My views on SupaPodia are all positive. There's nothing I could say that would be of interest to them. By the way, who are 'they', anyhow?"

"The Eliti, of course. All the systems of SupaPodia are controlled by the Eliti. They want to rub out all opposition to their rule, both in the OW and within the SupaPods. That is their High Director's aim. Hence the advance in the technology to make it possible. The OW's simple: you just allow it to degrade into starvation and chaos. The SupaPods, however, present more of a challenge. They don't like anyone in a SupaPod who won't accept its way of life entirely and unthinkingly; in fact, they will change the whole process of thought to achieve that. That's your job – Re-Education. A prime job, you have – one they will watch you doing most carefully."

Again Julian felt a stab of fear. He wanted to dismiss Peter's words as the ramblings of a sick, discontented man, yet part of him was not sure. His own conversion to SupaPodia – he had to admit – was not yet complete.

"Who is the High Director?" he asked in a croak. His throat was suddenly dry.

"No one knows his name or where he lives. He's probably thousands of miles away in one of the Southern Hemisphere areas. They say he rarely visits a SupaPod."

"Does he have a daughter?"

Peter laughed "A daughter? He may have. I don't know. Why do you ask?"

Julian thought, I will keep what Tina told me to myself.

"Be very careful of anyone who says they know the High Director," Peter said. "For it's unlikely they do, and they'll either be mad or trying to get something from you." He looked at his timepiece. "I must be going now. I'll be in touch. I feel I can trust you. I hope you will be able to help me with what I asked earlier."

"Let's see," said Julian heavily, his new world dissolving once more under the impact of what Peter had told him. If Tina said she was the High Director's daughter, that had to be true, whatever warning Peter had given him. To Julian, she represented pureness and light. It was much more likely it was Peter who was mad, or on the road to madness.

Yet, even with that internal reassurance, why was he still so troubled?

* * *

More time passing. He was used to life in his Pod by now – the lift and sliding shoot, the bouncy couch, the steel vending slots, the cleansing routines, the clothing orders and deliveries, the journeys to the EECs and often, later, by elevator to the Upper Deck. His training was going well. Stanley had told him he was a 'natural' and that he wished he could have had him under his wing "aeons ago" (the latter was probably a discreet non-use of SupaPodia time terms that could – Julian realised – mean anything).

Marion, as his Inculcator, was clearly pleased with him as well, dispelling his earlier fears that her sexual attentions would pass on to someone else. She stayed with him in his Pod several times, the two of them pressed together on the narrow couch like "frigging sardines" – as she had put it. While, clasped together, they had rocked towards a united climax greeted with unrestrained screams. "Jules, you're fucking marvellous! For an oldie, you've more stamina than a twenty year old." He had not quite known what to make of that, but he had judged it as a compliment.

He continued to see Tina, who always greeted him with a smile, but who seemed to maintain a distance from him now, even when he was giving her training in presentation and teaching method. The ethereal quality he had noticed in her from early on seemed if anything more pronounced. She usually wore her hair brushed back and tied by an elasticated band. She looked clean and wholesome, the perfect 'girl next door' whom he would like to care for and fuss over, but who – he had to admit to himself shamefully, buoyed by his success with Marion – he would wish to rut with as well, just to break up that unsullied demeanour, to bring some redness to her cheeks, some sweat to her brow, to see her legs in the lilac skirt, kept so carefully pressed together, wide apart for him. At least that was his – very occasional – fantasy.

It was never to be, Julian knew. She glided to her faith groups carrying a black-covered book in one hand, and the Podders came to her like dogs, with lowered heads, sniffing at her as he would have liked to have sniffed. Yet she was pure. He knew she was pure. Peter's warning had been as dust thrown up by the wind. His words had been nonsense. No mention of any new implant had come to him either, although he had searched for information on his Screen. He had asked Marion too.

"Who told you about that?" she asked quite sharply.

He hadn't wanted to mention Peter. Hadn't he promised him he would say nothing? "Oh, I just overheard something about it. I can't remember where. Perhaps in the Lilacs' Lounge." She had looked her disbelief at him, but said no more.

At one Orange segment, Marion took him by passage way and elevator – a lengthy walk – up to an Upper Level where he recognised the Staff Portal which he had entered when he had first arrived from the SupaPodia Express. From here, it was just a short journey by the glass-sided cabin train to the railway terminus, with the moving walkways that moved relentlessly downwards, taking their burden of new Podders into the outer entry halls of the SupaPod. As he looked at the long railway platforms stretching away before him, he saw the bullet-shaped front of a SupaPodia Express coming in.

"Quickly, Jules!" said Marion, pulling him by the arm. "We're just in time for a new influx of Podders. Do you remember I told you that your job would involve their first induction? Well, you'll be able to see how it works, so you can put in a shift or two yourself soon."

At the bottom of the crawling walkways, she led him into a large empty hall, the size of a football pitch, at least. It was lit by long strips of electric lights set amongst the beams of a raftered roof. Around the plain grey walls were rows of hooks, beside metal hatches that Julian recognised as those covering disposal shoots.

"Here they come," Marion said. "We're only just in time. It looks like only a small intake. They're prize winners, I think."

Through double doors, flung open by accompanying Lilacs, came a flow of Podders in their garments of the OW, most carrying cases or with packs on their backs, small children holding mothers' hands, babies borne along in carrying cots. Their babble filled the air, above which could be made out the shrill voices of the Lilac girls calling out "Club 34, over here!"; "Lotto 89, follow me!"; "Windfall 103, here against the wall". Coloured boards showing these identifications were thrust high, while the Lilacs gathered their groups about them.

Music started up from hidden speakers, with words clearly intended to catch the spirit of the occasion –

'Welcome to SupaPodia,
You are such lucky folk,
What fun you're going to have with us
Away from grit and smoke.
Now get all that clobber off,
There's plenty of new gear;
All's fun and games in SupaPods,
So Cheer, you Podders, Cheer!
Let's hear you CHEER!! CHEER!! CHEER!!

Some cheers were indeed beginning to break out amongst the people as they began stripping off their clothing. with the Lilacs holding out to them the baggy orange suits that were to be their uniform from now on.

"What size do you want? – 'Big', 'Extra Big', 'Average', 'Child'. One size fits most, lady. They stretch. Your kid can grow into it, mister. Come on. Come on. We must get you down to your teas."

Julian watched in a type of horror as he saw men and women, girls and boys, stripped to their underclothes, some even fully naked, mostly totally unabashed, although he did notice one or two family groups vainly trying to screen themselves.

A clapping of hands, "Come, come. No one has any secrets here. We don't mind a big bum, do we missus, large tits or even a small willie? It'll all be done soon, and then, after your welcome tea, we'll show you to your Pods."

Another pause as the re-dressing continued. One woman, Julian saw, watching fascinated, was having a problem zipping her large bosom into the orange blouse of her suit. At last, with the help of a petite Lilac girl, she succeeded. A chorus of giggles about her. "Thank you, darling. I've always had trouble with those."

"It's what we're here for," said the Lilac, and then, looking across at the watching Marion and Julian whom she appeared to notice for the first time, she clapped her hands. "Shush! Shush! Everyone. One more thing. Before your teas, you must meet our Education staff."

A chorus of groans rose up from the new Podders

"The system's been slipping," Marion said grumpily to Julian. "It'll be your job to put it right. All you have to do is welcome them to the SupaPod while I hand them a leaflet. Give it a go."

"What, now?" Julian said, suddenly anxious. "What do I say?"

"You'll think of something. It'll be a test for you. It's the best way to learn."

"Really," said Julian, unconvinced. He thought, if she's said that once, she's said it a hundred times. What the hell am I going to tell this mob?

He looked at the swirling bodies and faces before him, their old clothes now being thrust down the shoots. They were calling out excitedly to each other. The woman with the big breasts was sliding her blouse zipper up and down, laughing with a fat man beside her, whose face was covered in tattoos like a spider's web. At their feet, a boy and girl rolled about together.

"So get up there!" yelled Marion against the noise, indicating to Julian a high rostrum against the far wall. "Just give it to them. Anything. Providing it's hopeful and reassuring. Tell them they'll have jam with their tea. They probably won't know what jam is, anyway. It comes with crumpets. Go! Go!"

Julian found himself propelled onto the rostrum, standing up high facing the mob before him. There hadn't been time for him to be nervous. He had no idea what to say, but he thought something would come. Stanley, in fact, had given him some training in speaking about the benefits of SupaPodia.

A terrible noise, like an old-fashioned factory siren from one of those grainy, archive films Julian had seen, suddenly filled the hall. From his vantage point, Julian could see Marion squeezing the bulb of a portable klaxon horn.

"Attention, everyone! Attention! Your Educator will address you." She raised an arm towards Julian, who stood looking down at them, and the babble of noise slowly died away. Julian now felt the fear enfold him. What the hell to say?"

"Welcome, everyone! I am Julian, and I will soon be getting to know each of you. I will be your Educator. I will be teaching you about SupaPodia and how to get the best out of it."

So far, so good. They were looking up at him quietly, hope shining on their faces. Even the excited kids had stilled themselves, their eyes above their drooping, dribbling mouths wide and expectant. The cry of a baby was shushed into silence by its mother. She took out a breast to feed it.

He saw Marion below bringing out a pile of leaflets from a cupboard in the rostrum. "All that will come in due course," he continued. "Marion here will give each of you a pamphlet that sets out the essential things you need to know about living in a SupaPod." He saw Marion on cue indeed handing out the leaflets, as hands reached out around her to grab copies.

Julian felt strangely empowered: his nerves had fallen away like leaves drifting from an autumn tree, only, of course, SupaPodia knew no such seasons, untidy and messy as they were.

"Get yourselves settled in and enjoy your welcoming tea. There will be jam and crumpets!" He saw the faces smile at that, turning to each other to share this pleasurable announcement "Yes, it will all be fun for you now. You have become Podders, joining a worldwide community of those living the new way of life. The days of struggle are over for you. We – the Lilacs – will look after you in everything. Just come to us if there is anything you need or have problems understanding. Girls, lead these good people away."

The last was directed at his pretty colleagues from Reception who had been attending this new influx. He was pleased to see them leap immediately into action and begin ushering the Podders out of the hall. Some tried to pick up their cases and bundles, but were told to leave them: they would be delivered to them later, or so Julian heard one Lilac say to a young woman who was endeavouring to hang on to her rucksack. Soon the hall was empty. A giant of a black man in a bulging, lilac boilersuit was already going around the abandoned suitcases and bundles, pitching them one by one into the shoots.

"How are they reunited with their belongings?" Julian asked him. He genuinely didn't know.

"What?" the man grunted. "Where the fuck you been, mister?"

Marion had been helping to stuff some of the smaller items into the shoots. One bag had split open, showering a pathetic collection of underwear, a tortoiseshell-backed hand mirror, a teddy bear with floppy ears, and various cosmetic bottles onto the floor. She held up a pair of knickers with sequins sewn to them "Very exotic. Might as well keep those." She stuffed them into her trouser pocket. The rest of the items she threw into a shoot.

Julian was scandalised. "You mustn't steal other people's property."

"I'm not stealing. I'm salvaging. It's all going to the furnaces, anyway."

"But…." Julian really did not know what to say. A horrifying reality hung over him, a first real awakening.

"They get everything new," Marion said. "They'll soon forget their old stuff. New life, new things. Everything from the OuterWorld has to go. No memories, nothing, only what we give back to them in Re-Education. That's SupaPodia policy."

"But why are they not told that before they come in?"

"Because they would only try to smuggle stuff in, or we might have a riot on our hands. It's best to tell them they can bring so much, and then we seize it and dump it."

"Don't they protest?"

"Not often. They soon understand. The first experience of a SupaPod is so enormous there's not much room left for memory – which is as it should be, of course, because most things in the OW are bad, and who wants that brought in here?"

Julian felt very uncomfortable, very uncertain. "We Lilacs are allowed to bring stuff in," he said. "Not much, I admit, but some mementoes, at least"

"Yes, but we're Lilacs and they're Podders. As Lilacs, we need to deal with the past as well as the present. It's part of my work and yours too. There is a difference between us, but that's just on account of our job, not because of any intrinsic inequality. Otherwise, we're all the same – Podders and Lilacs."

Julian looked at her. Did she really think that, or was she just repeating what the system demanded of her? What about the Eliti? he thought. They seemed to do exactly what they liked. It was they who set the policy for SupaPodia and controlled it. Rules and regulations were necessary in every society. Someone had to set them and someone had to enforce them. Was it then really any different here?

His head swum. He didn't know what he thought. At times, he didn't want to think at all.

Later, he had to admit to finding the knickers Marion had taken very attractive around her white thighs. Suffused in his Pod with sex, a rump steak, and half a bottle of white wine, he thought things were not really too bad at all. As he fell asleep, he had just one last thought of what the owner of those spilled possessions might be doing now.

* * *

"You're going Outside," Marion said at the next Red segment.

"Outside? What to the OW? Really!" Julian was genuinely surprised. He had thought such an opportunity would only come much later.

"Yes, you've passed all your assessments with flying colours. Stanley says you're ready to learn about OW Re-Education."

"What is that exactly?"

"It's when we go out to the OW to assess potential new Podder intakes and their educational needs. SupaPodia runs a course on the subject at one of its Academies in the OW, and that's where we'll be going."

"Aren't the Podders' backgrounds all much the same?"

"No, of course not. There're many sorts of ethnic and cultural groupings. We have to be sure how they can be fused into a SupaPod."

"Fused? That's a strange word."

"No, not really. It's the one we use when a diverse group meets with a common norm and has to be merged in."

"I see." Julian did really see at all, but he had already learnt with SupaPodia not to worry about the exactitude of anything until he had actually experienced it, and then it normally made sense – or if it didn't, then that did not really seem to matter. "Am I going by myself?"

"No, Stanley will lead you, and Tina will come as well."

"Oh," said Julian, brightening. "Good."

Marion looked at him closely. "You fancy her, don't you? She's far too young for you and she's probably a virgin anyhow, so keep your cock in your pants."

He winced at the vulgarity. "I simply enjoy her company," he said lamely.

"Yes, go tell that to the fairies."

"You're the only one for me, my love."

She laughed openly. "As if you have any choice." He felt suitably deflated. She was right. After the delectable welcoming party, when he had been surrounded by friendly and eager young women, there had been no sign of any of them since, not even in the Lilacs' Canteen and Lounge of Level 19. Most women he met there now wore lilac business suits and seemed elderly and care worn, scarcely looking up from their edibles taken from the vending machines. Marion's periodic visitations were thus very welcome, although he suspected she flitted about from Pod to Pod like the proverbial butterfly.

He was summoned to Stanley's office, at one bar past Yellow. He was pleased to find Tina there seated at a Screen, her hair hanging loose, as he liked it best. On seeing him standing in the doorway, she gave him such a beatific smile as to almost melt him to his knees.

"We're going back into the OW, I believe," Julian said.

"Yes, isn't it exciting?" She looked exceptionally fresh and fragrant, wearing a short lilac tunic dress.

Stanley came into the room, rather stern and unsmiling. He said something to Tina, leaning over her rather too closely – or so Julian thought in an anguish of sudden jealousy – and then addressed both of them.

"Right, you're both with me Outside for some primary Re-Ed instruction. Pack for two full colour Sweeps away. We'll be starting at the next Orange 2." He handed them each a paper document headed, PORTAL PERMIT. "You'll need to produce this at the Staff Portal. Meet me there. We'll be travelling by SupaPodia Express. Any questions?"

"What part of the OW are we going to?" asked Julian.

"What? Does it matter?" Stanley looked sternly at the expectant faces of Julian and Tina, and then seemed to relent. "Yes, I suppose it does to you. It'll be to the SupaPodia Academy near King's Lynn, in Norfolk District 7. SupaPod 33 Hunston is close by, but I doubt if there'll be time for a visit there."

King's Lynn! Julian had never visited the town, but he remembered hearing during his last years in the OW that the Fens which surrounded it, once drained for prime agricultural production, had flooded again. There had been no money to service the dykes and the pumping stations, and briny sea water had leaked across the former fields, mixing disastrously with rising inland waters.

"How should we dress?" Tina asked. "Will we need outdoor clothes?"

"Yes, of course. Haven't you got any? Really, I can't think of everything!" He was scratching his head in exasperation. "Well, go to your Pods and order some now." He looked at his timepiece. "You'll be in time – just. A raincoat and some warm woollies, in case it's cold. You never know. I'm not sure what season it is out there."

"Late spring," I think, sir," said Julian, uncertain why he used the 'sir'. Stanley was clearly a man of parts, unruffled and friendly at one moment, then agitated and hostile at the next. The one followed the other without apparent cause. Tina, he thought, must by now be wary of him as she worked so closely with him. He looked at her, but she didn't meet his gaze. She stood quietly, with her hands clasped before her against the slight swell of her belly.

"Well you'd better get on with it." Stanley was showing signs of further testiness. "We'll talk more about the purpose of our mission on the train."

'More', Julian thought. He hasn't said anything yet. Perhaps Tina will have some detail. He was pleased to see she was preparing to leave the office with him. "Do you know anything about what we'll be doing?" he asked her, when outside. Her face held her habitual half-smile.

"You're my superior," she said. "You should be telling me."

He reddened a little. Why her sudden, unwarranted sarcasm? It was entirely out of character for her. Was it a sign she was suffering in some way under Stanley?

"What's your boss like to work for?" he asked.

"He's fine," she replied at once in a clipped tone. "Now, if you'll excuse me I've got a lot to sort out." And she turned away in the opposite direction to his own, leaving him even more confused and not a little hurt. He knew that was as ridiculous as any other of his feelings for Tina.

When he got back to his Pod, he found that Marion was waiting for him. "You'll need some new clothes for Outside," she said.

"I know. Stanley's just told me that."

"Here I'll help you order them."

From his Screen, they selected a very nifty-looking lined coat in brown, with a fur-fringed hood. "You should have some stout shoes as well," Marion said. So to the order was added a pair of calf-high, tan-coloured leather boots, such as might have been worn by a builder in those old days of the OW.

"You'll be wearing your lilac uniform, of course," said Marion. "And make sure you have your identification badges pinned to your blazer."

In a very sort time, his order, marked 'urgent', arrived. He had been so engrossed in 'other activity' with Marion that he did not notice its arrival down the delivery shoot. Later, she helped him try on the coat. "A perfect fit," she said, pulling the hood up over his ears. "You look quite the man. Now don't go wowing any of those King's Lynn Lilacs. And don't make a fool of yourself chasing after Tina."

He thought after she had gone, all this is very flattering, but it's degrading too. It's not what I want. It's as if she's using sex as an anaesthetic – perhaps that's what I'm doing as well. After all, what else is there to do in a SupaPod but indulge in self-gratification? Everything is aimed at the physical need rather than the intellectual. There is as little mental stimulus for me here as in a cardboard box. There's not even a library of proper books that I've ever found. Is this really where I want to spend the rest of my life? Now, this was heresy coming into his mind that he had better not speak out, or he might end up on those Lower Levels which Peter had warned him about. What exactly was it that happened there? And who had the power to commit you to those depths, and for what exact misdemeanour?

These thoughts disturbed him enough to keep him from sleeping. When the alarm on his time piece buzzed at Green 3, he was already risen, dressed and ready. The anticipation of seeing the OuterWorld again sent sharp shocks through his nervous system. After ensuring his bowels were as empty as he could make them, he made his way out of his Pod and to the elevator that would take him to the Staff Portal – the place where he had first entered the SupaPod from the tainted, yet still so desirable, OuterWorld.

9

It was only when Julian reached the Staff Portal that he realised he had not told Peter he was going out to the OW, as he had promised. Oh well, he thought, it's not really my fault. I have been rather caught on the hop by this. Peter would just have to find some other way of getting his message Outside. If he was honest, he was glad he was not going to be involved. But Peter had sounded so very desperate and his tale of the new implant that would record all your speech as well as your movements, well that had been most disturbing. As ever with SupaPodia, Julian found it difficult to make a subjective judgement. The next time he was sent Outside, he determined, then he would help Peter.

There was no sign of Stanley or Tina at the Staff Portal, although he checked the hall in front of the exterior doors. There was no one either to check his Permit to be there, or indeed to prevent him from going outside. I could come here instead of the Upper Deck, he thought. At least I'd be able to breathe fresh air.

The Guidance in his chip began to shrill in his ears at that moment, and he realised that it was the implanted chip, and probably camera surveillance, that stopped people leaving the SupaPod at will. The sound was merely unpleasant at the moment, but presumably it would get worse, making it impossible to continue. He hoped Stanley would be able to turn it off. But first he had to find him, and Tina too. Oh, why was nothing in SupaPodia ever clear and straightforward?

Once through the outer doors, he found the air chilly and he was glad of his thick brown coat, which had admittedly brought him some stares when he had first left his Pod. Let them stare, he thought, they do not have jobs that allow them Outside. Looking at their pallid, spotty faces under the eternal electric light of the SupaPod, he bet they wished they could join him too. No one spoke, however. Indeed, it was a fact he had not really registered before that people – the Lilacs, anyhow – talked very little away from their communal areas. It was as if they were frightened of faces they did not know.

Then he spotted Tina. She was standing on the concrete apron that stretched from the platform head to the entry doors. There were only a few other Lilacs about, some evidently having just descended from one of the glass-sided cabins that ran from the SupaPod's rail terminus.

"Hello," he said, walking up to her. "Stanley not here yet?"

She didn't answer him. She had pulled her black coat tight about her against the chill of the wind sweeping the platform, and was absorbed in looking out over the distant sea, which was rolling white with angry breakers, half-hidden by mist and spray. On her head was a round woollen hat, topped by a pink bobble; very fetching, he thought.

"Have you seen Stanley yet?" he asked again.

"Oh, hello there. Sorry, I was miles away. No, I've only just got here."

"How are you feeling?

"Not good. I've got a terrible buzzing in my head. It's getting worse all the time."

"Me, too."

"Stanley told me he'll bring a device that turns it off." She looked around her. "But where is he?"

"He's not on this cabin, is he? It looks about to go."

"I don't think so. We can't go, anyhow, until he's de-activated us." Julian had never heard her sound so distressed. "Ah, thank God! There he is now."

Stanley emerged through the sliding doors from the Staff Portal, a briefcase in one hand, a file spilling papers in another. He stopped to pick them up while Tina hastened to his side to help.

"Thank you, Tina. Good morning. Oh, blast it! Get that one!" This last as a sheet was whirled upwards by the wind, spinning in rising circles before Tina succeeded in catching it in her hand above her head "Thank all the gods, old and new! That's got all the notes for my speech on it. Well done, Tina." He kissed her on the cheek, while Julian stood by resentfully.

"Our chips are giving us merry hell," he called out.

"I'll deal with that just now! Get on the cabin or we'll miss our connection."

They boarded just as the door-closing signal began sounding, and the cabin rolled off, picking up speed and entering the long tunnel that Julian remembered. They stood, saying little, the only group of Lilacs in the cabin. When they had reached the train terminus and were standing on one of the platforms – a small group of Podders had just arrived on an opposite platform and were making their way noisily to the moving stairways – Stanley took out his CP and passed it over the right arms of both Tina and Julian.

"This switches off the Guidance function of your chips," he said. "I should have done it earlier. Sorry, you've had some discomfort, but I've been in a bit of a rush. At least you'll understand now the absolute imperative of only going to those places for which you have permission."

"I never thought anything else" mumbled Julian, rather testily. The noises in his head had thankfully ceased, and he could see Tina looking as relieved as he. Yet he was cross. Why was everything with SupaPodia so disorganised, or was it just Stanley who created that effect? He found his manner infuriating. This was a most important matter, affecting the health of his staff, and should have been dealt with properly at the right time. Presumably, Stanley, as a senior officer – a Commander – had been given the power of altering chips, otherwise reserved for medicos.

It seemed that no one in SupaPodia could ever provide the full information without having it forced out of them bit by bit. Marion was just as bad. Looking across at Tina, hoping for support, he saw she had turned away, apparently disinterested now the noises in her ears had stopped.

"Once we're on the train, I'll brief you about everything," Stanley said. He had lost some more papers, which Tina was dutifully scrambling after. He's hopeless, thought Julian, while reminding himself it was in his interests to keep on the right side of him.

The Express, a short train of only two silver-sheathed carriages behind its bullet-nosed locomotive, was waiting for them at the far end of the platform, its attendants in Lilac uniforms, with braided peaked hats. "Sirs, Madam," said one, touching the peak of his hat, "This door, please."

"But can't we go in the front, in the observation lounge?" Stanley asked.

"Sorry, sir. That's reserved for Eliti we'll be picking up at London North."

"Rotten luck," said Stanley, looking round at Julian and Tina ruefully. "Still we'll be comfortable here. There don't seem to be any other Lilacs."

He was wrong. The front section of the carriage they entered, which included the bar, proved to be filled with a noisy crowd, some lilac-dressed, some semi-dressed, a few of whom seemed to have already passed out over seats, or – incredibly to Julian's fevered gaze – were indulging in sexual activity, with others watching and cheering them on.

"Hell," said Stanley. "It's a crowd going off on furlough, probably to a camp. I'm not standing for this. He turned back to the attendant. "I'm a Commander. My people have important work to do. We're *going in* the front carriage. Now *make it happen!*"

"Yes, sir." The attendant touched his hat and led them further up the platform. As the door here slid open with a hiss, he said in Julian's hearing. "This is on your own head, sir. I shall make a report."

"Make what you fucking well like," raged Stanley, who to Julian's incredulity had changed in a moment from a fumbling incompetent to a firm, decisive leader – a SupaPodia Commander indeed!

In the carriage now, further attendants hastened to receive them, ushering them to luxurious seats that fully reclined, offering them drinks and food. Looking through the window nearest his head, Julian could see the train was now in motion. The branches of trees flashed by, a rusty railing, a man in a tattered raincoat, a broken bicycle lying on its side in mud, a terrier dog chasing a rat; the near scenes were speeding up so that Julian had to raise his vision from the trackside to see anything clearly – a bridge, its central arch fallen, two overturned cars without wheels at the bottom of an embankment, a shack of boards and corrugated iron, smoke billowing from its roof, with barefoot children standing, watching them passing. As Julian looked, one picked up a stone and threw it at the train. Now, there were fields, some flooded, a few with green crops, an old quarry, a wood with trees fallen into a fronting marsh, a sudden flash from metal-sided barns where tractors were dragging tumbrils filled with workers – a SupaPodia farm estate, thought Julian,: it was the only thing he saw in this miserable scene of dereliction and decay that looked to be working and prospering.

The change in Stanley seemed not to have been just a freak happening, perhaps occasioned by a rush of adrenalin, for it remained with him, for the present at least. He was much more attentive to his two charges, much more considerate, much more aware of their joint incomprehension. With a drink in his hand, leaning back against the plush cushions of his seat, he addressed Julian and Tina seated opposite him.

"SupaPodia offers new freedoms, but we still require controls. Of course, we have to watch out for anyone trying to get into a SupaPod illegally, and we have to watch out as well for anyone trying to get out. You may find the last pretty unbelievable. After all, who would want to leave a SupaPod and return willingly to this swill heap of the OW?"

Stanley waved his hand at the scenes rushing by, seen through the wide viewing window at his elbow. "But some do find such an urge, in particular new Lilacs and some unsuitable Podders. However much they like the new, they can still miss the old, which seems to want to pull them back to their former misery. So we have to stop that in their own interest. No one can get away for too long from a SupaPod before their chip would begin to disable them: it would sound like bedlam in their head, and, if they could endure that, would then start to shut down basic life function – breathing, heart, that sort of thing. So you see why I had to de-activate your chip – at least the Guidance part of it. We won't be away for long enough for the other nasty things to happen."

Julian felt fear at this information. A sheen of sweat broke out on his brow. He looked at Tina, but she seemed to be sitting calmly enough. Had she heard, had she understood, he wondered? They were now prisoners of SupaPodia. There was no escape other than through death.

He saw Stanley's eyes on him. "Are you alright, Julian? I haven't alarmed you, have I? None of this will affect you, for I'm sure you'll never want to leave us. You're going to be a valuable asset to SupaPodia, I know that – a very valuable asset. And you too, my dear." He reached across and patted Tina on her knee in a casual, familiar way that made Julian furious, but all he could do was smile and say, "Thank you, Stanley. It's good to hear you say that."

He was wondering, though, if what Stanley had just told them about the chips was really true, or just a story to frighten Lilacs and Podders alike. Perhaps it had no substance in fact, yet, of course, the implants were real. He tried to find a way through the murk of unease in his brain, but all he could think of was that Stanley was a Commander and should know. But who were Commanders, anyhow, and what powers did they have? What was their place in the control structure of SupaPodia?

Seeing that Stanley's relaxed, benevolent mood was continuing, he asked, "Stanley, did I hear you say you are a Commander? I don't know – and perhaps Tina doesn't either – what a Commander is. Would you be kind enough to tell us?"

"What?" A mask seemed to fall over Stanley's face, clouding the smiling eyes, curling down the corners of the mouth. Then he clearly made an effort to smile. "Of course. You need to know. Particularly you, Julian – forgive me, Tina – for I would already judge you to be of Commander potential." He wagged a finger. "But don't go getting any ideas yet above your station. It's taken me a long time to reach Commander".

Stanley leant forward, his elbows on his knees. His broad, florid face, topped by thinning strands of blond hair plastered to his forehead and scalp, exuded, Julian thought, an essence of perfect stupidity. If he was a SupaPodia Commander, the competition surely could not be all that great.

"Commanders control the Q-Levels," he said. "A Q-Level is made up of four individual Levels. In other words, every four Levels has its own

Commander. I'm the Commander for Levels 18-21. I manage all matters relating to the welfare of Lilacs and Podders, their accommodation Pods, their servicing, their entertainment, their work schedules, and their discipline. And all movements in and out too. The work occupies me more than my Education role, which is why, Julian, I have so welcomed your arrival."

He went on, "Commanders report to the Control Station. Ours is No. 15. It's separate from the SupaPod but within its outer precincts. We have regular meetings there. There's one due on my return. Come to think of it, Julian, I could take you there. Commanders are always being asked to put forward candidates who show promise. At least you'll be registered for training, even if the reality of progress towards higher rank will take a long time. "After all…" – he laughed "…you've only just arrived and I've been in SupaPodia all my life"

And I've already got one job to learn, thought Julian. Do I really need another? Still, the higher I rise, the more freedom I may have, like Stanley, to get out of the SupaPod often.

The Commander had slumped back in his chair and closed his eyes. Soon the steady sound of his breathing indicated he was asleep. Just like that, Julian thought. Oh that I could sleep as easily. Instead, I am left more confused than ever. He looked across at Tina, who did not appear to share any of his concerns. She had taken out the black-covered book he often saw her with, and was reading, a shiny nail tracing the words along each line. She was mouthing the words too, her lips fluttering with their sounds. How lovely she is, he thought. What a shame she's so tied up in that Christian nonsense. Even if her father is who she says he is – and Julian found it hard to believe what she had told him – she will only get herself into trouble eventually, and then she'll be in a hell of a mess, perhaps even expelled, or consigned – he remembered Peter's warning words – to the Lower Levels. Yet Stanley – he was now snoring gently – does not seem concerned, and she does what she does in front of him, so perhaps I am mistaken.

Julian looked over Stanley's shoulder through the broad window, where he could see the sky now clearing of rain, and bars of sunlight piercing the scattered clouds in columns of gold. He caught his breath at the loveliness of the scene, the sky shining above a fringe of dark woodland rushing by, a stream glinting silver, a lane with an old wagon and two heavy horses, some rough pasture bordered by houses, perhaps once a village green where cricket – the game he had loved when young – would have been played. Now they were deep within houses, and rows of streets, smoking chimneys, and rubble heaps, people walking with downcast eyes, a few battered-looking vehicles, a boarded-up church – or was it a mosque? – roads empty and going no where, a small river choked with rubbish and foam.

The train was slowing and Stanley opened his eyes. He groaned. "My head, my head..." Tina was evidently trained for this – as Marion had been – for she rose and squeezed herself in beside Stanley, taking his head in her arms.

"Oh, shit, I feel dreadful." He buried his head deeper against Tina's small breasts. "Such comfort. How can I stand the strain? How I want to rest."

What a charlatan, Julian thought angrily. He's just a dirty old man – a youngish man really – who likes to get his face in a place of choice. Why do these women let him? He gestured angrily at Tina, who looked up at him questioningly.

She said, "It's a small thing to help."

Well, help me as well then, thought Julian angrily. I can't stand any more of this, and he stumbled off up the train to find the toilet.

When he returned, Stanley was sitting up, and Tina had returned to her seat. She had resumed her reading as if nothing had happened. Stanley had a sheepish look on his face.

"I get such pains in my head," he said, clearly feeling an explanation was needed. "It's migraine, I'm told. It clears quickly if I'm quiet and comforted. Tina is very kind and has lovely hands."

Well, that's lucky for you, Julian thought. Just so long as you don't expect me to take her place.

The train had stopped. A long concrete platform stretched away beside them. Nothing happened. It reminds me of a poem I read once, Julian thought. There was nothing on the platform, the poet had written, but the station name. Here, though, there was not even a name, and no birds singing either, or flower-decked summer views of Oxfordshire and Gloucestershire. Indeed, those counties did not exist any longer, having been gobbled up into Midlands (Diversity) Garden City 3.

At last, through his window which faced the platform, Julian saw movement. A group of people were coming towards the train, some riding in small scooter-cars, others on foot, dressed in formal clothes, men in dinner jackets, ladies in full-length dresses and furs, jewellery flashing at their wrists, their necks and in their hair. Some younger women amongst them were squeezed into the new narrow tube-dresses, their hems high across their thighs, their loose necklines very low across their unfettered bosoms: it was a fashion only rumoured to him before he had left the

OW, and now he was seeing it for real. All this wealth, all this luxury, this outrageous clothing, he realised, could only mean one thing – these were members of the Eliti. And they were coming into that part of the train where he sat, where plain Lilacs should not in fact be.

Julian tried to issue a warning to Stanley, but before he could do so the doors to the carriage had hissed upon and the first of the new arrivals were being helped in. A lady in a green turban-style hat with a yellow feather, on spying Stanley, who was pulling himself up straight from where he had slumped in his seat, exclaimed in a loud voice, "But there are *other* people here." An attendant said something to her, which Julian could not hear.

"I don't care *who* they are. Get them out."

Stanley began to rise to his feet, "Madam, if you'll allow me…"

"Henry…." the woman called out in a shrill commanding voice.

"Yes, my dear." This was a man in a tweed suit behind her.

"Get rid of these people, Henry. The train guards won't do so."

"I say, you, people, jolly well hurry on out of here." Henry, with his wife's furious eyes on him, looked suitably determined. "You have your own – er, Lilac – places to go to. This carriage is for Eliti only. That's us," he added, as if there was any doubt.

One of the young women in her metallic silver tube-dress, coming down the carriage from the far door, her wobbling breasts almost totally exposed, now flung herself onto the seat opposite Julian.

"Hurry on out, you creepy little man," she said, chewing gum, "or I'll squeeze the last drops out of your balls. Assuming you've got any, of course." She emitted a shriek of laughter.

Julian, horrified, began to gather his coat from the seat rack, as he saw Stanley was also doing. The train attendants stood around, wringing their hands. "I told them, I told them," one kept saying, and Julian, feeling sick, would have liked to have hit him.

"Surely there's room for all of us," Julian said plaintively, looking up the carriage, which had many spare seats – whole rows of them, in fact.

An older man in evening dress, with a red drink-fuelled face, his lips curled up into a snarl, thrust himself forward, "Why do you think we'd sit with people like you? You may not be so bad as those dreadful Podders, but you're not quite our type either – are they, Pamela?" The last was to an elegant looking lady in a long dress, her arms bare, a silver ornament laced into her curled, orange-blonde hair.

Pamela, who was turning away from the distasteful scene, wanting simply to seat herself after a tiring visit to SupaPodia International (London), and wishing her husband, Rupert, was not such an unpleasant, pompous twit (the word 'prick' had lingered for a millisecond in her brain, but she hated coarseness such as that dreadful girl, Staceybelle, was showing here in such appalling abundance), suddenly started back, amazement showing on her face.

"Why, Christine. It *is* Christine, isn't it? What *on earth* are you doing here?"

Tina, who had put her book to one side during the skirmish about her, looked up with a start. A red flush spread over her cheeks, surprising Julian, for he had so seldom seen her discomfited before.

"Yes…", she began cautiously, and then struggling to regain her composure. "Yes, I'm Christine. I prefer Tina now. And it's Lady Lascelles, isn't it? I remember you. You're a friend of my father. You visited us all those years ago. I used to know you as Auntie Pamela."

"Why, darling, yes." Pamela had brushed aside Rupert and leant over Tina, planting a kiss on her cheek, leaving a round red mark. "Are you doing a job for daddy then?"

"No. I'm not." The hubbub had died away at this development, and Tina's words were icy clear. "I'm on the staff of a SupaPod now. I'm trying to make a difference there."

Pamela emitted a gasp, her long neck extended like a chicken. Her earrings trembled. She clutched at her throat in an exaggerated expression of horror. "Surely not! Joshua would never allow that."

"He doesn't know. He has no idea where I am."

"What possessed you, darling?" Pamela's eyes fell to the black book in Tina's lap. "Oh, no! You haven't taken up that praying nonsense again?"

"It is not nonsense. It is truth."

"Of course, darling. For those who believe in it, anyway."

There was silence after that, and the Eliti party, faces subdued, began to search elsewhere in the carriage for their seats. Even Staceybelle departed, looking sulkily behind her. The train attendants thankfully turned away to attend to their duties elsewhere. The train moved forward. Pamela, who had not moved, perched herself on the edge of Tina's seat, her face close to hers.

"It *is* truth," Tina said again quietly.

"Your father would have a stroke, if he knew. It's against SupaPodia's constitution, you know."

"Of course I know. I'm simply trying to do good from what I believe in. In everything else, I am SupaPodia's servant. The Podders, though, are coming to me in increasing numbers, wanting to learn."

"You're only tolerated because of who you are…"

"No one knows who I am."

Oh, come on." She lowered her voice to a whisper, but Julian still overheard. He thought Stanley did so too because of his sudden stillness. "Someone must know you're the High Director's daughter? They *must* do."

"No. I came in on my own merits under a false name. I am simply known as Christine Munro."

Tina looked up at Julian, and then at Stanley, realising she had now revealed herself. Stanley's face was a mottled mix of uncertainty and disbelief, with – Julian thought – just a hint of anger behind his eyes.

Pamela stood up. "Well, I suppose, you must do what you must do. Your father would be distraught, I know."

"You won't tell him." Tina's calm unflappability was penetrated for a moment.

Pamela looked at her for what seemed a long minute. "No, I won't, dear. But I expect he will learn now. Just remember, you can come to me at any time if you get into trouble and want to escape. Who is your superior?"

Tina stretched out an arm towards Stanley. For a moment, with a lurch of his heart, Julian thought she was going to indicate him as well. Stanley rose to his feet as Pamela addressed him.

"You are…?

"Commander Stanley Gaylord, ma'am..I mean, my lady."

"Ma'am will be sufficient. Here, I will give you my card." She fumbled in the small, pearl-encrusted bag she carried in one hand, and produced a plastic card, the shape and size of one of the credit cards upon which the OW had once floated. "As you will see, I am Lady Pamela Lascelles, SupaPodia Commissioner. Put my details here into your Screen, Commander, or whatever it is you carry for data, and contact me at once if your charge – young Christine here – has any problems. You may have learnt who she is, so make sure you look after her."

"Yes, ma'am. Of course, ma'am." Stanley's hands fluttered in his efforts at earnestness and sincerity.

Pamela leant forward and kissed Tina's cheek once more, ruffling her hair lightly with a bejewelled hand. "My child, I look forward to seeing you again under happier circumstances – when you have got all this nonsense out of your system. SupaPodia International's annual convention will be at the Cape next summer – that's their summer, our winter. You could come out with me. Your father will be there, of course, and you could make your peace with him and have a good high time with your own people, instead of … instead of…" She looked around distastefully, encompassing Julian in her gaze, wrinkling her nose and saying no more.

What a dreadful, insolent woman, thought Julian, the urge to say something in defiance of her strong upon him, but knowing that to do so would probably end his new career in one fell swoop.

Tina, her face composed once more, said simply. "Aunt Pamela, that's not going to happen. You must believe me."

Pamela backed away, her mouth snapped tight. She turned and waved her hand, and then was gone. Looking down the carriage Julian could see her settling into a seat alongside husband, Rupert. What a couple they make, he thought. Both must have been suckled on poison.

* * *

The trip continued with silence reigning in the carriage, broken only by an intermittent scream and outburst of giggles from the young ladies of pleasure in their tight dresses. Julian could see Stanley occasionally looking up thoughtfully at Tina, but she sat quietly, and apparently contentedly, as if nothing at all had happened, still tracing out the words in her book. Eventually, the train stopped again and the Eliti prepared to disembark. Julian saw Pamela, hitching up her long dress to descend the step to the platform, look across meaningfully at Tina, but Tina's eyes were still on her book.

"I wonder where these Eliti are going," he said out loud, expecting Tina to offer an answer, but to his surprise it was Stanley who spoke up. "This station is Audley Garden City. There'll be off to the estate of Commissioner Soubray: he owns all the land around. There's a big balloon fest going on at his residence – Audley End House. Look, you can see the omnibuses that will take them there."

As the train glided forward again, Julian could see parked beyond the station a line of golden-sided motorised buses with shining blue windows. Rough looking people in ragged clothes – mainly unemployed young men, by the look of them – who had gathered around the buses were being pushed back by harassed-looking police, some on horseback.

"They'll call out the Guard if those louts don't disperse," Stanley said. The British armed forces had been abolished, but Guard units, formed according to the old system of counties, were still trained to quell civil disorder. Julian remembered they were noted for their brutality.

As the line of police met the rioters, banners were thrust up above the many jostling heads. Julian was able to read a couple before the scene disappeared behind a line of trees – 'More SupaPods Now' and 'SupaPods for the People': the words flared for an instance in his vision, and then were gone.

"What's a balloon fest?" he asked a little later, recalling the information Stanley had given

Stanley rubbed his eyes. He suddenly looked very tired. "Oh, a balloon fest is a big jamboree for the Eliti. They take off in their hot air balloons, which have all sorts of strange shapes – a whisky bottle, a steam loco, a unicorn's head, a beer can, a pair of breasts, an upright johnny, a dog's turd, – er..what else have I seen? – a piano, a guitar, a side of beef, a cow's head; and so on, and so on. They try to outdo each other with their balloon creations. I once saw a willy that went from flaccid to erect as it rose up (literally!). That was really funny! The Eliti like to float about and watch people come out to look up at them. The countryside's safer for them to hover over now because so much of it is owned by the Eliti and has been cleared. A time back, I heard, one balloon came down over a city – LeedsCentral, I think it was – and its voyagers in their basket underneath were never seen again. Drones were sent in to try and spy out the crash site, but they were shot down by yobs with old army rifles. Apparently. there's lots of military gear lying about.... Not safe at all really, not safe...." His voice tailed off and his head slumped to his chest. As if on cue, Tina jumped up to take it in her hands.

"You shouldn't do that, Tina," Julian protested.

"Why not? It helps him. He's a clever man and needs my care."

"He's a fraud and he's useless. He just wants you to touch him." Julian spoke the words out loud before he could bite them off.

"I think you're unkind," Tina said.

Julian bent over, looking at Stanley's drooping head closely. His eyes were shut. He looked asleep. But had he heard his comments? If so, they could get him into a lot of trouble. Why the hell hadn't he followed his own advice and kept his mouth shut? He clicked his fingers next to Stanley's ear, where Tina's delicate hands were massaging his temples. There was no response. He certainly looked unconscious.

After a lengthy period of anxious watching, Stanley's eyes flickered open, and he sat up with a blissful smile on his face. He raised his arms, stretching, and gave out a vast yawn, "Oh, what a beautiful sleep. Where are we now?"

"I d-don't know," Julian said, stuttering in his relief at his Commander's re-emergence to the world. No, Stanley could not possibly have heard what had been said.

A mixed pattern of rough pasture and heathland was flashing by as the train reached express speed. Streams and creeks, wriggling away to a blue horizon, looked like so many bright, twisting snakes in the sunlight. "It won't be long now," Stanley said. "We're entering the Great Marsh."

A flooded landscape, with sheets of water interspersed with dark clumps of trees standing like islands, crossed by the occasional timber path, told Julian that this was indeed the Fens – the once long-drained Fens, now returned by neglect to their original condition. It was a sorry sight – buildings, sunk in water to their upper windows, a small island occupied by tumbled barns, a once broad road disappearing underwater, broken bridges, a fallen wind pump, cattle standing forlornly on the grassy strip beside the railway line, a dead cow being scavenged by large black birds, more birds wheeling in the sky.

Dry land emerged again, covered by huge blocks of concrete flats, with clothing hanging from windows and balconies, and crowds of huddled people at their base, kids kicking tin cans about, snarling dogs pulling at the ropes tying them, a woman spread out on a patch of grass, her skirt pulled up, three men above her. Slowing now, they slid into a vast, domed station, its curved roof like an aeroplane wing. This was SupaPodia Terminus – King's Lynn.

A shiny silver road vehicle met them at the outer gates. The driver wore a cap with the SupaPodia spearhead badge on its peak. He was in shirtsleeves and his forearms were broad and hairy, covered with writhing tattoos of sin and sex. Julian felt nauseated. Was this really the OuterWorld he had known, debased now to mere survival, oiled by images of death and fornication? Where now was the comradeship, the striving and the debate that had once lingered here? Such indications of a more stable humanity must be present somewhere. If they could not be seen here in the forefront of the view, they must lie hidden away in the background. Or there could be no hope left in the OW.

As they left the Terminus, some people rushed at their vehicle, twisted hands and faces appearing at the windows. "More SupaPods NOW," was the cry that Julian heard most. He looked across at Tina. She was showing her usual imperturbability, but her face looked sad. She still clutched her book in one hand. Fat good that book will do you, Julian thought, if the mob breaks into this vehicle. Fortunately, the tattooed driver knew his job. He accelerated, horn blaring, at the people still trying to surround them: one or two solid bumps against the vehicle showed the success of his manoeuvre. Looking out the rear window, he could see figures bending over a fallen man in the road. A last hand clawed despairingly at the windscreen, and then they were free.

It was not far to the SupaPodia Academy. It stood in a compound, tightly ringed by wire fencing, and with armed Guards at the gate. These were obviously Guards employed by SupaPodia, the first such Julian had seen, for they wore the same colour of lilac as all its other staff – a shiny jumpsuit, with shin, elbow, and chest protectors of a deeper purple, and a round, visored helmet that was such a deep purple it was almost black. They held automatic weapons, carrying them with familiar ease. The sight was a particular shock to Julian – even more so than the police battling the rioters he had witnessed earlier – for he had thought SupaPodia conducted itself without the need for arms, part of a new world order where reason prevailed. He realised now his delusion.

* * *

The two-day course at the SupaPodia Academy (it was correct to measure its time by days here as the sun did rise and set over this part of SupaPodia) passed in a blur for Julian. He had been split away from both Stanley and Tina, and he felt a tug of concern – or was it jealousy? – as he saw the two of them go off together. He was placed in a communal Pod, which supplied all the practical things he needed for the stay. He shared the Pod with three young men from Scotland, who talked much amongst themselves but little to him. He wondered why they were here. One did tell him he worked as an elevator mechanic at a SupaPod near Oban: this did not qualify him, Julian thought, for a role in Re-Education. He felt offended that he, as an academic, was forced to mix with mere mechanics.

He fretted over what Tina was doing, and where she might be laying down her lovely head; not on Stanley's shoulder, he hoped. So he was relieved to meet up with her the next day at the lectures, when Stanley reappeared also as one of the lecturers. Such was the general air of boredom and indifference about the course – emanating as well from the other two lecturers, if not Stanley – that Julian wondered why it could not simply have been given back at their own SupaPod in Ramsgate, instead of their having to make this long, difficult journey. Still, 'theirs not to reason why' was the motto he was beginning to adopt.

Re-Education appeared to consist – so Julian interpreted the lectures, realising with some alarm how rebellious he was becoming – of undermining everything he had been brought up to believe in and turning it inside out, so that black was white, and white black. If warfare had been considered courageous, it was now cowardly; if there had once been a belief in kings and bishops, they were now thought of as subservience and superstition; if there had been tenderness, that was weakness; morality was bigotry; celibacy was sexual repression…and so on, and so on.

The more Stanley's honeyed words beamed at him, the more Julian found himself in turn veering back into opposites, even beginning to pick up and accept again those much earlier beliefs of his which he had long since dismissed as populist and phobic. The other lecturers, feeble thin men with pins for brains – that was Julian's estimation – were even more direct than Stanley. According to them, the whole world before SupaPodia had been one long manipulation of humanity for the personal gain of a privileged few, whereas now, through SupaPodia, it was the many who held the superior status, leaving the earlier 'few' dispossessed of their history, which was trashed and traduced by the constant use of the word 'evil'.

How such stuff and nonsense could be believed alongside a SupaPodia global empire controlled through and by the Eliti, Julian could not even begin to imagine. He looked across at the placid Tina, wondering what thoughts were crossing her head. If ever a person was one of the privileged few, it was she. Her father was one of the leading Eliti and the High Director of SupaPodia also. That was a lot to shuffle off, pretending a compassion based on equality. She might as well throw her stupid black book away for all the relevance it had to this arrogant new world, controlled by lies and obsessions, a world that he realised – with great concern at how his views were changing – he was coming increasingly to hate. For the first time, he was thinking: how can I escape it?

On the last afternoon of the course, some Podders, who had been bussed from SupaPod 33 Hunston, were brought into the lecture room, shuffling uncomfortably in their bulky orange clothes onto the platform at one end of the auditorium. The lecturers fired questions at these Podders, and the Lilac delegates were encouraged to throw in their comments too. The questioning was aggressive. Julian felt ashamed of it. What had these people ever done but sought security in a SupaPod? You could not blame them if they remained apathetic to Re-Education and the other cerebral activities offered them.

"What were the Great Wars of the 20th century fought for?" asked one of the lecturers. "You, the fat man on the end, what's your answer?"

"They were fought for Britain," quavered the man uncertainly.

"Wrong! You dolt. Have you learnt nothing? They were fought for the ruling class, so that it could make money and keep down the ordinary man, sending him off to die by the million."

"Yes, of course, I know now."

"So why did you say what you did?"

"Because they were fought for our country too," he ventured doggedly.

"You're joking, aren't you?. Country is wrong. Nationhood is wrong. Patriotism is wrong. Now go away and repeat that to yourself, or you may find your SupaPod place is removed from you."

"It's luvverly here," spoke up a buxom woman whose auburn hair was enclosed in a net. Her aim was probably to deflect attention from the man who had just so lamentably failed.

"Why's it so *luvverly* then?" asked one of Julian's fellow delegates with something of a sneer.

"'Cos we have good food and new clothes, and there's plenty to look at...."

"What about the society you're part of?" yelled out another delegate. "Do you like its diversity?"

"Oh, everyone's very friendly, dear. We all get on well together."

"And why shouldn't you?"

"'Cos many of us is, like, from different backgrounds, so it can be hard to mix."

"That's because of your prejudices!" bellowed Stanley, joining the fray, his face shining read. "It's your prejudices we want to rid you of."

"You can't change people," the woman said defiantly.

"Oh yes we can, and we will! Or you won't be allowed to stay in a SupaPod."

The woman retreated to the back of the stage, her eyes welling with tears.

The questioning went on like this for another half hour. Julian did not say anything, although he knew he should do so, if only to keep in the lecturers' good books. He was growing worried about what a report on him might say. Yet Tina was silent too, her eyes downcast for much of the time. He couldn't imagine Stanley giving *her* a bad report, in particular in the light of what Pamela had said on the train.

At last it was over. They trooped out of the auditorium. Julian manoeuvred himself to be beside Tina. "I'm tired of this," he mouthed to her. He was surprised – and alarmed too – when she did not reply, but simply gave him a look which he construed as disdainful.

He did not see her again until they were on the train journeying home; for 'home' had to be considered his Kent SupaPod by the sea – now and forever more. Unless, of course, he thought, I am thrown out, or I escape – whichever may come sooner. The last idea was already forming in his mind. SupaPodia, once for him a dream of utopia, was turning rapidly into a nightmare of horror. How could he have been so foolish as to think otherwise? The realisation pierced him like nails hammered into his flesh.

On the journey back, the three of them had the train entirely to themselves. There was only one carriage, and an attendant each to wait on them, so both Stanley and Julian gorged on chocolates, canapés, and vintage champagne. Tina wanted nothing, however, and sat quietly with her book. For a reason he did not understand, Julian thought she was now being unfriendly to him. Emboldened by the champagne, and seeing that Stanley was asleep and snoring softly, he went and sat beside her. "What are you reading?"

"The word of God." She said the words, quietly, patiently, as if they were the most perfectly normal thing for her to say. If she anticipated criticism, there was no hint of it in her outward manner.

"And what does God say?"

She turned to him and looked him in the eyes. Her own eyes were very clear and blue. He felt his head drawn into them as if into a vortex. "God will speak many things – to you, perhaps one matter, to me, another; yet his words to both of us will say the same, that He loves us and that He wishes us to love Him and all His creation."

"*I* love you for sure," Julian said, the champagne pulsing in his veins, sending the foolish words into his mouth. Seeing the light fade in her face, he immediately realised his stupidity.

"You have to be ready to receive God's love," Tina said. "Julian, I do not think you are ready yet, for otherwise you would not endanger your soul by mocking truth."

That stung him – he had only tried to be friendly – and he would have liked to have shaken her a little on her plank of righteousness, but he could not think what to say. She looked so pretty seated there, with the light from the window in her pale hair, the book on her lilac lap, her smooth, round knees cut neatly by the hem of her skirt. He *did* want to love her, but God was in the way. Despite his disbelief, he knew it would be a mistake to challenge God through her. He tried to settle his revolving senses. More sensible it would be to ask her questions about her faith, instead of seeking ways to try and belittle it.

"How do you hope to bring the people you talk with to God – I mean the Podders, of course? What do they have to do?"

"They don't have to do anything. All they have to do is to understand that God is with them always, and that they can call on Him when they are in trouble and He will help them."

"And they don't have to do anything in return for this?"

"God likes them to pray, and to meet together in worship, for that helps to build and strengthen his Church. All people, whether of the OuterWorld so-called, or here in SupaPodia, are the same to God; whatever their background, their race or creed, they are all equal in His sight. Outward expressions of worship are not essential. God will know your heart. He will know your soul. All you have to do is believe in Him, and call out to Him, and He will be there for you – always."

"Tina, what are you hoping to achieve with this mission of yours?" He made his voice sound serious, for he knew the matter *was* serious. SupaPodia did not approve of religions, in particular evangelising religions. SupaPodia expounded its own morality of equality and diversity. It could well consider Tina's work a threat, and then what would happen to her? Perhaps even her father would not be able to save her. Such a scandal with SupaPodia International could even affect his position as High Director and undermine his credibility.

Tina answered, her voice calm and unemotional, "I am simply trying to help spread God's love. I have no ultimate objectives. I do not seek to convert those who do not wish to be converted. I only wish to proclaim that God is here for everyone. He is not superstition, or imagination, but a true source of love, who will help them through their troubles and their pain."

"What type of pain will they find in a SupaPod? Julian asked. "Do you mean their pain at being in one, of what might happen to them there, or some inner pain that can beset them wherever they live – SupaPod or OuterWorld, or even in the superior, golden lands of the Eliti?"

Now it was her turn to look at him sharply. He realised he should not have implied any criticism of the Eliti, or that her teaching might be of value in resisting an atheistic order.

"Humanity's condition does not matter," she answered. "We are all equal before God whatever our transitory status, and we all share the same pain of the world, whatever the conditions under which we live."

"Well, I admire you, Tina. "I must tell you that. Even if I think you a little misguided at times. I wonder – indeed, if I'm honest, I'm fearful – how long SupaPodia will tolerate you."

"Thank you," she said, giving him a smile. "I do not worry, so you must not."

"You know you can call on me at any time should you need help. About anything," he added.

"I know. You are a sweet man." And to his great pleasure she kissed him on the cheek. He returned to his seat opposite Stanley, who purported still to be asleep although he had stopped snoring, and Julian could see his eyelids trembling. He hoped he had not overheard any of his conversation with Tina. But, if he had, then he would realise that, for all his vacillating weaknesses, he was at least loyal to SupaPodia's secular values.

Stanley, though, was someone he felt he could never trust.

10

As the train came closer and closer to the Ramsgate Terminus, Stanley, on waking, seemed to grow increasingly agitated, rising to his feet and walking the length of the carriage, and back again. Tina watched his pacing with only a mild flickering of her eyes, but Julian was immediately concerned, as if he knew Stanley's restlessness boded ill for him. And so it turned out.

On arrival at the Terminus, Tina was sent packing with Stanley's files to board the cabin train for the Staff Portal, while Julian was led away by Stanley to a kiosk on the platform that served coffee, not out of a tube here but produced from a machine operated by an Oriental-looking vendor. The coffee was hot and surprisingly good, the best coffee, in fact, that Julian had drunk in a very long while. Coffee in the OW had become virtually unobtainable, and the coffee of the SupaPod itself was usually over-frothy and sweet.

"What did you think of the Re-Ed training?" Stanley asked, sipping at his coffee while leaning against a metal upright that supported the kiosk's canopy roof.

"Oh, very good. Excellent. Essential." Julian piled on the praise words, certain Stanley was leading up to something else.

"I was disappointed you didn't join in the final Shout-Out."

"Shout-Out? Oh, you mean the event where the Podders were brought in."

"Yes, exactly. It was the main test of your data input and motivation. The Podders provide a live practice, until you have to do it yourself for real."

"Oh, I didn't know that. I thought it was the lecturers who performed the role play, not the delegates."

"That's what you were meant to think, but we hoped you would show initiative. And you, for one, didn't," he added in a flat voice.

"Nor did Tina, or..or...some of the others," Julian said, beginning to flounder and ashamed of his betrayal of Tina.

"Tina's my assistant," snapped Stanley, his face suddenly red and angry. "You are my protégée, my understudy. I was going to get you an early introduction to Control Station 15, but now I'm not so sure."

Julian felt devastated. He may have had strong doubts about SupaPodia, but he did not want his professional record to be tarnished unfairly. Why couldn't Stanley have made clear what had been expected at that so-called Shout-Out and then he would have joined in without reservation.

So we're not going to the Control Station?" he said somwhat plaintively.

Stanley looked at him and did not reply. His silence continued, broken only by his occasional slurping at his coffee.

"If I say I'm terribly sorry and it won't happen again, will that wipe out the blot I've made?" Julian asked, increasingly desperate.

He felt he was between two worlds. If he made a mistake with either, he might be dropped down a cleft in-between and not be heard of again. It was all very well wanting to escape back to where he had come from, but he had to make sure that former world was still there for him – or that it could even be reached. For all its faults, recognised now by Julian so clearly, SupaPodia had been quite fun. It had been secure, at least physically so, and he had had plenty of challenges to meet and colleagues to relate to, which included the delights Marion had provided. Where could he obtain that in the OuterWorld? There, you might have no one to talk to, passing other lost souls like ghosts in the grimy, litter-strewn streets. If you dropped down dead, you would simply become part of the litter, picked over by vermin, your body boiling with maggots, until dragged away with hooks. He didn't want an end like that.

"I've mentioned only one matter," Stanley said suddenly as he drained his cup. I might accept your apology for that, but the other is far more problematic."

"What do you mean?" Julian, who had only had a few sips of his own coffee, tensed, spilling some onto his new brown coat.

" 'He's a fraud and he's useless.' " Stanley said the words in a dull monotone, making Julian's blood freeze. "Isn't that what you said about me when you thought I was asleep."

"I'm s-sorry. I didn't mean it."

Stanley grabbed Julian by both lapels, pulling his face towards his own. "Yes, you did, you arsehole. Remember Stanley never sleeps. He knows everything. I could get you banished for that, abusing your superior, your Commander too; for fuck's sake it's against every SupaPodia rule, but…" – his face broke into a smile and he took Julian's face between his palms, patting his cheeks – "….I won't. You're mine now. You'll do exactly what I say, and if I ever hear another sour word from you, another criticism, you'll be off to the Lower Levels – and I doubt if you'll ever come back."

He laughed, high-pitched and wild, and Julian realised in that moment he was mad. Like a madman himself, Julian had fallen right into his trap. He fought the rising panic in him, aware of Stanley eyes and manic grin on him all the time, thinking how can I get out of this, how can I escape? I can't go on like this. My life will not be worth a shit.

"How can I atone, sir?" he asked in his most small, grovelling voice.

"Atone, eh? How do you propose to do that? Suck my cock? I'm sorry, I'm not gay. Wipe my arse? I'd rather do it myself. Oh, I'll tell you what you *can* do, for I expect your fingers are much stronger than our Tina's, is rub my head. I feel one of my very worst headaches coming on."

Stanley bent his head forward, and Julian, smothering his feelings of revulsion, began smoothing his hair and pressing his fingers into his temples, as he had seen Tina doing.

"That's good, that's very good," Stanley began to groan. Julian was aware of the knowing smiles of other Lilacs at the coffee kiosk, who had just arrived off a second train. He kept up the massage, however, realising it was perhaps his last chance to save himself with Stanley. It seemed to have worked, because eventually Stanley, straightening up, said, "Enough for now. Time we left for Control Station 15."

Vastly relieved, his hands trembling from administering the massage – or was it from fear? – Julian followed dutifully in Stanley's wake. They climbed a spiral stairway from the concrete apron where the kiosk stood. The stairway had concrete steps and a low metal railing, and Julian became dizzy as they climbed higher, seeing the drop opening up beneath him, with the upper works of the SupaPod's entrances now laid out below. He could see the blue sea stretching away and the dark, curving line of the great Bar that ran out far into the ocean across the sand islands of the Goodwins, with the humps of its turbines like the many heads of the great Hydra. How clear were the white cliffs seen from here, with the green blur of the land opening out beyond them. A sudden flash within that blur told of another train approaching the Terminus, or perhaps going from it; Julian could not be sure.

They reached a broad platform in the hillside. It was crisscrossed with wires attached to tall metal posts, and amongst them taller masts with antennae and receivers of many shapes, the wires all leading to a white-painted, one-storey building set against the hill. It had the look of a large domestic bungalow, only with a flat roof and two projecting wings, its windows blocked out by steel shutters. Beside it stood several van-like vehicles with the SupaPodia name and logo on their sides.

They crossed the platform, twisting between the many posts, approaching the far side wing where there was an open doorway with 'Control Station 15' stencilled in black letters on the wall alongside. No one was in the small entrance room inside, but Julian was aware of a red flickering light somewhere above him. "Our chips are being read and re-activated," said Stanley. "It won't take a moment."

A far door slid back, and they went through into a broad passage, where several individuals, men and women, were coming and going. They wore a boilersuit-type uniform, similar in style and lilac colour to those used within the SupaPod, but with broad red lines along the jacket sleeves and trouser legs. A short, tubby man, with a bald patch at the centre of otherwise plentiful black hair, so he looked to Julian like some jovial monk of olden times, greeted Stanley with a hail.

"Hi, Stans, old chap. I heard you were coming."

Stanley introduced Julian. The man's name was Gerry. "Pleased to meet you," he said. "I've heard you're the Commander's favourite." He gave a wink that brought a sense of unease to Julian and a sick feeling to his stomach. *What* exactly had been said about him?

"All clearances in order?" asked Gerry. Stanley nodded, but Gerry said, "Sorry, must check." He ran a hand scanner over the two of them, and examined the result in its viewer, pursing his lips. "OK. All's well. Follow me."

He led them along the corridor and through far doors into a large open room, the sides of which were filled with enormous screens covered by twinkling lights. A number of operatives sat around viewing the screens or manipulating controls.

"This is our Location Monitoring Unit," Gerry said to Julian. "Some 70% of our work is carried out here, but that percentage will increase soon, as you may have been told."

He looked expectantly at Julian, who stood dumbly, not understanding. Stanley said, as if in explanation, "He's heard the outline but not the detail."

"I see," said Gerry. "The Second Implant is still not general knowledge to Lilacs then?"

"We've had no directive yet."

"It'll come soon, I'm sure."

Julian was thinking: what are they talking about? Obviously, something about that awful new implant I had mentioned to me by Peter – the one that records and transmits all conversations, and everything else around you, automatically. It sounds as if it'll be introduced soon. Hell – fear was rising in him again – I must get out as soon as I can. But that's easier said than done. What chance of relocating to the OW is there? Would they allow me to do that? Almost certainly not.

Someone was saying something to him and he was too full of his own thoughts to respond. Come on, Julian, get a grip. Or they'll dismiss you as an idiot, and there's no future in SupaPodia for an idiot – perhaps only as a Podder, and that I most certainly don't want to be.

"Would you like to see a representation of fine-tuned positional monitoring?" Gerry asked Julian again, giving no sign of any impatience. He knew it took new inductees a while to comprehend the inner workings of a SupaPodia Control Station.

Julian looked at Stanley, who was standing with his arms folded. "Well answer him," he said testily. "It's what I've brought you here for."

"Of course. Yes, please," Julian said hurriedly, thinking, what on earth is this about? Surely I could have received some sort of general introduction first. But that never seemed to be the way with SupaPodia.

Gerry led him over to one of the wall screens. "I'll show you an example of both Inner and Outer positioning," he said.

"Excuse me," Julian said. "What do you mean by that?"

Gerry did give Julian a second look now.

"He's a bit slow," Stanley said cruelly. "Or perhaps, to be fair, he's still very new."

"Of course," said Gerry in a flat voice. Addressing Julian, his round face close to his – he has vile breath, Julian thought, wanting to turn his head away but needing to focus on the screen – he intoned, "Positional monitoring comes from the implanted chip given to everyone in a SupaPod – Lilacs and Podders – or who works Outside for SupaPodia, and that includes a large number of Externals, who might never actually go near a SupaPod – farmers, manufacturers, carriers, freighters, members of the Guard militia, and so on. It doesn't include Eliti, of course."

"Why not?" Julian was emboldened to ask.

Gerry looked at him, then slowly shook his monkish head as if bewildered or sorrowful. "Because they are our controllers and their exact location at any time is of no concern to anyone but themselves."

"Yet, it might be," Julian persisted, then saw the look on Stanley's face and made an abrupt reversal. "Sorry, I shouldn't have said that."

From their expressions, both Gerry and Stanley clearly agreed. All Stanley commented, though, was, "Think a little more clearly, Julian, please."

"I really am sorry."

"Anyhow," Gerry continued, "Control Station 15 receives the data of all within the broader SupaPodia area centred on the Ramsgate SupaPod. That data is put out to SupaPodia International and combined with the totality of data it holds, first within Britain alone and then, if required – and this is rare – throughout the entire globe. Here is a typical result. We'll use as an example the monitoring data of – let's see…" – he studied a paper printout in a black folder beside him – "…of one Wendy Brownlow, a Lilacs' catering operative here at Goodwins. She joined the SupaPod three and a half years ago…" – Julian thought it interesting that years were still referred to at the Control Station – "…from employment with the now defunct company, Transfood, in the OW. Let's see, she has the SupaPod reference L38/121/796/175Z, so we can find her straightaway." He tapped some numbers into a pad below the screen. "Ah, yes, here she is."

The screen's image had collapsed inwards with amazing rapidity. Large clumps of light were resolved as smaller clusters, then separated into individual pinpricks. The screen rushed down on one such pinprick, now divorced from all others about it, and then showed that particular single light, close up, within a space framed and labelled with the reference Gerry had sought – L38/121/796/175Z.

"Ah, there you see," Gerry chortled. "Our Wendy Brownlow within her Pod, by herself, perhaps viewing her screen, perhaps sleeping, perhaps…. She's not in motion, anyhow. Who knows? We can't pick up exactly what she's doing. Not yet, anyhow. The Second Implant will help a lot in that regard. Then, we should have both sound and vision."

Julian was amazed, horrified by the implications of what he was seeing. And this was just the beginning.

"Now – and I'm using OuterWorld time measurement units – if we go back minutes, hours, days, we can see the movements of her existence" Gerry was rapidly pressing some buttons. "You see, an hour and a half back, she was here." The screen had altered to show a different outline and a different reference. "This is a communal staff washroom. She was perhaps having a shower. You see there are some other lights alongside, other Lilacs doing the same. Now further back, let's say 12 days, 22 hours – I'm moving at random, for I have no idea of her typical movements – you see, she's back in her Pod, but there's another light conjoined with hers. Let's see its reference. That's it, L37/298/2353/169Q. Let me search for it…Yes, here we are, one Archie McBray, a fellow Lilac from catering. He must be her lover, unless he's just visiting for tea, and that's unlikely."

Gerry gave a horrible greasy chuckle, which sent a sick feeling through Julian, who was beginning to realise the enormity of what he was seeing. Gerry then would be able to work out how he had linked – was that the right word? – with Marion in his Pod on several occasions. What Julian had been dreading was now confirmed. There was no movement you made in a SupaPod, and even outside, that could not be followed and interpreted.

Wendy's movements could be picked up everywhere, as were those of everyone with whom she came in contact. The lights flickered, weaved and zig-zagged on the screen. Speeded up, they made a pattern like fireflies in the evening gloaming. Wendy had left the SupaPod to attend a course – as Julian had done – and she could be followed there as well in the OW. Her bedroom in the college appeared to have been invaded by three other lights – "All men", Gerry had chuckled. "Group bang by the look of it." – and so it had gone on, Gerry sweeping the data back in time until the moment Wendy's implant had been made and the device first activated. It was a total record of a life, and more than that, of all the lives that had conjoined with hers, or passed closed by, either by intent or by coincidence. And that was just the record of one person.

"How long do you keep the data?" Julian asked.

"For ever" was the reply. "Storage space is minimal. It's all highly compressed. The movements of the whole of SupaPodia International and its external workers could be placed on an old-fashioned memory stick, and there would still be space over."

"And now," Stanley said, "we're due the Second Implant. Gerry, do you wish to tell Julian more about that, or shall I?"

Gerry looked at his watch. It was an old-style watch with numbered hours and hands that moved around the dial. "Could you do it, Stans? I've got some figures to get together before the meeting."

"Oh, alright." Stanley sounded a bit grumpy. With a sinking heart, Julian remembered what had happened between them earlier, likely far from forgotten. Stanley led him from the location monitoring room into another much smaller square room with a central table, two chairs and little else. Someone had stuck a poster on the wall, perhaps not an official one for it was hand-drawn and read, 'MMM – 'Monitor (All) Misguided Mutts.' Julian wondered what a 'Mutt' was in the eyes of the Control Station. Was he one of them?

"Just briefly, Julian, for I haven't much time. Give my temples a pressing would you? You've got fingers of gold. If I didn't have Tina in post, I'd offer you my assistant's job. Ouch! Not too hard, you prat. You nearly had my eyeballs out."

"I would have been honoured to accept the job," Julian said, trying to keep his voice level and normal. Stanley's thin blond hair and scalp were greasy to the touch, and he knew he would have to disinfect his hands later to cleanse them of all feel of him. He thought unhappily, my academic posting to SupaPodia is now downgraded to body servant.

"Alright! That's enough for the moment," Stanley called out. "Now, this Second Implant business. Not everyone will have it. Commanders, such as myself, certainly not. It'll be on a trial basis at first, but I'm putting you down for it. If I could have trusted you more, I wouldn't have done so. But you have proved yourself to be rebellious, and you're – to put not too fine a point on it – fucking about behind my back. You've already got into Marion – well, everyone does that sooner or later – but I know you've got plans for Tina, and I really can't allow that. She's far too valuable a property. So I have to keep an eye on you."

"You're quite wrong, Stanley," protested Julian, aghast. "She's half my age. I like her, that's all. I try to help her."

"Don't be fooled by all that religious mumbo-jumbo. She's a clued up girl, far too good for such crap. It's just a shield for her, I think – a cover."

"I think she's perfectly sincere," Julian said, but doubts were creeping into his mind.

"Just watch it with her. We'll come down on you very hard if you do anything stupid. She's safe because of who she is, but you're not. I look after her. It's not my concern what she gets up to. If others at the top allow it, then so do I."

"I understand. I'll be very careful, sir."

"And no fiddling about with her, meeting her in secret, as I know you have done. And no more trying to get into her knickers, or at least fantasising about doing so, you know what I mean?"

"I have never done anything like that and never would!" Julian was really angry at the suggestion and of being traduced in this way.

Stanley laughed, and he realised his superior – his Commander – was deliberately provoking him. His face flushed, and he wanted to walk out of the room; but where to? He didn't know, but anywhere to get away from Stanley. However, he didn't dare.

Stanley continued remorselessly. "The Second Implant will record and transmit everything you say, every sound you make – so no farting, please or loud wanking – and, what is more, everything that is said to you and all other external sounds around you. Soon, they'll be able to add pictures too."

Is there anyone more crude, vulgar and hateful than this man? Julian thought, his fists tightly clenched, not to strike Stanley but to keep a hold on himself. And yet at that time when Stanley challenged the Eliti on the train I quite respected him. What the hell is going on with him? His mood alters like a chameleon changing its colour.

"What's the exact purpose of the new implant?" Julian asked, desperate to stick to the facts, awful as they were, without the unwanted addition of Stanley's sudden hostility.

"Well, control, of course – as ever. We need the control to keep SupaPodia efficient. That'll be a main consideration at the meeting I'll be going to just now. In such a tight-knit community as ours the slightest dissidence can easily upset the order of things, spoiling life for everyone. We have to monitor rigorously to ensure all is in harmony."

"And what happens to any dissidents?" Julian dared to ask, knowing he might not receive a straight reply.

Stanley's answer, however, was direct. "They'll go down to the Lower Levels and are unlikely to cause trouble again."

"What exactly goes on down there?" Julian could not hold back the question.

Stanley gave him a long look, seemed about to turn away with the question unanswered, then suddenly thrust himself forward, so his face was inches from Julian's.

"I haven't forgiven you yet, you twerp. You've got a great deal of atonement to make yet."

He took a couple of steps away and then swung back. "It's a great pity, Julian, for I had quite liked you. Tell you what I'm going to do, so you won't want to speak badly of me again. I'll take you down to the Lower Levels and then you can see for yourself what can *happen* to those who upset the order here and speak ill of their superiors. Now, I've got a meeting to go to and you must get back to the SupaPod. Don't worry, I'll be in touch!"

Julian watched him walk away. He had to sit down because his knees felt weak and he found his hands were trembling. When he had recovered himself a little, he left the room and stood in the corridor outside. He did not know where to go. How could he make his way back to the SupaPod?

He managed to find the Control Station's outer door, and stood on its step blinking in the sunlight. A body of men in purple uniforms were drawn up in front of the building. They carried laser guns slung across their chests and held plastic shields. They were practising drill movements, forming from line into square, the shields of the front rank thrust forward, then the square advancing at a running crouch, the shields of the rear ranks raised above to make a defensive roof. They finished with a great shout.

One of the men detached himself and marched up to Julian. "What are you doing watching us?" he demanded. Julian saw he had 'SupaPodia Guard' embroidered in white on the shoulder of his purple tunic.

Julian explained as best he could. He did not really know the proper answer to anything now. The thought passed through his head that all this was rather like one of the nastier scenes from 'Alice in Wonderland', a film he had viewed many years ago. Had he then fallen down a hole in the ground and found a new fantastical world? Well, in a way he had. He could see the upper buildings of the SupaPod before him shining in the reflected glare from the sea, the same SupaPod that descended deep into the bowels of the earth, at the bottom of which he might find any manner of things. But who would be ruling there, that was the question? Tina's loving God or the devil?

The Guard commander was a man with a florid face and a short clipped moustache. As Julian, rather dazedly, told him his purpose, his features relaxed.

"You'll need the tunnel, sir," he said.

"The tunnel?"

"Yes, sir. Not the steps. You shouldn't have come up those, anyhow. There're for Terminus staff only."

"I see. Sorry."

"Not your fault, sir, I'm sure."

He led him round to the rear of the Control Station building and pointed out a tunnel mouth in the hillside. "That, sir, is what you need. It'll take you right into the SupaPod. Bring you out where you'll be able to find your way."

"Thank you." Julian felt almost tearful that someone was being kind and helpful to him.

"Don't mention it, sir. Others, like you, get lost here."

"So I'm not alone, thought Julian, feeling immediately better. He headed for the tunnel, leaving the Guard to begin their drills again, the dark, geometric blocks moving purposefully over the high terraced ground, against a background of blue sea and distant white cliffs. He heard their shouts, and then, as he entered the tunnel, could hear them no more.

The tunnel was brightly lit and had a moving floor going down steeply, forming stairs in places, and carrying him eventually by a further steep flight of stairs to a place he knew well, the long promenade of the Upper Deck, which he entered by a sliding door at its furthest end – a point to which he had not ventured before. From here, it was a lengthy walk to the main Upper Deck hall, passing the places where he had stood with Tina looking out over the sea. He hoped she had returned safely. From the hall, an elevator took him down to the Level of his Pod. He had tasted the OuterWorld once more, but now was firmly back in the sunken vaults of SupaPodia

The navigation of his chip was working again. It took him a while to get used to it. After the distances and the relative freedoms of the OW, the enclosed chambers and tunnels of the SupaPod, for all their bright embellishments, seemed strange and menacing. He didn't like that feeling at all. He was certain now: he had to get out – the next time for good.

In his Pod, his Screen was playing an old Hollywood movie. He heard the song,

'If I knew you were coming,
I'd've baked a cake…'

repeated over and over again, but whether this was on the Screen or in his head, he did not know. He could not think what it was he had to do next, or whether the time was Green, Orange, Red, Yellow, or Blue, or any other combination of colours. He couldn't find his timepiece and for the moment he did not care.

After a while, he fell asleep.

11

The lofty palace of the High Director of SupaPodia – it had been compared by one cynical American journalist with the fortified Eagle's Nest of that mythical tyrant, Adolf Hitler – occupied most of the southern slopes of a mountain called Inkwelo in the Lower Drakensburg of South Africa. The nearest town had been Volksrust, named after the white Racists who had originally taken the land from its peaceful inhabitants and had used it as a 'resting place' before going on to steal the gold that lay further north, using African slaves to dig the deep mines that followed the strata of gold. In recent years, those same deep mine shafts had been turned into three of South Africa's SupaPods, and the very first Podders that were admitted, as a mark of honour to their history, had been the last inhabitants of Volksrust. Now the site of the former town provided one of the broad drives of a great game ranch for the High Director's shooting friends and colleagues coming from all over SupaPodia International.

Close by was another mountain, Amajuba, rising like an enormous flat-topped pyramid. On the summit of this the High Director had had a rotunda of white marble built, so he could walk its curving colonnaded portico and look out over all his lands to the north, and all those to the south, seeing the grey-green grassy hills rippling in the heat of the African sun, and all his lands to the west too, and to the east where the hills were cleft by the mighty Buffalo River.

Strange it was, thought the High Director, seated on a marble bench of his portico and looking down at the green and golden roofs of his Inkwelo palace below, that his surname was Collyer, and that it had been a General Sir George Pomeroy-Colley (such a remarkably similar surname) who had led a British army up this mountain of Amajuba more than two hundred years ago, and been defeated there by the Racists. In celebration of this remarkable coincidence, which, being no scholar at that time, he had found out by chance from an old history book, he had added the name Pomeroy to his own, so he was now Joshua Pomeroy-Collyer.

He had turned down all Eliti titles (they had wanted first to make him a Sir, then later an Earl), wishing to be thought a mere 'man of the people, but otherwise High Director and First Person of SupaPodia International – which by now was really the whole world. His daughter Christine, however – his only child by a vicar's daughter, whom he had seduced early in his political career 'in a moment of madness' – refused to accept the name Pomeroy, for she judged the late General, who had died on Amajuba with a bullet in his head, to have been as much a Racist as those who shot him.

It had been difficult for Joshua bringing up Christine – or Tina as she had liked to be known from a nursery age – by himself. He had not allowed her mother to have more than a distant connection with her. Of Scottish birth, he had been introduced to politics and to SupaPodia by an associate of his father, who happened to be a member of Britain's top Elitist organisation, the House of Lords. By diligence, some luck and much ruthlessness, his rise within the fast developing SupaPodia of Britain had been as rapid as the proverbial meteor. Within ten years, he had had the satisfaction of sending the House of Lords into extinction, together with much else of the corrupt, abusive British politics of that period, and had moved to Southern Africa, which he had made his base to further his global ambitions for SupaPodia. A further ten years passed and he had taken control of SupaPodia International as its third High Director. With the quick development of South Africa's SupaPods, he had moved from his Matopos Headquarters to a new SupaPodia Administrative City at the Cape, which had also offshore the world's then largest SupaPod of Robben Island.

For much of that time, Tina had been at school in Britain or in Zimbabwe, or been coming of age in Switzerland. He had seen her occasionally in her holidays, but never for longer than to kiss her on the cheek and ask her a few questions, and then there was a further obligation that took him away. The situation was not helped by the fact that he kept a string of mistresses. One of these was his lovely Pammie, his most expert and fluent lover, with whom Tina, rather surprisingly, did achieve some sort of bonding. The three of them had spent the occasional Christmas together earlier on, but, as this was a religious holiday that SupaPodia frowned upon, even those meetings became difficult, and he came to communicate with his daughter mainly by message and Screen. He saw less and less of Pammie too, although she remained a close, but distant and now re-married, friend.

It was with some alarm, not long after work had begun on his new Inkwelo palace, that he learnt through an anonymous message sent from SupaPodia Central Control that Tina was seeing her mother, a notable

Christian activist, who was imbuing her daughter with her religion – not just the ethics and morality of Christianity that SupaPodia did not proscribe, but all the superstitious ritual as well that it most certainly did not allow.

And then Tina had disappeared. He could get no answer from her, and no one even at SupaPodia Control knew where she had gone to. Her mother had laughed in his face when he had jetted from a symposium in Canberra seeking information from her at the old, decaying vicarage, lost in the muddy, overgrown lanes of Suffolk, where she still lived.

"She has more wisdom in her tiny foot than you have in your whole serpent's body," the grey-haired matriarch had told him. He had not known if that was a quotation from the great black Bible she kept on a lectern in the crumbling church next door, with its leaking roof long-stripped of its lead.

Not long after that, Tina's mother had died, still hugging her Bible to her breast. The High Director had attended the funeral, hoping that Tina would turn up, but there was no sign of her at the church, or anywhere else for that matter, although the news of the death had been broadcast widely by SupaPodia Media. Tina, in fact, was in hiding with a Christian organisation – the Brethren – who practised their worship in caves in the West Country. To them SupaPodia was the Anti-Christ. Tina volunteered to spread the word in a SupaPod, not as a militant – a soldier of Christ – but as a disciple and a teacher. "By tiny drops, the evil will be dispersed," she had declared. No one with the Brethren knew her background, and nor did SupaPodia until, by the merest chance, she was recognised by an Eliti – one Pamela ('Pammie') Lascelles, former mistress, still a close friend to Joshua, now High Director of SupaPodia International.

So now the secret was out of the bag. At least it would be when those who knew, such as Pamela herself, or Commander Stanley Gaylord, dared to spread it. Until then, there was still time. Tina was safe, surely – her father would allow no harm to come to her – but what of those who countenanced her teaching, and for fear of her position and not daring to test her father's reaction, did nothing about it? And that most certainly included Stanley Gaylord, her Commander at SupaPod No. 16 Ramsgate, together with Dr. Julian Foster, Educator Grade 2, of the same SupaPod, Level 19.

12

It was for Julian now an eternity of dream, nightmarish dreams that licked his inner vision with fire. He saw the devils below him feeding the fires, deep within those Lower Levels that the arch-demon Stanley had spoken of. His time passed in quiet acceptance of the Re-Education tasks that he must perform. Sometimes he saw Stanley; for a long time he did not; then Tina was there, looking at him with a quiet smile, more beautiful than ever with her hair tied back with blue ribbon, and then she was gone. The fact that she smiled at him perhaps showed he was forgiven, although he quite forgot why it was he had to be forgiven – was it because he had questioned her beliefs? – but he was happy to receive and return her smile.

Marion was with him most often, sharing his Pod, her needs increasingly urgent and frenzied. He found it hard to satisfy them. He suspected she had her own inner demons from which she was seeking release, but, if so, she told him nothing of them. Occasionally they resorted to viewing images on the Screen to provide extra stimulus, but these left him afterwards feeling disgusted and broken. He thought: oh, where is the fineness now of the things I used to enjoy? –sunrises and evening skies, the majesty of billowing clouds, the long green slopes of hills, dark woods full of secret sounds. I have none of these now. I read no literature beyond the hideous, staccato, monosyllabic sounds that make up the instruction manuals of SupaPodia, and their flaring posters that tell you how to move, to think, and to fart. I hear no music either, other than the shrill dementia of some jibbering, jabbering, twisting, rocking group, akin to monkeys in a zoo but without their grace and intelligence. Their noise is everywhere in the Podders halls as if it is essential for life. If it stopped, then the world would stop too – and, in truth, would that not be a good thing?

At some point – it must have been only a relatively short time after his journey to the OW, as his memories of that occasion were still harsh in his mind – he met medico Peter once more in some long passage, lilac-lit, when he was on the way from somewhere to somewhere else. Peter stood, hands on hips, hairy legs protruding from beneath his short tunic hem.

"Well met," he said. "I have been looking for you."

"What for?"

"Are you due for the OW yet?"

"Oh, Peter. I'm sorry. I quite forgot what you asked. I've been and done it."

Peter scowled. All his former heartiness seemed drained from him. "That's a great pity. I'm trying to get a message out."

"I know. You told me."

"Are you due to go again?"

"I don't think so. I haven't been told anything."

"Well, I must make another plan. Are you willing to help me?"

"I think so, Peter. What is it precisely you are trying to do?"

"Get out of here. What do you feel about joining me?"

Julian felt so confused, so full of worry and fear, remembering all Stanley had said to him and the Control Station above ground he had visited, and…and…well, everything, even Marion's insatiable onslaught on his overworked body, her haunches settling once again upon his sore genitals, her skin slippery with their conjoined sweat, that he blurted out. "For Christ's sake, Peter, help me escape from this before I go mad!"

Peter placed a hand on his shoulder. "Hang in there. In the meantime, whatever you do, don't say anything but the right things to anyone. We'll have a meeting." – he looked at his timepiece – "The next Green, at two past. Green 2. I'll meet you at L18/122/69/101/C2. Input that into your CP now."

Julian did as he was told, seeing how his fingers trembled over the buttons.

"We'll have to move fast," Peter said. "I'm down to do one of the first batches of the Second Implant soon. There's a technical hold up at the moment, but it won't take long to resolve. Once the Second Implant is part of the system, everything will become impossible. We won't even be able to talk like this without the Control Station knowing."

"That's appalling."

"And you know," Peter went on remorselessly, "the implant will be made directly into a vertebra. So there'll be no way of removing it without major surgery, and that might endanger the spinal cord."

"Fucking hell!" The crudity, which did not come easily to Julian's lips, seemed the only adequate way to express his horror.

"Talking about fucking," said Peter drily, "are you still at it with Marion?"

Julian looked his astonishment at him.

"You see, nothing is secret," Peter said, lowering his voice as a couple of Lilacs approached them along the passage. "Her promiscuity is a joke here. People take bets on who's next. You've lasted longer than most."

"I don't believe you." Julian felt a sudden urge to burst into tears.

Once again, Peter's consoling hand was on his shoulder. "No harm done. I don't believe she's setting you up for anything. It's just a release for her. She's as much a victim of SupaPodia as we are. But don't tell her anything, will you?"

"No, of course not."

"Well, until our meeting then."

Julian, more confused than ever, saw him retreating down the passage, exchanging a greeting with another Lilac. He re-checked his CP, for he had completely forgotten where he had been going. When eventually he got back to his Pod, he found Marion was there, already undressed. Despite all his forebodings, he was quite unable to resist her.

Marion, satiated for the moment, raised herself on the bouncy, rubber couch, and said to Julian, "I hear you've been a bad boy."

He looked at her – the light-brown skin of her shoulders and neck, her tousled short black hair, her narrow face with its pointed noise and dark eyes, her small breasts with their hard, brown nipples, the creases running across her navel, one arm flung out, fingers extended – and he thought, Who are you? What are you doing here with me? He rose, and poured her a tea from one of the taps in his Pod.

"How is that?" His heart fluttered. What had been said about him?

"Stanley says you've been rude to him and you've been trying to seduce his assistant."

"Oh, that's all nonsense." He moved about the Pod jerkily, feeling vulnerable in his own nakedness.

"I told you to keep that to yourself – or to save it for me, at least." She made a grab for his penis, but he ducked away. He pulled on a pair of underpants, hoping she would not notice his arousal. But, of course, she did.

"Well, Jules, as I've said before, you certainly have stamina for an oldie." As she worked on him, his mind remained calm and detached. My life is reduced to physical gratification, he thought. There is no mental stimulus here at all. What happens when the fucking stops and the food runs out and the eternal entertainments are turned off? What happens, indeed, when the lights go out? There will be nothing here but utter blackness and a thousand, thousand lost souls shrieking in terror. I don't want to be part of it any longer.

"Stanley says he'll take me down to the Lower Levels," he said, when at last she had finished with him.

"Oh, yes."

"He says it'll teach me to be obedient."

"Really, what have you done wrong?"

"I'm not sure. Can you speak up for me?"

"I'll have a word with him. He obviously doesn't know what a good boy you can be."

Julian was pleased by that. He was sure – as Peter himself seemed to think – Marion was harmless, and didn't represent a threat to him. He could just play along with her, which wasn't entirely unpleasurable. She was dressed now in her lilac skirt and blazer and was preparing to leave. She pressed herself against him, with a last, affectionate squeeze of his anatomy

"Keep that for me and watch yourself," she said." She gave him a peck on the cheek. He didn't know whether this was a warning or simply a casual farewell. There was too much else to worry about.

* * *

Tina was passing Julian in a passage near the Lilacs' lounge when she put out an arm to stop him. She was dressed in a lilac pinafore dress, with white embroidery across its front, and a white blouse beneath, a mixture of official and casual wear, he thought. She was carrying her black book in her hand.

"I wondered if you would like to attend one of my Bible-reading groups." Her look was almost appealing, and he found it hard to resist those calm blue eyes.

"I'm not sure I should. I mean…."

"Stanley doesn't mind, if that's what you're worried about. I've got clearance from him"

"What for me?" Julian was somewhat alarmed that Stanley should know of this. After all, it was Tina's request, not his. He had little interest in learning about a religion that talked of saints and sinners presided over by a distant, capricious divinity.

"For anyone. It's open to all, but only Podders have come so far. I really need some Lilac support."

"What are you preaching?" Julian was suspicious. He didn't want to be part of something needlessly subversive of SupaPodia that might get him into trouble. His visions of possible escape did not include getting lumped in with a bunch of hymn-singing weirdos, however good their intentions. But then Tina was certainly no weirdo. She was just misguided in her utopian vision of a better order, perceived within the compass of some supreme being – her god, any god, it would all be the same. If she was indeed the High Director's daughter, she must feel there would be no consequences for her, whatever she did. She probably thought genuinely she was doing good – God's work – and no one would come to harm as a result

"We just read the Bible – mainly the New Testament – choosing a passage at random. And then, if people wish, we discuss it, or we just take away the words within us."

"And why do you want me there?"

"Because I know you are a thoughtful man and will benefit from something that takes you beyond these concrete walls."

Julian found this irritating, indeed, patronising. But she looked so sweet, he could not deny her. "When are you doing this?"

"Now. In a Podders' hall one Level down. It's only for one Red segment."

He looked at his time piece. He was aware of his meeting with Peter which was coming up at Green 2 and he needed to get some sleep first. "OK, OK. Providing it's no longer."

"Thank you." She took his hand. "You'll come with me now?"

"Yes, alright." The feel of her fingers against his palm made him forget everything but the immediate need to be with her. He walked to the elevators beside her. Now, was that a look of quiet satisfaction on her pretty face?

It was a small alcove off the Podders' hall that they went to. There were already three Podders in their orange suits awaiting them there, and two more came out of the depths of the hall to join them, so seven of them in all seated themselves on the cushioned bench seats around the semi-circular end of the alcove. Outside, the big Screens blared out their noise, mingling with that from adjacent alcoves that had Screens offering 'adult material'.

He concentrated his gaze on Tina who was welcoming the group, and then introducing him. "I have brought a fellow Lilac from Education. Brother Julian. Please show your love to him." They all rose in turn and came over to kiss him on both cheeks, even the two men, one elderly and grizzled. He tried not to shrink away. A full-bosomed woman gave off a heavy perfume which made his head swim. "Welcome. Most welcome."

"Who will choose our passage today? Brother Julian, would you like to open the Holy Book?"

Julian hesitated, then seeing everyone's eyes on him he picked up the Bible, and opened it towards the rear, which he somehow remembered was where the New Testament was placed. The page he had found showed 'St. Luke: Chapter 11'.

"Would you read to us, Brother Julian?"

"'And it came to pass, as he was praying in a certain place, when he ceased, one of his disciples said unto him, Lord, teach us to pray.'"

Julian could not quite believe the voice uttering these words was his. In a flash, those days of his youth when he had attended church came back to him. It had been an old, soot-stained building, wedged between boarded-up shops at the centre of the city. Inside had been rows of wooden benches set before a plain altar with a bronze cross. The church had long-since been stripped of its original fittings. The officiant was a thick-set bearded man wearing an embroidered gown. He had exuded an air of calm and dignity, telling of an uncorrupted faith, which had impressed itself upon Julian. He had gone to the church more to hear the man speak, for the beauty of his speaking, than to worship God, although he realised the two things should go together.

"'And he said unto them, When ye pray say, Our Father which art in heaven, Hallowed be thy name, Thy Kingdom come, Thy will be done...'"

"On earth as it is in heaven," continued Tina, signalling to the others to join in, which they did, some faltering over the words.

"And lead us not into temptation," said another voice. "Indeed *NOT*."

Julian spun around. Standing at the entrance to the alcove was Stanley, and beside him three burly men in deep purple: he recognised the uniform of the Guard he had seen at the Control Station.

"Take him!" said Stanley, pointing at Julian. "Leave the rest. Well done," he said to Tina.

"Julian, I didn't know!" cried Tina, her face red and contorted, her mouth open wide. "He told me to get you here. For your good, he said. That's why I invited you."

"Be quiet, Christine!" snapped Stanley. "I haven't deceived anyone. It *is* for his good, for our good." – he pointed accusingly at Julian – "For this man would bring harm to SupaPodia."

By now Julian had been seized by two of the Guards, his arms bent up behind him.

"My father will hear about this," said Tina angrily. Had she forgotten no one was expected to know who her father was? Stanley would remember, though. Perhaps he was aware too of how long she had been out of touch with him. Her threat seemed to weigh upon him as lightly as a feather.

"How gullible can you be, Christine. Your father – any father – would only commend me and spank your bottom. Perhaps I should do that myself because you have let me down by your own foolish actions.

Tina flung out her arms at his words. "May God forgive you," she said.

"And all the little elves and fairies too," Stanley sneered. "Now take your silly book with its oldie worldie words and get back to my office. I'll speak to you later. And you…" – he turned on the frightened Podders who sat huddled in the alcove as if they had been blown there by some mighty wind – "get back to your Pods and don't get led astray again, or it will be the worst for you!" They scuttled off like frightened mice, or, in the case of the large-bosomed lady, wobbled away like an orange jelly tipped from its plate.

Julian had been propelled down the passage from the hall by the men in purple, his arms still painfully twisted. At the elevators, he was pushed into the first that arrived. A group of Lilacs waiting for an elevator looked on with blank faces. Julian, scared as he was, particularly noticed those expressionless looks, entirely drained of emotion, either of fear or pleasure, or of anything else really, just indifference. It was a characteristic of the Lilacs, which he had noted before when they were not in their own, often raucous, company. They were usually very quiet, with a bleak inner concentration that seemed to deny the outer realities about them, as if to accept reality would create a void into which they might fall and be swallowed up.

A lone Podder trying to enter the elevator was pushed roughly away. One of the Guards inserted a key into the control panel. As he turned it, lights flashed and the navigation function of Julian's chip began to shriek in his head, so much so that he cried out, "Stop it! Stop it!" He was ignored. Once in motion, through his pain he could see the direction of travel by a series of green arrows flashing downwards. The elevator seemed to go on for ever. Terrified, Julian guessed where they were heading – to the Lower Levels that Stanley had spoken of.

At last the flashing arrows stopped. The door slid back, and Julian's right arm was twisted once more up into the small of his back. He was pushed out into a narrow, grey-painted corridor. The pain from his chip had ceased. He did not know why. Perhaps it did not work at these depths. Perhaps, here, control was enforced in other ways. Reason still tried to burn its bright spark within Julian's brain.

He was frightened – of course, he was frightened, of the unknown and the abyss – but he thought reason would reassert itself, and sense of what was being done with him, and why, would emerge. Perhaps this was meant just as a lesson for him, a sharp shock to convince him that the rules of SupaPodia must be obeyed at all times. Otherwise, he had been doing well, hadn't he? Marion, his immediate boss, had told him she was very pleased with him – in more ways than one; and he groaned inwardly at the sudden realisation of what might have been recorded of him with her, in pictures and in sound. What a fool he had been! They could use it to blackmail him whenever they wished: he felt sick at the thought.

His stomach did, in fact, rise to his throat, and he tried to double up to stop the sickness, but they pulled him upright and the vomit came, but only as an acid dribble out of the corners of his mouth. His head was filled with a great roaring sound that he thought must come from innumerable fans set in the walls and ceilings. The ventilation was probably very poor at these depths, he realised, and air needed to be pumped here at great pressure from higher up. If the pumps and the fans failed, then the air would soon run out and everyone here would choke to death.

They came to a steel door, and, with no word said, it was opened and he was shoved inside. This was clearly a detention cell, as the police still used in the OW, but he had not expected to find in a SupaPod. But then, he knew almost nothing of the policies of a SupaPod towards non-compliance and other crime. What happened to those who fell out with the system and tried to oppose it, as he knew he had begun to do?

He sat on a hard concrete seat looking at the walls. They, and the door, were painted what was once known as 'battleship grey'. He found himself reflecting on that term. It was probably as antiquated now as the battleships themselves. SupaPodia had striven to outlaw warfare, whether by land, sea, or air. It was one of its big achievements that had first attracted Julian to the organisation. If violence flared now, it was not at a national level, but between local communities struggling to survive while feeding the insatiable SupaPodia machine.

A long period passed. He looked at his wrist timepiece. He had been due to meet up with Peter at Green 2. It was already Blue 3. Would they let him out in time? Would they let him out at all? Of course, they would. They were simply teaching him a lesson. Perhaps Commanders like Stanley had that power. Then, suitably chastised, he would be set free again to carry on his

Re-Education work. After all, that's what Stanley had said he needed him for, and urgently too. Who, otherwise, could take his place?

Then in a moment of clear vision, penetrating the grey murk that was otherwise his comprehension, he realised that he was not needed at all. Re-Education was a fiction. The whole of SupaPodia was a fiction, a great bubble of nothing, dreamt up to keep the Podders – the masses – subservient. From a first positive aim of controlling overpopulation and of lowering harmful atmospheric emissions, and of providing 'all mankind' with food and somewhere to live, SupaPodia had grown into a huge artificiality of thought and existence, wanted by no one, least of all by its principal denizens – the Podders, if they could only realise they were just being kept, fed, and entertained as animals might be, reared in vast underground sheds, away from the fresh air and the wide earth that it was their right to roam, just awaiting the end time that would send them into oblivion.

His thoughts shocked him. Why had he not seen this clearly before? The fiction had been there to understand even in the OW. He had been blinded by the prospect of an escape from hardship and struggle, his mind befuddled by an idealism that he could not then see as untruth and manipulation. Manipulation by whom? By the Eliti, of course. They were the main villains in this preposterous new world, failing those they assumed control over from their first entry into a SupaPod until their death.

And another thought – one that had scarcely crossed his mind until now – what happened to Podders when they died? With so many thousands locked up within the teeming Levels of a SupaPod, death must be a frequent visitor amongst the living. How were their bodies disposed of? Were they cremated in huge ovens, the smoke of their burning jetted to the outer air through massive steel chimneys?

A rattling at the door. It pushed open with a high pitched squeal that caused Julian to place his hands on his ears. Stanley stood there, looking down at him, a taut smile on his face.

"Well, are you repenting yet? You soon will be. There are things I can show you that may make you want to cover your eyes as well as your ears. Are you ready?"

"I need the toilet, Stanley."

"Oh, do you? And call me 'sir' from now on. I offered you comradeship, but you flung it back in my face."

"I'm sorry, sir."

"I bet you are! You can do it here. On the floor. Up against the wall. I don't care. You can clean it up on your return."

Julian had no choice but to urinate in a corner, the liquid running into a spreading pool on the concrete floor. He shuddered, feeling the degradation penetrating to his very core.

"Done?" Stanley had turned his head at the door, smirking when he saw the mess. "Just as well you didn't need to poop then. It'd have taken you a while to lick that up."

The horror showed on Julian's face. Stanley laughed. "I do but jest."

Outside the door, they were joined by one of the purple Guards. They proceeded down a passage, the ceiling of which was scarcely higher than Julian's head, so he felt he must walk bent forward. The concrete walls were left unsmoothed and undecorated, save for occasional stencilled reference in tall red characters that were meaningless to Julian. The lights, in a strip along the ceiling, were low and flickering. Fear swept like a wave through him. What if the lights went out and he were left here? The blackness would be that of the tomb. There would be nothing he could find or understand to save himself. It would be like spinning off into outer space without even the stars for guidance.

At last the light began to brighten, and they came into a much broader part of the tunnel that was lined with white panelling, and here people in lilac tunics and robes came and went, some bearing clip boards which they were scanning intently as they walked.

"This is Lower Level 02//22," said Stanley grimly, stopping suddenly so that Julian collided with him. "Known to the Lilacs who live and work here – which will soon include you, dear Julian – as Hell Hole 22. He gave a sudden yelp of laughter. "You understand, don't you, 'LL' makes a sound like 'Hell'. There is also a Level 01, which some consider far worse." He chuckled again.

Through his fear, Julian thought, this man is mad. The whole system here is mad, and it is evil too. How could I have been so deluded. As if there could ever be some utopian world built without the need for rules and discipline and punishment to ensure conformity. And what is that conformity? It is not an equality of vision and delight, but a tiered structure, like the SupaPods themselves, of privilege and position and corruption as harsh and uncompromising as anything that ever existed in the OW. Only out there, there might be some escape. Here, there is nothing but torment – forever. Eternal hell.

"Follow me," commanded Stanley. He whispered something in the Guard's ear, and the man saluted him with a raised hand, and fell back.

They passed through double doors, and came into a large brilliantly-lit room like the ward of a hospital, with beds against the walls and spaces with screens around them. Away from the beds, there were desks and chairs where Lilacs were gathered, some talking into CPs, others consulting Screens, all very busy – and yet there was little noise, just the rustle of a uniform, the creak of a bed, or the low mumble of a voice.

Julian looked along a row of beds. The patients lay there on their backs as if on parade, their heads neatly against pillows, their bodies swelling in similarly-shaped mounds beneath the lilac covers – bed after bed after bed.

Stanley led Julian up to one of the desks in the centre of the room. A bald-headed man, wearing dark-rimmed spectacles and a loose lilac coat looked up at their approach.

"Stanley, old chap," he called out. "How nice to see you again." They shook hands. His eyes took in Julian. "And this is one of your people you are *putting forward*?" The small, cold eyes behind the glasses examined Julian closely. "Fit are you?"

"What? Yes, I suppose so." Julian, surprised at being addressed, did not know how to answer. He had expected to be instructed in some duty as a punishment. Perhaps he would be a cleaner-up, an emptier of bed pans, something to humiliate him further.

"Any particular specialism you offer?"

Again, great confusion in Julian. "I've no real knowledge of medical matters, sir," he said, his voice quavering with anxiety. "But I can probably be useful if you give me a plain task to do."

The cold eyes continued their stare, then the shiny round face broke into a grin, and he pushed his glasses up onto his forehead, rubbing each eye with his fist. "Well, I never. Stanley, you're quite a card, aren't you? How do you manage it?"

Stanley's face had also relaxed into a sleazy smirk. "Just genius, Hector. Sheer genius."

"You really don't know why you've been brought here, do you?" Hector said to Julian.

"No, I don't." Julian gathered himself to state that fact in a calm voice, while all the time he could feel his heart racing. What evil was going to happen to him in this clinic of the damned?

"Well then, I'll tell you what we're about and what we need, and you'll be able to choose. People – Podders normally – offer us parts of themselves in return for favoured treatments upstairs. By 'upstairs' I mean in their Pods and communal halls. They might also look to receive some freedom

Outside, for instance to get on a football team or into athletics training to compete in the OW – that's very popular. Generally, they just want better facilities – clothing, food, and the like – in their Pods, or – and this is the most popular of all – sexual favours, a twenty year old stud if they're an ageing woman, or, if a young man, some feisty, mature lady to show him the way to do it, or perhaps, a nice young virgin for the older man. It's all possible, you see, depending on what you are prepared to offer. But we don't normally get Lilacs here. So you're a rarity. Whatever your sin has been, you'll be offsetting it with what you can offer us. What's he done, anyhow, so wrong to end up here?"

The last question was directed at Stanley, whose smile-wreathed face immediately took on a serious look. "Disobedience. Undermining SupaPodia in his thoughts. Spreading superstition."

"My, my," said Hector. "You have been busy. Have you been implanted?"

"I have a chip, sir," said Julian, hoping meek compliance might save him from whatever horror was proposed.

Hector stepped aside to hold a conversation with Stanley, the two of them talking into each other's ears like conspirators in some ancient drama. The two white faces placed together, glistening in the harsh electric light, gave Julian a particular sense of terror. He knew now he was indeed in hell – a sadistic living hell of bodily experiment, such as he recalled the all-powerful, all-evil Nazi Racists had once practised.

Hector turned back to him, a smile flickering on his face. "We are agreed. Your punishment – or should I say, correction? – is to be the first Lilac to receive a Second Implant, about which you may have heard?" His voice rose in a question and he stood staring at Julian as if expecting some confirmation, but Julian just looked back dumbly.

Shrugging his shoulders, Hector continued, "You see, the implant has been given to a trial batch of Podders, but the method and placement were not successful. We had been making the insertion point the upper arm, but the buggers have been cutting off more arms than we can possibly have use for – for our spare parts programme, you see." He gave a high pitched giggle, which sent a shower of spittle into Julian's face. "Now we are to use the spine. The nerve uptake is much better there, but it is a far more complex procedure, and dangerous too, which is why we need to experiment. Of course, we have designed a programme using Podders, but a Lilac might provide us with better feedback. You are an intelligent man, I am sure, otherwise you would not be a Lilac. You will be our first articulate guinea pig." He giggled again and more spittle was expelled against Julian's cheek, which he did not dare to wipe away. "Come man, what do you say?"

"What *can* I say?" croaked Julian. "I am in your power? I have done nothing wrong. I have tried my best to adapt to SupaPodia, but you think I have failed."

Stanley thrust his face forward on hearing this. "We don't *think*. We *know* you have acted against us! Admit it!" His words came out in a shriek, terrifying Julian, because the sound, as much as the words, confirmed how unhinged he was.

"Is there not some other way I can make amends?" he asked, desperate to try and play these mad people along, to get them to change their minds and send him back, suitably chastised, to his comfortable Pod.

Stanley, however, continued his hissing, screeching attack. "What has been proposed should be an honour to you; to be given the chance to *help* SupaPodia by supporting the Second Implant programme. But even that you want to resist, in the same way you have been against SupaPodia from your very start here."

"That's not true, sir…" Julian began desperately.

"Yes it is!! You have been overheard speaking against the ethics of SupaPodia: it is clear you don't like its diversity and equality, you think you're fucking superior." He looked Julian up and down with a look of distaste on his face. "I can't think why. I've looked at some of the images from your Pod, and you don't even do *that* well."

Julian felt himself shrivelling into the floor like a grub pecked at by a bird. So his sexual activities with Marion *had* been viewed. by Stanley – and by how many others? Had Marion, therefore, been a willing accomplice of Stanley, a mere honey-trap?

"I'm sorry, I'm sorry…" was all he could repeat.

Unexpectedly, Stanley adopted a softer tone. "I'm trying to give you a way out," he said. "The Second Implant may go very well, and we Lilacs will look to you for your advice when you have recovered and the procedure has settled into your system. It could be a way to get yourself noted by SupaPodia, by our Eliti bosses even, as I think you would like. In any event, the alternatives are not good."

Seeing Julian's ashen, despairing face, Stanley said, "Come with me." He made his farewell to Hector, and led a stumbling Julian, whose knees felt suddenly weak, out into the centre of the hospital ward – if that indeed was the correct term for it. They paused by a block of beds, whose occupants lay still like wax models, some with faces bandaged, but others expressionless, only their eyes moving – one woman, one man, one elderly person of indeterminate sex, one much younger, the empty eyes following them as they passed.

"These Podders have made their donations," Stanley said, "Kidneys in the main – the Eliti love their booze, but it doesn't love them – but an eye here and there, bone marrow, a hand or a lower leg perhaps, a bit of liver, a penis even…" – he chuckled – "…like a butcher's shop, isn't it? Do you want to be one of them? I don't think so."

They passed a Screen and came to another block of beds. "And these are some of the recipients, Lilacs most of them, for the Eliti don't come here but get their donations sent straight to them Outside. Look at how cheerful they are now."

Indeed, from one or two of the lilac-covered beds a hand or two waved as they passed. Most, however, lay dazed, some with head-sets on, occupied with an inner transmitted world that consumed them entirely.

"I know that man at the end," said Stanley, indicating a large male figure who lay with his lilac covers raised by a square box underneath. "He's from my Q-Level. He got the penis. Alright Victor? Soon be back in action, eh?" Victor gave a rather feeble wave of his hand. "Probably already jerking himself off."

"So, when I said I'd show you the alternatives, you now know what I meant," said Stanley most casually, speaking over his shoulder as he crossed the hospital floor. You're lucky, because if we'd had a current Eliti order for a particular part – something special which you might have supplied – then your punishment could have been worse, very much worse. That might have been *your* penis, for instance."

He gave a guffaw of laughter and slapped Julian on the shoulder. "But a little too well used, perhaps. Most of the older, wrinkly Eliti want new faces, and those are very hard to find, and yours would hardly do, anyhow." He chuckled again. "There are even worse things, though, I might have sentenced you to. I tell you what, I'll show them to you, so you'll know just how fortunate you've been."

Outside in the corridor once more, they descended even lower by a small elevator, with a silver metal door marked 'XX Cleared Staff Only'. The journey was short, only a single green flash of the control light, Julian noted, his disorganised brain in a further whirl of fear, so he found himself pressing his finger nails into the balls of his thumbs in his efforts to steady himself. The tunnel when they emerged was very dimly lit, the walls of rough hewn rock but with an even gravelled floor that scrunched beneath their feet. After a few yards, the walls became tiled, with huge white curving panels, and the light grew brighter. They reached a steel door where a Guard sat in a black sentry box. She came to her feet at their approach. She carried an automatic weapon slung across her front.

The Guard checked Stanley's chip with a hand-held instrument, and then his own. He heard a double click sounding in his head as the instrument was passed over him.

"Is he a one-way?" she asked. She had an attractive face, Julian thought, beneath her shiny helmet.

"No, he'll return with me."

"Very well, Commander." She pressed a button and the steel door slid open.

They came immediately into a room with steel-framed bunks in tiers against the walls, and a large wooden table at its centre. Around the table, sat a number of Lilacs drinking tea – at least Julian assumed it was tea, a large, chipped enamel teapot being on the table. They shuffled to their feet at the sight of Stanley.

"Another one for us?" a Lilac asked. He was a short, scruffy-looking man in a stained uniform, with straw-coloured hair sticking out from a peaked baseball cap.

"No," Stanley chuckled. He turned to Julian. "He thinks you're going to work here. It's a punishment detail for Lilacs, you see. They're the ones who have to superintend the Podders here, and it's not pleasant work, is it?"

He received a couple of affirming nods from around the table. At least two of the Lilacs were female, Julian saw at a quick glance. One had long golden hair, which she had released from her cap. He met her eyes, but she looked away hastily.

Stanley was looking around the room. He went across to one of the bunks and prodded the shape that filled it. "Get out when a Commander's present!" he shouted, his voice rising to a shriek. A figure fell to the floor, then rose reluctantly. It was a girl, arms across her breasts, wearing only a pair of brief pants. Stanley prodded at another bunk. This time the occupant was a young male, stark-naked: he stood with his hands over his genitals.

"Get dressed," Stanley commanded the two, turning away. "Don't let me find you in bed again."

"They've only just come off shift," said the scruffy man with the yellow hair, a note of defiance in his voice.

"I don't care what they've been doing," Stanley shrieked. "What's your name?"

"Albert, sir." He stood, legs apart, his face expressionless."

"Are you in charge here?"

"Yes, sir."

"Well you won't be much longer if you don't run a tighter ship."

"No, sir."

Stanley seemed suddenly to lose interest. He watched the girl he had roused from bed scrambling for her clothes. "Nice arse," he muttered, then turned to Julian. "Follow me."

They left the room by a door in the far wall, and came out onto a steel platform, raised on scaffolding above a deep pit. As they descended a flight of twisting metal stairs, Julian could see into the pit, which had been hidden in blackness from higher up. Lights were now flashing on, showing that the pit was both broad and long, and was filled with rows of bodies that stretched away into darkness, so that Julian could not see where they ended. The smell hit Julian first – an awful smell of human waste, of fetid air, and putrefaction. He could see Stanley was holding a handkerchief to his nose.

They were on a level with the bodies now. They lay under orange, rubberised sheets on plain stretcher-type beds. Only their heads showed, propped up on bolsters. Plastic-coated wires ran away from the beds, forming a spider's web of conduits that led to a thick black cable running the length of the walls. There was no noise. The mouths did not open, the few eyes that were not closed were wide and unblinking.

Stanley paused by one of the first of the beds, and pulled back its cover. The head was grey-haired, the body was of a woman; her breasts sagged on her chest, her hands twitched against her sunken thighs, her pubic area was enclosed in black rubber, shaped like a baby's nappy, with a pipe running from it.

"That takes the smelly out-pourings away," Stanley said, as if the sight needed an explanation. But Julian was still too full of horror to comprehend. He looked at the wires coming out of this lady's chest and side, and then suddenly realised the enormity of what he was looking at.

"It's the regular power of the beating heart muscle that SupaPodia wants," Stanley explained, "far better than any human treadmill for it never stops – well, not until death, anyhow. This is a major experiment for SupaPodia and it seems to be working. Already more than 2.5% of all our electrical power comes from this source, and SupaPodia will extend and make the process far more efficient – efficient, that is, in the way the power is generated and the number of human body units needed. Discipline is getting better in SupaPodia – a good thing, but bad at the same time, as there are now only so many Podder recalcitrants available. We can't use animals, as to keep them sufficiently quiescent is impossible; they waste away too quickly."

He looked at Julian, and gave out his shrill giggle. "Which is why you might well have ended up here if I had made a big enough case for it.

SupaPodia normally looks after its own, but bad transgressors have been shown little mercy of late by our Eliti bosses. Needs must be, you see, and what they want is more power for more SupaPods. Generation from the old carbon-based sources of the OW is undesirable if the planet is to survive, and the tidal and wind turbines for each SupaPod are increasingly inadequate. Human-sourced power may, therefore, be the answer. There are already plans to obtain it by a less destructive and more humane method, but for the present...." – he flung the cover back over the woman – "....the bad ones are punished in a way that makes them useful. Of course, most don't last long, however well we look after them, but normally long enough for more 'bad boys' to become available to take their place."

"You're all mad!" said Julian suddenly, the words compelled from him. "And evil beyond belief. Is this what the dream of SupaPodia has become?"

Instead of reacting angrily, as Julian cringed to expect, Stanley said quietly, "Every civilisation is built on the suffering and sacrifice of some. Look at the great cultures of the past. How many depended on slavery? Those who lived in wealth and finery, and those who created that wealth and commissioned great works of art and architecture, often did so by the blood and toil of others whose lives were short and unpleasant. But what would you prefer? Museums full of marble statues and exquisite jewellery, or just a legacy of dirt and squalor? All art, all beauty, all order is founded on other people's suffering. History shows us that, over and over again, and our SupaPodia world is no exception."

Julian could say nothing. Stanley's words floated through his mind in shreds of disbelief, like snowflakes falling in summer heat that would never settle. Surely, a truer evaluation of history would show him to be wrong.

"You may wonder about the mechanics of it," Stanley continued, his voice still calm and level, adding to Julian's sense of disbelief, for he might as well have been talking of mundane things, such as what coat to wear for a walk on a rainy day or what medicine to take for an upset tummy. "Of course, we drug the Podder recalcitrants to make things as merciful as possible. They scarcely know what's happening to them. The punishment Lilacs, whom you briefly met, look after them, affix their body drains, give them food and water, take away those who are clearly ill and dying, collect the dead bodies. Naturally, we have medicos on hand to make the heart connections and ensure that everything is working properly. Look, there is one coming down the aisle now."

Julian saw a lilac-clothed individual approaching them in the half-light of the wall lamps, and, with a sense of ever-growing incredulity, thought he recognised its bulky shape and the thick legs protruding from the uniform tunic. As the figure came up to them, he realised he had been right. By what must be a truly remarkable coincidence, this was Peter – the Peter who had asked him for his help and whose message he had failed to take to the OW, and with whom he had talked about escape. He had been due to have a meeting with him – hadn't he? – before….before all this latest stuff had happened. Now what had that been about? He raised his hands to his head, thinking it would overflow with all the thoughts, half-remembered, of things not done and those yet to learn.

"Commander," said Peter with the utmost deference, "Greetings"

"I recognise you, if I'm not mistaken," said Stanley. "You are based on Level 18, are you not?"

"Yes, I am. Dr. Peter Clayton at your service."

"That is good. You come at a most propitious time."

Peter looked his enquiry, glancing at Julian for the first time, his face inscrutable. "May I help you then?"

"I hope so. It will speed things up, if you can. This Lilac here, under my direct command, is due for punishment. I have just been showing him to where he might have been consigned. But he is fortunate. the decision I have agreed now with Dr. Bogunovich…that is, Dr. Hector Bogunovich; do you know him?"

"He is my superior, sir."

"Excellent. The decision is that this man…" – he jabbed a finger into Julian's side – "…will receive the Second Implant instead. He will be our guinea pig, so to speak." He chuckled. "Can you organise that and the necessary monitoring to follow?"

"I certainly can," said Peter. "It is my speciality. I have already worked on Podders. A Lilac presents more complications as the procedure is more complex for that class, but I shall be very pleased to have the practice."

"Good. Good," Stanley said, rubbing his hands. "I had been wondering about the correct channels to go through, so meeting you is exceptionally fortunate."

"All you need to do, sir, is to hand him over to me. I can give you a body receipt. Do you wish him back after he is implanted and first monitored?"

"Oh yes. I still have a role for him in Re-Education when he is suitably chastised and I am sure of no further transgression."

Peter looked at Julian thoughtfully. "What was his crime, sir?"

"Ask him yourself. It will be encouraging to hear his confession."

"Mutinous thoughts," mumbled Julian, looking at the ground. "Attending a superstitious meeting and speaking ill of SupaPodia."

"Lucky then to have your mercy, sir," said Peter, looking severe. "When can you deliver him? I have received the prototype chip and have practised its implantation procedure under Dr. Bogunovich's direction – as he will, of course, confirm. So I'm all ready to go live, as it were."

"As soon as I get back to my office. I'll give you the address. You can collect him from there. Make sure you have the right documentation for handover."

"Of course, sir." He looked grimly at Julian. "You'll be mine for experimentation. You've only got yourself to blame."

Julian, whose head had begun to turn in slow circles at the impact of this conversation, wondering if Peter could be trusted now and whether he had fallen from the hearth into the fire, or just possibly the other way around, thought it best to make no reply.

There was a noise behind them on the steel stairs, and, turning, they saw the punishment Lilacs descending, carrying various bundles and canisters. Each Lilac was now clothed in shiny plastic overalls that creaked and cracked as they moved.

"Gentlemen," said their leader in his baseball cap, "You must move now, I fear. It is inspection and replenishment time."

For a brief while, the three of them watched as hoses were deployed, floors were sprayed, covers lifted, connections checked, food and water sloshed into mouths that opened like the beaks of unfledged chicks in the nest. Away in the gloom, Julian could see one thin body being lifted upright from its connectors and pushed into a body bag. He shuddered and turned away.

Peter came up beside him. "Keep your spirits up," he whispered. "It couldn't have worked out better. Play the game until I come for you." Julian looked at him dumbly; he did not dare to react.

Stanley had not finished with him yet. There was more horror for him to witness.

* * *

Julian had returned to Stanley's office. He was dumped into a small armchair in a windowless outer room and sat there with his limbs trembling, his head held in his hands. He thought Tina should be here somewhere, if Stanley has retained her as his assistant. He heard the sound of someone moving about the other side of the door – the scraping of a chair, the closing of a drawer, the buzz of a CP and a voice answering, too indistinct to make out, but he thought it was female.

Was Tina alright? She had dared to argue with Stanley and she had made reference to her father and the power he held over them all; not that Stanley had seemed unduly in awe of that, indeed just the opposite. Yet it compromised her surely and whatever it was that she was trying to achieve. So what would happen now? Would Stanley continue his dismissive attitude to her, or would he see what advantage he might gain out of his knowledge.

Stanley would be careful, though. Oh yes, Julian thought, deep in his despair, he will be very careful, as he could not know which way all this might work out – in his favour or against him. Tina would be safe, though. Stanley surely would not dare to harm her person. Yet, Stanley was clearly unbalanced and there was danger in that: he was liable to give way to irrational tantrums and urges. It would be far better if Tina were able to remove herself entirely from him. But how could that be done?

Julian groaned aloud in his agony of thought and fear. He couldn't help Tina now, for he could not save himself from what had been threatened. If he was to receive the Second Implant, that might finish him off entirely. There could be no escape for him after surgery, which might immobilise or even kill him. And with the new implant activated, he would be controlled even further, every movement monitored in image and sound, every word he spoke listened to and recorded.

His only hope seemed to rest with Peter. Peter had indicated that his sudden appearance amidst that hell of the Lower Levels had not been a sheer coincidence. He had planned it, perhaps? But how and for what purpose? Would Peter be able to save him, and get him out of the SupaPod altogether?

The OuterWorld seemed to him now a most desirable place to return to. He had truly turned full circle. SupaPodia had once been the utopia he sought, but he realised now, with an intensity that burnt him to the very quick, what a flawed and foolish vision that had been. SupaPodia, he knew now, consisted of every evil of which distorted mankind was capable, compressed into a space like a buried honey jar, teeming with frenzied ants, in comparison with the broad spaces and limitless beauty of the world Outside – however much wrong and suffering was laid upon it.

It was not the world that was wrong. It was mankind. Mankind corrupted every space to which it ventured. There was no escape underground; the wrongs there were only intensified. The old struggles, therefore, to redress those wrongs must continue. There was nothing left but to fight – for freedom of thought, for freedom of conscience, for the very basic freedoms of life. The fight must come now while there was still some power left to do so, for it was the Eliti who were expanding fast to control the entire surface of the globe, consigning much of humanity to a conformity of existence that, while superficially attractive, was controlled through fear and punishment. A trashed, traduced mentality was the result – one that shamed the human creation and its long social evolution.

What Julian had been shown by Stanley after Peter had left had shocked him most of all, unlikely as that might seem after the horrors he had already witnessed. A chamber, larger even than the two others he had entered on these hellish Levels, contained cubicle after cubicle where Podders lay dying, huddled together on mattresses on the floor. Many deaths were from illnesses, Stanley had told him, while nonchalantly unveiling these new horrors – illnesses mostly left untreated – but many too were at the individual's own request, although physically healthy; a very much smaller number from simple old age.

As they died, those who were still capable of doing so watched a full programme of SupaPodia entertainment on large Screens in their cubicles, ranging from the inappropriately humorous, to the sickly sentimental, to the graphically pornographic – the latter even in the face of death, the frantic sexual movements of anonymous bodies seeming to mock the dying from the coloured, flickering walls. Was this the type of death you would wish for your own family, thought Julian? What had happened to human dignity? The rituals of bereavement had been abandoned, solemnity replaced by comedy and debauchery, even in the very moment of life passing – and after that only thankful oblivion.

Some bodies, Julian was told by the Lilac in charge of 'Death Disposal', were consigned down a shoot into pits that had been bored during the SupaPod's construction deep into the rock. Others, though, were burnt in mighty furnaces, which opportunely provided another important power source for the living. Their ashes were made into a fertiliser delivered free to the farmers with SupaPodia contracts slaving in their fields Outside.

The door to the room where Julian was being kept opened suddenly. He looked up eagerly, hoping Tina would be there, but he saw it was Marion, and his heart fell like a stone.

"Well, well. What have you been up to? Naughty boy." She wagged a finger in front of his face. "Stanley tells me you've got into trouble, but he's going to get you out of it."

"Did he?" Julian's voice came out in a croak. "I think he means he's going to finish me off."

"Don't be so silly. He won't want to do that. He needs you to work for him. Re-Education's getting behind target and some of the big bosses are complaining."

"I'm to be the first Lilac for the new implant."

"Oh that! It'll be a bit unpleasant perhaps, but we'll all have to have it in time. Don't worry, it won't be as bad as you think. It goes to show how much Stanley values you that you're to be the first."

Julian looked at her, trying to keep his tired eyes steady on her face, feeling himself swaying in his chair, the ground unsteady beneath him.

"Stanley's seen us at it," he said.

"What?" She laughed – a bit nervously, he thought. "You mean?…No, no. Of course, he hasn't. There's no monitoring of the Lilac Pods I've ever heard of. He says things like that deliberately to cause confusion, to get one over you if you've upset him in some way, as you must have done. It's happened before, with….with….". She didn't finish. "Anyhow, we've done nothing wrong. We haven't broken any rules."

"It gives him power over me." Julian's mind was very clear on that point. "Were you part of his plan then to set me up?"

He face clouded and her eyes became sharp. "Of course not! How could you say such a thing? I'm here to help you, as I've been helping you from your very first day with us. You're an idiot, you know. It's your poisonous thoughts that are getting you into trouble."

"*My* poisonous thoughts! Stanley showed me what happens on the Lower Levels."

Seeing the distress on his face, she softened her tone. "Yes, that can be disturbing, I'll admit. It upset me for a while too when I first saw it, but you need to get it into perspective with the totality of SupaPodia's operations. I bet, for example, you didn't go to mortuaries, crematoriums, hospices, surgical wards, even abattoirs and the like, in the OuterWorld. Here we try to show you everything, so you'll achieve a more rounded and realistic picture of life – and of death too – in a SupaPod. But try not to worry. I'll keep an eye on you from now on. Get the implant over and you'll be sent back to me for further inculcation."

"But I don't *want* any more implants. I don't *want* any more inculcation!" His words were shrill and high. He knew he was at the edge of collapse. Oh God, would this endless circle of lies and half-lies never close?

"Well, I'm afraid you will have to have them. And that's an end on it." And with that, she rose, smoothing down her short lilac skirt, and went to the door. She left a perfumed trail behind her.

"Get a grip, Julian," she said over her shoulder, "and all will be well. If you don't, then I can't help you. You'll be lost."

The door closed. He sat there, feeling even more frightened and despondent than before. He seemed to have lost everything, both of his old world and the new. SupaPodia was rejecting him and destroying him. It was his former life, however awful it had been at times, that he wanted back.

His only shred of comfort was to remember Peter's words, "Play the game. Until I come for you."

Would this be a way out of his troubles or was it just another misunderstanding, another delusion?

13

"What do you think I should do?" asked Pamela. She had told the story of her meeting with Tina on the SupaPodia Express. "She's such a beautiful girl, but so impressionable, so full of idealism. Others will take advantage of her. I dread to think what she might have been up to in that awful place."

The 'awful place' was, of course, SupaPod No. 16, otherwise regarded by Eliti, such as Pamela, as 'a model of enlightenment' where all would be 'enthralled to live', if only it were possible to build enough SupaPods to contain them and give them the 'freedoms of life' they deserved.

"I really think you should let Joshua know you've seen her," said Zara.

They sat on the terrace of Zara's marbled mansion, looking out over the green expanses of Romney Marsh. On the horizon, the wrinkled sea rose against the sky to merge into an encompassing blueness. A coloured bird in a cage hanging from a beam above their heads gave out a fluting song. Over and over it sounded. A cynic might have thought it was singing, 'Let me out, let me out, let me out….', but any such interpretation would have been lost entirely on the implacable consciences of Zara and Pamela, and all the others of their privileged ilk. They were of the Eliti, and the world was largely theirs to enjoy as they wished; a fact becoming increasingly true as the remaining blots (admittedly, still very large blots in places) on the societies and landscapes they now controlled were slowly cleared.

"You have a special connection with the HD, don't you?" added Zara, who had heard the widely-related gossip that Pamela and Joshua had once been intimate.

"Yes, darling," purred Pamela, looking pleased rather than outraged that her secret was known. "If it wasn't for Rupert, I think I might, er.. approach him again, if you understand my meaning. I doubt if he's living a celibate life, but that doesn't really matter, does it? I'm sure he'd want me again. "

"I do understand you perfectly, my dear. Only why should you let Rupert stop you? You don't love him, do you?"

"Oh, no. No more than any other man. But we are married."

"Why, you old-fashioned thing. I didn't know."

"Just for convenience. To keep things tidy. It doesn't mean all that much. I know he takes pleasures elsewhere."

"Well then, why shouldn't you?"

"It's such an effort," yawned Pamela, stretching out her arms. "I think you and Roberta have it best. Where is she by the way?"

"She's taken a cruise to the Aegean. A small boat, you know, crewed by Greek gods."

"And you trust her?"

"Of course. She sends me Screen messages every day. The gods look a bit scrawny to me. They give her massages, but that is all."

Pamela laughed, disbelieving. "And what about you?"

A male servant, a dark-haired Adonis, bare-chested and wearing a sarong, came onto the terrace, carrying a bowl of fruit and a terracotta pitcher of wine.

"I take what I can get when it is easily delivered."

"You know," said Pamela somewhat later, "I think I *will* seek out Joshua. I'm sure he'll see me. I can always say I have a role in organising the forthcoming convention. That would make sense. Prepare the way, so to speak."

Zara refilled her mouth with grapes.

The Adonis had gone, leaving his sarong draped over a chair.

14

As had been arranged, Peter came for Julian only a short while after Marion had departed. Stanley led him into the small room where Julian was confined. Peter stood behind him, his arms folded, his face severe. He wore a stethoscope about his neck and a circular metal scope attached to a head strap above his brow. The result was to make him look clinically evil, like some deranged doctor out of a horror movie. He showed no personal recognition of Julian, only as an executioner might view his next victim. Julian's heart raced. Had he been deceived again? Were Peter's earlier expressions of help just part of a general game to get rid of him? Somewhere in the background, through the now open doorway, he thought he caught a glimpse of Tina, but then she was gone.

"Off you go," said Stanley in a disinterested tone. "And when you come back, I'm sure you'll be a better man."

"I hope so," said Julian, the words sticking in his mouth, but trying to play the game Peter had spoken of, hoping against hope that his advice had been sincere.

"Come with me," called out Peter in a deep, dead voice that once more sent Julian's nerves fluttering. He followed Peter into Stanley's outer office, and there indeed he now saw Tina, a pile of papers in her arms, standing against the far wall. Her face held a frightened look, but as his eyes met hers it took on what he took to be a smile of encouragement.

"God bless you, Julian," he heard her say, her words so soft he scarcely caught them. "I'll be praying for you."

Seeing Stanley turn sharply to her and raise a hand, index finger extended, as if to warn her, Julian knew that those words had been said at some cost to herself. Whatever the protection her father's position afforded her, Stanley still had the power to make her life most unpleasant. She might even be made to disappear. A thousand, thousand deaths in this place, he imagined, could be ascribed to accidents – accidents that would never be investigated and would be long forgotten before the High Director even got to hear of the one that had led to the ending of his daughter's life in a SupaPod. If Julian had understood Tina properly, he had no idea she was even there. He decided not to endanger her further by making any reply, but steadfastly turned his face away from her, following Peter to the outer door.

"I'll get him back to you as soon as his recovery is complete and the necessary diagnostic tests have been made," Peter told Stanley who was standing at the door.

"How long will that be? I've got no replacement for him yet."

"Fifteen, perhaps twenty, Sweeps," Peter said.

"Don't let him get away from you," said Stanley sternly, asserting a Commander's authority. "Dr. Bogunovich has approved this transplant experiment, as you know. And you're answerable to him."

Peter replied placidly. "Don't worry about that, sir. I'm fully briefed. I'll look after him well." His voice even contained a hint of menace, which Stanley clearly approved of through a nod of his head.

"Don't bring him back unless the Second Implant's a success," he said cruelly, deliberately raising his voice to make sure Julian heard. "I don't want any cripples on my staff."

"That won't happen, sir. But, if it should, we'd follow the set procedures for detachment and disposal." Stanley nodded his approval again.

Through the door, Julian saw Tina's shocked look, her hand raised to her mouth. The door closed and he was left in the corridor with Peter.

"Walk with me, don't speak," the doctor said out of the corner of his mouth. "I'm taking you to my surgery on Level 18. We'll discuss what's to happen to you on the way."

It seemed a long journey for Julian. The elevator Peter used was one Julian had not seen before. It was much smaller than the main elevators, at the end of a side passage that had seemed to go on forever, its walls after a distance tiled white, so that Julian suspected they must have entered a medical area. He noticed that there were no directional buzzes in his ears; perhaps Peter's presence counteracted these. He couldn't ask: it didn't seem important now, anyhow. They passed no one. In the square space where the passage ended was the narrow green door of the elevator, and nothing else but a sign in red letters reading, 'Service Use: Not for Personnel'

"Ignore that sign," said Peter, pressing the lift button. "The elevator's slow but it's perfectly safe. It's not used much. I prefer it for getting about."

After what seemed to Julian a long wait, during which Peter did not speak again, the elevator arrived with a heavy clunk and the door slid open. There were some boxes inside labelled 'Hospital 7: L20/2334/9Z'.

"Ah, that's good," said Peter, entering the elevator and pulling Julian in beside him, the two squeezed between the boxes, with heads bent owing to the low roof. He pushed a button on the control panel and let out a long sigh as the door closed. "These are bound for my hospital," he said, thumping a box beside him. "From the External Delivery Portal –EDP to you and me – on Level 7. It means we can accompany them directly there with no other halts. God's shit, how I'm glad to get away from that awful man! I'm sorry to have seemed so hostile to you while we were with him, but it was necessary – very necessary. He's an idiot, but at the same time he's no fool, if that makes sense."

Julian nodded. "I agree."

Peter's crude blasphemy had grated against his ear, so recently filled by Tina's soft blessing. Peter clearly had his own way of dealing with the dangers of SupaPodia. Julian wondered at the process of this man's disillusionment, which must have been even quicker than his own. What was his aim, he wondered, in seeking renewed contact with the OW? He had said he wanted to escape the SupaPod. Would he be able to help Julian get out too?

Peter said, "We can talk now with no fear of being overheard. There's no monitoring in the service elevators, which is the main reason I like to use them. Once we're in the hospital, though, I will only be able talk to you as doctor to patient – in your case a prisoner too – so it all has to be official stuff. So listen now to what's going to happen, as I won't be able to repeat it."

"But…"

"No 'buts' now. If you wish to get away from here, you must do *exactly* what I say. If you don't want that – in which case, you must believe me, your life will scarcely be worth the living – then you must tell me this instant."

He looked challengingly at Julian, who said straightaway, "I want to get out of here! I *do* want that so very much." He felt tears rising to his eyes and shook his head as if to rid himself of such weakness.

"Good! I believe you. Now listen to me. Once we reach the hospital, you will be given your own screened bed space. Say nothing to anyone but to answer your name and give your SupaPodia service details. No one should ask you anything else, anyhow. Don't talk to any other patient. Pretend unconsciousness, if necessary, but no one should disturb you as you'll be out of view of the rest of the ward, and the patients will have their own problems to contemplate, anyhow – some as serious as yours, if not more so. You've seen what they can do to you here – 'they' being SupaPodia's medical establishment into which I am ashamed to have been recruited."

The elevator all this time must have been continuing its slow descent, but Julian could feel no movement at all. The flashing lights on the control panel suddenly stilled, and Peter stiffened, but the door did not open and the lights started up again. "A call for the elevator," he said, "It'll go there next once we're out. Don't worry, we won't be interrupted. There's still plenty of time."

"Now, where was I?" he continued. "Ah, yes. I will come for you and have your bed moved into one of the operating theatres. Don't worry, I will be with you all the time. There will be other medicos watching – I can't prevent that – including possibly the utterly bloody Dr Bogunovich, my superior, who gave permission for the Second Implant to be tried out on you as a punishment. So much for his Oath! You will be sedated. It will put you right out. You will, in fact, be conscious but you will not remember a thing of the operation."

Seeing Julian's worried look, he added quickly, "You don't have to be concerned. I'll make sure you don't say anything inappropriate, not that you would anyhow because your conscious mind will be working. It's the memory function that is temporarily frozen with the type of anaesthetising drug I will be using. I will then remove your present chip and prepare to insert the Second Implant."

He held up his hand as he saw Julian about to protest. "Only it will be faulty." He chuckled. "You see I've already disabled the one unit delivered to me in a way that will seem a technical fault. I will have to go ahead with the actual insertion, though, otherwise questions will be asked. That will be made by a surgical punch into the second lumbar vertebra. It's a tricky procedure but I know it well. I won't cripple you as the delightful Commander suggested. He knows that has happened with some Podders."

He looked at the flashing buttons that were slowing down in their movements. "Now, quickly, because we don't have long. Are you clear so far?"

"Yes," said Julian in a strangled voice. He felt sick. "But how do I...?"

"Get away? I'll tell you that later. I've got it all worked out. A good plan. I just hope you have a good head for heights. Do you?"

"No, not really." Julian felt his head swimming already at the words.

"Well, not to worry. I'll be showing you what you have to do. It'll be a piece of cake once we're underway."

Julian realised how little he knew about Peter and his motives for doing what he was. It was too late to ask him now. His 'piece of cake' reference brought into Julian's mind the crazy party song that had been playing over and over in his head: *'If I knew you were coming, I'd've baked a cake, baked a cake…'*. Hell, this is all mad, isn't it, he thought? Which is madder, SupaPodia or me – or are we one and the same in lunacy?

"I can't tell you any more now," Peter continued, speaking fast, "only that our escape will start from your Pod, to which you will be taken after the Second Implant procedure. You'll need at least three days before you can be back on your feet: I'm using the old term, not those crappy time segments some SupaPodia prick thought up. Your Commander and the others – watch out for that Marion, as I've warned you – will know the details and won't be expecting a signal from your new chip straightaway, only when I – your medico – say you're fit enough for it to be switched on. By then, we should both be right away."

"Shouldn't I be checked on during my recovery?" Julian asked weakly. "Where will that take place?"

"I'll be doing the checking. I'll come to your Pod. They'll want you back there under supervision, anyhow, not taking up bed space needed for others. If it's a success for you – and, of course, it won't be, as we know – a big programme for Lilacs will get underway. The Podder programme is not so demanding and is already being implemented. It's much less complicated, as their chip does not require sound and vision transference; it's really just a minor upgrade to their present chip. You see, subversion is much more suspected in Lilacs than in Podders. Podders are fed everything they ask for so that they will conform. Personally, I think the average Podder is far more intelligent than that, and one day…."

Peter's voice stilled in mid-sentence. The elevator control lights had ceased flashing and changed colour. The door slid slowly open. Outside was a brightly lit passage. Julian saw passers-by in lilac medical coats and tunics.

"Remember," breathed Peter, "Play the game, and we'll be alright. I can't guarantee anything, but it's worth a try, isn't it?"

"Yes…," began Julian, but Peter silenced him with a cutting motion of his hand across his throat.

"That's enough, Dr. Foster. Quite enough. Clasp onto my wrist now and do exactly as I say."

* * *

Everything went as Peter had said it would. As soon as they came into one of the SupaPod's large open medical wards ranked with many beds, all occupied by silent patients lying prone, Peter was greeted by colleagues who were clearly expecting him. Julian was taken at once into a cubicle formed of shiny white curtains that were then closed around him. A female nurse stood by him as he undressed, and gave him a narrow lilac loin cloth to wear in bed. Then she helped him under the covers. "Make sure you lie still," she said. "Always flat on your back. There's water by the bed, if you need it."

"What if I need the toilet?"

"Sound the buzzer." She indicated a press button on the bed-head. "One of us will take you."

He had not long to wait. After a short while, the curtains were pulled back and Peter stood there in a long lilac coat with his stethoscope still about his neck, but the sinister-looking scope now removed from his head. Two porters – one male, one female: they wore lilac tunic tops tucked into floppy trousers – accompanied him. With Peter assisting as well, they pushed him in his bed across the ward and through double swing doors into a broad, white-tiled passageway where groups of medicos, all in short sleeved tunics and trousers, mostly green in colour, but a few in lilac, stood around talking. Some broke off to look curiously at Julian passing in his bed.

"Your first transo implant, Peter?" one called out, a well-scrubbed, pink-faced man whose bald scalp reflected the arc lights shining above.

"Yes," Peter called back cheerily, waving the hand not pushing at the bed. He mouthed to Julian beside him, "Transo, you should know, my friend, is what we call 'sound-light transmission' here, or SLT, the proper acronym for the Second Implant."

The information hummed into Julian's ears, but he had grown too fearful to take it in or even give a grunt in reply. He was at the very edge of what he understood, about to enter a world he did not know at all – a course of action that might end in disaster and extinction, despite Peter's optimism.

He now found himself being pushed through more doors into a bay lined with various pieces of equipment – black flexible tubes, shiny chromed vessels, a red extinguisher, a yellow cylinder like a small torpedo, a steel trolley with glass shelves piled high with plastic boxes. Above all, hung a timepiece, showing one black hand firmly within the Orange segment and another circling the dial at some speed. He felt his bare arm being taken and something being rubbed into the fleshy bend of his elbow by a person he hadn't seen before, a figure, large-bosomed, in a full length, green robe and wearing a white mask. She held a needle poised in one hand.

"Help!" Julian called out in sudden fear.

He was reassured to see Peter's face appear immediately in his line of vision. "Everything's fine, Julian. Relax now. The next you will know, this will all be over."

The needle went into his arm. Some seconds passed and nothing to Julian's consciousness had happened, other than that his bed was being pushed forward again through metal-framed doors into a much bigger room where the light was very much brighter and a ring of faces were looking down at him. Amongst these, he recognised the doctor – Hector something or other – who had agreed this procedure as his punishment, and then the world suddenly boiled inwards like misty foam and he felt himself sinking down and down until he was not there any longer – although, very strangely, he heard his own voice talking, "Yes, I am Dr. Julian Foster", and then no more.

His eyes opened slowly, uncertainly. He did not know where he was, aware only of a greyness shot through with light, which slowly peeled back to reveal scattered, jagged parts of clearer images. Then he saw Peter's round, cheery face float into view, and he was comforted by the sight. Other images out of the corners of his eyes showed he lay on his couch in his own Pod, On the shelves set in the far wall, shining in the glow of the ceiling lamp, stood the items he had brought with him from the OW – the glass dish, for instance, that seemed to flash a light of surety to him, the steel paper knife, that gave him a feeling of solidity and strength. They spoke out to him: 'We are here still from your old life to your new. We are constant. We are tangible. You can hold us and remember. We shall not leave you.'

He heard Peter's voice. "Good, you are coming round. How are you feeling?"

"What happened?" said Julian feebly. Then, as the blurred memory of why he was here returned to him, he stiffened. "I didn't say anything, did I? I didn't…" – his voice rose in sudden terror – "…say anything silly, give the game away?"

Peter laughed. "No, you were very sociable, quite chatty really, but it was all innocuous chit-chat. I seem to remember you asked Hector if he liked to read poetry. You even quoted some at him, *'The old order changeth, yielding place to new…'*, if I remember correctly. He'll probably put it forward as a tag line for SupaPodia. They like to make use of memorable quotes such as that to add a gloss to their new state."

"*'Less one good custom should corrupt the world,'*" continued Julian in a hollow voice.

"Oh, is that the next line? No, they wouldn't like that. But as it is…" – he stood up over Julian, applying his stethoscope to his chest and listening – "…you've come through the Second Implant procedure very well. But, as you'll remember, we couldn't actually activate the new chip as it was faulty, much to everyone's disgust. The manufacturers are going to get such a blast. So you're in limbo from now on – no chip at all. There's no way now of monitoring your movements."

He stepped back from the couch, leaning against the wall of the Pod. "I'm the one who reports on you now. Once you've recovered, they'll expect me to re-instal your first implant until a replacement for the second one arrives. But, of course, I won't be doing that. So this Pod is totally clean of insidious bugs of any sort. Now all you have to do is recover from that punch I made into your vertebra. Your back will be stiff for a while, but another two full Sweeps (48 hours, that is, for hell's sake), and you'll be fit enough to move. And you're going to need to be. That, I'll be coming on to when I see you next. The plan's worked well so far. The next bit won't be for the faint-hearted, though, but I know that's not you, young man."

"Young man!" groaned Julian. "I wish I was."

Peter chuckled. "Rest now. No one will disturb you. Doctor's orders. I'll be back soon, and then we'll implement the plan. Don't worry, I'll have everything ready for you. Now get some sleep"

"Peter," said Julian drowsily. He felt sleep like rippling waters, warm and sunlit, beginning to close in over his head.

"Yes?"

"Nothing you've just told me can get out from this Pod, can it?"

"No. I've just told you that. Why do you ask?"

"Only Stanley told me that Marion and I had been overheard here, and seen too."

"That's nonsense. The only transmission from your Pod would have been of your location, to be viewed as a spot of light on some distant control board. Even that's extinguished now. And mine won't show, as it's another system entirely, which I can switch off at will."

"So, why should he lie to me?" Julian could hardly get the words out. Huge dreams were already forming up like coloured clouds as his consciousness retreated.

"Because he wanted to frighten you, to ensure that he had you under his control. But – as I've told you – be very careful of Marion. She's likely to be working on Stanley's orders. She's not your friend, Julian, but your enemy."

"I liked her," he dimly heard himself say. And then he struggled to add, "She can't be all bad", but sleep overwhelmed him.

Peter sighed, and left the Pod, making sure the emergency lock, to which only he had the combination, was firmly activated. He descended by the exit shoot to the lower hall floor, arriving on his hands and knees alongside a pair of shapely, stockinged legs, cut by the hem of a semi-transparent lilac dress. Rising to his feet, he saw the legs belonged to Marion, who stood with arms folded across her chest, her dark head jutting forward with more than a hint of aggression. Fuck it, thought Peter. If anyone will wreck my plans now, it is she. She has the brains, she has the intuition. You could run a cart full of cow shit under Stanley's nose and he would not smell it. Marion would pick up a whiff of something bad at any distance.

"How long before he can receive visitors?" she asked.

"Not long now."

"How long exactly?" She tapped her foot impatiently.

Above her head, the stack of Pods hummed with movement. External lifts moved up and down, steel shoots ejected their occupants or sucked them in. Groups of Lilacs stood talking, or were moving off individually into the connecting passageways. The lilac colour was everywhere, on the many uniforms, in bands on the walls, in strips on the floors. Even the air seemed to hold a lilac tinge that Peter thought he had not noticed before. It seemed to catch in his throat. Probably it was air filled with polluted dust and, fuck only knows, what other harmful residues.

All of us, he thought, are probably being poisoned here day by day. SupaPodia never seems to check the quality of the air in their SupaPods: it's continuously sucked in and out, and pumped around, from the great orifices on those vast, concrete roofs. When were the pipes ever cleaned? They must be filled with contamination. In every way – physically, technically, morally, practically – SupaPodia is already decaying. It will take but one great push to bring the whole system down. Could that push be precipitated from the OuterWorld? Did it still have the energy?

That was Peter's dream now, all that he lived for since his own great disillusionment. No doctor could work here, and see the evil being done supposedly to create a fairer, more ordered society, salvaging a ravaged, exploited world, and not rebel. He had one chance now to try and initiate that great push – that revolt. No sleek, dark-haired bimbo like Marion, the perfect product of the SupaPodia system, her mind closed, operating by slogans, believing propaganda as reality, would get in his way.

"Two Sweeps," he answered Marion. "Possibly three. I'll know more at my next consultation."

"And when will that be?"

"I don't know yet. Really, it's none of your business."

"I'm his Inculcator."

"You *were* that. Not now, you'll find. Dr. Foster's being disciplined. It's my job to implement his punishment under close medical supervision. Speak to your Commander, if you're in any doubt."

"I have. I will."

She flushed, and turned on her heel, while Peter laughed out loud behind her. Later, he realised he'd been foolish? He had made a real enemy of her when he could have played her along. There was danger still, both for himself and his patient.

The latter, though, slept on with no idea at all of the perils ahead.

15

From the broad windows of the tower room, the sea light swirled misty-grey this dawning, the haze covering the gardens below. On a clear day, the tight, geometric shapes of lawns and flower beds might be seen sweeping down to the edge of the marsh, and, further out, beyond that broad expanse of reeds and twisting water-channels, surged the open, white-rimmed sea. This morning, however, all seemed shut out from the world, as if the house was cocooned in wool, which only the rising sun had hope of piercing. A brighter light in the eastern sky was already dissolving the mist into tatters, so, drawing back the curtains, Zara thought it would not be long before the haze cleared.

She turned away from the window, then glanced sharply back, for had her eye not caught sight of some movement below seen through the dispersing mist? No, surely not; there was nothing there, only the long trails of white still covering terrace and balustrade, wreathed amongst the statues by the fountain, veiling the long, pergola-lined path leading to the apple bower. Then, as she watched, a sudden shift in the mist revealed the grey outline of a man standing on the far side of the terrace, and other men as well beyond him on the lawns, some lined up against the tennis courts, where the nets slumped limply.

Zara's hand flew to her mouth. Who were these? They were far too many to be her own workers. Were they then other workers from the town come to beg of her, or, worse, escaped Podders? There had been a Podder live-music event, she had heard, further along the coast – at Hastings, wasn't it? – but that was a long way away and they should have been well-escorted. Why in any event would they want to come here onto her land, unless they were simply lost? Perhaps that was it. Podders were notoriously stupid, being like young children really. Out of their own controlled environments, they would be as confused as animals escaped from a zoo. But dangerous? Of course not. She would deal with this situation calmly.

She descended from the tower room and went into the Red Bedroom – so-named by Zara from its decoration of crimson satin on the walls, from the red panels, chequered with white, on the hand-woven carpets brought back from Nepal, and from the curtains of its four-poster bed, which she stood before now.

"Roberta," called out Zara, making her voice sound light and untroubled.

"There was a stirring in the bed, and Roberta's tousled brown head appeared from the covers, then her upper body with a pillow clasped to her breasts.

"What is it? Are you not getting back in, my love?" She thumped the bed beside her petulantly with one arm. "It's still so horribly early."

"Don't be alarmed, but there are some people outside and I will have to find out what they want."

"What!" Roberta shot straight upwards in bed, the pillow fallen from her arms, her full breasts hanging free.

Zara leant over Roberta, kissing each nipple in turn and then her mouth. "Just stay here. I'll be back as soon as I can. And then we'll make love again."

Zara hurriedly changed her silk pyjamas for a loose woollen top and a pair of cotton trousers. She turned to reassure Roberta again, but saw she had already disappeared back under the clothes. Downstairs, she found two of her servants setting the dining room table for breakfast. One was her Adonis, whom she liked to dress in a sarong. This morning, however, he was wearing dark trousers and a white tee-shirt.

"Philip," she called out. ('Adonis', she reserved for other occasions). "Who are those men outside?"

He looked puzzled, his oiled features under lanky black hair set in a frown. "What men, Madam?" He looked at his companion, who shrugged her shoulders.

"There are men in the gardens. I saw them from the Tower. Come with me."

She strode from the room into the long stone corridor with its floor of mosaic fronting the house, the two servants following her – Philip with his long strides and Maria, short and petite, almost running. Before opening the grand front door, with its two leaves of blackened oak studded with iron, she paused and said to Maria, "Get all the servants together, the garden staff as well, and meet me outside."

Zara's hand hung for a moment over the mahogany cabinet where the panic button was positioned, but then impatiently she moved away. She did not know if there was anything yet to be alarmed about, and there had never been any cause in eight years or so to call out the Militia Guard. There had been no rumour of anything wrong, a robber band on the loose, perhaps; nothing like that at all. Her Screen had been very quiet on local news: just a few deaths from a collapsing building in Ashford and some children poisoned by a leaking sewer. Whoever those men were, there must be some mistake. She would deal with them herself and chase them off her land. She had some stout gardeners, if necessary, who could thrash them with their spades and sticks, and give them a broken head or two to make sure they never returned.

She stood outside on the gravelled drive, her staff coming in ones or two to form a group about her. Philip was closest to her, the skin of his smooth, tanned arms beaded with moisture. Peering into the mist, which was now being torn into strips like ragged cloth by a rising breeze, she could see nothing at first, and hear nothing, but then saw suddenly, advancing through the gardens, a group of men coming straight at her across the lawns, silent on the grass, with two other groups on their flanks. They paid no attention to the flowerbeds and the plants, but marched right through them, leaving destruction in their wake – crushed stems, broken trellises, trampled seedlings.

"You, *stop there!*" yelled Zara in her sternest, most commanding voice, which had once stilled a frightened mob when a village she owned was being cleared by a unit of the Guard. "Who are you? How dare you *trespass* on my land?"

One of the men at the front gestured to his followers to halt. They stood before Zara, but some were still encroaching upon her on both sides. With her small band of retainers in a bunch about her, she could see she was greatly outnumbered – by at least three to one, she estimated. This was no causal invasion of vagrants, but men carrying clubs and bars, with hatred on their sullen faces. She wished now she had pressed that panic button. She whispered to Philip. "Run back. Find Lady Roberta. Send an alarm."

He made to move, but the men were watching closely and two ran to intercept him, beating him to the ground with sticks and kicking him in the body and the head. The oiled torso under the ripped white shirt writhed briefly, then was still. A chorus of shrieks arose from Zara's people. The intruders had spread inwards now to ring them entirely.

The man who seemed to be their leader stepped forward. He looked in mid-life, about forty, wearing a frayed green shirt and corduroy trousers. Above his heavy boots were black gaiters. On his head, a broad-rimmed hat, with a feather in the band, was set at a jaunty angle.

He spoke in a low voice that was acid in tone and sneering. Zara had to lean forward to hear him, strands of her long, brown hair lashed about her cheeks, her face pale and frightened.

"You see, missus. That is the trouble. You have it in one. You call this your land, when it is my land and that of these others here. We held it and farmed it long before you and your spawn came here and seized it to build your fancy big house."

"And what's more," he went on, "we don't like the way you live here neither, with all that you have that we don't, and your servants and the poncey toffs who come here and live off the fat of everything, and we have nought."

"But you have the SupaPods!" cried out Zara, determined not just to stand here and listen, but fling the argument back. "We've given you so much and now you want *more!*"

Turning her head, with her hair whipping out in the breeze, she saw Philip – her lovely Adonis – had not moved. Oh, God! These people were murderers. Was she about to be killed too, and darling Roberta, unknowing, still tucked up in bed? Oh, how could she summon the Guard? They would come in riding their black helidrones and put this vermin to the sword.

The leader of the invaders laughed, and others about him guffawed too. They were all men, Zara noted, unshaved, their faces covered in sores. Where did they come from? Where were their women? Their skinny, ugly women in black dresses. She saw them whenever she had to pass through their towns. They smelt and they urinated in the streets, and their children played amongst the shit. Wasn't it for people like this that she, and the other Commissioners of SupaPodia, had developed the SupaPods? Now they weren't even satisfied with that, but wanted a share of what the Eliti possessed as well. Well, it had to stop, and right here now!

She stepped forward and slapped the man before her, once, twice across the face. "*Get out of here!* Before the Guard comes. They are on the way. I don't want you on my land alive and I don't want you dead. *Go now!*"

The man, who had stepped back before her assault, seized her by the wrists and held her struggling. "You're a brave lady," he hissed, "I'll grant you. But that was a big mistake."

Zara screamed, and that set off other screams from the female servants. The men, many just boys, turned to find a way of escape, but could not get through the strengthening cordon. Some of the gardeners, hardier than the others, started laying about them with the iron tools and staves they had hurriedly picked up. They were attacked in turn with long-handled clubs.

Soon a general melee developed, at the centre of which was Zara, held now by several men, raised up high, her trousers dragged down, her breasts pulled out, a man wearing a greasy, peaked cap cupping and pummelling them in his grimy hands, laughing and shouting. Her body fell to the ground, and a scrum of men were bent over it, her screams muffled by the wall they made.

Little Maria was being raped too, by a young man with ginger hair in a blue boilersuit who used his engorged penis like a sword, thrusting at her until he was spent. Others then covered her like flies. And so it went on until Zara was still, and Maria too, and all the other servants, spread over the dark grass in red pools of flesh and torn clothing, some of the gardeners still writhing and groaning until smashed over the head again with clubs; only two boy servants who reached the edge of the marsh and hid in the reeds, lived to describe what had happened.

It was they, with eyes floating on the water's surface, frozen in fear, who saw the great house go up in flames, gusts of fire bursting from its windows, dark, frantic shapes, trapped, framed momentarily in the openings, a wall falling outwards in a shower of stone, then the heat beginning to bubble at the water's edge, so the watchers must retreat and swim away.

And at last the air was filled with the sound of rotors, and the helidrones summoned – was that by Roberta's hand before her body puckered and charred? – swooped in like great vampire bats, not that there was much that they could do. The fire lit the morning sky for miles around. It could even have been seen from Ramsgate SupaPod 16, if there had been anyone watching from its Upper Deck.

But at that very time, Dr. Julian Foster, who had once looked out from there at the sea cliffs and green countryside of the OuterWorld, seeing it once more as a land of hope, was asleep in his Pod, with a journey before him, of which as yet he knew nothing at all.

16

Julian awoke. Someone was in his Pod with him. He heard their breathing. In the pitch blackness, he could see nothing. "Peter," he called out. "Is that you?" Alarmed, he scrambled with his left hand for the button of his couch lamp but before he could do so the whole Pod was suddenly filled with bright light, so that he had to fling his arms across his eyes, groaning.

"Sorry, Jules," said Marion's familiar voice, but I had to get to you." Julian took his arms from his eyes and saw her standing over him in her lilac dress.

He struggled to regain his senses. It came back to him in a rush, the long channel of recent events with Peter's face at the forefront: Peter who was due to get him away from here, Peter who was himself in rebellion against SupaPodia. So how…?

"I was able to override the lock," Marion said, guessing his question. "Stanley got the code from Peter's director – a doctor something or other. You see Peter thinks he controls these matters, but he doesn't. He's a danger to you, Jules, and I'm going to get you away from him. But we must be quick!"

Julian had sat up, shaking his head with this new puzzlement filling it. Peter had told him he was saving him from Marion, and now Marion was here, at Stanley's say-so too, to protect him from Peter. What the hell was going on? He slid one leg over the side of the couch, and groaned. He remembered the Second Implant which had gone wrong, deliberately so he had been told, or was that still true? His back and his side were very sore. Peter, he thought, was not due back for another full Sweep at least – although he was far from certain about that. He should still be recovering. So what did Marion want him to do?

"I'll help you up," said Marion, taking his hands in hers. "And get you downstairs. There'll be a stretcher for you there, and we'll take you to a safe place. Stanley's expecting you."

It was the name Stanley that flared across Julian's mind like a red warning light. He remembered the evil of Stanley. So, if Marion was acting for Stanley, what she was doing must be evil too. She *was* evil. That's what Peter had told him. He should wait then for Peter to come for him, as he had said he would. But that might not be for a long time yet. He must not let Marion take him away!

He had an idea: how he could delay Marion and hope Peter would arrive. Peter had perhaps been warned of Marion's sudden move and be on the way to him even now. He reached out his right arm from the couch and forced his hand up her dress between her thighs.

"What the hell are you doing?! There's no time for that! Haven't you heard me? We have to move!"

Everything was fuzzy in his head. Perhaps it was the drug they had given him. Her struggles excited him.

"It's been such a long time." His voice came out in gasps. Despite the pain in his back, he had managed to pull her onto the couch and pin her there, half on top of her while she writhed beneath him. "Stop it! Stop it! You fool!"

He didn't know what had been in that drug but he lusted for her now, with a force he had not known before. All his pain had left him and he felt reinvigorated as if he had woken from a long sleep. He got astride her and tried to pull up her dress, but it was too tight. He heard the seam tear. He seemed to have the strength of devils and he laughed in the freedom it gave him. Marion was hitting him now, with her hands. She tore at his groin with her nails, and that *did* hurt. He hit her across her face with the flat of his hand. He could see the fear in her eyes but he was quite beyond caring.

"Stop it!" she shrieked. "Fuck! They've made him mad!"

She managed to drag herself from under him and staggered to her feet in the small space beside the couch. The top of her dress was torn from her shoulders, one breast exposed. He had dragged her pants down around her thighs, and she made an effort to pull them up with one hand, staggering as she did so against the entry door. It opened and Peter came in. Behind him was another head – that of Julian's neighbour, Oscar, from Servicing. Julian recognised him straightaway, although he had seen him only rarely since Marion had first introduced him. Oscar's eyes were bulging wide.

Sanity returned to Julian with a rush. Hell! It was not seemly – Marion, whose body he had enjoyed, exposed to others like this. He pushed at Oscar's head and it disappeared back through the door with a squeak of dismay.

"I'm sorry, Peter," Julian gabbled. "I was asleep and she came in."

Peter looked grim. He didn't answer Julian, but spoke to Marion in a voice hard as steel. They were wedged so close together their faces were virtually touching. "Woman, do you never do anything with your clothes on? Do you have any conscience, any beliefs, that are not centred in your cunt?"

Marion's face was taut with fear, but her dark eyes still sparked back. "It was not me, it was him. He was trying to rape *me*. He's mad."

"Oh, yes," said Peter, spitting his disbelief. He jabbed his hand at Julian, who had now collapsed back onto the couch. "Look at him. He's just had a major operation and is still recovering. You've come here, against all medical orders, to try and subvert him, and he's resisted you. That's what happened."

"We know what you're up to," Marion said defiantly.

"Oh, is that true? Who's we? You and that vicious sod, Stanley, I bet."

Marion did not reply. She had managed to pull together her torn clothing, her strength returning. "I'm leaving now. You'd better watch out for yourselves because all this is on Recall. I wouldn't be in your shoes."

"Stop!" bellowed Peter, placing himself between her and the exit. "You're going nowhere!"

She attacked him then with her nails, trying to gouge his eyes. After a short tussle, he was able to get his arms around her, flinging her onto the couch beside Julian, in fact on top of him at first until he was able to wriggle free of her thrashing legs. She let out three terrible screams, then her body collapsed and she burst into tears.

"What are you going to do with me?"

"I don't know yet. It depends on how you behave. If you try to interfere or attack me again I'll tie you up and gag you."

"You wouldn't dare."

"I would, you know. I'll rip your dress up and tie you with that, and shove your knickers in your mouth." Peter laughed as he said this, which made his threat only more menacing, not less.

Julian was thinking: is this the same jovial Peter that was? He seems as demented as I was just now. What has he got planned for me? I'm sitting here next to Marion, who used to be my friend, and now she's not, and I have no idea what's going to happen other than that Peter said he'd get me away from here. But perhaps he's madder than she.

"Stay out of the way on the couch next to Julian," Peter commanded. "I've got to get Oscar in now. I hope he's still outside or there has to be a change of plan. This is serious now, *thanks to you*." The last words he

171

bellowed at Marion, who backed away from him on the couch, her back against the Pod wall, her raised knees against Julian's chest. Absurdly, Julian reached out to comfort her.

"Get your hands off me!"

Such was Julian's confusion, he did not know what he had done wrong. The pain had come back, stabbing him in his lower back. He must clear his head. Realisation was returning to him that whatever was to come now would be critical to whether he survived or not.

Peter had slid open the outer door to the Pod. "Damn it," he said. "He's not in the lift. This could be the end for us if he's left and starts blabbing... Ah, thank the heavens, there you are!" He had spotted Oscar in the side shoot and hauled him up by the collar. He pulled him, red-faced and scared, into the Pod.

"Thanks for your patience, Oscar," he said recovering himself. "We're ready for you now. Do your stuff, will you?"

Oscar may have been thoroughly scared by everything he had witnessed, but he did not hesitate. He said not a word, but pushing between the couch and Peter's legs, he knelt at the far wall, where the steel lavatory pan was positioned. From a pouch attached to his belt, he took out various tools, screwdrivers and spanners of differing types, the working ends of which fitted into slots in the plastic panelling. After a brief period of knocking, twisting and tugging he was able to strip away a section of panelling, perhaps a yard high and a yard wide beside the pan, which was now loosened at its base and tilted to one side. Revealed was a central void, the sides of which were lined by the twisting service pipes coiling away into the blackness.

"Good, good," Peter said, rubbing his hands together, looking very satisfied, a look that only increased Julian's wonder and fear. He thought, surely that's not the escape route. It's too small. I'll never fit in and there must be a hell of a drop. This is just insanity.

"In you go, Oscar," Peter commanded. "Lead the way. You know the tunnels better than anyone."

Julian saw Oscar try to shrink away, but he was blocked by Peter behind him. "I don't want to go in," Oscar quavered squeakily. "I said I'd help you but I've done that, haven't I?" He began to whine.

"I'm afraid you're compromised now, thanks to her."

Peter gestured at Marion beside Julian on the couch. She was struggling to sit up now, fresh determination showing on her face. Julian noted with alarm the brightness of her eyes and the way her arms had begun to thrash against her sides. Seeing her eyes flick across to his possessions in the niche beside the Screen, with a sudden shock that pierced the lingering fuzziness of his brain he realised what she might do.

"Oscar, help me!" shrieked Marion, with a sweep of her arm seizing the bright silver paper knife from the niche and launching herself against Peter.

"Watch out!" yelled Julian, his voice returning in a full-throated roar.

Marion stabbed Peter in the chest before he could turn to protect himself. The handle of the knife snapped off, clattering onto the floor. Peter gasped in pain, the narrow blade sticking from his tunic, blood already staining the lilac cloth. Whatever the injury caused to Peter, for the present it did not seem to affect his movements. He seized Marion in his bull like arms, forcing her towards the hole that Oscar had opened up.

She shrieked. "Help me! Help me!"

Oscar had sought to escape the Pod, but the exit shoots were now locked tight. Feebly he plucked at Peter's tunic, then took out one of the tools he had just used and tried to stab him in the back. Julian, reaching forward from the couch, was able to grab Oscar's arm, while Peter, still holding Marion about the neck, swung a fist into Oscar's head with such power that it sent him like a stone to the floor. He did not move again.

"No, Peter. No!" cried Julian in horror, realising now what Peter intended.

Marion's head was already forced into the black hole, with Peter pushing at her from behind as she tried to cling on to the pipes at each side. "You bitch!" he snarled. "You know where you're going? To the depths of hell".

She shrieked over and over again as Peter chopped at her hands and wriggled her forward as if he was trying to stuff a lumpy parcel into a post box.

"No, Peter!" cried Julian again, off the couch now, stumbling over Oscar's prostate body while trying to stop Peter by grabbing at his waist.

"Get off, Julian! She's got to go. She'll give us away otherwise. It's you or her."

"Can't we tie her up? Drug her?"

"No, we can't. Ouch!" He cried out in sudden pain from his wound, the blood soaking his front. "See what the mad bitch's done to me."

He heaved convulsively at Marion's struggling body, which suddenly slipped forward into the void and dropped away. Her terrible shriek went on and on, dying to a distant echo, and then there was only silence, broken by Peter's heavy breathing and Julian's sobs of horror.

"She was good to me," he cried. "I loved her."

"She was your killer," Peter said grimly, trying to twist his head to see his wound, touching the end of the blade sticking out of him, his hands running with his own blood. "And she's mine as well."

Peter staggered away from the hole, stumbling against Oscar, whom he knelt beside and examined briefly, before collapsing onto the couch. "I'm sorry about him. I didn't want to kill him. He could have guided us. He knew all the inner workings of the Pods here."

"Is he dead?" Julian's voice was shrill with anguish.

"One blow. He must have a thin skull." Peter gasped the words, holding his side, the blood wet on his fingers.

"This is terrible," Julian sobbed.

"Yes, it is. More for you than me, I think," said Peter, calm despite the terror about him. "She's caught my heart, I'm sure. Got the left ventricle, I suspect. I won't survive for long without help, and I can't get that now, so you're going to be on your own." He sank back onto the couch. "Julian, get out of here, as we planned. I won't be able to make it now. So listen to me. *Listen, man!*"

He reached out and clasped Julian's arm. "Do this for me as much as for yourself, to make a blow against the evil of this place. Let one of us at least get out to tell the truth about the SupaPods – how they are hell on earth, not places of paradise. *The people must know this! They must rise up against them!*"

He fell back on the couch, panting with the effort to speak. Blood was spitting from his mouth. He tried again, the words coming in gasps. "You have to get out through one of the portals – a freight portal will give the best chance: you can't get to one the normal way, for they're all guarded and only warehouse Lilacs are allowed there – you'd get lost anyhow without a Guidance chip. But there's another way, I've learnt, difficult and dangerous, but just possible, so poor Oscar told me…."

Julian placed his hands over his head in his despair. He wanted to die too, to be away from all this, free from everything of this present and this past. There was no future now but horror, all-encompassing horror, which he did not have the strength to bear any longer.

Peter, his voice breaking, his face ashen, his blood seeping into the cloth of the couch, croaked, "Memorise this! You can't write it down in case they catch you. First, getting out of here: Oscar's route. Go through that opening. You'll find there's a steel ladder at the side beyond the service pipes. Descend to a platform – it'll be a hundred feet or so down, so hang on tightly, take it slowly, and you'll get there. Remember you're still weak after your operation and the drug I had to give you. The platform occupies half the shaft, so I understand from Oscar, and there's a side shaft from it running off horizontally, you'll have to crawl along it, which won't be pleasant, but after some way – I'm not sure how far – it will broaden and you'll probably be able to crouch at least. There'll only be pipes and cables in the shaft, and perhaps a rat or two – Oscar said they eat the cables and much of his time was spent mending them. Ignore all side shafts and eventually the one you're in will get much wider and you'll come to a steel hatch, which *should* be open – I asked Oscar to unbolt it – but if it's not, you're *stuffed*."

He coughed, emitting a shower of blood, gasping for air, then summoned up a further effort. "*Quickly now.* On the other side of that hatch, you'll come into a warehouse. You should rest there and see how the land lies. Hide yourself amongst boxes, or whatever else is there. If you're lucky you might find food and drink; that's what Oscar said, anyhow. You *have to* survive. Be canny. Use your wits. You'll be in a freight portal where transport comes and goes. There should be a chance to get on board some truck or other, and *get out* into the OW. Remember, if you don't succeed, you are dead. They will kill you if they capture you. No doubt about that. They've been kind to you so far, that bloody Stanley and his perverted henchmen."

Peter gasped deeply; the front of his tunic now drenched with oozing blood, which dripped from the couch onto Oscar's body on the floor. "Promise me, you'll get away."

"Of course, I promise?" Julian repeated, despite the desperation he was feeling.

"There's much more to let you know." Peter giggled now, as if he was telling some great joke to which he had yet to give the punch line. He took Julian's hand. His fingers were sticky with blood. "I don't know how much time you'll have before the alarm's raised. Because Stanley's alerted, maybe not long before they come and check here and see this shambles." He indicated the Pod with a feeble gesture of one hand.

"What about Marion? Won't they find her?"

Again, Peter's giggle. "No. She's gone forever. I expect she's still falling."

Julian felt sick and retched.

Peter managed to raise himself a little from the couch. He pulled from a crimsoned pocket of his tunic a yellow plastic object, which Julian saw from its lens was a small torch. "You'll need this. It'll be so black where you have to go, you'll see nothing at all. It'll be like a wall about you. Get used to that black wall, force yourself through it by feel until you reach the platform. After that, when you've a hand free, you can use the torch."

"You must get dressed now," Peter said suddenly and urgently. "There's not much time. Put the torch in a pocket, so you won't drop it."

Julian obeyed. He stood, his head spinning at first, found his clothes in his wardrobe, and dressed as quickly as he could in lilac trousers, shirt and pullover, and a lilac zip up jacket. He pulled on the pair of boots he had worn on the training trip Outside.

"Good," said Peter, watching him. His voice was very low, his breath coming in faster and faster gasps. "Now, this is the last of what I have to tell you. At all costs, you must remember it. Seek out Nemesis. Their leader is Adrestia. You can find her in Canterbury at the White Swan. Now, repeat that back."

"Nemesis. Adrestia. Canterbury. White Swan," said Julian quickly.

"Correct. Keep saying it yourself. Do not forget."

"No, I won't," said Julian, feeling suddenly quite calm. The terror seemed wondrously to have lifted from him. He had no choice now. He was committed.

Peter sunk back, a half smile on his bleached, hollow cheeks, his breathing shallower and shallower.

"Repeat it."

"Nemesis. Adrestia. Canterbury.White Swan," Julian intoned dutifully.

"Good, good."

"What do I say to this Nemesis?"

"Tell them what you know of the SupaPod," Peter spoke urgently and tried to raise his head. "No one who has gone into a SupaPod has ever come out with the knowledge you have now. Every detail will be invaluable to them."

"I see," said Julian. "Are they going to attack it?"

"Yes, yes, perhaps so, perhaps so. They need data to plan."

"I can tell them about Control Station 15 and the Guard that drills there."

"Yes, do that. And…." – he coughed and a great stream of black blood came out of his mouth – "tell them what goes on at the Lower Levels; what you have seen and experienced yourself."

"I shall."

There was a lengthy silence when Julian thought Peter, whose eyes had closed, must have passed away, but bending closer to him he thought he heard the continuing whisper of his breath. The blood was clotting darkly all about him, so he lay on the couch like a red flower with a black centre, like a poppy from a long ago war.

The eyes opened. "Who's there?"

"It's Julian."

"Repeat."

"Nemesis. Adrestia. Canterbury. White Swan."

"Then I am content. You *must* go now. *Go!*"

176

The last word came as a long-drawn out hiss, and when Julian turned back from the edge of the hole to look at Peter he could see clearly from the white stillness of his face that he was dead. He felt tears coming to his eyes, but steeled himself sternly against them. Peter had placed his trust in him and he would not let him down. There was no time to lose, no time to dwell on anything but what he must do.

Making sure the torch was safe in his pocket, he reached into the hole and located the top rungs of the ladder with his hands, then, bending his body, pulled his legs through too, hanging for a while by his hands only while he found the rungs with his feet. Trying not to think of the vast drop beneath him, he started step by step down into the void

* * *

Blackness deeper than any night, encompassing him, suffocating him, only the thoughts that swam in his brain giving him substance, and the touch of his hands and feet on the iron ladder, on and on down the long shaft into the black oblivion to which Marion had fallen, the shock of which still shrilled in his nerves. Reality now had to be imagined, through this feel of steel, this rush of breath, this fast beating of his heart. So easy it would be to let go, to soar into the blackness, to find an escape through death.

The feel of his feet meeting a surface broader than a ladder rung told him he must have reached the platform. His hands were clenching the ladder so tightly, at first he could not let go, but after a while he was able to release one hand and feel around, finding what appeared to be a high steel wall all about him, forming a type of box into which the ladder had descended. He freed the other hand, his arms and legs aching, his body bent rigidly forward. Tentatively, he pressed down with one foot to see if the floor of the box was solid. It seemed to be: he could find no indication of the ladder continuing down. He freed himself entirely from the ladder. He did not fall.

He took the torch from his pocket, holding it with trembling hands, terrified of dropping it. He found the sliding switch and pushed it on. A beam of white shone out, slicing the blackness like the first starlight of creation. He found the side shaft straight away, a black hole seen in the torchlight within a tangle of pipes. Its entrance was low. As Peter had told him, he could only crawl in. If he got stuck, he could probably not reverse. Fear swept over him, trouncing all his previous fears. His body seemed to empty of identity, without substance or form. By breathing deeply, he steadied himself. At least the air was fresh. He could be trapped, he could fall, he could suffocate. Which death might come first?

More terror. Was it possible? As he swept the torch beam around the steel platform, confirming the curving sides topped by a rail to shoulder-height, he saw a strip of cloth hanging from the rail, cloth stuck within a mass of something red and dripping. With such shock he could scarcely breathe, he realised that this must be where Marion's body had struck the edge of the platform in its terrible fall.

He was sick, a slimy mixture of bile dribbling down his front. Out of this horror came thought of a greater horror – that Marion's body might have hit the platform itself, and burst open where he had to stand now. There was no way he could have passed over that. He was sick again, then, wiping his mouth, he crawled into the side shaft, knowing it was the only thing he could do, desperate to escape from all traces of Marion's disembodied ghost.

He crouched amongst cardboard boxes in a warehouse. The tiers of boxes stretched away, for as far as he could see in the dim light from his place of hiding. His journey here from the vertical shaft had been every bit as claustrophobic and frightening as Peter had indicated – in utter blackness to begin with, the passage in places hardly high enough to crawl through, his chest against the floor, his shoulders almost as wide as the space between the various pipes, gaining the purchase to force himself forward virtually impossible – but he *had* succeeded and the passage had widened eventually, just as Peter had said it would. He was then able to bring out the torch and light his way, proceeding at a crouch. He was fearful of the rats Peter had mentioned, but he had seen none, so at least that was a mercy.

His fear had grown most acute when he had reached the steel hatch mentioned by Peter. He had examined it with his torch, fearful it would prove unmovable if Oscar had not done his job of taking out the locking bolts. That could only mean a retreat to the ladder, and a long climb back to his Pod – and what would he find there, after his role in the killings, but his own execution?

The hatch was set at an angle to the floor, beneath pipes that went on through the solid wall ending the passage. He had turned its handle and pushed, and there had been no movement at all, so that his heart pumped hard in his fear, and then he had thought to pull, and the door had creaked open inwards, just wide enough for him to wriggle his body through. On the far side, he had fallen several feet to the floor, protecting his head with his arms and landing on his right side with a thump that sent the torch clattering out of his hand.

He had lain still, knowing he must be in the warehouse that Peter had told him about and fearing the noise he had made would have been heard. All, though, remained quiet about him. When at last he had risen to his feet, his body aching, his clothes torn and dirtied, and retrieved the torch, he found that it would no longer work. Luckily the warehouse was lit, although the light source must be some distance away, for it was a shadowed darkness that was about him. As his eyes slowly adapted to the grey light, he could make out boxes rising above him, and all around him, on row after row of shelving. Hurriedly, he had crept in amongst the boxes on a lower shelf nearest to him, not knowing if he was well hidden, or indeed hidden at all. He stayed here for a long time, trying to make up his mind what to do next. He was fearful of going out into the open amongst the rows of shelves, as he had no idea what dangers might be present there.

The sudden sound of voices and footsteps, accompanied by whining machinery, disturbed him, and he retreated as far as he could amongst the boxes. As the voices and other sounds grew more distant again, he climbed up to a higher level on the racks, whincing at the pain in his side and back. He found a place behind boxes on the topmost rack and settled down there. He thought he would now be hidden to a casual glance from below.

From his perch, which was higher than most of the stacks around him, he was able to view the length of the warehouse. He could see light spilling through open doors a hundred yards or so distant, so bright that he had to shield his eyes at first. He thought he saw men moving against the light, and vehicles too. Possibly they were unloading goods to bring into the warehouse. Lorries from the OW might come right up to this freight portal, or even rail wagons. Peter had suggested getting inside one of these as a way of escape. He had to find out. But how to do so without being seen?

Should he not wait until it was dark outside? Then, surely he would be better hidden and the work at the warehouse doors would have ceased; or would work go on all the time, night and day? He had to get used again to the sequence of night following day, a concept almost lost within the SupaPod.

He was exhausted and very thirsty. Peter had suggested he might be able to find foodstuffs in the warehouse. But where and how? He knew if his escape was discovered – and that might be very soon, should Stanley investigate why he had not heard back from Marion – then there would be a security clamp down and searches everywhere, in particular at the portals of the SupaPod. Had anyone ever escaped before? Probably not. All dissidents ended up in the Lower Levels, where there would be no chance of escape at all. It was much more likely that people would be trying to find their way *into* a SupaPod, rather than their way *out*, such was the continuing lure of SupaPodia.

Julian knew that his priority had to be getting away as soon as an opportunity presented itself; finding food and drink must take second place. But what opportunity could that be? The answer began to show itself almost straightaway. High up on a wall to the left of where he crouched amongst the storage boxes, there was a walkway made of steel planking with an open railing. A door at the end of the walkway suddenly opened. Julian had no time to do anything but freeze his body and remain stock-still; he was without any cover at all from a sightline above. A line of Podders emerged onto the walkway, recognisable from their baggy orange clothing. To Julian's quick glance, it seemed they were a mixture of men and women, young and old, perhaps twenty of them. A man in a lilac boilersuit was at their rear, "Come on! Come on!" he was calling out, "Down the steps. You won't fall. If you do, we'll scrape you up", followed by coarse laughter. The Podders disappeared from Julian's view. No one seemed to have noticed him, although he knew he would have stood out like the proverbial sore thumb if anyone had looked.

He heard a second man say, "What you got there, Jake?"

"Punishment Orangies. For warehouse service. To be reclothed, repodded."

"Shit, we've no room."

"Get them togged, anyhow. Dirty gear"

"Wait on then."

It was not reason but sheer instinct that impelled Julian down from his perch. The descent, hand over hand, from shelf to shelf of the stack was much easier and pain-free than he had feared. Considering his recent operation, he was amazed by his own adroitness, making little noise. No one called out. No one rushed at him. He reached the floor and stood listening.

He heard the second voice once more. "You lot! Put these on over your other clothes. One size for all. If it's too big, roll it up, if it's too small swap with your neighbour. You're going to be scrubbing out intrays; hasn't been done for a while, so these will keep you nice and dry. There, you see, you should have behaved yourselves better. Better than what some get, though, ain't it Jake?"

"That's true, Des. That's fucking true."

Julian came round the end of a row of stacks and saw the group gathered in a small open space around a heap of black overalls with attached hoods and clear plastic face masks. One or two were picking up the overalls and trying them against themselves for size. Others stood watching, blinking in the light that streamed here from the far end of the warehouse. Some had their hands over their faces. Poor people, thought Julian. They've probably only just emerged from the SupaPod and perhaps haven't seen daylight in years, if ever. No wonder they look stupefied.

"Hurry up all of you, get them on." Julian saw Jake shake his head despairingly at his mate, also in a lilac boilersuit. They turned and walked a distance away, talking, their backs to the group.

Julian took his chance. Emerging from between shelving, he came quickly up to the Podders, seeing some turn to him, startled; others, though, intent on the new overalls, did not seem to notice him.

"I've been a bad Lilac," Julian said, as cheerily as he could muster, only too aware of the colour of his torn and grubbied trousers and blouse jacket. "I've been ordered to join you for punishment."

He got some reluctant grins at that, and one well-figured woman, who was pulling on her overalls, called out, "Glad t' 'ave yer. We're's t' be a dirty gang, so get these on yer."

Julian wasted no time. If the supervisors saw his lilac clothing, he would be lost. Covered up by the thick, plastic-coated overalls, he might not be noticed. Did they have a count of numbers? His heart raced as he picked up a pair of overalls, hoping they would be a good fit and he could pull them over his clothes before the supervisors returned.

He stepped into the trousers (they were a little tight under the crutch but not too bad), and pulled up the tunic part, which fitted him well enough across the chest. It fastened with sticky tabs. The hood with its face mask hung back against his shoulders. His brown leather boots were a bit of a giveaway, since the Podders, he saw, were all wearing chunky white trainers, but there was nothing he could do about those now. His socks, though, were lilac and, because of the short trouser legs, were clearly showing. No Podder wore lilac-coloured socks.

He looked along the row of stacks. The supervisors were still talking, although one had turned, looking back. Julian sat down on the floor and pulled off boots and socks. He was just in time, for the supervisors were now returning. He unstuck a tab of his tunic and stuffed the socks inside. Hurriedly, he pulled his boots back on. The supervisors had now returned. They noted him sitting whilst all the rest were standing. While one harangued the group – "Now come on, come on, my black-arsed beauties. Who hasn't finished? Missus, that's too tight, or your tits are too big. Try another." – the second came up to Julian and stood over him.

"They's fancy shoes you got, mate. What's your normal line?"

"Library work," said Julian, thinking fast. "I have to dress up for that as Lilacs use the place."

"Really. Library, eh. Didn't know we had one. What did you do wrong? Stamp the wrong bleedin' books?" He laughed out loud, his head tilted back so Julian had an unpleasant view up his hairy nostrils.

Julian thought it best to join in the laughter. "Something like that," he said, but the supervisor had already lost interest and had turned away.

Jake was clapping his hands. "Right, all ready?" Seeing a couple of Podders with their hoods and masks in place, he said, "Leave your hoods down for now. You're going to get some grub before you start. Then it'll be all work until you've done."

He led the group, squeaking and creaking in the stiff overalls, into a room where food was being dished out into metal cans by a fat Podder woman. Julian picked up a can and had it filled with a brown mixture topped by what might have been potato mash. He took it to a trestle table where others were eating in silence, shovelling the food into their mouths with their fingers. Julian did the same, surprised to find the food tasted good, a type of shepherd's pie. He washed it down with water from a white enamel jug on the table. The water was warm and seemed to have specks of rust floating in it, but at least it eased his thirst. The woman he had spoken to earlier sat beside him.

"I knows yer, don't I? Didn't I used to do for yer?"

Julian was thunderstruck. Of course. He recognised her, although he had only seen her a few times at work in his Pod. "You're Sandra, aren't you?"

"That's right. You'se remembers. And yer…?"

"It doesn't matter," Julian said quickly, suddenly frightened of disclosing himself.

"What's you'se 'ere for?" she asked. "I means you'se a Lilac, ain't yer?"

"I had an argument with my boss."

She laughed. "We've all done's that. Must've been a bad scrap."

Julian, wasn't sure if he should say more; indeed he felt he shouldn't be talking at all. Everyone else was sitting in awkward silence in their heavy suits, lost far away in their own thoughts.

"Why are you here, Sandra?" he did ask after a short while.

She laughed, as if he had made a joke. "For not washin' the 'allways. Level 21, you'se knows. Bleedin' washin' floors, me who'se was a dressmaker to the Eliti with my own little shop."

"Why did you come to a SupaPod then?"

"They'se made me. Said the Eliti would only continue their orders if I was in a Pod. But when I'se come in 'ere they tooks all from me – all me fabrics and tools – and put me in a Pod stack with furriners, some not e'en Christians."

"Hell that's bad," Julian said, but was really thinking she's an idiot. They were just getting her out of the way. Did all these Podders think they could have the good things of their previous lives carried into a SupaPod? It was all about dumbing down here, not raising up. If you objected, you went into the punishment squad – or worse – as had clearly happened to Sandra.

"They'se said I was stuck up," Sandra said. "Me, who'se grew up on a farm with pigs. They'se worse than pigs."

"Shh," Julian cautioned. "They may be able to hear you."

"No, not 'ere. Nothin' like that 'ere. I've done's a stretch 'ere afore, you'se see. All you'se got to worry about 'tis not lettin' one of they'se Lilacs get atween yer legs." She cackled again. "Or in's yours case, up's some's other part of yer."

Hell, thought Julian. Nothing gets any better. Wherever you turn, there's a new nightmare. Yet if Sandra was genuine, she might be able to help him. He looked around. Jake was busy talking to his mate, both with mugs in their hands. Others at their table had got up, some removing their overalls perhaps to use the lavatory signposted through a far door. There was no one near to them.

"I'm trying to escape," he whispered to Sandra.

Instead of looking shocked, she replied, "What, gets right out?"

He nodded, his nerves fluttering, knowing he had committed himself now and this might have been a fatal mistake. But all she added was: "Will you'se take me with yer? I wants to get out as well."

"Try and keep with me then? Have you done this dirty work before?"

"Yes."

"And you know where we'll be doing it?"

"Yes, in t' rail wagons that comes in 'ere."

"And they go out again?"

"I thinks so. They must do."

"Do they keep a close check on everyone?"

"I don't think so. They'se keep an eye on t' women mosts of all, to see what sex they'se might get. They likes t' watch us after-like in t' showers."

"God, what a place this is!"

"'Tis everywhere, believes me. In t' Pods, out of t' Pods. Cameras everywhere recording pics of yer. 'Tis not SupaPod, 'tis SupaPorn."

"I believe you. I've seen the evidence myself." He had a flash of memory of Marion, and then thought of her bloodied flesh spread across that awful platform rail.

"Are yer alright?"

"Yes," said Julian, gulping back his nausea.

"Right, get finished! Get finished!" The shouts came from the two supervisors, walking down the line of the tables, one sounding a portable klaxon that made a loud, penetrating noise. Several of the Podders pressed their hands over their ears.

"When you hear that sound, stop what you're doing and wait for new instructions. Now, get your hoods up and follow me."

Supervisor Jake led the Podder work gang in a straggling line out of the warehouse onto the sunlit concrete apron beyond. Half-turning, Julian saw through his face mask the other supervisor bringing up the rear: there could be no chance of an escape yet, and to where, anyhow? The concrete stretched away like a white sheet under the sun, so bright after his recent confinement that he had to screw up his eyes. Like swollen black ducks, their stiff overalls crackling like newly lit fires, they approached a vast open-ended, low-roofed building, on the far side of which Julian could make out the slow, steady movement of rail wagons coming and going. They entered the building over a high step, which caused one or two of the Podders to trip and fall.

"Come on, wake up! Watch what you're doing!" Julian heard the shouts clearly through his hood. He helped up one Podder, a young girl judging from her frightened face seen through her mask. Sandra was close to him, her overalls rustling against his. He pushed back his hood, "Keep with me," he said to her, almost pleadingly, not wanting to lose this unexpected ally. He thought she had not heard him and was relieved when she raised a gloved thumb to him.

"Keep your hoods down!"

They were at the edge of a concrete pit filled with large metal trays, each dark with slime and muck. Around two sides of the pit were long black hoses mounted on stands, their steel muzzles dangling low, like – and it was Julian's first crazed thought – the flaccid penises of men awaiting arousal. Beyond the hoses stood lines of rail wagons, each with open sides. Other work parties, Julian could see, were removing trays from the wagons and placing them in heaps. Further pits with their attendant hoses were positioned to right and left. Through his hood, Julian was aware now of noise filling the vastness of the building, muffled booms and sharper clangs, men shouting, the groans of straining metal, the rushing of water, and above all the high-pitched howl of the klaxons calling.

Julian found himself, along with others, pushed by Supervisor Jake into the pit in front of them, while others were lead away to other pits. He looked around him. Was Sandra there? He could not recognise her: everyone looked much the same in the black overalls once their hoods were in place. What if she was with the other Podders and going to betray him? And then he thought he saw her – at least the buxom outline of her – on the far side of the pit he was in, but he could not be sure. A klaxon sounded near them and Supervisor Des, in charge of their pit, yelled out, "Everyone grab a hose. And get busy washing out them trays!"

Julian reached for the nozzle of a hose, finding it unrolled easily as he tugged at it. There was a lever on the nuzzle, and he pressed at it, seeing others doing the same. Jets of water soared in all directions, some upwards, some directly at the ground and into the trays, splashing up the muck within them. Some Podders were knocked over by the force of the water, losing control of their hoses, which whipped back into their stands. Des was doubled up in laughter, until a jet came up suddenly high from the pit and hit him squarely in the chest. His laughter changed abruptly to roars of anger. "You dozey fuckers! Grip them hoses hard. Get cleaning. Anyone else spraying me is for the chop!" He retreated from the edge, mopping at himself with a grubby rag.

The Podder gang soon worked out how best to employ the hoses. Used with full force directly against the trays would result in dirt flung up over the operator and their neighbours. With the jet directed at more of an angle, however, it was possible to sluice out the tray steadily until its lining was silver bright, although everyone's overalls were soon running wet. As the trays were cleansed, they were picked out of the pit by a team of boys, naked but for loin-cloths, who seemed to appear from nowhere – had they been one of the gangs Julian had noted earlier piling the trays? They appeared to enjoy their work, splashing and laughing amongst the water jets, working together to lift the heavy cleaned-out trays and replace them with dirty ones. The skill they showed indicated to Julian that they had been doing this work all their short lives. What hell hole in SupaPodia did they come from, he wondered? – yet possibly a relatively happy one.

In between flushing out the trays, Julian glanced up to see the clean ones being returned to the rail wagons, this time by a team in the standard Podder orange. Some lines of wagons, when refilled, moved off and others were shunted into place. The system seemed to work without a hitch, co-ordinated by the supervisors' shouting and the screaming of their klaxons.

At last, Des called a halt. Hoses sprung back into their stands and the black-covered work gang, dripping water, collapsed against the sides of the concrete pit. The tray boys melted away as quickly as they had come, to where Julian was quite unable to see. He thought they might have a place somewhere underground beside the pits: one minute they had been busy, calling out excitedly amongst the clattering trays, and then they were gone. He wondered: is all this real or is it just some fantasy of light? And then he remembered Marion, and Peter whom she had stabbed, and the long tunnels of the SupaPod, and what he had seen on the very lowest Levels there, and all that he had endured himself to be standing here now – and he knew these nightmares were indeed formed from a central core of reality. If he had had any momentary doubt, Des's crude voice cut across his senses.

"OK, you buggers. Out of the pit! Hoods back! Follow me!"

Des led them towards the distant rail wagons. As they trailed along in a line, exchanging glances, Julian was desperate to find Sandra, which to his vast relief he soon did – she gave him a wink of one large brown eye – then they were joined by others of their original work gang, some talking, others blowing out their cheeks in their exhaustion.

"Stop that fucking noise! No talking!"

Close to a line of lilac-painted wagons, with their central doors slid back and open, Des halted. Jake joined him here with the last of their work parties.

"Right, my hearties," Jake called out. "Enough of the fun. Now for some real work. You're going to unload goods next, so take your overalls off. Leave them here on the ground, and they'll be collected."

Julian saw Sandra looking at him. She was clearly thinking the same as he. Taking his overalls off would reveal his lilac clothes. What to do? He felt a surge of near panic. Jake and Des had turned away: they were watching a group of skimpily dressed girls, who were picking their way on bare feet towards a nearby pit, presumably to take over the work the boy team had been doing. Another work party in black overalls had arrived there and were being instructed.

"Why can't we get *that* fucking detail?" Des was saying.

"Why d'yer think? It ain't good for you."

"It fuckin' would be."

"In your head, Des. It ain't allowed, mate. They'd put you in with the pervs."

"I wouldn't mind."

Coarse chuckling followed as the two sets of eyes followed the nubile girls with their budding breasts.

Sandra, who had removed her overalls, hissed at Julian, "Get ye's up 'ere with me!" She had climbed into the nearest wagon and pulled him up beside her. "Hide yerself at the back behind t' boxes."

In a real panic now, he did as he was told, forcing himself between a row of boxes and sliding behind an extra-high carton by the far wall, labelled in red 'Refrigeration Defective. RETURN'. Another Podder, thinking that he had to follow as well, jumped up onto the wagon.

"Start takin' those out!" Sandra whispered fiercely at this Podder, indicating the piles of boxes at the far end. As he turned dumbly to obey, she slid down the wagon to crouch beside Julian, but they were at best half-hidden from the door.

The attention of Jake was clearly back on them, for they heard him yell out, "Hey, you! Get out of there! Not that wagon, that stuff's going back!" As the Podder, confused and frightened, jumped down again, they saw Jake's face briefly at the door, and the box that had been taken out was shoved back in. He looked around briefly but could not have seen Julian and Sandra against the interior gloom, for the door was slid to with a crash. The sound seemed to reverberate for a long time within the steel hull of the wagon. Even through his thick, clammy overalls Julian could feel the trembling of Sandra's body beside him. Instinctively he wrapped his arms around her. She smiled and wriggled closer to him behind the cases sheltering them.

Time seemed to have no meaning now. They waited for something to happen, for movement onward, for discovery: there was nothing they could do but accept what was to come. The wagon was lit by small ventilation openings in the roof: pools of sunlight flickered from these points onto the steel walls and onto the jumbled heaps of cardboard and wooden containers on the floor, some empty, others with their contents strewn untidily about them. Julian could see close to him a hairbrush, a carton of sanitary pads, two legs of a broken chair, the bowl of a lamp, a white plastic phallus protruding from a box labelled 'FunFinger'.

From time to time they heard shouting outside, and feared the doors would be suddenly flung open. Had that errant Podder reported their presence in the wagon? Had a count revealed at least one orange body missing? But the shouting died away. Occasionally, too, there was a thud somewhere close outside, which made them jump and cling together more tightly, but again nothing further happened.

Julian's bladder was bursting, and he knew he must relieve himself soon, but did not dare to move. Sandra was beginning to wriggle too and he suspected she had the same problem. Just then there was a clash of sound from outside and the wagon rocked slightly. Another breathless wait, and then came a low rumbling noise and a feeling of vibration, and they realised they were moving. They were being hauled away from the freight portal, they were on the way out, back into the OuterWorld: they were escaping. They had done it!

Julian sought to rise. His bladder agonies had returned. "We're not out yet, luv," Sandra whispered in his ear. "There may'se still be checks."

"God, I have to go." He stood and pulled down the vile black overalls, and fumbled for his trouser fly beneath. His piss arched in a yellow stream over the box with the 'FunFinger'.

"S'easy for you men," grumbled Sandra, squatting in the same corner. Her urine flowed in a rivulet to join his.

The wagon rumbled on, gathering speed. The sounds of movement became steadier, the hiss of the wheels louder.

"I don't thinks we'll stop now," Sandra said, pulling up her orange trousers. He noticed for the first time how lovely she was, a shaft of light bringing out a reddish tint in her dark brown hair. He staggered over to her, feeling his way between the boxes, and kissed her. Frantically, he sought her body, and she, his. They conjoined. Nothing else then mattered, only the release.

The wagon train tore on.

17

Sandra and Julian —one of the lesser of their intimacies had been for him to tell her his name – slept, careless now of anything but sleep itself and the oblivion it brought. A sudden change in the tempo of their journey, however, transmitted through the steel vibrations of the wagon and the hiss of its wheels, at last brought them to consciousness. Sandra sat up and shook out her hair. It trailed over her breasts. She smiled at Julian, awakening and watching her, pulling the tresses of hair over her nipples as if in modesty.

"Welcome back, my'se soldier: my'se most upright, fine soldier."

Julian's waking pleasure, his full feeling of manhood, was shot across at once by a bolt of fear, knowing that the railway engine which drew them was slowing. A thought, known earlier but suppressed, surfaced in his mind. He should have asked before, for it was vital.

"Have you been chipped?" He saw her smile vanish to be replaced by a look of puzzlement, the hand that had reached for him returned to her side.

"Chipped? What yer mean?"

He reached for her bare right arm and saw what he had not wanted to find – the square mark where a chip plug had been inserted. She followed his eyes.

"Oh, that. We all's 'ad that. Innoculation, ain't it?"

"No. It's so they can track you; know where you are."

"Surely not. Hell, I'd 'eard of it but did'na believe it. None of us did."

"It's true, I'm afraid. Their Control Station will be able to see where you are."

"What's e'en away from t' bloody Pod?"

"Yes, especially that. You'll be a bright dot of light moving across one of their Screens."

"What about you's then?

"Mine was removed by a medico. It's how I was first able to get away."

"I don't feel nuthin' bad, like".

"That's good." Julian had been worried she would be in pain from noises in her head, or worse "Perhaps it's not working then."

"I do 'ave sum 'isses and buzzes in my ears, though. Like the wind blowin' or t' sea on't shore. Only just noticed 'em."

"Oh." He thought, so that's not so good, after all "You'll let me know if it gets worse."

"We's slowing right down," she said urgently. He could see the sudden worry in her eyes.

"I know. They might have found us on a Screen. Perhaps a signal has been sent out to stop the train."

"You'se must get out and make a run for't. They'se be looking for me: it'll give yer a chance."

"I'm not going without you." Julian said the words firmly. She had saved him in the warehouse and got him into the train. He wouldn't abandon her now.

He went to the door of the wagon and pushed at it. It moved, opening a crack. Thank God – any god – it was not locked. Why had he not checked before? Had all sense been driven out of him? He remembered Peter's words. They would kill him if they caught him. And probably Sandra too.

The wagon wheels were squealing now, the brakes applied, coming gradually to a halt. Julian had no idea how long the train was. He could see through the crack they were on a straight stretch of track, but he was unable to see the head of the train or its rear without leaning out. And he did not wish to do that. He had no idea who might be watching, from the train itself or by cameras fixed outside. When the train was finally at rest, or perhaps just before, then would be the time to make a move.

He decided all this in a flash, his brain, so long pummelled into apathy and disbelief by happenings so outrageous it was impossible to absorb them, was hardening at last into decision and action. It was Sandra who had achieved this for him; she had brought him back to life and given him renewed self-belief. At all costs, he had to look after her.

"Stand alongside me," he commanded, one hand grasping the edge of the sliding door. She came obediently to his side. When he judged the train was almost at a halt, he drew back the door with all his force. It rumbled open with a crash, disguised by the final shriek from the locked wheels. Grabbing Sandra by the arm, he leapt out. She fell with him onto a grassy bank that sloped steeply downward, at the foot of which was a deep ditch thick with rank vegetation. Into this ditch their two bodies tumbled together, the breath knocked from them, their hands and faces stung by nettles, their clothes muddied and wet from the trickle of water in the ditch.

"Ouch!" Sandra squealed, trying to free herself from the nettles and rise to her feet.

"Shhh," hissed Julian urgently. "Get down. Bend double like me."

He led her along the ditch, its canopy of green like a tunnel hiding them from above. After some fifty yards, the ditch bent to the right and they came to a brick arch under which they sheltered, crouching, their knees in the rivulets of water. They could now hear the sound of voices, which steadily came closer, with the stamping of boots and the swish of vegetation being pushed aside.

"Bloody gone and stung myself," one voice complained. "They ain't here."

"Must be. The wagon door's open. Someone's pissed inside. They've jumped for sure. Keep searching."

"Quick!" said Julian in Sandra's ear. He led her further away from the bridge to a point by an overhanging oak tree, its leaves golden in the late afternoon sunlight, where the ditch divided, one arm running aongside a hedgerow. They followed this. The hedge was thickly overgrown, the field beside it uncultivated and filled with tussocks of grass. Deep within the hedgerow, they stopped, panting. Julian raised his head cautiously and peered out through the tangle of branches. In the distance by the oak tree he could see the men still beating the first ditch. There were three of them; none was looking his way.

He peered to right and left. He had not felt so alive for ages, his blood throbbing in his veins, his eyes judging, his brain calculating. Sandra lay by his feet, awaiting his decision. He felt confidence restored to him. Whatever the perils, he was in control now. He decided to take a chance.

"Are you ready?" he asked Sandra. "We've got to make a dash for it. Keep by me."

He rose from the ditch, waiting for her to do the same beside him. Together they burst from the screen of the hedge, crossing the field at a run, zigzagging between the grass-topped mounds. No shouts came, no shots, no alarms. They couldn't have been seen. They reached the far hedgerow and found a broken gate, which Julian half-climbed, half-vaulted. He pulled Sandra over behind him. They lay on their fronts on the damp grass. Ahead of them was a lane, its tarred surface a mass of potholes with weeds growing through them.

After gathering their breath, they followed the lane until they came to the ruin of a barn: sheets of rusting corrugated iron were scattered about it. Enough of the barn still stood for them to find a refuge inside. They

191

collapsed upon the rotting remains of some sacks. Julian knew that at the best this would be a temporary refuge; they had to find a better shelter and they needed food and water. But how? He knew their hunters would renew the search for them soon. Sandra's chip would give them the information they required.

He went outside the barn and looked back across the bleak, abandoned landscape they had just crossed. In the far distance, he could see the line of the railway embankment and the silver wagons upon it. Even as he watched, they began to move. He blinked his eyes to be sure. Yes, the train was continuing its journey. But their hunters would still be somewhere around. Even now, reports of the position provided by Sandra's chip might be coming to them. He knew he and Sandra should move again at once: the hunt would not be held up for long.

He went back inside the barn. Sandra was sitting up. She had removed her orange top and the shirt she wore underneath, and was looking at her right arm. "It's this we 'ave t'get rid of," she said, "Can you's cut it out of me?"

"Hell, no. I haven't the skill or the equipment for anything like that."

"Then tis me who'll get us caught an' killed." She said this in an expressionless voice, looking at him directly.

"No. We'll find a way. We'll keep ahead of them and I'll get you to a doctor who could do the operation. We'll have to find someone who'll sympathise with us and be prepared to help."

"Then they'd be arrested too," said Sandra matter-of-factly, as if she was talking of something mundane, like milk going sour.

"Believe me. We'll find a way," Julian said stubbornly, but he did not know what that would be. Sandra was right. The chip would track them wherever they went, on the land or at sea, even in the air. But there had to be something he could do.

Julian looked at her, her bare breasts milky white in the gloom of the barn, her long tangled hair catching the sunlight filtering through the broken roof. And he loved her. She seemed to represent everything of normality that it was worth fighting for, for a life away from the grasping hands of SupaPodia and its controlling Eliti – forces that were increasingly destroying every decent impulse of humanity and the very naturalness of the earth.

"Wherever you go, I will go," he said. If they catch you, they will catch me. I will die alongside you."

"My hero," she said, and kissed him. But her face was still troubled, and he thought she must be in increasing pain from the noises in her head. He suspected too that she might be working out some other plan to try and protect him.

He was right.

* * *

They had left the barn and taken up a position in a dried out hollow ringed by trees some score of yards away. Julian had hoped this would give them a chance should the hunters come for them. SupaPodia's positioning system was unlikely to be so pinprick accurate that they could distinguish between the barn and the immediate countryside around. They would be likely to break into the barn first. He had propped up the collapsed door with a balk of timber and a corrugated iron sheet as if an attempt had been to barricade it. This subterfuge should at least give them a head start if they kept alert.

Julian, however, fell into a deep slumber. He was hungry and thirsty, as he knew Sandra was also, but there was nothing he could safely do until night fell. Then, they might hope to seek out some isolated house or farm where they could find food and drink. Sandra had nestled down beside him in the hollow, her dark head resting against his torn and dirtied lilac shirt. He had taken off his zip-up jacket, also muddied and crumpled, and wrapped it around her shoulders, pleased to see her eyes close straightaway as she drifted into sleep. And so he had slept too.

He woke with a start. Something was wrong. There was no pressure now against his body. Where was Sandra? She was not beside him. It was growing dark and the hollow was in deep shadow, but there was enough light left to see she was nowhere close by. He scrambled to his feet, his heart thudding. Perhaps she was relieving herself somewhere. But looking out from the copse he could not see her or hear her. There was only long silence. With the coming of night, the whole world seemed to have stilled. No bird sang, not even the gentlest breeze stirred the tree tops and the long grasses.

Then he found it. It was folded into his jacket which she had left on the ground: a pencilled scrawl on a scrap of lined paper she must have kept in her pocket. She had clearly had trouble writing it, perhaps pressed against her own knee, as the words, only lightly inscribed, were not in lines but rose and fell across the paper. In the half light he struggled to make them out.

'My luvly man, am sorry to go. I hav to do this. Mays see yer agin, if works, or else not but worth it to giv yrs a chance. Luv always. Sandra xxx'.

What did she mean? He sat with the note, his hands trembling, tears starting to his eyes. In the silence came a noise, a sweeping sound like a sudden wind rising, then a clatter like the call of an animal, far off, only this, he knew, was no animal but a train passing on the line nearby. In that moment, with sudden shock, he realised where Sandra had gone. The fear shook him so violently that he felt he would be sick, and he twisted and turned in the hollow at first, wondering what to do, before gathering up his jacket and setting out at a run, open and exposed in the field, towards the railway line. It was the way, he knew, Sandra would have gone.

When he reached the embankment, he climbed its side and came to the single track, which stretched away to right and left. The parallel rails were catching the very last of the light, gleaming silver either side of him before disappearing into darkness. Where was she? He feared. His heart was racing so much it must surely tip out of its cage.

Then he saw her, or what he thought was her, a dark shape coming towards him by the track, staggering and falling. Even as he looked, it fell again and this time did not rise. He bounded across the intervening darkness. "Sandra!…Sandra!…."

"You'se should nay have come."

He saw now what she had done, the open, crushed wound draining blood, the one arm left clasping the stump, the blood seeping between the fingers, her head bloody with one ear torn and dangling, the hair a tangled, dripping mass.

He caught her up in his arms and carried her to the grass strip at the embankment top where he lay her down. He knelt beside her, tearing at the jacket he carried, which would not rip, so he pulled off his shirt and tore that into strips instead, with which he tried to bind what was left of her upper arm to stop the blood flowing, but all he had in his hands was a soaked bundle of cloth and the blood still came. Pressure point? There would be a pressure point somewhere. But how? Where? He did not know. His arms were black with her blood in the darkness.

Her eyes were open, her lips parted in a smile. " 'S funny. I thoughts I could do it and stops the blood. Come back to yer armless, chipless. And we'se could go on." Her face collapsed. "But it wouldn't work. The train caught my 'ead too."

"Shhh, my love. Be quiet now. Are you in pain?"

"No. Funny, ain't it. I's feel I'm floating and you'se somewhere beneath me."

All he could do was wrap his arms about her and hold her as tight as he could, hoping by that to stop the life blood that was draining from her. She did not try to speak now and he hoped that at least he was comforting her. Then her body heaved suddenly as if to throw him off, but he clung on and she fell back, and there was a long gargling sound in her throat and she died. In that very moment of her death there came a breath of wind on his cheeks, which stirred as well the bloodied grass stems where her head lay. He said through his tears, "Good bye, my love. I thank you." And later when he had laid her body at the foot of the embankment, and covered it with grasses and leaves from the bushes, he said. "I have to go from you now. I will never forget you or what you did for me. I will love you for ever."

A train was coming; he had heard the rails begin to rattle. He left her and pushed his way across the blackened countryside, his body doubled up with grief. Behind him – although he did not know this – the train, of one carriage only, stopped, and men, some of them from the Guard, got out. They found her where he had laid her, and they wrapped her up to hide her wounds and bore her most carefully onto the train. The person they really sought, however, had gone.

There was no easy way for SupaPodia's Guard to keep track of Julian now. This was the sacrifice Sandra had made for him.

18

Joshua Pomeroy-Collyer lay in bed staring at the information being projected from one of SupaPodia International's news feeds onto the ceiling above him. He frowned. The High Director was disturbed to learn of the number of revolts that had been breaking out against the benign influence of his organisation. Podders were inexplicably growing ungrateful of the great benefits bestowed upon them. Worse, it seemed they were being increasingly incited by the OuterWorlders to protest against some imaginary condition or other in SupaPodia. The OuterWorlders, of course, would employ every tactic to try and get themselves inside the SupaPods and the present Podders ejected. That had to be the main reason behind these small rebellions – envy of the beneficence bestowed by SupaPodia. Oh, if only there was room for everyone! It would take many centuries yet to fulfil that dream.

Joshua turned to Lucinda beside him. Her head was half buried under the pale yellow damask sheets against the morning light, her long black hair spread out like a pool of ink. She was the latest in the line of Eliti supamodels who were privileged to share his bed. Lucinda was a little different from most. She came with a clear intelligence, having gained a doctorate in racist and sexist literature from the now defunct OxCam University before its recent re-creation as part of Goring SupaPod 33, bored deep under the bed of the River Thames.

"Darling," he breathed to her, so her fine olive-skinned head and dark-tipped breasts emerged slowly from beneath the sheets. "What am I to do about all these annoying troubles that are occurring in parts of SupaPodia?"

"Do?" said Lucinda in her husky voice. "Find out who is responsible and shoot them!"

She realised this was not the response expected of an educated diversifier committed to universal equity and beneficence. But she was tired. Joshua's fumbling and inadequate attentions to her body last night had meant only a modest number of hours before the light of a new day had awoken the Inkwelo Mountain palace. The horns had sounded out, the beautiful people in their flowing, coloured silk assembled in the various stone-paved courts; golden balls tossed about according to custom; bread, wine, and fruits served by black servants, their oiled skin glistening under the rising sun….while all Lucinda wished for was peace in order to sleep on. Oh, rather for her the quiet solitude of her own Cape estates than the noisy, rollicking jabber of this palace, which Joshua seemed not to hear other than as a necessary background, rather as the sea surges or the wind blows.

"I couldn't do that," chuckled Joshua, accepting that Lucinda's comment had been jocular rather than serious. "It would have to pass SupaPodia's ruling council, anyhow, and they would be unlikely to agree to summary executions. You must remember, my darling…" – he swooped suddenly to outline each of Lucinda's pert nipples with his tongue before nuzzling his face between her breasts: "you are so very beautiful," he murmured, although the words were largely lost in those muffling depths – "….you must remember, SupaPodia is all about enlightenment and progress, not repression and punishment."

"Of course," said Lucinda, her earlier irritation replaced by the need for placid agreement. She knew that in time she would be replaced. She did not wish that to happen too soon, however. She thought of the island in the Indian Ocean she hoped to acquire, where eventually she would be able to entertain her friends and share things of the mind as much as of the body. At this moment, though, how her flesh ached for the shaft of a virile man.

She left the bed and padded to the shuttered window, which she pushed open, feeling the heat of the day on her already fevered skin. She looked out into the grassed jacaranda court where the servants spent their leisure. As she had hoped, two were already copulating beneath the trees, his black penis huge against her white thighs. Another couple – two maids by the look of them – were pleasuring each other against the far wall. Such a garden of earthly pleasures should be forbidden, she knew. It was unseemly, improper, within the palace of the High Director. But, as with so many other things, Joshua was unaware of it.

She came back to the bed aroused enough to convince him that it was his ardours which had excited her. So, for the moment, the pretence continued.

19

Julian was exhausted, without sleep, without food, only a mouthful or two of water from the grimy bottle of the lorry driver who had brought him here. He knew he had been lucky to be picked up at all. The steam lorry, rattling and belching smoke, had come up the potholed highway as he had waited in the night, hoping for deliverance. That deliverance had come when the grizzled driver stopped at the sight of him tottering in the black road and taken him on board, with no apparent curiosity, no questions asked, other than a conversational "going far?"

"As far as you are going," he had answered, forgetting for the moment the address he had been given by Peter and only wanting to separate himself from the fatal railway line where poor Sandra had bled to death for him. He was sure SupaPodia would be looking for him, but now they would be hunting blind. Would they – could they – set up roadblocks, organise patrols to seek him out? He did not know what forces they controlled in the OuterWorld. There, he remembered, the ordinary police were as run down as everything else, and were very few on the ground, more often than not besieged within their own stations, scared to venture out into the most crime-infested streets and housing estates. He couldn't see them acting as agents for SupaPodia.

The SupaPodia Guard, he thought, only operated in the immediate vicinity of their Control Stations, as he had witnessed himself. So, the further he got away from a SupaPod, he reasoned, the safer he would be. He had no idea what network of spies and informers SupaPodia might employ in the OuterWorld. It would be best, therefore, to keep as low a profile as possible until he made the contact Peter had so earnestly put to him. He would deny he had ever been in a SupaPod, let alone on its staff. He would need to find a change of clothing, though, as soon as he could, or otherwise his scruffy, lilac appearance would create suspicion.

SupaPodia did have its fleet of helidrones that could deliver the Guard speedily to any trouble spot, as their trains could do also. Even as Julian sat in the darkness of the lorry, wedged between two dustbins slopping with the intestines of pigs (or so the driver had told him), he heard the roar of engines somewhere above them in the night, perhaps attracted by the lorry's feeble lights, but no machine landed to demand who they were and where they were heading.

In the first light of dawn, the driver had put him down at the edge of a town, which lay in a valley enfolded by high downland. Revealed now in daylight, his appearance, with his dirtied lilac jacket hanging open showing he was shirtless beneath, must have looked very odd, but the driver made no comment. Julian hurriedly zipped up the stained jacket against the morning chill.

He walked into the main street of the town. A few people were about, some wheeling handcarts, others picking glass off a pavement from a broken shop window, a dog or two, a skeletal ginger cat, a small child, naked below his grubby tee-shirt, looking out along the street as if waiting for Father Christmas. Even as Julian watched, he squatted and delivered a squirt of faeces into the gutter. Then he cried, and a stab of such pity pierced Julian's chest that he knew he would have cried too if he had not forced himself to tread steadfastly away. As he had feared, in his dirtied and torn lilac-coloured garb he attracted some curious stares.

He came to a river, where some terraced houses backed onto the river, their gardens overgrown, the fences fallen. In one garden, closest to the road, a washing line drooped between two leafless trees, and on it hung the answer to this first of Julian's problems – some freshly-laundered clothes. Could he beg these off their owner? No, unlikely. Dare he then take them, as his need was so great?

He pushed through the broken fence, and seized a white shirt, a pair of jeans, a nightdress, and some underwear, dragging them from their wooden pegs. As he did so, there came a woman's shriek from the house, and she appeared in the garden, naked, hopping on bare feet, breasts flopping, her mouth wide open yelling curses at him. But he was gone, clutching his haul and running over the river bridge.

"Come back, you bastard!" "Stop him!" he heard behind him, but no one did so. The only people on the bridge, a man holding a young girl by the hand, moved rapidly to the other side as he passed. He thought, theft is probably as common now as winter rain and broken sewers. He saw two dead rats in the road, and swung away from them in front of a battered car with boxes on its roof rack, which blasted its horn at him.

Under the cover of a brick wall running around what looked like a disused office block, he tried on his new clothing. They clearly had been worn by the woman who had yelled at him, for they were too small for him. He managed to pull on the shirt – or was it a blouse? – although he could not button it up. He took off his trousers, but was unable to force the jeans over his thighs, so discarded them, deciding instead to rub dirt from a spilling waste bin over his lilac trousers to disguise their colour. Before putting them back on, he took off his foul underpants and pulled on the woman's knickers, relieved to find she must have a big backside for they fitted him and his male apparatus snugly enough. He put on his lilac zip-up jacket, which, despite its dirtied appearance was still distinctive by its style and colour, yet it was the only outer garment he possessed. The last item he had stolen, a blue woollen nightdress, he bunched up and draped over his shoulders like a shawl. It looked peculiar, he knew, but it did at least partly hide the jacket. He knew from those grim, poverty-stricken days before he had entered the SupaPod that others, scraping together whatever clothes they could find, would be as equally bizarrely dressed as he was now, and he was unlikely to stand out except as another beggar tramping the highways.

It was the best he could do, anyhow, and like this he now had to seek out Adrestia of Nemesis at the White Swan in Canterbury. He was relieved to find that, despite all he had gone through and his exhaustion, he recalled Peter's instructions. He committed them again to his memory, repeating them several times in his head, just to make sure he did not lose them now.

Having seen to his clothes and confirmed his purpose, his next big problem was to find sustenance, without which it would be impossible to attempt the journey to Canterbury, in whichever direction that city lay – and he did not even know where he was now. That last problem, at least, was solved straightaway by a direct question to the first person he met on emerging onto the road again, an elderly man wrapped, despite the sunny morning, in a thick black coat and with a peaked baseball cap on his head. A small white terrier he held on a lead was sniffing frantically at something rotting beneath a hedge.

"Dorking, mate. Where's it you come from then?"

Julian ignored the question as he ignored the man's curious look. "Thanks," he muttered and shuffled off. His feet were hurting him. He was wearing his leather boots, but he realised now the soles were only thin, suitable more for indoors than outside; typical SupaPodia tat, he thought angrily. His mind swept back to the SupaPod from which he had escaped and the trail of death he had passed along. There was Peter, who had started him on the journey. He was dead, and Sandra too now, their blood flowing out from them like crimsoned water. And Marion – it was with shock he remembered her – she had been hurtled into oblivion, reduced from sensate flesh to smashed pulp, the remnants of her body now littered in some obscene deep pit.

Further on, Julian came to another bridge over the river, where the town ended and the open countryside began. A steep-sided hill rose above the river like a cliff. Julian stood looking up at it. In the piercing clear light of the autumn morning, the bare white chalk that seamed its green flanks hurt his eyes. Casting his gaze down, he made out at the foot of the hill what seemed to have been a small hotel. A sign still hung at an angle from a metal post, but he was unable to make out its wording. The building was fenced off, its broken roof showing signs of a recent fire and the white walls beneath were scorched black. He pushed at a metal gate in the fencing, expecting it to be locked, but to his surprise it opened. A sign in red letters – 'Keep Out' – lay on the rubbish-strewn path beyond.

At the back of the building, which he reached by passing between a burnt-out car and two rusting skips overflowing with rubble and smashed wood, he found someone had been here ahead of him, because a window had been forced open, its glass smashed. With difficulty he crawled through it, and found himself in a room that must have been a kitchen, because it was surrounded by fitted cabinets. He opened one of them and was knocked back by the smell from inside. Beside a brown furry mess, writhing with maggots, were some cans of soup and one of sardines. He picked these out carefully and placed them on a counter top that stank with the green mouldering contents of several jugs. He found more sealed cans in other cabinets and added them to his growing pile.

Searching frantically in a drawer, he found some cutlery, a fork, a wooden spoon, and a very worn, rusting knife. Deeper in the drawer was a can opener. It was rusty too, but he hoped it might still work. While he was casting around for something in which he could carry his haul, there was a sudden crash and the door flew open. A man, bare-chested wearing only a pair of underpants, stood there swaying, a bottle in one hand.

"Ah, I thought so. A thief! Wanna drink, thief?"

Julian put down the knife he had clenched in his fist, of which the man had seemed unaware, and followed him down a passage into what may have once been a bar or a lounge. Broken bottles were everywhere, glass scattered over the remaining strips of a carpet, shattered light fittings fallen to the floor. In a corner, lying on a rug, was a woman in a dirty pink dress, her knees raised so Julian could see she was wearing nothing underneath. She was swigging from a bottle that seemed to be of gin or perhaps vodka.

"Wanna drink? Wanna fuck?" the man said. "Found a stache of booze here, they'd all missed. Help yourself." He indicated some bottles spilling from a broken box.

"I'll take some with me, if I may," said Julian, his words not seeming to belong to him. He thought, I must get out of here. There may be others. I could be trapped.

" 'Ave a drink with us first, then take what you want. Here, put it in this." He indicated what Julian had been looking for – a sack on the floor, made of some fibre or other, but with plastic handles. When Julian bent to pick it up, a furry creature rushed out over his arms, and he let out a cry of horror. The man and woman laughed.

"Worse than that 'ere, mate. Now, what's your poison?"

"Is there a beer?"

The man leant forward to examine the bottles, tottering so he nearly fell. His underpants were stained, his genitals half-exposed. Julian felt sick.

" 'Arvey's fucking Ale, its says. Will that do yer?"

"Yes, thanks."

"Posh, ain't yer. Ever had a posh bloke, Lizzie?"

The woman on the floor guffawed. "No never. Out of me class."

"Now's your chance if… What's your name, mate?"

"Mike," Julian said quickly, plucking the name from mid air.

"If Mike wants you. Feel the urge, Mike?"

"No, thank you. No offence."

The woman giggled. "You sure?" She pulled her dress right up while using the bottle she was holding in the way of a phallus.

"Quite sure."

"Pity. You men, got no lead in your cocks. Not good for a girl"

Julian looked away from the offensive sight, his stomach churning. Seeing the man making a move towards the woman while pulling down the front of his pants, he hastened from the room, carrying the beer and the sack with him into the kitchen. Hearing the shouts, the grunts, and the giggles that were now coming, he hastily stowed away as much of his loot as he thought he could carry, heaved the sack out of the window, and followed it in a headlong fall. As he escaped around the building, he brushed against two other scantily-clad women and a greasy, long-haired lout who must have been coming to join the party. How lucky he had been then to get in and out as he had. At least he had some food and drink now. With that, perhaps he would survive.

An hour later, Julian stood on the summit of the hill. He had borne the sack up the steep green slope, gasping for breathe, realising how unfit he had grown in the confined tunnels of the SupaPod. He took in great breaths of air to steady his reeling senses. Once he reached the woods that crowned the summit, he went a little way into their shade. The heavy sack he flung down beside him; one of its plastic handles had pulled off and some of its contents, he realised, might have tumbled out during his climb. Still there were some tins left. He realised he was too tired to eat, even to drink. He settled back on the woodland floor, his head amidst a clump of dying bracken, and he slept.

When he awoke, the sun was high in the sky. He felt marvellously refreshed. Peering out from the trees, he saw the bare slopes of the hill were empty of life. Tumultuous clouds sailed high overhead, their edges puffed out like pillows. Between them, the deep blue fell away into infinite distances. As he stood looking, he became aware of a staining of the nearer clouds as they drifted like swollen swans above him. A column of grey smoke was rising and spreading from the land below. He could not be sure, but it was likely the ruined hotel he had left behind him was burning.

The tin opener worked at the second attempt. He clawed open the half-cut lid of a can of mushroom soup and poured its contents into his hands, licking it up with his tongue. Then he twisted the key of a tin of corned beef and levered out the pressed mass of meat and fat with the help of a twig, consuming it in two or three bites. Furiously thirsty now, he knocked off the top of the bottle of ale and slurped it down, using his teeth as a filter in case of any slivers of glass, but found none. 'Harvey's Ale' was strong. He felt light-headed now.

He repacked the sack with as many tins as he felt he could carry given its broken handle, disposed of the rest in the undergrowth, and continued his journey. In a valley below, covered by woodland, he found what he was seeking – a small stream with brown-coloured water. Careless of the danger of contamination, he sucked water out of his cupped hands until he had drunk his fill. Then, by noting the position of the sun from a clearing in the trees, he took a path towards what he hoped was the east, the direction – if his memory of the geography of the south-east of England still served him well – where the city of Canterbury could be found.

* * *

Julian finished the last of his food on the third day of his journey from Dorking. His stomach was bad, probably on account of the water he had drunk from streams. On one occasion he had swilled from a broken water main gushing unattended in a village street, filling as well two plastic bottles he had picked out of a rubbish bin. He had kept away from people as much as he could, still fearing a call would have been put out to look for him, and that someone, alerted by whatever means were still possible, would turn him in.

On one occasion, three helidrones had flown low over him, so low he had seen the black-helmeted pilots looking out of their bubble-sided cockpits, and he had hidden for the best part of a day in the heart of a wood. Nothing, however, had happened, and he came out of his hiding and continued his journey. He was following the old track running beneath the North Downs known as the Pilgrims Way, although whether any of the old-time pilgrims had ever followed it was unlikely. They were much more likely to have been on the paved roads to the north than on this track at the base of the hills, often deep in mud and making detours at times into the adjacent fields.

When Julian realised how his walking amongst the mud and fallen trees and spreads of sharp flints was affecting his thinly-soled boots – one sole had ripped up at the toe and flapped open like a hinge – he decided to risk greater exposure and take to the lanes that led north across the Downs, hoping to get onto the main highway that he remembered ran straight towards Canterbury. He needed also to find more food.

He came to an isolated cottage and waited amongst the brushwood behind it until he saw the woman who lived there leave with her two children, pedalling away on an antiquated bicycle, with the infants propped up in baskets at front and rear. By now, his mind was cauterised against all normal feelings, and he managed to break down the back door by kicking at it, which action tore the sole completely from his boot. In the lady's larder he found bread and some fresh beef on a saucer, and tins of pilchards, and a packet of biscuits labelled 'for SupaPodia consumption only'. Because of the latter, he did not feel quite so bad stealing these things. He also found, behind the kitchen door, a pair of good rubber boots, of a size that fitted him and must have been owned by a man who lived there too. He pushed his feet into them gratefully. He might have looked for more clothes but by now was growing fearful of discovery, and he set off at a half-run with his haul.

The sunshine with which he had begun his journey changed to a cold, penetrating rain, and he was grateful of the shawl that he had fashioned from the nightgown. Now, by tearing it at the neck and slipping it over his shoulders, he was able to hang it about him like a cloak.

Like this, and with several more stops to beg or steal food, he came at last to a great concrete highway that curved away from him through the green countryside, its two double lines of carriageways blocked in places with heaps of earth and broken machinery. As he plodded along in the direction of the rising sun, he came across fallen bridges – grotesque piles of twisted metal and shattered concrete slabs, which he had to climb over. Others were doing the same, in both directions, some carrying bicycles on their shoulders, one with a small motor bike that fell over and spilt fuel, so that it burst into a sudden bright ball of fire.

Drunks and vagabonds preyed upon the road, and he joined up with a group of other men and women going the same way as he for protection. At one point, they had a running fight with some desperate raiders, waving clubs, who poured down an embankment at them. Julian, who now carried an iron bar he had pulled from a wrecked tractor, beat down one young man who ran at him, leaving him screaming on the grey concrete. Another, trying to escape, he chopped the legs from with his bar, finishing him with a blow that shattered his skull. For these acts, he gained an immediate status with the group, and found himself being given food without having to ask for it. That night, as they sheltered under the surviving arch of a bridge, a woman came to him, and he took her without thought within the pulsing blackness, lifting her clothing and heaving himself upon her as a stag might take a hind. The next day, after he had decided once more to branch out on his own, she tried to follow him, a distant figure behind him, dressed in a long ragged skirt, but he sent her away with a wave of his hand. When he looked again, she had gone.

Two days later, following a wide trunk road which was busy with traffic – gas and coal-driven lorries, pedal trucks, cyclists, horse-drawn wagons, even some modern heavy vehicles powered by electricity, each marked with the SupaPodia logo of 'SP' intersected by a slanting spearhead – Julian came to the top of a hill, and pushing himself amongst trees away from the crowded road, saw ahead of him across a blur of countryside the shining grey-white towers of a great church, which he knew must be the cathedral of Canterbury. He stayed here that night, drinking from a well he found which still gushed amongst broken stones. In the morning light, after a meal of crushed biscuits and an oily pilchard, washed down with water, he removed all his clothing in a grassy space amongst the trees and rubbed himself down with the remaining rags from his lilac shirt. He re-dressed himself as well he could in his ill-fitting clothes, putting on the black rubber boots and stamping over to the well where he bathed his head, rubbing the water into his hair and his sprouting beard. Refreshed, he went back to the road and set out on the last lap of his journey.

After only a mile or so, while passing between an abandoned petrol garage and a shuttered food store, its sides bedaubed with strident graffiti – 'Pods for the People'; 'Fight Poverty, Build more SupaPods' – a man, emerging from a side street, suddenly confronted him. He wore grey trousers and a grey zipped jacket, and his wide-peaked baseball cap bore the slogan, 'I ♥ Pods'. So abruptly did the man come up to him that Julian feared he wanted to assault or rob him, and he stepped back, dropping the bundle he had made of his sack, his fists raised, ready to defend himself.

"Julian?" The man said. "You are Julian, aren't you?"

"Who are you? Why do you ask?"

"We were told you might be coming. I've been watching out for you."

"How would you know who I am and what I'm doing?"

"We know," the man said with a touch of smugness, and Julian feared the worst: he was being intercepted by some agent of SupaPodia.

"Get away from me!" Julian's fear was now replaced by anger. Over the past days, he had learnt well the art of survival. He had turned into a hard and desperate man. He had killed and was prepared to kill again.

He turned and walked hurriedly away, then broke into a run. He crossed the road, dodging between the traffic, forcing a pedal truck to swerve and upset its load. Amongst the mayhem caused, with street urchins rushing forward to loot the spilled goods, Julian ran down a side road. Turning his head, he was alarmed to see the man was still close behind him, running easily. Julian's breath was already coming in gasps.

"Come back!" the man yelled. "I have a message for you."

Julian turned into another street, lined by tall buildings with washing lines stretched overhead between grey, grit-panelled balconies. Grubby children were kicking a football about. The street was a cul-de-sac ending in a high brick wall. Julian turned at bay. The man came up to him, his hands raised in a gesture of peace.

"Just listen to me." He came close. "Hear me now. It is urgent. You must *not* go to the White Swan."

The words shook Julian. The White Swan formed part of the instructions he had been given by Peter.

"Who are you?" Julian asked again. He suspected this man was not a friend, but could be leading him into a trap.

"It does not matter who I am or who I work for. I understand your caution, but a friend of yours has asked me to find you, and that is what I have done."

"You talk in riddles. Give me some facts."

"The facts are that the White Swan has been broken. It is not safe now. I will not say any more, but the names you have been given still flourish. They will contact you."

"Contact me where?" Julian was determined he would not reveal anything Peter had told him. This man could well be trying to get the information from him.

"I will take you to a place. You must trust me?"

"How can I trust you? I don't know who you are."

"We have a mutual friend."

"How can that be? Who is he?"

Julian felt he should not be talking but trying to escape, bursting past this man who clearly knew so much about him. His information could only have come from SupaPodia's Security Services. They must have been following him all this time.

"It is not a he, but a she. Her name is Christine, although you will know her as Tina."

Julian's world dissolved, then slowly took form again. How could this be?

"You must trust me," the man repeated, anxiety written large on his face, which, as Julian's senses returned, he found reassuring. This man was either a consummate actor or he was being entirely honest.

"After all," the man continued. "What alternative do you have?"

And that was true.

20

Tina stirred in her narrow bed. A breath of air in the small stone room had wakened her. She saw the flickering candle flame in the greyness by the shuttered window. The candle moved, lifted upwards. The cowled figure who held it came to the bed.

"Sister Christine," she said softly. "The time is for prayer."

Tina slid from bed, sluiced her face with water, let the habit held out for her fall over her head, smoothed her short-cut hair with her fingers, and followed the other nun from the room. Down the dark passage they walked, their way lit at intervals by narrow windows through which the light of the new day was already filtering, like fingers pushing through prison bars.

In the Church, they joined the line of other nuns, and on silent, slippered feet walked to the Chapel of St. Thomas, where they knelt in prayer. Outside, a blustering, high wind boomed on the stone, filling the flickering spaces within with a sense of dread, that what was without might yet penetrate this cloistered place.

Sister Christine rose to read from the Bible. She wore the simple grey habit and white linen cap of a novice, having been received here less than two weeks ago.

"For thou hast been a defence for the helpless, a defence for the needy in his distress, a refuge from the storm, a shade from the heat; for the breath of the ruthless is like a rain storm against a wall."

She paused, looking at the shadows playing across the image of St. Thomas beyond the hanging cross made of swords.

"The branch of the terrible ones shall be brought low. The Lord God will wipe away tears from all faces; and the rebuke of his people shall he take away from all the earth: for the Lord hath spoken it."

She added now her own chosen text, as the novices were encouraged to do.

> *"In his hand are the deep places of the earth: the strength of the hills is his also. The sea is his, and he made it: and his hands formed the dry land. O come let us worship and bow down: let us kneel before the Lord our maker."*

After the service, Sister Alice told her she had read well. "The storm has blown out, but there are trees down in the close. The men will have a job cutting them up and taking them away."

Tina's face was fallen, her eyes on the stone floor.

"What is wrong, my dear?"

"Has there been no message?"

"I know only from my nephew that he is out. The place is in an uproar. Lives have been lost."

"Is he safe?"

"We do not know. Yet he will come, as he has been instructed, if God is willing."

"We must warn him."

"I shall see what I can do, but these affairs are not ours that we should be involved."

"They are mine because of who I am."

"Then, my dear, you should not be within these walls."

21

Many Eliti enjoyed seeing the Podders in the OuterWorld. It was good, they thought, to bring Podders out from time to time into the unrestricted fresh air, providing they were suitably controlled. Under escort, usually travelling in SupaPodia charabancs, they came from their SupaPods to attend events such as concerts of wild music (so-termed) and sporting events, of which football was by far the most popular. The UK Podders produced teams that could match any that still played in the OW, although most of the Leagues there had by now been discontinued. Generally, however, they were pitted against teams from the Overseas SupaPods, who were airlifted in by one of SupaPodia's fleet of commercial air ships.

A match of Brazilian SupaPodders was in process against one from the Cuckmere SupaPod No.58. It was taking place at a stadium on the flats below Lewes. This town on its high hill had been acquired years ago by Lord Grimscott, who, with Lord Rand, had been one of the original founders of UK SupaPodia. He had had it flattened and cleared, and had built a great house on top of the hill, incorporating the old castle buildings. The slopes of the surrounding hills had been planted with vines, the fruits of which had produced a label Grimscott was happy to export to fellow Eliti around the world. It had been his personal initiative, and some at least of his own money, that had led to the stadium being built beside the River Ouse. Grimscott had a weakness for football, which was inherited by his children, Priscilla and Nigel. After their father's death, they had established these regular contests between teams of Podders. At this present match, they were seated in the Founder's Box. Brazil were winning 3-1.

As Brazil were celebrating their third goal in a running, tumbling heap of green and yellow-clad players, there came a sudden sharp, staccato sound, repeated again and again, which many of the spectators around the stadium thought at first was from firecrackers released to celebrate the goal. Those nearest the playing surface, however, saw a line of men, dressed in black, at the edge of the pitch firing automatic weapons – the old type that projected steel-tipped bullets – at the Founder's Box. The heads of Priscilla and Nigel, and their guests either side, disappeared in a trice, shot down like coconuts in a shy. Blood spattered the lilac-covered backdrop to the Box. Some spectators nearby turned to try and help, while others fled backwards through the seats in panic, the shooting continuing all the while; more bodies fell, some tumbling down the aisles or caught up writhing on the barriers and guard rails.

There was no Militia Guard at the game, only unarmed attendants whose job it was to control the crowds. Many of these nearest the shooting were targeted by their SupaPodia uniforms. From the control room of the stadium, a message was flashed to the nearest Guard control station. By the time their manned helidrones began landing on the pitch, the assailants had fled, leaving heaps of the dead and the dying behind – some 107 killed, it was determined and 489 injured, many by crushing. Amongst them were Priscilla and Nigel, their friends and entourage. The Grimscott family was extinguished.

Worse was to follow. As the crowds streamed out over the stadium park by the river, desperate to get away, some saw smoke begin to arise above the castle mansion on the hill, darkening the sky, and then the flames appeared, red and lurid, like boiling blood. All along the line of the hill the flames burnt, until the day was like night under a cauldron of fire, and the vines shrivelled on their terraces and the earth was covered inches deep in ash. Ash was reported falling as far away as Selsey Bill and the Isle of Grain, and even on the streets of central London, not that it was noticed much there as a pall of smoke and soot hung over the former capital now for much of the year.

SupaPodia UK's Security Services attributed these outrages to a group called Nemesis, the reported aim of whom was the overthrow of SupaPodia International and the reinstatement of the paramountcy of the OuterWorld in human affairs, at first locally, then eventually globally. This was the largest, most blatant and most deadly of Nemesis's terrorist operations to date. The organisation was tracked down to Canterbury, where the well-known inn, the White Swan – said to be a meeting place of the terrorists – was raided. No terrorists, however, were captured. Nemesis, and its shadowy leader – reported to go under the name of Adrestia (whether man or woman, unknown) – for the present lived on. However, SupaPodia had every hope of extinguishing these murderous traitors very soon. OuterWorlders were warned that anyone assisting Nemesis, either directly or by any association whatsoever, did so at the peril of their own lives.

The High Director read the report of the latest attack in SupaPodia UK while seated on his golden toilet throne in the alabaster-lined bathroom of his private rooms. Reports could come to him wherever he moved within his Inkwelo palace, and even, if he wished within his Amajuba rotunda, although he seldom called for them there; he was determined to keep the colonnaded rotunda as his ultimate retreat and place of enduring inner peace. Communications were projected onto whatever surfaces he selected to receive them: these could be walls or floors or table tops, or, as here, the side of the porphyry bath in which Lucinda was lying beneath a deep white tide of skin cleansing foam.

There were too many reports coming now of unrest, from all quarters – or so it seemed – of SupaPodia International's growing empire. He had heard of resistance to a SupaPod in Fiji and clamour as well for what were termed 'better conditions' in the SupaPods in Australia: one at Darwin had been calling for more fresh-air activities, including an area for al fresco love-making, without which, it was said, the SupaPod populations might dwindle. There was all this sort of nonsense going on, while in other parts of the globe, including here in South Africa and, of course, in the old Britain, people were clamouring to *get into* SupaPods, not seeking to modify them. As regards actually trying to destroy them, what was happening in Britain, his own country of origin, was unbelievable. Why should it be? Why did most of the violence seem to be happening there, and not in places with more volatile populations, such as Russia perhaps, or the Far East, or even in Germany, noted for its overly aggressive outflows in the not too distant past? But those areas appeared to remain very quiescent and relatively content.

Joshua worked the cleansing jets of the golden throne, then rose and stepped away. He was about to walk over to speak to Lucinda in the bath, and perhaps give her some of the attentions they had used to share but which had been lacking of late, when another report, to which he was alerted by a pinging in his ears, appeared against the background of the white Turkish cotton of a towel hanging on the door.

He read:

'For the urgent attention of High Director and Executive Committee, SupaPodia International'

'GLACIER FLOODING DANGER: Monitoring by SupaPodia Climate Research indicates that a Great Ice Sheet in Antarctica could be about to collapse entirely. URGENT. Sea levels could rise significantly WITH IMMEDIATE EFFECT.'

'SPCR recommend that no more SupaPods be built in coastal or river environments until further notice. All future underground accommodation silos should be drilled on upland sites only. Consideration should be given to immediate EVACUATION of existing SupaPods in danger areas, as deemed necessary.'

Damn it! thought Joshua. We can't have that. We haven't built some 65% of our SupaPods at the edge of the sea in order to abandon them now. There must be something that can be done. He thought awhile. But what? Panic began to stir in his stomach, jumping along his limbs, into his toes and his finger tips. What the hell can we do? We can't pump the water out. We can't be like Canute wishing the tide to retreat? No, it *won't* happen. This is just alarmist claptrap from the SPCR. It's high time they were abolished, anyhow. Their next report has to be much more hopeful or I'll get rid of them. Fuck them. I *will* abolish them. No discussion. I'll tell the Committee this is fake news. They'll be sympathetic. After all, most of them have big estates on the land we would have to drill for new SupaPods. It would take an age, anyhow. No one wants that to happen…so it *won't*.

He switched off the message. Without its contamination, the Turkish cotton now gleamed freshly white and purified. He took the towel over to Lucinda and bid her to rise. She did so, the water draining from her fine tanned skin. He wrapped her in the towel and carried her back to the bed. He had not felt so aroused for months. Perhaps he should receive more messages about pending catastrophes. As he rolled onto Lucinda, hearing her small squeals of anticipation, he realised catastrophes were an aphrodisiac.

Roll on Armageddon, he thought. Armageddon will never happen. He remembered the old joke. If it does, "I'm a-gettin' out of here."

But where would he go? It is me who is responsible. It is me whom they will crucify.

The thought flattened him, leaving a most disappointed Lucinda beneath him.

22

"How did you know where I was?" Julian asked Tina.

He was amazed to see her again, here in the shaded cloister where the shadows cast by the portico columns lay in dark stripes across the worn flagstones. He had scarcely recognised her at first. She had seemed swallowed up by the grey habit, her face a small white oval beneath the headdress. He thought she looked pale and strained, but her face still held that calm look of peace he had become accustomed to, lit now by a flash of welcome in her eyes. She sat him down on a seat beside her, her hands resting in her lap.

"I had heard from the SupaPod. I still have many sources there, you see, who wish to help me."

"Not Stanley, I hope."

"No, not him. Certainly not. I could not work for him any longer. If he had not commanded me to leave, I would have done so, anyway."

"Would they have allowed you to go just like that?" Julian thought of his own painful journey of escape and the punishments he had had to endure.

"Oh yes."

"Because of who you are, I suppose?"

"Yes, because of that and because they know I have no master but Christ."

"They must have been pleased by your departure then."

"Why do you say that?"

"Because you were probably seen as a focus of resentment amongst the Podders."

She sounded quite cross. "That was never my purpose! I thought it my mission to spread the good news of our Lord, who rules all things and all people, whatever their status and their place."

"Quite." Julian thought it best to say no more. Then a thought.

"You have warned me, I understand, not to go to the White Swan."

"That is right."

"If they – that is, the secret intelligence units of SupaPodia, however they are known – if they suspect I might go to the White Swan, which is under their scrutiny, to meet up with whoever – I only have a codename – then why will they not be watching you as well; indeed might have seen me coming *here*?"

He felt a sudden fear at his own words. Everything had been happening so fast, after all the perils he had survived and Sandra's terrible sacrifice for him, his mind was quite turned upside down once more; there had been no time to think anything through.

She laid a hand on his arm. "Because they do not know where you are. They do not know where you have headed. I have to confess to misleading them. I told Stanley that you and Peter had been planning to go to Lincoln to meet a contact there."

"Lincoln! Why on earth that place?"

"Oh dear." She crossed herself. "The Lord forgive me. I told them I had heard Peter say he had friends there. It was where he had used to live, you see."

"I hope that doesn't lead then to a witch hunt amongst the eastern SupaPods."

"I hope so too. But I had to tell them something, or else they would have been suspicious of me – or rather more suspicious – than they were. All they really wanted, though, was not to have to worry about me any more."

"Stanley never asked you then if Peter had ever divulged anything to you? He probably knew you had spoken with him."

"No, he didn't." She looked down as if feeling shame. "I think he trusted my innocence."

"You know Peter was killed, don't you?

"Yes, Stanley told me at the time I left the SupaPod. And two others, he said, who tried to stop Peter."

"Did he tell you of any role I played?"

"No, just that you had escaped." She looked Julian in the face. "What *did* happen?"

"Nothing", Julian lied. "I got away ahead of Peter. I don't know what happened to him. I thought he was behind me"

"So how then did you know he was killed?" Tina asked quietly, her eyes on his.

He looked away and was silent. There was nothing he could say to her of what had happened in his Pod, not now, or very likely ever. Different threads of truth and lies were being spun. Which could he believe, and which Tina? Wasn't it enough that the both of them lived and were for the moment safe, and had hope for the future?

"It is of little consequence now," said Tina eventually, matching his own conclusion. "God will know the truth." She looked at him meaningfully as she said the last words.

A horror filled him at what Tina would think of him if she knew of his part in several deaths, of his thieving as well, and of the wildness so recently of his bodily depravity. All this Sandra had sacrificed her life for, that he could go free to commit more sin. Such confession, in whole or in part to Tina, could surely never be.

"So why did you come here to this Church?" he asked at length, to change the direction of questioning.

"Because I have known the Prioress of St. Augustine's for some time, and she had sent me an invitation. It was a pure coincidence that I learnt of the details Peter was planning with you."

"How *did* you learn of them?"

"He told me, as he told you. He wanted me to support him, join him in what he wanted to do. He told me too much really. I think he liked me."

"We all loved you," Julian said without thinking, and he noted how Tina blushed. So, she was still a woman of flesh and feeling.

There was a pause. A sister in a black habit passed, looking at them and smiling. A flock of small birds squabbled together on the cloister grass, fighting over a scrap of bread. Their cheeps rose loudly, until all at once the quarrel was settled and the birds flew away.

"Come with me," Tina said suddenly. "Don't follow the route of violence that Peter proposed."

"You know the names then he gave me?"

"Yes, I think so. The White Swan, I do remember. I knew that place was watched because of the recent atrocities in this area."

"Atrocities?"

"Yes, some fearful killings. And great brutality by SupaPodia in return. It happened quite recently, I've been told."

"Hell, then they *will be* watching this town."

"You must be careful when you leave. They have no cause to think you're here, yet they may be able to pick you out as 'unusual' and worth investigating." She looked at him critically. "I can still make out the Lilac uniform despite its camouflage." She wrinkled her nose. "What have you been using?"

Julian looked embarrassed. He had not thought he smelt. He had thought his efforts at concealment were more successful than this.

"I'd rather not say."

"Oh, how you have suffered." She reached over and placed her hands on his head. For a moment he thought she would kiss him, but perhaps she was simply blessing him. He would have preferred a kiss.

"I can help you with fresh clothes," she said, replacing her hands in her lap.

"Really? That would be marvellous."

"Yes, we keep a small store here for those who come to us seeking alms and sanctuary."

"Is there anything I can do for you in return?"

"That is not necessary. We give in the love of Jesus Christ. Your thanks should be to Him. Love Him in return, that's what I would ask of you."

Julian sat uneasily under Tina's earnest scrutiny. "What I would really ask you, though," she said, "in Christ's name, is not to join any resistance group using violence. That should not be the way to redress wrong, to add even greater layers of injustice that might endanger the innocent."

Julian was somewhat startled by this admonition. "What would you have me do then?" he said. "You have witnessed the evil of SupaPodia. You know their strength, and you know how they are consuming the whole world. Any small pinprick we can make against them will be a victory. And it can only be achieved by force; there is no other way. Not by argument, or reason, or prayer. They proclaim a democracy for the SupaPods, but the reality is coercion, enforced by punishment of the most degraded type. I have seen it at first hand. Violent resistance is the only way to hope for change, even though innocents may suffer too. That has always been the way in wars, even just wars."

"Violence can never be the answer," Tina said softly. "I have a plan in my head that I know will help. I would like to attend the next SupaPodia Convention at the Cape. There, I would seek to be reconciled with my father and to speak to him to soften his heart. I would like you to come with me. Together we would be able to open his eyes to the many wrongs of the organisation he controls. He is a reasonable man. I am sure that much is kept from him. When he hears the truth that we will bring him, he will set things in motion that will turn SupaPodia back from evil to the true ideal of its founding purpose."

Julian was astonished. "Wouldn't we be stopped before we had got half way there? I would be for sure, even if you were allowed through."

"Not if we travel incognito and only make ourselves known at the Convention. Many Eliti, I know, would like me to attend. They are sad there has been such a long rift between me and my father."

"No one would welcome my presence with you when they learn of what I've done."

"What *have* you done? You have not raised a hand against SupaPodia, have you? You have simply managed to escape from a SupaPod, with a mission not to destroy the SupaPods but to reform them. You don't seek harm to anyone – Podders, Eliti, or the servants of SupaPodia. What you seek is reform, and I shall be there to help you."

"I will have to think about it."

"Of course. Promise me then you will not contact any group intent on violence."

"I cannot promise you that, Tina. As I say, I must weight everything up when I have rested."

"Of course. You will be able to stay here at St. Augustine's overnight, if you wish, when you can make your decision. But now, for the present, I see I have been remiss. I have not offered you refreshment." She rose to her feet, taking him by the arm. "Come, we will see first to your clothes, then we shall visit the refectory and, after that, book you into our guest lodge."

An hour later Julian was newly clothed, in a plain suit of grey trousers and a matching jacket, worn but clean. A pair of brown shoes that fitted him well enough was found, and a pile of underwear, a towel, a darned grey pullover, and a small cardboard box containing toiletries. Looking in a mirror, he realised how it might have been hard to recognise him. Tina had greeted him without comment on his appearance. Yet, she must have wondered at this scruffy scarecrow, with the bristling cheeks and chin, when he had first stood before her. He tidied up the stubble but decided to remain unshaved. It served to disguise his face should descriptions of him have been circulated.

He was undecided what to do. Tina's offer was both tantalising and tempting. He could probably stay with her, later travel with her, and perhaps try to help her put across measures for SupaPodia's reform. But, by doing that, might he not run a great danger of being found and recaptured and sent to eternal torture in those deepest Levels of the SupaPod? He remembered the terrible things he had witnessed there, and he *knew* what he must do. First, though, he would spend the night here, as he had been offered.

There was only one other occupant in the male section of the guest dormitory. He was an old man who had lost both his legs and had to be helped by a nun in and out of bed. While out, he was able to wriggle his way along the floor on his bottom. Julian struck up a conversation with him, learning he had once been a sailor and had travelled the world. This was when SupaPodia had been in its infancy.

"I couldn't have stood being shut up in one of them places," he told Julian. "But now I'm old and it's hard to manage, I long for a rest in one. Do you have any contacts? Could you get me in?

The man's eyes were appealing. Julian felt a fraud. Perhaps, then, there was a need for SupaPods, as good places where people who were really in need could go to be looked after. But how would this man manage amongst the corridors and elevators of a SupaPod? Who would look after him there? Wouldn't he simply be consigned to the depths for terminal disposal?

Seeing the hope in the old man's eyes that he must disappoint, Julian was more certain than ever what his course should be. SupaPodia must be overthrown and physically destroyed. It was too corrupt and dangerous simply to be appeased, tampered with, or modified. And its rulers – the Eliti – they must be destroyed too, and the lands they had stolen given back to the people. It would be a long battle that must be fought to achieve these things, one that might occupy a whole generation, or more, but it had to start somewhere at some time. Indeed, from what he had learnt, it had started already.

Violence had always been instrumental in settling the affairs of the world. So, regrettable as it might be, it was violence that was needed now. He could not be involved with anything less. It was all or nothing. He knew that he wanted to use the rest of his life – however long he might have left – taking part in this great crusade for freedom.

The name to be called upon was not Christus, Prince of Peace, but Adrestia, handmaiden of Nemesis, goddess of revenge.

* * *

Tina's face was one of sadness when Julian gave her his decision the next morning.

"Then may the love of God give peace to you even now," she said, taking his hand.

"It's not that I don't think you are right," Julian said, "that is, in a perfect, shining world run by ideals. Yet, such a world is yet to be, and will certainly never come through SupaPodia. SupaPodia is evil, and, since we are all sinners rather than saints, the only way to overthrow evil is by direct action to root it out, not fine words."

"I disagree, Julian," she said, her small hand still in his, looking up at him with her wide, shining eyes. "A sword swung to cut out cancer may cut innocent flesh as well, and the disease will likely spread again. The way to destroy evil is to alter human hearts, and that can only be achieved by showing people better ways."

"But that will take far too long," he protested, "even if it works at all. In the meantime, the suffering goes on from generation to generation. In the SupaPods, even the framework of the real world is soon lost. What chance then for education about a better way of life that no one can recognise at all?"

"You would be surprised, Julian," she said gently, "at how fast things will happen once God's will is put into practice."

He said no more. He did not want to challenge her beliefs, but he was beginning to think she was more than deluded. However much he loved her, he was fearful that her dreaming was the result of some mental imbalance rather than a faith arrived at through reason. It was impossible for him to respect what she wanted of him. He might as well throw himself off a cliff. He *had* to strike a physical blow against SupaPodia.

Seeing the look in his eyes, Tina said, "If I cannot stop you, I can bless you and pray to God to keep you safe. Remember, Julian, if you are in danger and in pain, I shall always be here for you. I shall pray for you."

He left her, and looking back, found his sight blurred by tears, her small figure in the grey habit outlined against the deeper grey of the Abbey walls. She raised an arm to him and he waved back. Then he passed through the gateway into the busy street beyond.

The man who had met him when he first came to Canterbury was waiting for him. Julian had half-expected this, although he had said nothing to Tina of his next moves, and indeed he had no clear plan, only that he must now seek out Nemesis and its leader, Adrestia.

Who then was this man in his peaked cap and grey zipped jacket? He had a look of ages in his shrewd, dark eyes. Surely he could not work for both Tina and Adrestia, the one of peace, the other of violence. Was he perhaps just a personification – a spirit, a force, an ennabler – originating out of Julian's own brain, putting into effect the inevitability of his decision, acting between life and death?

"Who are you?" he asked as the man stepped out of the shuffling crowd in the street. He looked solid enough. "Why do you wait for me?"

"As we wait for most things, master," he answered cryptically. "I knew you would come, for we have need of you."

With that Julian had to be content. The man walked ahead and Julian followed him. He realised he did not have to follow. He could have easily stepped aside and gone his own way, but a strange sense of destiny made him keep the grey jacket in sight.

They pushed through the crowds in the main street, many pushing barrows piled with boxes, others with children on their backs, beggars against the walls, their arms extended, an occasional mule laden with panniers dropping dung, a group of women with tight short skirts and reddened lips giggling by a fountain, a man juggling wooden clubs close by. The scenes swept past Julian's eyes as if he was watching them on a screen and was not part of them at all.

They turned into side streets, lined by old houses, some of which had collapsed into heaps of bricks. An abandoned police station, its doors and windows boarded up, still had its blue lamp hanging outside. Even as Julian passed, a pack of small boys were shying stones at it. A man with a barking dog on a leash shouted at them to be gone. Further on into these back streets with their derelict buildings, they came to a small overgrown park, its steel railings twisted and broken down, bushes, once neatly trimmed, now wildly intertwined. Overlooking the park were the ruins of a public house, its sides shored up with timber posts, rusting scaffolding against its front, dark green tiles still surrounding its boarded windows. A fallen sign, coloured with the picture of an aeroplane, was propped up on the pavement. Through sprayed graffiti, it announced 'The Spitfire Arms. Shepherd Neame. Master Brewers.'

The man halted here and waited for Julian to catch him up. It was the first time he had turned round since leaving the Abbey.

"We must go round the back," he said, looking around furtively, causing Julian a twinge of anxiety. What was he to expect here? A meeting with Adreista? He pictured a boldly-featured woman with long flaring hair. Or betrayal to SupaPodia? He could see Stanley, with his sneering face, reaching out to seize him by the collar while his purple-coated Guard beat at him with rubber truncheons.

They went down a passageway running between a high wooden fence and the brick wall of the building, and, rounding a corner, came to a peeling, green-painted door, which was opened at their approach. A large, bearded man wearing a khaki-coloured pullover stood there, his arms folded across his chest. He looked at Julian, his face expressionless, and grunted at the guide, "What took you? You're late."

"Traffic."

The big man nodded. "Always fucking traffic". Julian did not understand what was meant.

"Go down." He waved Julian and his guide towards wooden steps curving below from a narrow hallway. At the bottom was a further doorway, which opened into a large stone-walled cellar, lit by a single opening high in one wall. Two steel beer casks, which, from the rust on them, looked as if they had been here for many years, stood on the floor. An old cooking range of blackened metal was set into a side wall, its tubular chimney rising through the grubby, plastered ceiling.

Removing his cap, the guide sat down on one of the barrels and waved Julian to sit on the other. "It won't be long."

"What won't be long?"

The guide scratched at his scanty hair. He didn't answer.

Julian felt annoyed. Why couldn't he be told what was to happen? He bit his lower lip and stared down at the stone-flagged floor. The dust lay thickly in its grooves. How many feet had passed here, he wondered, stepping in and out of time? Now it was his turn. Perhaps Tina had been right. It was best not to force yourself against time but to accept its inevitability, seeking belief in a divine creator whose ultimate purpose was yet to be revealed.

When he looked up again it was to see a man standing before him. He was wearing a sleeveless leather jerkin over a grey shirt, and grey trousers with zipped pockets, and he carried a short-barrelled gun slung by a webbing strap over one shoulder.

Julian scrambled to his feet, "I'm sorry I didn't see you." Then he noticed his guide was no longer beside him. Had he then fallen asleep? No, he had only cast his eyes down for a few moments.

"Where on earth have you come from?" he called out.

The man made no answer. His face was thin, he looked tired and there was stubble on his cheeks. His head was covered by a floppy, olive-green cap. Julian thought he could be any age between thirty and fifty. When he did speak, his voice was harsh.

"First lesson. Keep alert. Doze off and you die. Where have I come from? That's for me to know, not you. Who are you and what do you want?"

Julian, much to his disgust, found his voice quavered. "I have escaped from SupaPod 16. I was on the staff there."

He told the man the circumstances of his escape and how Peter had told him to seek out Adreista of Nemesis at the White Swan in Canterbury.

"Are you Adreista?" he asked at the last, wanting to sit down on the barrel again, as he felt sick and his knees were suddenly weak.

"I am the Major. That's all you need to know. I ask the questions here, not you."

"Of course. I'm sorry." Julian shuffled his feet, feeling awkward and out of his depth, beginning to regret being here at all. This was not what he had expected.

"Nemesis is our purpose," the Major suddenly barked out "Is that your purpose too?"

"If you mean revenge, sir, yes it is." Julian used the 'sir' instinctively, thinking it might help him. If he was rejected by this man, what would happen to him then? Already he must know too much. "I believe I have information that may be of use to you," he said in a rush.

"We shall see." The Major laughed suddenly. It was so unexpected that Julian jumped in fright. "We shan't kill you then." He called out, "Come!" and to Julian's astonishment the black range in the wall twisted round and two men appeared out of a hole behind. They were armed too.

"Take him to Pandora," the Major said. "Treat him well. He's come a long way to be here." He turned to Julian, "Pandora is where we interrogate new recruits. If you survive Pandora, you will survive anything."

For the first time, there was a flicker of humanity about the Major's lips.

Julian was escorted by the two armed men, one short and thick-set, the other tall and lean, along the passage that led from behind the cellar range. Turning his head, Julian saw that the Major had not followed. The brick-lined passage had a high curving roof, which only the tall man had to bend his head beneath. Light filtered in through gratings set at intervals in the apex of the roof; it was just a grey, murky light, not open daylight, so Julian thought it was perhaps coming from within other buildings they were passing beneath.

Despite the warning about Pandora, his spirits were rising. This passage was nothing compared with those tunnels he had wriggled through from the SupaPod. I have found Nemesis, he thought. What may come will undoubtedly be dangerous, but I have a new purpose and I *will* survive. He remembered Tina and his tearful farewell from her. Would he ever see her again? Something deep within him told him he would. He felt almost happy walking the tunnel, one guard ahead of him, one behind, their guns now unslung and held across their bodies.

The passage ended at a steel hatch, which the first guard pushed upwards, and they came out into the open air within a small, weed-covered enclosure surrounded by broken brick walls. Beyond the walls lay an open patch of wasteland surrounded by high razor wire Adjacent to this perimeter, and outside it within its own wired compound, stood the high, grey concrete slab of a tower block stripped of its cladding and due for demolition. At least that is what a large board on its side proclaimed, adding that this was being done on behalf of 'SupaPodia Resettlement'. By screwing up his eyes, Julian could just make out some other wording beneath:

Don't Live in Squalor.
Live the SupaPod Way in Comfort.
A POD FOR EVERYONE, EVERYONE IN A POD.
Apply for a Pod in SupaPodia NOW!

Julian suspected the former inhabitants of this tower would have thought themselves particularly fortunate to be removed into a SupaPod.

They crossed the wasteland, keeping close to the wire fence furthest from the tower block. The guards must feel confident of themselves walking here in the open, Julian thought. They're clearly not frightened of anyone watching – of eyes in the sky, or anything else like that. Perhaps the technology available for SupaPodia's security operations in the OuterWorld was limited. Perhaps most such resources went into the SupaPods themselves. He suspected that combating insurrection in the OuterWorld was a fairly new requirement. Yet he knew SupaPodia would soon gear itself up for it. If the Eliti felt in danger, then everything would be deployed to protect them. It was the Eliti who had most to lose should SupaPodia fail. Yet was such a failure really likely?

So what was this Nemesis he sought to join planning? What sort of action had it taken so far and would seek to take in the future? Its title meant revenge, but was that really possible? Revenge for what? For what the Eliti had done to the OuterWorld or for what they were doing within their SupaPods? Would that not do more harm than good? How did Nemesis see the future? What were its ultimate aims?

Julian did not yet know the answers to any of these questions. He was worried now he would be as disillusioned by Nemesis as he had been by SupaPodia. Would a second escape, this time from Nemesis, be any easier than his first?

His guards brought him to a gate in the wire. Beyond was a broad concrete strip stretching away in both directions where the sun flashed on tall buildings in the distance. This place looked as if were once an airfield, he thought. The clamour, the noise, the many peoples had gone. There was only emptiness now and stillness. As the guards opened the gate, the rattling of their keys and the drawing back of the bolts were almost painful to his ears. Rising through that sound came the sudden sharp trilling of a bird, and, looking up, he saw a lark hovering high above on frenzied wings, pouring out its song, a tiny speck against the huge blue sky. The sight gave him strength. It is only the smallest fragment of life, he thought, but it flies triumphantly. It is not weighed to the earth as I am. Yet I hope to rise again too.

Another hidden metal cover presented itself; once lifted, there were further steps deep down into a concrete passageway smelling of wet and mould, with rooms leading from it. Julian was brought up to a metal door, black with traces of blue paint. A name had once been stencilled upon it: all that could be read now was 'W/Cdr Tho----'

A guard banged with his fist on the door. A voice called, "Enter". He was pushed inside and the door clanged to. A man was sitting at a table. His head was down and he was writing. Even before he looked up, Julian knew it was the Major. Now, how on earth had he got here first?

The Major made no greeting. He did not refer to their first meeting.

"This is Pandora. Here *we* do the questioning, you answer. If you satisfy us, we train you. If you don't, we get rid of you. So it will pay you to have no secrets, for we will find them out. Far better for you if you tell us first. Any traitors, we get rid of. Do you understand?"

"Yes, sir."

"Go through that door. There's a doctor there. He'll examine you. When you're done, we'll take you to the next step."

"Yes, sir."

"Oh, Foster." Half way to the far door, Julian paused, surprised to hear his surname spoken. Had he given it earlier? He didn't think he had."

"Yes, sir?"

"Have you ever killed?"

"Yes, sir."

"When was that?"

"On the way here, sir. It was necessary for my own survival."

The Major looked intently at him, then actually smiled. Julian noticed one of his front teeth was missing. Perhaps that's why smiling came hard to him.

"I think we may be able to make something of you, Foster."

"Thank you, sir."

The Major looked down once more and returned to his writing.

That's not much of an encouragement, thought Julian, but at least it's a start.

* * *

Stripped naked, passed fit by a bleary-eyed doctor who coughed over his stethoscope, interrogated by the hour in the concrete chambers, where water dripped from a roof black with mould, Julian was at last released into the open air once more. He slept in a round bell tent under trees, somewhere – he did not know where: he had been taken there after dark, with others, in the back of an old petrol-driven lorry that leaked fumes. He had been fed at an outdoors canteen where a brawny woman in white overalls had ladled stew onto an enamel plate. The stew had been good, with real meat and carrots. It had made him fart; his stomach had not known such food for a long time. Others in the sleeping tent had farted too. It had brought a chorus of giggles as if they were a pack of teenagers out on a spree.

They were a mixed lot, five of them, two very young as if they should have been still at school, another older man like Julian, who read from a book of poetry he carried in his pocket, and a younger man, who affected a high-pitched voice and a mincing gait. Now what was *he* doing here? What were any of them doing here, for that matter, even if they knew where 'here' was?

Julian had told his interrogators everything he knew (he had no secrets he was aware of) – about his own background, how he had been taken into the Ramsgate SupaPod, what he had experienced there and what he had learnt. The interrogators were particularly interested to hear about the Control Station he had visited. The Major came into the room when he spoke about that, asked some questions, then left slamming the door behind him.

He described his escape; how Sandra had cut off her own arm so she could get away with him without their being tracked; how that had gone so terribly wrong; how he had come to Dorking, found food and clothing, and headed for Canterbury, being attacked on the way and defending himself and the group he was with. He then described being taken to the Abbey, which had given him temporary sanctuary.

What Julian did not talk about, however, was Tina. Perhaps he should have referred to her. This close link with the High Director of SupaPodia

International was surely of great importance. Did they know about her, anyhow? He suspected they did, or otherwise how was it that the guide sent by them, who certainly knew Tina's name, had been waiting for him? He glossed over how he had been helped at the Abbey, and no questions about his stay there were put to him. That was strange itself, but then everything here was strange.

He wanted to keep Tina in a separate compartment of his brain. Tina represented to him the peace he most sought. Her ways were of peace. He did not want his thoughts of her to be contaminated by the violent path he had chosen to follow. Julian knew he could not hope to reach any blissful plain of peace without passing through struggle first – a struggle that was likely to be far greater than anything he had yet endured.

They were taken to another site, which, judging by the long journey in the rumbling lorry, half poisoned by fumes, was at a considerable distance. It was an abandoned farm deep in the countryside, in a narrow wooded valley hard up against a range of hills. There were still five of them, but one of the 'schoolboys' had gone (thrown out, it seemed) and had been replaced by a woman, a beefy woman, perhaps in her 30s, with red hair that she wore up in a coil on her head. She was known as 'Boadicea'. They had all been given code names. The man who read poetry was 'Alfred'; the remaining 'schoolboy', 'Lancelot'; the effeminate one, 'Marilyn' (it did not seem to concern him he had a female name); and Julian, 'Cromwell', which pleased him. These names were accorded by the Major in person. The Major now took a personal role in their training.

They were put into black fatigues of loose blouse and trousers, with thick-soled trainers on their feet. They learnt unarmed combat. On account of his fifty odd years, Julian found this difficult. He could not absorb the rough and tumble as he might have done if he had been even ten years younger. He was paired with Boadicea for practice. She threw him time and time until the Major was roaring with laughter. He did laugh quite often now, normally at the sight of someone else's distress. Julian had better luck with Alfred, flinging him over his head while rolling back with his foot in his stomach. Marilyn then managed to throw Boadicea. Julian decided he was a harder man than he seemed at first.

That first evening amongst the farmhouse ruins, the Major gave the group a lecture. He was assisted now by a big brute of a man in camouflage clothes known to everyone as the Beast. The Beast had arrived on a motor bike, which was one of those models with long, high handlebars so that the rider leant backwards in the saddle whilst riding it. This was hardly travelling incognito, Julian thought, but then perhaps the Beast was only based a mile or so away.

The lecture was about methods of killing, using knives, bottles, clubs, and bare hands. The Major demonstrated the techniques with the Beast. It was all very realistic. At one point Julian though the Beast had finished off the Major during a demonstration of strangling, and was relieved when at last his body shivered once more and he rose, swaying a little, to his feet. It would not be good to be leaderless without the Major whose personal unit Nemesis appeared to be. Although it was never spoken, Julian thought that 'Adrestia' was very likely the Major's own code name: wings embroidered on the sleeve of his combat suit might be those of a goddess of revenge.

After the lecture, the Major handed around some photographs. The pictures were mostly blurred, although some stood out in sharper detail. They showed a house being burnt down, and many people milling about before it. Groups of men, with arms raised holding weapons, stood over prostate figures. One shot showed an area of bloodied grass with body parts spread over it. A man held up a head – a woman's head, from its long hair.

The room was now in near darkness. The Beast, with Boadicea's help, lit some stubs of candles.

"What you must do will be every bit as bloody as those pictures," the Major intoned, standing up very straight. "You must kill without mercy, as Nemesis did in that action we photographed. It creates our reputation, which goes before us and makes the Eliti – the unthinking, stinking rich, the hell dog agents of SupaPodia – tremble in their beds."

They slept amongst bales of hay in an outbuilding. The hay had long turned green with mould: it smelt of decay. Julian found it hard to sleep. He talked with Alfred for a while, then stumbled outside into the moonlight and relieved himself. There, on a patch of grass under the silvery light, lay the Beast on top of Boadicea. Close by, another couple groaned and threshed – Marilyn and Lancelot. Hell, thought, Julian, am I the only one now not getting it? He went back inside the barn and found there was nothing to do except talk poetry with Alfred. After a while, the Major joined them. Something had caused him to unbend. He seemed to want to talk.

"'Oh, God be thanked who has matched us with His hour,'" he intoned, breaking in upon Julian's own poetic musing, which had been of a subject much more peaceable. "How grateful I am of the chance to get even with them. They took my whole family, you see – my mother and father, a brother and sister, and an uncle: they had been sent into the Portland SupaPod. They hadn't wanted to go. An Eliti bigwig was clearing their village to create a ranch for his racehorses. Three years ago, they were sent back in cardboard boxes – just a few of their ashes; you'd get more from a couple of pigeons. I reckon they cut up the rest of them for spare parts. Nemesis is all I have left. You understand, don't you?"

Both Alfred and Julian nodded. Julian could smell the alcohol on the Major's breath.

"Were you a soldier before this?" asked Alfred.

"Christ, no. I was a warehouse man in a furniture factory. When it closed down, I had no job. I was offered a place in a SupaPod, but I had the sense to keep out. They got the rest of us, though, the bastards."

The others were creeping back into the barn, other than for the Beast who, if he was not topping Boadicea, always slept alone.

"Get some sleep, my beauties," the Major said. "I don't care what you get up to here, but I do care about you being on parade at 06.00 hours, fresh as a daisy, alert as a guard dog. Got that?"

"Yes, sir!"

Julian was beginning to think the Major was fully human after all.

The training continued. They were introduced to weapons.

"These are old kit," the Beast growled. "But they work. They kill."

They were guns from the period of the 20th century, the time of the great world wars. "We found an arsenal at Blandford buried in an abandoned army base," the Major told them. "It had been kept from the last century into this one, then forgotten. There are enough rifles, light machine guns, grenades and explosives to start a war. If used properly, we can outgun the SupaPodia Guard. Many of the Guard have laser weapons, but these will kill just as well if you can get in close enough."

They learnt how to strip down and clean bolt-action rifles, Sten and Bren guns. They threw wooden blocks as practice grenades, prepared satchel charges with dummy explosives, went through the motions of fixing pretend fuses to them and strapping them to targets. All this was far from the real thing, however, for there could be no live firing, no explosions.

"SupaPodia don't know our location," explained the Major, at the end of one day's training. "Long may that continue. They come over in their helidrones from time to time, but there's nothing they could see of us to attract their attention. As you will have noticed, all of our training we do under tree cover. If we made a noise, though, they'd be sure to get a report and be here to investigate: they're much better now at getting raids together. We can't take too much of a risk, which is why we'll have to move again before long, then show them we're still in business. You're the last five fighters I'll train for the present. I've got enough now for another show. This time, it's not a soft target we're going for, but a hard one, a very hard one. We'll be going against a SupaPod and its Guard this time, so there'll be some real fighting, not just killing. So, *look to your training.* It may save your life and those of your comrades about you."

The Major eyed Julian. "It'll be your SupaPod. I'll need some more input from you."

"Of course, sir. I'll give you everything I know."

As the Major dismissed them, Julian felt a particular thrill at being singled out in this way. The information he had brought out of the Ramsgate SupaPod so perilously was going to be acted upon: there was to be an attack. He hoped it would target only the guilty. The Guard would fight back. Innocent Podders and Lilacs might get caught up and be killed. It was more than likely *he* would be killed.

He didn't want to die. Yet the cause was surely worth fighting for. He could see Tina shaking her head disapprovingly, invoking her pacifist creed. She was wrong. Change only came by the use of force, rooting out evil. And that meant fighting and death.

'Greater love hath no man than this, that a man lay down his life for his friends.'

In a good cause, surely that was the greater truth.

23

"We can't wait for the SupaPodia Guard," said Lord Clive de Vere. "We have to be organised now."

"For our own survival," he added, with a jut of the family chin that had once been the terror of foreign invaders, gypsy trespassers and starving poachers alike, hanging all he could catch in rows on the various Gallows Hills about the de Vere estates.

He wore a uniform cleverly devised out of portraits of his military forebears. The blue patrol jacket had epaulettes of golden braid, the polished brown harness was hung with pouches and revolver holster, the trousers were camouflage patterned, bought recently by Lady Sophia de Vere in a salvage store. She was present at this meeting too, bulkily clad in a suit of khaki once worn by her great-great grandfather to storm Germany.

The Eliti were reaching back into their family pasts – those, of course, who had such pasts and had not joined the Eliti ranks much more recently, for instance out of popular entertainment – whining, shrieking singing perhaps; or kicking a football about; or running half a mile faster than anyone else; or cycling even faster – or acting as a conscience for a 1001 heartbreak causes; or telling children how to change sex and have an abortion (but not at the same time); or possibly just through being in a politicians' Forum with a thoroughly liberal conscience, embracing all parts of the world except those occupied by populist, bigoted, fascist, racist, thoroughly unfashionable OuterWorlders.

"Have we got weapons?" a voice called from the back of the hall.

"We've enough to stop a raid," Clive answered, trying to sound confident, knowing that the shotguns and rusting rifles of that ancient 20th century yeomanry, the Home Guard, he had found in one of his attics would not hold off a determined attack for too long, even if the raiders were just armed with knives and clubs. He did not even know the rifles would fire, and the clips of ammunition that went with them seemed mainly to be drill rounds.

"We've got some automatic guns," yelled out a shrill voice, and looking warily into the throbbing audience before him, Clive could see the voice came from that old boot, Pamela Lascelles, whom the rumours said had some sort of link to the High Director of SupaPodia himself. Well, good luck to her if she had been able to get modern weapons out of him, although he'd heard the HD's idea of shooting was something else entirely.

"I've my own unit of Amazons," Pamela continued to shout. She waved her arms towards a platform at the back of the hall, where a line of grey-uniformed girls in short skirts was standing, each with a snub-nosed weapon slung between her bosoms, and a pot-like helmet perched prettily on her head. Remembering a quotation he had once read, Clive thought I hope they scare the terrorists as much as they scare me.

However, he shouted back over the noise in the hall, "Good, very good. Now things are really shaping up."

If those words held even a hint of a double meaning, it was certainly not intended. Things were growing far too serious for that. The Eliti of the South East had been subjected in recent months to a wave of terror attacks by dissidents. The situation was confused. At first it had not been clear if the violence was on account of people not being able to get into the SupaPods, or was some sort of revolt against the conditions there. Surely, it could not be the latter.

It was only later that it became clear that these armed attacks were coming principally from discontented OuterWorlders who were *excluded* from SupaPodia entry, because they were needed to do work for the Eliti to make the whole system work. They were the disadvantaged ones, who had none of the benefits of SupaPodia and no security, Denied entry to a SupaPod, they must live on, giving their labour for a pittance, while paying taxes to SupaPodia in an OuterWorld that was crumbling all about them. Even the densest of the Eliti – and there were certainly many of them – could see that now.

"What about the Guard?" yelled out a long-haired man with a tattooed face, a heavy golden chain about his neck: Clive de Vere recognised him as the Earl of Westsussex, whose estates now incorporated much of the old New Forest. "What are they doing to protect us? Are they going to be reinforced?"

"The answer to your first question is, 'everything'", snapped Clive, who didn't like Rolly Batwing, ex vocalist with the SexyBoys, one little bit. Rolly had been favoured by Prince Ojo of the Royal House of Tamworth, lineal descendant of the Windsors, who had given him the Earldom of Westsussex to show how much he had liked his 'moosic', much to the green-eyed jealously of others of far greater rank, many of them media celebs, vying to be part of the Eliti world.

"And to your second question," Clive said, deepening his voice to sound more manly, "Yes, reinforcements of trained personnel are being helidrone-borne to all local areas, together with the latest defence equipment, including laser rifles that can seek out and destroy any insurgent up to 2000 yards."

"But the Guard can't be everywhere," wailed the Earl of Westsussex. "The nearest Guard Station to me is at Southsea SupaPod, twenty-five miles or so from my Shat-o, so what if these rebels come onto my land, burning and raping?"

"Keep your backside to the wall," some lout or other called out, to titters.

But Clive, knowing the seriousness of the question, kept his face as stern and commanding as he could. "Set up your own defence force then," he said, "as you hear others are doing. And make sure you have a clear emergency signal to the Guard. That way, you can see off any attack until you get help."

Rolly, Earl of Westsussex, looked as if he was about to cry. Clive realised he could not even make himself a slice of toast, let alone organise the defence of his Shat-o, his land, many mistresses, dogs, exotic pets, and racehorses. Oh well, he for one would not weep too much if, like the unfortunate Zara and Roberta so recently, Rolly was spitted and burnt. Perhaps he could sing as he died. What a last performance that would make!

"That is what you ALL have to do!" Clive exclaimed wildly, swinging round on the platform to take in his audience, seeing the rows of flabby faces and drooping jaws staring back at him.

God! (yes, the old deity who had once protected the aristocracy should come into this) – they were all so hopeless. Luxury and pleasure and too many servants had stripped the power of self-reliance from them, just as it had done to those poor benighted cretins who, so hopefully, had descended into the buried silos of SupaPodia looking for salvation. Clive saw it all so clearly now: it was the OuterWorlders who retained the power of thought and determination. Stripped willow thin, they had learnt the art of survival, how to bend to the wind, merge into invisibility when required, appear with whiplash force when the time was right. And that time was *now*. Here in Britain change was coming, a change that was also emerging elsewhere in the SupaPodia empire, if the reports he had read were true. The rule of the Eliti through SupaPodia was entering a new and probably decisive phase. It was a time for resolution and for action. Only the fittest were likely to survive, whatever their rank, whatever their situation – Eliti, Podders, or OuterWorlders.

24

Julian had been put in a hut with fifteen other men, all strangers to him. Alfred, Marilyn, Lancelot, and Boadicea were no longer with him. They had gone to other huts. He was sorry to lose their company, in particular Boadicea whom he had grown to like a lot, even if he had come nowhere near achieving what the Beast had so easily claimed.

They had left the farm training camp at night, and, led by the Major, marched at first across moon-drenched grassland, then deep into black fir plantations, their way picked out by the Major as readily as if he was walking them across the palm of his own hand. The huts were in the middle of the woods, four of them in a row with the coniferous canopy of the trees above them like a vast green umbrella. Even when it rained hard, as it did the following day, only a spattering of drops reached the woodland floor.

They did not leave their huts that first full day, other than to go to the brick built ablutions and latrines that stood behind the huts. Instead, they sat or lay on their bunks and played cards, or chatted and got to know each other. They used their real names. Whatever had been the need for the earlier code names, that did not seem to apply now

In the beds closest to the one taken by Julian were Bert and Colin, both in their thirties – Bert with a broken nose like an ex-boxer and Colin with the sharp-pointed face and furtive look of a ferret. They had come into Nemesis at much the same time, by chance discovering that both had once been policemen serving in and around London.

Bert's patch had been Woolwich, where the air stank with the sulphurous vapours rising from the poisoned waters of the Thames. In consequence of that pollution, his family had been high on the list for the new Tilbury SupaPod, but Bert had had to remain at his job, since growing disorder in the OuterWorld meant all police entry to SupaPods was denied. His wife, Elaine, had stayed with him, sharing his quarters that were a single portakabin, without light or water, dumped with other kabins in the former station yard. His own house had been cleared for riverside 'improvements', so termed, which were realised as a block of expensive Eliti apartments raised up high above the river. Elaine had been killed during a Guard's raid on the Thames-side warehouse where she worked: it had been suspected (incorrectly) of supplying counterfeit goods to SupaPodia. She had been shot accidently by a Guard using a laser weapon, her eyes burnt out and her brain penetrated. She had lived on only a short time. Bert had vowed revenge on SupaPodia, a revenge that had brought him by various routes to Nemesis.

Colin's story was equally dramatic. He was unmarried – like so many other men in the OuterWorld these days – and had got out of the police when conditions in London had plummeted to the extent of affecting his health. (Julian, hearing this, suspected he had, in fact, deserted, but who could blame him?) He had found a job on a farm near Faversham, where all the produce went to SupaPodia, leaving scarcely enough to feed the farmer or his workers.

Most of the workers sought a ticket into a SupaPod, but Colin thought differently. He loved the land, and the fruits of the land, which his hard work had contributed to, and hated to see how the demands of SupaPodia destroyed the fertility of the soil and gave little back to the people who had lived and farmed there for generations. He did not want to go into a SupaPod, for he could see how the voracious demands of SupaPodia were stripping the land bare and destroying the villages and the towns, with the estates of the Eliti gobbling up more and more of what had once been free, open land to walk over and enjoy. An unguarded protest about this in a tap room – all that was left of a once fine coaching inn – had brought him to the attention of a SupaPodia agent. When a knock had come on the door of his small flat one night, he had left by the back window, leaping down from balcony to balcony and making his way eventually to Canterbury, where he had been fortunate in finding, and being taken in by, Nemesis.

Many of the other men in the hut – their age range was from 20 to 60, Julian being one of the oldest – had similar stories to tell of hardship, deprivation and resentment.

No one, however, had escaped from a SupaPod, as Julian had done. When he told Bert and Colin his story, leaving out certain bits such as Sandra's death – which he could not bring himself to describe – they were aghast. It seemed only snippets of information, much of it rumour, had yet emerged to the OW from the SupaPods. Podders were rarely allowed to send messages to the Outside, other than through the formal SupaPodia postcards which had standard printed phrases, such as 'I/We are coming on very well here' or 'No troubles here, all SupaPod fun.", which they could tick or otherwise highlight.

Julian's account, therefore, brought home to his new comrades the graphic reality of the SupaPods, about which they might have had many suspicions and heard many stories, but received no first-hand confirmation until now. It brought tension into their faces, a whitening of cheeks, a rippling of muscles along jaw lines. And, Julian thought, they understand only a fraction of it yet. They are prepared to fight against SupaPodia already. How many more will rise up when the full truth of SupaPodia comes out? He thought of telling them what he had seen on those Lower Levels, but feared he would not be believed and they might think he was trying to rouse them by false propaganda.

On the second day – it was the second day for Julian, but the others, he learnt, had been in the hut for a full day longer, having been trained at, and marched from, another location they were forbidden to divulge – they were ordered by the Beast to parade in a clearing some fifty yards away from the huts, where a brick building, with steel shutters at its door and windows, stood beneath a great oak tree. Thick ivy grew against the brick walls and made a green mat on the flat roof. The recruits of the other three huts came to the parade as well. Julian was surprised to see how many women there were; in fact, they had a whole hut to themselves. He saw Boadicea and waved an arm at her, but perhaps she didn't recognise him at a distance (his beard was quite thick now), for she didn't wave back.

They formed up by hut on the flat forest floor, standing on strips of concrete between which emerging bracken shoots uncoiled towards the light. Some drops of rain pattered upon them. Through the swaying pines, Julian could see the greyness of the sky. Yesterday's rain had not yet cleared.

Some of those on parade began calling across to others they recognised.

"Keep it quiet!" snarled the Beast. There was instant silence.

The Major appeared. He wore a dark green camouflage uniform and black rubber-soled boots. "Three things," he said without any introduction. "Teams, Kit, Weapons. First – Teams. Sergeant-Major – that was to the Beast – "Mark them off."

The Beast came down the ranks. "You, you, you, you together." – there were four in a team – "You, you, you, and …" – he pulled across a woman who looked about sixteen – "You."

Soon there only a few left who had not been allocated to a team. The Beast had his hand on Julian's arm, "You. With him and him. And her."

Julian was pleased to see he had been placed with Bert and a man with close-cut ginger hair from another hut, and – wonderfully – with Boadicea.

They stood looking at each other speculatively. "Welcome, team," said Boadicea, and, rather self-consciously, they all shook hands.

"Enough of that!" yelled the Beast. "This is not a tea party. It's a killing party. You're killers. Know your other killers. They'll kill for you, you for them."

"And who do you WANT TO KILL?" It was the Major, standing legs apart, hands on hips, who yelled this out.

"There was a silence at first, as if everyone was embarrassed to say, to speak first.

"The SupaPods….the Guard…" Various voices spoke out at last.

"NO!!" bellowed the Major. "You want to kill the ELITI. The Eliti control everything. So who do you want to KILL most of all?"

"THE ELITI!" came the combined roar.

They were issued with camouflage uniforms such as the Major wore. Even the Beast's bulky body was swathed in dark green camouflage. The uniforms came from boxes brought out of the hut and dumped in the open.

"Small, Medium, Large," shouted the Beast, "Take your pick."

Some changed in the open, some – mainly the women – in the hut. It was pretty miraculous, Julian thought, how everyone was soon clothed in suits that seemed to fit them, even if some looked a bit drowned by outsize jackets. All of them seemed to possess the same type of stout trainers he had been issued with; only the Major and the Beast wore high leather boots.

Underclothes had been handed out too, one size for all.

"What do I do with this?" giggled Boadicea pushing a finger through the fly of a pair of long johns.

"Put them on back to front," their crop-haired team member suggested: he had given his name as Rick.

Julian thought, I must keep a special eye on Boadicea: he still thought of her as that although she had said Carol was her real name. He remembered the Beast's body upon her. He didn't want Rick, or Bert even, to be the next. If anyone was going to have her, it would be he. But he doubted if there would be the opportunity for anything like that. He feared time for them all, like sand in an hour glass, was flowing out fast.

There were supplies of shirts too, collarless tee-shirts in the main, in greys, browns, and olive green. Julian grabbed a couple, which, when a break was called, he stowed away back in the hut with the few other things he had been able to keep.

They trained in their teams, ambushing each other amongst the deep bracken in small clearings in the trees. Rick proved a natural leader, so he was appointed the section commander by the common consent of Julian's team, confirmed by the Beast who watched broodingly over the small battles waged on the forest floor. Rick seldom used names, but simply, pointed, swore, and shoved in a way Julian found irritating. Still, as he led them to a victory over another team, whom they ambushed and beat over the head with socks filled with earth, Rick's apparent lack of social skills was soon forgiven.

They were now each issued with a Sten gun and live ammunition, which they practised loading and unloading. Rick and Bert also made up a two-man Bren gun team, using live rounds to practise charging magazines, clearing stoppages, changing barrels, but with the safety catches kept firmly on.

"The first time you'll fire your weapons," growled the Beast, "is when you go into action. We can't risk live firing before then."

Grenades, their cases deeply grooved, and with a ring pull at the top were also issued to each team, twenty or so in a wooden box. "They're primed," the Beast warned, so don't go pulling that ring until you're ready to throw one. And, when you do, keep the lever down until the bomb's left your hand, or bits of you will go up with the explosion."

They had already practised with dummy grenades. Julian wondered if he would be able to throw one for real – chuck it through a window, then fall flat. Or would he freeze with fear? In action would he become a trembling wreck and hide in a ditch? It was the old question all men – and all women – ask themselves when going into their first battle, knowing that they can be killed as easily as the enemy they will be trying to kill..

They practised all these things the whole day until in the evening the rain came down once more and they retired to their huts. Here they were fed – as they had been since first coming here – by two large women in flowered pinafores, who dragged around the huts a vast steaming cauldron set into a metal frame with two drawing bars. The food was slopped into chipped, enamelled plates, and delivered with a hunk of bread and an apple. This evening it was another meat stew. How it was prepared, and where the women came from and went to, was a mystery to Julian. He asked one of the women.

"Conjur'd up by magic, dearie," she said. "I jus' makes a spell and there it is. Ain't that true, Gertie?" And they both giggled and cackled like demented hens. Julian wondered why they couldn't simply give an answer. After all, it was hardly a top secret matter. Yet they were clearly following what the Major had ordered.

Just after Julian had finished spooning the tasty stew into his mouth, the Beast arrived at the hut door and told him the Major wished to see him. Julian followed the Beast out, leaving a chorus of catcalls behind him, "Promotion for you, mate." "Remember us poor sods when yer get your stripes up."

In the last of the line of huts, the Major and the Beast had their quarters, neatly sealed off from each other by walls of cardboard boxes. One space formed in this way held a large table – in fact, three trestle tables placed together with a grey, threadbare blanket thrown over them.

"Here's Foster, sir," said the Beast, saluting with his fist held to his temple.

"Thank you, sergeant major. Stay, will you."

The Major was staring at a plan unrolled on the table top. Beside him was a woman with short hair beneath a peaked forage cap, wearing camouflage trousers and a grey tee-shirt.

The Major looked up. "Ah, Foster. I need to ask you some more questions."

"Salute, damn you," the Beast was hissing in Julian's ear.

Julian raised his right hand to his head as he had seen the Beast doing, aware of the woman looking up at him as well. She acknowledged his salute with a casual wave of her hand. "Captain Bradwell," she said.

"Here is a plan of the Ramsgate SupaPod," said the Major, prodding a begrimed finger at the plan. "We need to fix the exact position of its Control Station."

It was a large scale plan, hand-drawn, that Julian viewed, bending forward over it. It showed the great block of the SupaPod's upper works with the long arm of its Bar curving away into the sea, each of the great power turbines clearly marked and labelled. Also marked were the freight and personnel portals to the SupaPod, and the positions of the railway and goods terminals.

"It's hard for me to judge …" began Julian.

"It's imperative we know exactly," snapped the Major.

"Can you remember the route you took there?" said Captain Bradwell. She had a pleasing lilt to her voice, perhaps Welsh.

Julian thought hard. He remembered arriving back at the SupaPod with Stanley, and climbing a steep stairway to a ledge in the hillside where the Control Station stood. Stanley's verbal attack on him at that time had wiped much of the surrounding detail from his brain. However, they had walked from the railway platform. He traced with his fingers the railway lines running into the SupaPod on the plan. The daylight, filtering through the one begrimed window, was fast fading to grey. "It's hard to see" he said.

The Major tutted, but the Beast had already produced a long, rubber-covered torch which he flashed onto the plan.

Julian stabbed a finger at the plan. "This must be where we disembarked for the SupaPod. Yes, you see here where the line for the cabin tram should lead on to the staff portal, only it's not been drawn in. We climbed a steep stairway, which must be over here." He swept his hand over an area of the plan marked only with the word 'Cliffs'. "The Control Station stood on a broad terrace in the hillside. Somewhere here. This plan was obviously drawn before it was built "

Julian saw the Major flash a glance at Captain Bradwell. "Good, that's what we hoped you'd say. It matches our own intelligence." He whispered something to the Captain, and she left the boxed-off room. They could hear her steps retreating over the floorboards of the hut beyond, then silence except for the Beast's heavy breathing and a belch of indigestion from the Major. "Pardon," he said absent-mindedly, his eyes still fixed on the plan.

"One other thing," Julian said. "There was a tunnel into the SupaPod from close beside the Control Station. I remember taking it and coming out on the SupaPod's Upper Deck, as it was called."

The Major looked quite startled. "What from the same terrace, the same level?"

"Yes, sir."

"Was it guarded in any way?"

"No, I don't think so. Certainly no one challenged me. I was quite surprised really. There was a moving floorway too that carried me inside."

"Really, that's most interesting." The Major's head was bowed over the plan. Then he looked up and forced a smile. "Thank you, Foster, for that information, which could be very useful at a later date. It won't form part of our present attack, though, as I'm reluctant to enter the SupaPod itself in a way that might endanger Podders. They need to be liberated, not killed. Now go back to your hut and get some sleep. We'll be parading at 05.00 tomorrow, then moving to our start line. Sergeant-Major!"

"Yes, sir."

"Inform all the huts."

"Yes sir."

"Operation Nemesis begins tomorrow." The Major turned to the Beast, who was preparing to escort Julian away. "This is it, Sergeant-Major. Tomorrow we'll either be dead or heroes. Perhaps both."

"It'll be worth it, sir, whatever the outcome."

The Major stretched his arms out wearily. "It'd be nice to have a legacy, though. Someone to tell the story."

"Get some sleep, sir."

"Send Captain Bradwell back in. There's still stuff to go over."

Julian arrived back at his hut with his brain in turmoil. So this could be his very last night. 'To do and die' – great in books or on film, but not much of a battle cry really for those called upon to fulfil it.

He said nothing to his hut comrades, although they pressed him. "Early parade, so get to your little cots!" That was what the Beast had said at the door.

Julian found it hard to sleep. He was thinking of Tina, and then she became conflated with Captain Bradwell, so he could not tell them apart. A voice somewhere at the back of his mind kept on saying, "Peace is the answer, not violence." And he saw a white face that might have been Tina's beseeching him, the eyes streaming with tears. The vision quite unmanned him, until at last he did fall into a deep sleep.

* * *

It was drizzling with rain the next morning. They formed up in their team sections, each fighter weighed down by his weapon, ammunition pouches, and grenades, the latter stuffed into pouches in a broad belt that ran diagonally across the chest. The Beast was in the store by the parade ground, handing out black woollen balaclavas. The fighters pulled them on, fifty or so masked faces turning to look at each other, features removed now, save for eyes and mouths. A murmur of conversation was shut off abruptly by the Major arriving on parade with his Captain.

"Weapons loaded?" he asked the Beast, who appeared from the hut saluting.

"Yes, sir."

The Major and the Captain walked round the ranks inspecting. Occasional a Sten gun was knocked up and pulled away from its owner. "Safety catch on, you fool! Keep it on until you need to fire."

The Bren gun teams carried their weapons with the front bipod folded up and a curved magazine in place. Further charged magazines bulged from the pockets of the teams' combat tunics. Captain Bradwell inspected the Brens in particular, checking barrels, safety catches, magazines. "Good, good…" she said, her voice clear against the softly pattering rain. She went to stand by the Major, while the vast frame of the Beast filled the hut doorway behind.

"Nemesis group. Shun!" Fifty pairs of feet stamped the soft woodland floor. The Major spoke, "Today is ACTION DAY. We'll travel in two lorries to our start lines. Our target is the SupaPod at Ramsgate. We'll attack their Control Station where their Guard is based. The aim will be to kill as many of them as possible and damage or destroy the building. At the same time, Captain Bradwell's teams will act against the Bar. The main targets there are the turbines. We'll use satchel charges against them. Even one turbine damaged will be a victory."

"I want volunteers," Captain Bradwell called out, her voice raised against a sudden gust of wind swirling the tree tops. She indicated the webbing satchels that were piled beside her, each about the size of a haversack, with a carrying handle and a red-topped plug. "Many of you have practised with dummies. These are live: they are charged and fused, each with 10 lbs of ammonal. You place the charge against the turbine housing, pull out the red plug and you have ten seconds to get clear. Volunteers now. The most agile of you who can get in and out quickly under our covering fire."

Several amongst the assembled ranks took a step forward. Amongst them, close beside Julian, he saw was Carol (or Boadicea as he still thought of her). "I need you with me," he whispered to her.

"I'll be more useful doing this."

"I thought we were a team."

"We are. I'll be back for you."

But Rick, Julian could see, was already looking around for someone to take Boadicea's place.

"Silence in the ranks!" The Beast had stepped onto the parade ground and was marshalling the volunteers together. "Those of you who've just lost section members will have to act in threes for the time being."

He means for ever, thought Julian. We're the 'forlorn hope', if I ever saw one.

A distant rumble, coming closer and closer, revealed itself as the transport lorries, old petrol vehicles grinding along the deep ruts of the one track to the camp site, their wheels spinning in places flinging up showers of mud. Eventually they were parked at the side of the clearing, steam rising from their bonnets. Their drivers in frayed, khaki denim suits got out; one, a woman, was wearing dark glasses.They disappeared into the end command hut.

There was a further inspection of the fighters, their equipment and their weapons, and then the order came to board the lorries. We'll never all cram into those old tubs, thought Julian, seeing the heavily encumbered fighters

242

climbing into the first lorry, handing up their weapons first, then being half-pushed, half-hauled up by the dangling tail board rope. He began counting the numbers, but then had to break off when he was ordered by the Beast to the smaller second lorry. Julian was one of the last to board, and found a place inside with difficulty, crammed up against the tailboard with the wet canvas covers, now dropped and tied, rubbing harshly against his cheek. The light was dim, coming mainly through the holes around the rigging lines of the canvas.

He looked into the interior, seeing the rows of fighters seated either side of the lorry, with others squeezed in at their feet. Their eyes, outlined by the black balaclavas, glowed in the murky light. He was glad to see Bert close to him, and he identified Rick as well, with a Bren propped between his feet, only three fighters further into the lorry. Julian cradled his own Sten across his knees, double-checking the safety catch was securely on. A weapon going off here would spell disaster. They might call themselves fighters, but most of them were rookies at this business of death – virgin soldiers, playing at killing, who had not even fired their weapons yet: soon reality would be upon them, and they must kill as if this was something they had done all their lives. Their initiation would last seconds at the most. Their enemies would die, their friends would die, they would likely die. Only survivors became veterans, and in this business those were rare.

The engine roared suddenly and the lorry lurched.

"We're off," someone said unnecessarily. It sounded a girl's voice.

Another voice: "Next stop Armageddon." There was a nervous titter at that.

The Beast's voice roared out over the noise of the lorry's engine and the creaks and groans of its shuddering body. "Silence! No noise from now on."

After that, there was only the quietest mumble and the sound of someone breaking wind, and the half-suppressed giggle that it attracted. Some ten minutes later, the pitching and rolling of the lorry, and the roaring of its engine, steadied, and they knew they were out of the forest and onto a road. Now the only noise in the lorry was of heavy breathing, an occasional cough, a throat being cleared. Julian's fear felt so palpable he thought it must show as an aura about him. He found himself wanting to pee, but there was no place to do so. He squeezed back at the urge and eventually it went away. He closed his eyes and his head seemed to float from his body. Like that, he was able to maintain his equanimity as the dreadful journey went on.

Occasionally they stopped. On one occasion there was the sound of voices outside, and they all tensed expecting the covers to be suddenly lifted and their purpose exposed, but in a short while the engine gunned back into life and they continued. A rumble of the tyres told them they were on some sort of corrugated, unmade surface. The rumbling went on for some time until at last it ceased, and they could sense they were going slowly now, until abruptly all feeling of movement ceased.

"Out! Out!" voices were calling urgently – the Beast, the Major, and the Captain combined. The canvas was tugged open. They helped each other down, weapons, equipment, jangling and crashing. At the other lorry, parked in front, there was a shot – an accident certainly – and a girl lay screaming and writhing, blood spraying from her neck, those about her scattered as if from the burst of a bomb. Pulling a handgun from his holster, the Major went up to her and shot her in the head. There followed a deathly silence, as heavy as lead.

The lorries stood beneath the high arch of a concrete bridge. Beyond, a mean street of ruined houses ended at a high fence. The corrugated iron was rusting and broken. As they looked, they could see its panels swaying wildly in the wind.

Seagulls screamed overhead. Julian smelt the tang of sea air. They must be at some point in Ramsgate – but where? A black cat, as thin as its own bones, was watching them with yellow eyes from a bank. Two rats, frightened out of a drain, scuttled amongst the fighters, some of whom had gone to urinate against a bridge pier.

The Major now called them forward to the corrugated iron fence where all fifty stood around him in a straggling group, their weapons in their hands. At the same time, Captain Bradwell with a female fighter carried the body of the dead girl back into the lorry. The wind shrieked around the bridge, and the spattering rain driven from a grey sky stung their faces. They stood tensely waiting for the Major's commands.

"Get into your sections. Bren parties with the Sergeant-Major. Detonation carriers with Captain Bradwell. The rest of the assault teams under my command."

There was some confusion, and even some chatter, as they obeyed. Captain Bradwell looked magnificent, Julian thought, standing up tall, her arms raised, calling out "My teams to me!"

Once order was obtained, and the noise died away, the Major said, "This is what we have trained and planned for. This is ACTION and this is NOW. Once we are past that fence, the battle begins. We will regroup here afterwards. The lorries will take us away. Anyone who does not make it back will be left. Do you understand?"

There was a murmur of assent. Julian's body begin to shake and he felt his blood running thin like water. He urgently wanted to pee again. But it was too late now. He looked at Bert and Rick standing close to him, but under their black balaclavas he could not judge what they were feeling. Bert, however, jabbed up his thumb at him, and he gained some reassurance from that.

"The Control Station is right beneath us," the Major continued. "It's protected by wire, which I will blow with a charge. A further charge will open up the building to us. My sections will go in with two Bren teams, and wreak hell. Kill everyone. Our surprise will be complete. Their Guard is unlikely to engage us. They will not be expecting an attack. If they try, we will destroy them. We will destroy them, anyhow –with bombs and bullets, hand to hand. While we are doing this, Captain Bradwell and her party will descend to the Bar and attack and blow as many turbines as possible. Two Bren teams will provide covering fire. It will be demanding, it will be dangerous: most of you will be firing for the first time, but IT CAN BE DONE; IT HAS TO BE DONE. When our targets are destroyed, I or Captain Bradwell or the Sergeant Major – whoever's your commander then – will signal a retirement to this point. We'll then get out and away. We should leave the bastards with more than a headache." A nervous chuckle or two at this. "Good luck to you all!"

The Major looked at his watch. "Right, this is it."

There was a general tensing of the fighters, a last checking of weapons; one or two even briefly shook hands. Eyes glinted through the black face masks.

The Major moved to a gap in the corrugated iron panels of the fence, and with the Beast's added strength forced the gap further open, enough to allow two fighters through at a time. They moved in their sections, following their commanders. Julian saw they stood on a green, grassy plateau, with the flat-roofed Control Station immediately below them, and further off the upper works of the SupaPod, with its wide-spread concrete aprons, piled with stores and seamed with the tracks of the trains that came and went. Beyond, the great Bar jutted out into the sea, with the grey wind-driven waves breaking against it. He did not envy Captain Bradwell that target. It seemed impossible that she would even reach it, let alone complete her attack. Yet the Major had spoken his plan.

Julian cocked his Sten, as he had practised so often, this time with a live round, a full magazine. He carried a further seven charged magazines in a belt round his middle, some 200 bullets with which to kill the enemy below.

He remembered when he had come here to the Control Station and been shown around, learning about how the control chips implanted in human beings could be monitored in that hellish world he had once been part of. Now he had returned to kill and destroy.

Julian saw that the Major carried two of the demolition satchels and had a Sten slung across his chest – the perfect fighting man. Captain Bradwell too, with her satchels of explosives and a pistol stuck in her belt, her eyes fierce, her uniform shiny with the rain, was clearly one who meant to do and return: no defeat in death for her.

They began the attack, each group moving nimbly down the steep slopes. Captain Bradwell was already far out in front, with her section, mainly of female fighters, about her. Julian was close behind the Major approaching the Control Station wire, with Rick motioning at him to keep low. The Major's charge exploded, and he burst through the gap created with Julian's team close behind him. Behind him, he heard a gun firing, a flat sound like a hammer knocking on wood. That lumbering ox, the Beast, must be covering them. A man wearing Lilac suddenly popped up in front of Julian as if he had come out of the ground. His mouth was set in an 'O' of surprise. Julian felt his Sten quiver, two shots only, as he had been taught. The man fell away, his 'O' spurting blood. It was his first kill. It was not to be the last.

The Major heaved his second satchel against a shuttered window. It burst in a cloud of white, shot through with red. The window gaped wide. The Major went through, with Rick close behind. Julian tore his thigh on the jagged steel, but fell inside after them. Gunfire filled his ears. All he could think was I've fucking wet myself – but it was his own blood running on his leg. He scrambled after the rest of the assault group, finding himself in the room with the bright shining Screens he had been in before. He fired at the Screens and they dissolved before his eyes, as if a stone had been chucked into a mirrored pool.

Out of nowhere, it seemed, some Guards appeared. They had clearly been surprised; one had bare feet and was in his underpants. A laser bolt hit the wall beside Julian. He fell on his face. A grenade burst, thrown by whom he did not know. The blast knocked the Sten from his hands. Scrambling for the gun, his hands slippery with blood, he shot the trouserless Guard in the legs, then, as he fell groaning, put two bullets into his head.

Rick was down, perhaps hit by a shot from his own side. He lay still. Bert had been blown aside by a grenade as if by a great wind: bits of his flesh were plastered against a metal cupboard. There was no sign of the Major. As Julian rose to his knees, a man rushed at him waving nothing but his fists.

It was the fat man, Gerry, who had once shown him around here. Julian gave him a burst of his Sten that dropped him like a punctured balloon. He changed magazines, as easily as if he had done this all his life, amazed at how steady his hands were. Taking a grenade from his belt, he threw it into the next room, following after it firing from the hip.

Where the fuck was the Major?

* * *

The Major was dead.

One of the Guard, trapped in the Station kitchen without his laser gun, had lunged at him with a bread knife after his Sten jammed. The knife had pierced the Major's neck, severing the carotid artery. He had fallen back into a corner jetting blood. He died not knowing the Control Station was taken. The last sounds in his ears were of grenades exploding. It was not the death he had wanted, but at least it was a soldier's death.

The Major's soul floated out to join those of all the other warriors killed since mankind had first made war. It was a very crowded place his soul found, yet only a tiny niche in eternity. Joining him there was fat Gerry whom Julian had killed. "Move over", some substance in the ether that was now Gerry seemed to say. "There has to be room for me too, and for very more to come. The killing goes on and will continue for a long time yet. I don't think it will ever stop."

So the Major doubled himself up to allow Gerry his place, and shook hands with him. It had been a fair fight, they agreed. Yet, a pity we were killed, for the world is a wonderful place and we would like to have enjoyed much more of it – but not now to be. And all the stars of the universe rushed down at them and they saw that the next life would be even more beautiful than the one they had just left, and they took a vow that this time they would not make a mess of God's creation. And so they slept, oblivious now of the affairs that until their last moment of life had so consumed them.

To his great surprise, Julian found he was enjoying himself throwing his grenades; kicking a door open, pulling the grenade pin, bowling it in underarm, the lever springing out and clattering down, the anguished cries within, then shooting the bursting, reddened figures with the Sten, their hands thrust out, screaming, appealing, legs collapsing, blood spraying – great fun! Other fighters were with him now, some of them women, who were good at this too. They shot two men together in a bunk; perhaps they'd been gay, now they were dead. One had his false teeth in a glass by the bed.

More fighters from the Major's teams were in the building. They shepherded outside into the slashing rain Guards and Lilac workers alike, men in pyjamas who had been sleeping, one completely naked, his hairless penis like a wagging finger, a rolly-polly of a woman who had been cleaning, two young bespectacled youths who had been punching in data at a keyboard – they were all grateful to be prisoners instead of dead. Lined up on the parade ground where Julian had watched the Guard drilling, the Beast then opened up on them with a Bren, the firing continued until the very last stopped kicking. The fat cleaner nearly got away until one of the fighter girls chased her and stabbed her in the back with a hunting knife.

The Control Station caught fire. Sudden flames swelled red at the windows. The Major! It was too late to bring out his body. With the other dead, his body burnt – a funeral pyre worthy of Valhalla. The remaining fighters – some twenty of them who had not been killed or injured: the Beast was going around with a Sten shooting the few who lay badly injured – moved forward from the burning building behind them, gazing down the hill which Captain Bradwell's demolition teams had descended. The Beast now pushed his Bren teams forward, firing on the rail trucks, the station buildings, and at the huddled Lilacs glimpsed scampering between buildings.

Through the rain and swirling smoke, Julian could see figures moving out onto the great Bar. Flashes rising like sparks told of a fire fight going on, then the figures were past that point running for the black bulk of a turbine's housing – Captain Bradwell and her Amazons, with the red-haired Boadicea amongst them.

There was an explosion at the turbine, a point of bright fire followed by a wave of buffeting sound, then white smoke rising, followed by another flash of fire and an echoing roar further off, and some figures on the Bar were running back. The chatter of the Beast's Brens opened up again. Some people by the rail tracks had fallen. Were they Lilacs? Were any of them Des and Jake, he wondered, wretched men from whom he had escaped that long time ago? He thought then of Sandra, and found his hands on his Sten were shaking. His right leg hurt, the pain tore suddenly at him, and he saw the bloodied mess oozing through his torn trouser leg. He heeled sideways and nearly collapsed, but another male fighter, whose name he did not know, supported him.

"Right on, mate. Keep going. It's nearly over."

The Beast was returning, as was Captain Bradwell and many of her demolition teams, their job done. Then, stark against the green slopes immediately below the point where Julian stood, he saw the Captain fall, hit by Guards' fire. They had got an old machine gun into action, set up behind a concrete shed. He could see its barrel poking out, whispers of smoke jetting from it as it fired. The Beast's Brens clattered out once more, covering the retreat of the rest of the party, but Captain Bradwell still struggled on the grass trying to drag herself forward.

Motivated by a force beyond anything rational, Julian found himself descending the slope, his own pain now just a dull background to this exertion, the hiss of his breath in his teeth, his gaze focused on the twisting, writhing body of the Captain just feet below him. He stumbled, dropping his Sten, but he was at her side, lifting her up. He found her body to be as light as a feather, and he hauled it up onto his shoulder and began climbing back. He saw a Guard some yards away to his right stand up out of the grass and aim at him, but fall away suddenly, shot down by someone else. Hands reached out for him as he reached the top of the ridge, and the burden he bore was lifted from him. He collapsed now onto his knees, his breath coming in gasps. Close by, another Bren was firing. Far below on the concrete aprons many figures had gathered. One group, which looked disciplined, were clustered around something or other – a gun, a large gun? It was hard to see.

"Get down," yelled a fighter. A jet of fire below and a great explosion on the stone parapet beside Julian, knocking his body sideways, crumpling him up like a leaf, pain such as he had never known searing him, darkness closing.

"Get back to the lorries!" he heard the Beast shouting, and there were rushing figures all about him – but he was in darkness and could not move.

He remembered being frightened of the Beast's coup de grâce, then even that fear receded.

25

He woke.

His eyes were out of focus. He could remember little of himself or what he had done, or where he was. *He did not know where he was!* That was serious, surely. Very serious.

He struggled to move but found he couldn't. He lay in a bed which cocooned him like a tight jacket. He had no movement in his shoulders or his legs. He felt trapped, and called out, but was aware of making only a spluttering sound. He tried again and thought this was a stronger, higher noise that might reach someone, so he relaxed and stared up at the ceiling with his muzzy eyes. Piece by piece the vaulted ceiling gathered itself and became clearer, so he saw he was looking up into a wave that was falling away in white spray on either side. The ceiling was dark in one place, a shadow perhaps, but he could see no greater light that might have thrown a shadow, unless there was a window somewhere and the sun was shining. The sun! He longed to feel the sun and have its warmth on his flesh, and hear the air breathing down the long shadows of some hot afternoon.

Where was he? Why did no one come?

He was piecing his mind together now, bit by bit, as he had pieced the view before his eyes together, and he remembered the battle and the Major's body collapsed back like a crimsoned puppet, the strings that had held him together snapped forever. And he remembered throwing the grenades and firing the Sten, and the power he had felt, as if high up on a cushion of air; and then the pain that had come, and the terror he had felt when his life was being sucked out from him down an ever-narrowing tube of darkness…. So how was it that he was here when he should be dead? – unless this was death, of course, but he couldn't see how it could be.

There was a sudden puff of air in the room and a sweet smell – a smell of cleanliness and order and comfort – a swish of clothing and a figure came into his sight, and he saw it was Tina – Tina in her grey nun's habit, as he had seen her last.

She smiled at him. Her face, he thought, looked older than he remembered, more care-worn.

"Tina, Tina, Tina," he kept repeating. "How…How…" There were a thousand questions that he wished to ask her, but the pain suddenly returned and stabbed at him, and all he could do was gasp.

"Here, drink this." She held out a glass of water, and helped him to take a gulp of it. Much. though, ran out over his bearded chin. She mopped at his mouth with a soft, white cloth.

"We are going to move you away," she said, "to somewhere safe. Here, at St. Augustine's, you have sanctuary only. I shall come with you. There is much I need to tell you."

Julian struggled to sit up. He tried to thank her. He wanted to know who had saved his life and brought him here. What had happened to his comrades he had fought with? Had their attack been a success? He remembered going out to help someone…..Of course, he had found Captain Bradwell on that terrible slope and picked her up and brought her back. Had she lived? He did not know. Did Tina know?

"Do you know what happened to me?" he asked.

"I have been told some details." She sounded reluctant to speak of this.

"Did the woman live?"

"You mean the person you saved? Yes, she did."

He sighed his relief. "That is good. That is very good."

He rested for a while as she looked on. Her face, he thought, is translucent. It is as if light shines through it. I should be able to see her blood vessels pulsing. But I cannot…."

Then he became agitated again. "Is there a war on now? Is SupaPodia avenging what we did?"

"No. The attack was put down. You did a great deal of damage and killed many people, some in the SupaPod when the power went out. But, as far as I know, there has been no SupaPodia follow up, no counter-attack. They want peace as much as anyone else. I did ask you – pray for you – not to take part."

He felt chastised. He felt hugely sorry to have upset her. He was very sad to have caused the death of ordinary Podders. Yet he made himself say, almost sulkily, "It was worth doing. To show them they cannot get away with their evil forever."

"Perhaps…," she said, and he was surprised to hear that word, even if it was delivered in a reluctant tone, "….perhaps, just for once, violence will lead to greater understanding, even to a new settlement."

"What do you mean?" His mind was still drowsy, but he sensed at once something new and unexpected might be happening.

"When you are stronger, I will tell you."

"Tell me now."

She sighed and rose to her feet, walking away from the bed to the centre of the room. He could now see her now clearly in her grey habit and plain white coif standing looking down at him. A wooden cross was fastened to the whitewashed wall behind her.

"Very well," she said after a lengthy pause. "Some of your fighters brought you to me. They seemed to know of our connection. Perhaps you told them. I do not know. They said they owed you a debt because you had saved the life of one of their leaders. But SupaPodia has since tracked them down and I understand most have been arrested. Their fate isn't known."

Julian groaned and covered his face with his hands.

"They would have arrested you as well, but I was able to plead sanctuary to them, which they have respected, although at first they threatened violence to this house."

"Who do you mean by 'they'?" Julian asked.

"Some officials from SupaPodia. They came here with Commissioner Lascelles, who knows me, and I her. She's high up in SupaPodia. Do you remember, I spoke to her when we were travelling that time to King's Lynn. I call her my Aunt Pamela because she was good to me when I was young."

"Oh, yes," Julian groaned weakly. He did remember her; a very unpleasant, arrogant woman, he had thought.

"But why would they not simply come and take me?" he asked. "They must want to wipe us all out." He said this with a great effort.

Tina walked back to the bed and bent her head to look directly into his eyes. "For two reasons. Because you were badly injured and they didn't want you to die. To move you again, particularly back into a SupaPod, would probably have killed you and they *want you alive*."

"So, now I've recovered, they could come for me at any time?" Bleak fear had returned to him.

"No. That will not happen. Because of the second reason."

"And what is that?"

"Because Pamela Lascelles knows who I am – that the High Director of SupaPodia is my father. She, and their security people, knew I had been working in a SupaPod, but they had not been sure when I had left or where I had gone to. Now they have found that out; it was not difficult – Stanley would have told them. They know everything now, and I have agreed that all sorts of communication be opened up. My father has been informed, and a plan has been drawn up."

Her voice took on a greater note of urgency. "You see, they want an end to the violence – to the attacks on the SupaPods and the Eliti estates that are becoming increasingly common, not just here in Britain but, it seems, elsewhere in the world. They see me as an important factor – an important link, if you like – in helping to put down the revolts. If the problems causing the attack on the Ramsgate SupaPod can be understood and resolved, then the grievances elsewhere might also be settled – peacefully this time. We will be able to create a new understanding between SupaPodia and the OuterWorld, of benefit to all."

"But how can that be?" Julian croaked. He felt very tired now. These revelations were almost too much for him to take in. "Nothing can ever be resolved unless the whole edifice of SupaPodia is brought down, or at least radically altered."

"Of course. And I think change will come. But in time...in time. My father has told me so himself."

"He has been in direct contact with you?" Julian said weakly.

"Yes. Through a Screen carried by Pamela. She maintains constant communication with SupaPodia, and with other Eliti as well. My father has now *invited* me to the forthcoming Convention of SupaPodia International; the one at the Cape I've already told you about. It'll take place in February; that's only three months away. I have told my father about your case, and he wants you also to come, so he can hear your evidence at first hand. What has been going on in individual SupaPods like Ramsgate has come as a great shock to him."

"And you believe him? You trust him?"

"Of course. We may have had our big differences in the past, but he's not a bad man. This will give me that opportunity to acquaint him with the real conditions of SupaPodia that I spoke to you about previously – before you set your mind to violence. Once he learns what has been really going on both within and without SupaPodia – the very reverse of the progress for humankind he would wish – then he will take steps to change things. It won't happen overnight, but it will be a start – a most important start. SupaPodia Media Services have even announced what is termed a 'New Initiative' for the Convention, and their notice, as much as my father's word, means it *will* take place. Let me see now, how did SMS describe the Initiative exactly? Oh yes, 'a much-needed cry for a more balanced and fairer world order.'"

Tina's eyes shone, her hands clasped before her as if in prayer. Julian thought I hope she is right. But a great doubt filled him, like a black boulder in his brain.

"I hope this works out," was all he could say.

"It's what God wishes," Tina declared beatifically.

He probably does, Julian thought. But sometimes His wishes take a very long time to be fulfilled, and in the meantime they can be twisted by humankind into whatever form seems most convenient. He did not think SupaPodia was going to yield any of its power so easily, nor would the Eliti of the world surrender any of their land or bountiful wealth without a fight.

"You are going to be moved to a place where you can better recover," Tina said. She looked much more relaxed now than she had seemed before. Probably, Julian thought, this news of a deal and reconciliation with her father had been a great burden for her to put to him.

"And two others will be transferred with you." Now Julian did look his surprise at her.

"Yes, we took in two who also suffered with you. One is a Captain Bradwell, whom you rescued, I understand, and the other is a woman who calls herself Boadicea. I don't think that's her real name."

"It's Carol," Julian said, waves of pleasure washing through him. So he wasn't alone here. Others had escaped with their lives and freedom as well.

"Ah, Carol. That's good to know. She insists on Boadicea, though."

"She's a toughie. Was she badly injured?"

"She had to have her arm amputated. Our doctor saved her life. She's still in the infirmary."

Oh God, Julian thought. "What about the Captain?" he asked, remembering how slight her body had seemed when he had carried it up the hill.

"Gun shot wounds only – flesh wounds, nothing too vital. She wants to come and see you as soon as you're up to a visit."

"Tomorrow perhaps," Julian said. "I'm sorry I feel very tired now. What you've told me has been quite a shock."

"Of course." Tina ran her fingers over his cheek, and then bent forward and kissed his bearded cheek. "Ring the bell…" – she indicated a handbell on a table by the bed – "…if you need anything. Someone will come and help you. Otherwise try and lie as still as you can, or you may tear your wounds open."

"How bad was I?"

"Some large gashes to your legs and your right side, but all healing up well. Our doctor had quite a job stitching you up. It's lucky he was here as he's now left to take up a post at Buckfastleigh. He's left precise instructions for your care. Your Boadicea told me you must have been too close to an explosion for it to do you more damage: it was the concussion that knocked you right out, lucky not to have collapsed your lungs, she said. You were very fortunate. Others, she said, were killed by the same shell"

"Yes, I have been fortunate, very much so."

"Tina…" he began.

"Yes?"

"Where are we to be taken?"

"To a Convalescent Home on the Hampshire coast – a high class one It's run by Pamela Lascelles: she and her husband Rupert live in a big house nearby. It was she who suggested you complete your recovery there, with the other two. I will be joining you a little later. If all works out, we will go on from there to the Convention at the Cape."

Julian felt so drowsy he scarcely reacted to the name, Pamela. Yet at the very back of his mind was an anticipation of something that was wrong, something to be feared.

Nonetheless, he drifted off into a deep, dreamless sleep.

26

The news from SupaPodia UK had come as a great shock to the High Director.

Joshua Pomeroy-Collyer read the reports carefully, feeling a trembling in his fingertips as he traced the lines of text on the paper sheets printed out from his Screen. He was greatly disturbed by the volume of unrest from all over the world, wherever SupaPods were already in place or where they were currently being built. There had been riots in Brazil where an enormous SupaPod in Rio Bay was planned, and riots as well in Namibia where a first SupaPod for the Khoikhoi people was proposed at Swakopmund.

Astonishment filled Joshua as he read on. Did these protesters not realise that the SupaPods were for their great benefit? Within them, peace and comfort for ordinary people could be found, with no need for struggle in the business of living; no need either for sinful money, or for bartering and dealing, and enough entertainment to fill all their days, even provision to secure a mate, so as to enjoy one of life's greatest pleasures: sex. There was security, and the company of their fellows about them, and purpose as well in representing SupaPodia in very many fields – in sports, for instance, or in theatre and singing and dancing, live events that were second to none. Why then, in the name of goodness, why then, even in the name of hell, were they seeking now to throw all this away? – just when SupaPodia's development was advancing to a fullness and maturity that meant it would soon be established as the supreme world-governing organisation of universal happiness on the planet, banishing forever all those antiquated nationalisms and religions that had been the cause of so much grotesque dissension.

Joshua's principal concerns, however, rested with those reports out of the country of his birth, SupaPodia UK, still known by some – the obstinate and obdurate – as Britain. Here, one of the very few armed attacks anywhere on a SupaPod itself had taken place: was this then a symptom of a discontent

– of rebellion even – that might grow very much worse and break out in other places?

He drew in his breath as he read: 36 SupaPodia staff killed, including 27 of the local Guard, 48 residents of the SupaPod also killed, caught up in the collateral damage, 15 of the terrorists killed or died of their wounds and 23 captured (held currently for further interrogation, pending their disposal): they came from an organisation known as Nemesis (whatever that name might mean), which had been responsible for other terrorist atrocities in the South East of the country.

He later called an extraordinary meeting of his innermost Inner Command to discuss the SupaPodia International situation in general and the UK attack in particular. The meeting was held in his palace on the Inkwelo Mountain, the various helidrones transporting the Command members piloted in remotely by the Cape's Control Station.

For this meeting Joshua wore a tan coloured, 'Supreme Commander' uniform with much gold braid and multi medal-ribbon rows, and a high-peaked cap set with SupaPodia's logo of a slanting spearpoint. The members of his 'top team' – as he liked to term them – emerging from the helidrones, wore similar uniforms, only differing in the amount of braid and number of ribbon rows, according to their lesser or greater rank.

The meeting took place in the Cetshwayo kaMpande Memorial Hall, once free-standing but now contained within the later palace, its walls hung with many buffalo tusks and lions' heads, and with assegais and knobkerries crossed against ox and cowhide shields. Murals showing the many defeats of the racist, red-jacketed white men by the mighty Zulu people also decorated the walls. A former SupaPodia Commissioner had agreed to the building of the Hall, and accorded it its memorial designation, in return for titanium mining rights under Zulu territory. These mines, when exhausted, then formed the first SupaPods for the Zulu people, occupying much of the Nqutu plain upon which one of their greatest battles had been fought. The Zulus had thus disappeared literally into a hole in the ground, but many subsequent SupaPodia monitoring reports were keen to emphasise their new contentment, greater than anything they had ever experienced in their long history.

The meeting proceeded smoothly enough at first, with various of the Inner Command team members reassuring Joshua that the situation overall with SupaPodia International was stable, both in terms of its Inner and Outer populations, and that any riots, in particular those involving actual violence, were down to localised rabble-rousers with self-seeking agendas:

such individuals and groups could easily be identified and eradicated. Joshua began to breathe a little easier.

As regards the climatology reports, SupaPodia's Inner Command technical expert, Maria Spallspotti assured the Command there was no immediate danger. Spallspotti was a fairly recent convert to SupaPodia, having entered as a former 'adult entertainer' who had had a vision of redemption on a walking tour of the Peruvian Andes. Thereafter, embraced by SupaPodia's sisterhood and possessing a High School grade A in botany, she had rocketed upward in SupaPodia's hierarchy. The so-termed Antarctica thawing danger, as originally communicated to SupaPodia International's Inner Command by its Executive Committee, she had reassessed as 'non-urgent': any immediacy of a melt-out that would lead to an 'historic' rise in sea levels was now discounted by a further Crisis Committee headed by Spallspotti herself.

Joshua let out a great sigh of relief at this. He had ignored the earlier warning, and now it could be seen he had been right to do so. If he had acted (he was forgetting he hadn't known how to act), then many people – SupaPodia personnel and Podders alike – might have been severely disrupted. If you emptied out a SupaPod, where would you empty its people to, anyhow? Many of the best areas of natural, scenic landscape were now Eliti estates, or were needed for intensive agricultural production. Other more marginal land was regenerated forest and reflooded marshlands, helping to restrict the massive carbon emissions that had been threatening to overheat the planet. It would be ironic, therefore, if these climatic considerations, which SupaPodia, had been so instrumental in challenging, should now have been identified as threatening its own existence. Joshua found Maria's words, therefore, immensely reassuring.

No sooner was this matter safely out of the way, then he was being asked by old, buck-toothed Priscilla Bowl, SupaPodia International's Manager for Global something or other (he could not quite remember what) about the matter that he had tried to keep very much to himself, namely his daughter's sudden reappearance on the SupaPodia stage. He had already received a tip off about this from Don Parowski, his Chief of Security Services (C-SS) and thought it had been dealt with already more than satisfactorily, but now here was this ugly old boot trying to put in her boot, as it were. What did she really want?

It turned out that she, and, it seemed the whole Inner Command team, were uneasy about recent developments in SupaPodia UK, in which a relative of a leading SupaPodia official – "OK, let's not prevaricate"; most particularly the High Director and Supreme Commander himself – might be involved. Joshua's decision to grant an amnesty to the terrorists recently captured in Kent UK needed confirmation by the Inner Command, although the HD's right of personal discretion in such a matter was acknowledged. However, more discussion about the decision was most certainly necessary.

This was bad enough, Priscilla Bowl had continued – showing greater disrespect than Joshua thought tolerable – but any agreement by the HD about meeting his daughter, with other representatives of the terrorists in a private conclave, leading perhaps to modifications in the structure and practice of UK SupaPods (and possibly by that parallel extending to the whole of SupaPodia International) was a most serious matter that required the consenting approval of the Inner Command team members, and then only after a full and structured debate. And so the Inner Command meeting had broken up, with Joshua having to acknowledge there was a need for greater dialogue.

Seated later on his golden toilet – his solitary throne that had always served him at times of troubled reflection when there was the need for decision making – Joshua groaned at the problems opening up around him: a revolt from within and without, the terrorist attacks on his beloved SupaPods, a lack of resources for the Security Services, the need to re-equip, retrain, and recruit SupaPodia's Guards, climatic regression, and now his own daughter, apparently having sided with a band of rebels, approaching him under some spurious cover of religious sanctuary, largely invented by herself (yet he knew, being of his own flesh, he could not deny her: it had been *so good* to speak with her again). This last provided clear cut evidence that the practice of SupaPodia, in one UK SupaPod at least, demanded urgent investigation and possible substantial regeneration. Hopefully, and very probably, Joshua thought, the malaise rested in this SupaPod alone. He had already asked for in-depth inspections to be carried out, using impartial investigators from a surviving non-SupaPodia and non-UK academic institution – in fact, a college in the USA, which had always been the slowest region on the globe to take up the SupaPodia model for the survival of society.

He had also consulted, via encrypted face to face messaging on his Screen, his most kind and supportive friend from earlier days, Commissioner Pamela Lascelles. She had reassured him and told him not to worry. Everything in the UK, she had said, was very much hunky-dory and under control: she would be accompanying Christine to the Cape for the Convention and they looked forward to seeing him again.

Priscilla Bowl had gained her position in SupaPodia through a ruthless manipulation of the weaknesses of her colleagues, which she had identified so easily within both their service and personal records. Joshua decided it would be as equally easy to remove her through a similar ruthless exercise, this time by the direct administration of his power. Rising from his throne and flushing it, he thought, never underestimate the High Director of the largest, most powerful organisation that the world has ever seen.

Once he had made his decision, he visited his colonnaded temple of peace high on Amajuba. One encrypted message from his Screen to Parowski ended Ms Bowl's career forever: she was last seen handing out cups of gruel to would-be Podders awaiting their turn to compete for a place in the new Bengaluru SupaPod. In due course, her former position was filled by one of Lucinda's Asian girlfriends, who had been looking for a job.

Still, the worries continued to haunt Joshua. He sat in his temple as summer rain mists rolled in across the Buffalo River, and thought that his world was no longer permanent; somewhere both beneath and around him the rocks were cracking and breaking up, and he might suddenly plunge down to he knew not where – perhaps the same place as Priscilla Bowl had gone. He shivered, and sent for a litter to bear him down the hill to the more secure warmth of his palace below.

27

They sent an ambulance to take Julian to the Convalescent Home of Commissioner Pamela Lascelles. It was a luxury vehicle with an electric engine, painted yellow and green. It had huge black side windows, which you could see out of but couldn't see in. Julian had turned away the stretcher sent for him and was able to walk to the ambulance with the help of a stick. He had been given a set of second hand clothes to wear – a checked shirt and yellow pullover, a tweed jacket that fitted him badly, and a pair of broad-legged woollen trousers that looked decidedly archaic; he had the feeling that their previous owner must be long under the earth. A pair of slip-on brown shoes, a size or so too large for him, made up the sum of his possessions. Freshly shaven, he was now ready to face the world again.

Julian was intrigued to see that accompanying the ambulance in a separate vehicle – open-topped, like those military jeeps of yesteryear he had seen on film – was a guard of four girl soldiers, dressed in camouflage-grey uniforms, each holding a short-barrelled automatic weapon that looked much more up to date than the Stens deployed by Nemesis.

Tina waved him farewell. She was dressed in ordinary clothes this day, her nun's habit discarded. She had told Julian her period of vocational duty at St. Augustine's convent was coming to an end and that she would be joining him shortly at Pamela's Home. Provided he had recovered fully – which should certainly be the case – they would then be setting out together for the Cape in a SupaPodia airship especially chartered for their party. The High Director was organising everything, she said, with a hint of pride in her voice. Julian was a little disturbed by that. To his understanding, it represented something of a volte-face from Tina's previous attitude to her father.

He had been even more concerned when, emerging at last from the mental confusion caused by his injuries, he had come to recognise more fully who this Pamela Lascelles was into whose care he was going. Something inside him told him to be very careful of what her true intentions might be. If anyone had seemed to personify the worst of the Eliti and the arrogance of that order, it had been she – and her husband too, for that matter. He found it hard to believe that Tina held such good feelings for her, confident, apparently, that she would take her side in a petition to the High Director for a radical overhaul of the SupaPods. Was Pamela not just leading on dear, idealistic Tina, who had only a hazy idea of the uses and abuses of power in the real world? But for what purpose could that be?

Julian had been worrying as well about Captain Bradwell and Boadicea, as he still knew them. Although allowed temporary sanctuary under some sort of truce (which he had yet to fully understand), he knew they, and he, were in effect SupaPodia's prisoners, but perhaps with some small hope of an eventual pardon. Realistically, though, Julian thought the latter unlikely, given that all of them had been involved in acts of terrorism, for which others of Nemesis – if he understood correctly – had already been arrested. What had been their punishment, he wondered? He feared the worst. Those hideous Lower Levels were clear in his memory.

He hadn't been able to see Boadicea, as the convent nurses had thought her still too unwell to have visitors. Tina had told him, though, she was now off the danger list and somewhat stronger: she would be coming to the Convalescent Home later in company with Captain Bradwell. Julian's concern was about what would happen to them in the longer term. Would Pamela, as one of the Eliti and a Commissioner too, not hand them back to SupaPodia where they might disappear forever, or was she genuinely part of a movement within the Eliti that sought progressive reform and an end to bloodshed? It was hard to know. Everything seemed to have happened so suddenly that Julian had little up to date information to make a judgement.

Captain Bradwell had paid him a visit (Jill, he learnt, was her first name). By abandoning the formality of rank and surname, she was able to avoid any embarrassment while thanking him for saving her life. She was dressed in a suit of white linen, and with her diminutive stature and her close-cropped hair, he almost mistook her at first for Tina. He had been out of bed and seated in a chair when she had come into his room, and she had immediately taken him in her arms and kissed him on the lips – a most unmilitary thing to have done if they had still been in uniform.

"You were very brave," he told her. "You destroyed that turbine, I think."

"We destroyed one and damaged another," she said in a matter-of-fact tone.

"And your wound? Is it quite healed?"

"I was very lucky. Nothing vital punctured or broken. If you hadn't rescued me, though, I'm sure I would have been hit again."

He could see now that her right foot in its loose slipper was heavily bandaged, the bandage continuing upwards under her trouser leg. She winced a little as she stepped away from him.

"What now for you?" he queried, wondering whether he should ask her that question.

"Full recovery at the Convalescent Home we're going to, then back to my job."

"What job is that?"

"I was a physical education instructor – for children and adults."

"Really." Julian was surprised. There hadn't been much call for that in the rundown area where he had lived. "Where did you work?"

"Chichester. Do you know it?"

"I don't think I've ever been there."

"Come and see me one day, if you get the chance. St. Richard's Academy on Stane Street."

"What about SupaPodia?"

"What do you mean?"

"Will they just let you go after what you – what we – did?"

"I hope so. That's what the truce is all about. I'm done with soldiering."

"How did you get your rank of Captain?" Julian asked, curious. "Were you in the Army before?"

"There is no Army these days," she said laughing, as if Julian had said something very silly. "The Major gave me that rank. I had to sleep with him to get it!"

God, thought Julian. Does sex determine everything? I thought we were fighting for the truth – clear eyed warriors of the new dawn, and all that. He said, "Well, he chose well. And now he's dead."

"Yes. he's dead. He was a brave man and a good commander. But that's all over now. We made our point. It seems they've listened. Hence the truce and the amnesty."

"Amnesty!" Julian was surprised. He hadn't heard that word used until now.

"Yes, amnesty. I only heard myself last night. SupaPodia have taken enough revenge, it seems. They know that to build again, they have to wipe the slate clean. We are the lucky ones. Many of our comrades were betrayed and killed, many innocents too. Things will recover now and get better.

That's the big hope, anyhow. You'll know more than me, as I understand from Christine you're to be part of the reconciliation process."

"I know very little," said Julian, a little sulkily. So Tina had been talking to Jill about him. Was Tina then the source of the amnesty information? If so, why hadn't she told him when they had parted?

"Do you really believe the worst is over?" he said. "I can't see the Eliti accepting change. They have a lot to lose. And conditions in the OuterWorld are so bad they will take an age to recover. And the SupaPods! They can't simply be *improved*. They have to be shut down completely!"

"What's happening now is only the start," Jill said. "You and I, and those others we were privileged to fight alongside, have helped achieve that. Things will slowly get better, but it will take a long time – a very long time. But we are at least going in the right direction now."

She paused, then added, "Tina confided in me that her father is very important in SupaPodia. That fact should help take the struggle forward without more violence. You have been friends with her, I understand."

"Yes, we have been good friends," Julian admitted. "I have tried to follow her advice, but sometimes I fail."

Something warned him that, like Tina herself, Jill's hopes were a little premature. For someone, so much grounded in reality, he found this surprising. He did not wish to say anything to contradict her optimism. Yet, she had not seen the reality of the SupaPods as he had. It would take much more than sanctimonious words from the Eliti to bring those edifices down.

"May God bless the two of you," had been Jill's parting words to him, surprising him. Had Tina been speaking of her God to her, he wondered? Perhaps then the power of God was the non-violent force that would eventually get rid of the SupaPods.

Somehow, he didn't think that very likely.

The ambulance, with Julian aboard and a female Guard beside him, her weapon resting on a steel shelf where it rattled alarmingly, accompanied by the jeep riding ahead, took several hours to reach its destination. Some of the roads were blocked by debris – a fallen footbridge, a washed out drain, a collapsed hoarding – and it took a while to go around these obstacles, even with the jeep acting as a horn-sounding vanguard. They passed through towns where crowds of onlookers watched them sullenly from the roadsides, but there were no shouts or missiles thrown: the girl soldiers with their pointing guns saw to that. What had once been a major motorway had been turned into a dumping ground for rubbish, where ancient tractors wheezed and groaned, pushing and pulling at huge piles of debris, while seabirds shrieked and swooped above. It took them a while to find a way onto the section of the motorway that was still open, and then they proceeded faster, entering Hampshire and reaching the coast at the town of Havant, from where they crossed a narrow timber causeway to the island of Hayling. Through the ambulance windows, Julian could see a dark mass staining the sky further west, which the Guard accompanying him said came from the smoking chimneys of Portsmouth and Southampton, joined together as one of the largest remaining cities in the southern half of OuterWorld Britain.

On the far side of the causeway, which had shaken and rattled alarmingly under the ambulance's wheels, Julian spotted a huge sign fixed to a concrete wall. It read:

HAYLING PROSPECT CONVALESCENT HOME
PRIVATE ESTATE
OFFICIAL AND APPROVED BUSINESS ONLY.
ALL OTHERS KEEP OUT.
24 HOUR SURVEILLANCE.

Some yards beyond, another sign appeared to contradict:

HAYLING PROSPECT
WELCOME
YOUR CARE, OUR CONCERN.

They followed a long, winding road passing through woodland, with only the occasional glimpse of a broader open landscape to right and left. Occasionally Julian saw evidence of fallen walls and exposed foundations where whole streets of houses appeared to have been demolished, their remains yet to be covered by the saplings newly planted about them. At last, they came in sight of the open sea, stretching away from broad shingle banks where the roadway, now just a narrow tarred drive, bent away to the left. Here, looking forward through the windscreen of the ambulance, Julian could see what seemed to be the shoreline of another island across a broad channel of smooth green water. Even as he looked, some three or four helidrones rose from there, like clattering black insects outlined against the drifting white cloud, hovering for a moment, then dipping their noses and flying out across the open water.

"There's a Guard's air base there," said the girl soldier accompanying Julian, pointing at the far shore. "We get good protection here."

"Protection from whom?" Julian knew the question was unwise.

"Why, the terrorists, of course. We have to keep on stand-by all the time these days." She showed no sign of knowing his own recent role.

The driveway had almost made a U-turn, and was now running parallel with the sea, so Julian could look out over the open ocean, the blue-green waters foaming towards the shore in rolling breakers, but empty of any shipping as far as the eye could see. Through the distant murk yet to be dispelled by a clouded sun, Julian could just make out another shoreline, a high dark smudge on the horizon.

"Where is that?"

The soldier was on her feet now, picking up her weapon and slipping the carrying strap about her neck. "Where is what?" She bent forward to look through the windscreen. "Oh, that's the Isle of Wight. Don't think you can visit there. The whole place belongs to SupaPodia. They say the High Director has a house there for when he's in this part of the world – Osborne Park, it's called."

"I went there once when I was very young," Julian said.

"Well you won't be able to go again. No one's allowed on Wight now, other than for high-up SupaPodia officials and other Eliti. I heard they're even going to build an underground holiday complex for them at Freshwater Bay It will stretch as far as the Needles and will cost a fortune."

"SupaPodia International can probably afford it," commented Julian.

The girl laughed. She was nice-looking girl, with a clean-cut square face and large eyes. "Yes, they can afford it for sure."

"Would you like to live there?"

"Me?!" Hell, no. I like the outdoors too much. I wouldn't want to be shut up in a place like that."

"Where do you live then?"

Commissioner Lascelles has a barracks for her private Guard. It's next to her House which we'll be coming to very shortly."

"What's she like to work for?"

The girl's face closed up. "You ask a lot of questions. I shouldn't be answering them by rights, but as you're for the Convalescent Home and not the Correction Camp, it can't matter."

""Where's the Correction Camp then?"

"It's a way off on the far side of the island. You wouldn't want to go there. It's run by Commissioner Lascelles and it doesn't pay to cross her … Now I *have* said too much. Look we're arriving."

The ambulance, led by the jeep, had turned onto a gravelled drive and, passing between immaculately maintained gardens, reached a large house. It had an exterior that looked to have been made from a giant's set of building blocks – huge concrete cubes, white-painted, pierced by square, green-shuttered windows at differing heights. At the centre rose a square tower, capped by a pyramidal roof. It looked out across a broad stretch of shingle at the sea, where beams of sun, released from their morning cloud cover, played upon the surging crests of the waters.

What a house! thought Julian. Not exactly to my taste, but dramatic and modern, and not out of keeping with this seafront and the dark trees behind. Is this the Convalescent Home, or…?

To answer his unspoken question, the vehicles passed the front of the house and entered a belt of woodland, where the jeep pulled off onto a sidetrack but the ambulance continued on until the trees ended and the shore opened up once more. Here stood the immense red brick pile of a building in late Victorian style, clearly much restored, with round towers at its corners, a projecting porch concealing a massive front door, and several floors of windows, each framed by pale stonework. On the roofline, various terracotta figures – griffins, dragons, and the like – stood between the high stacks of twisting brick chimneys.

"We've arrived. This is Hayling Prospect Convalescent Home," said Julian's guard. "It was once a hotel, I believe."

She jumped down from the ambulance, and helped open the rear doors as a party with a wheelchair emerged from the front of the house. Julian was surrounded by smartly uniformed nursing staff, who smelt of fragrant soaps.

"Welcome," one large-bosomed lady in a blue-checked dress said to him. "I'm Gillian. I'll be in charge of your care. Let's first take you to your room."

He was pushed in the cushioned wheelchair up a ramp into the porch, then through the double-leafed doors into a marble hall. Statues in white marble, of men and women, draped and naked, in classic poses, stood around its sides.

He was taken into a lift, then wheeled by a porter along a carpeted corridor, until Gillian opened a door and he entered a large, comfortable looking room, with a bed covered by a cheery red and white counterpane, a mahogany dressing table and mirror, and two armchairs set around a low table. Heavy cream-coloured curtains were drawn back to reveal the open sea across an expanse of well-mown grass. A half-opened door by a built-in wardrobe allowed a peep into an en-suite bathroom beyond.

"I hope you'll be comfortable here," said Gillian beneficently, her small hands clasped in front of her.

"Thank you. I'm sure I will be."

"A nurse will be with you shortly. In the meantime, if you need anything, please ring the bell."

The first thing he did was to go into the bathroom and have a much needed piss, marvelling at the toilet bowl with its cushioned seat and button flush that set jets of blue water gushing out from all around the rim. He had not urinated in such luxury for a very long time – probably ever.

When he came back into the bedroom, staggering a little on his injured leg, it was to find a nurse there, pretty with an oval face and black hair pinned up under a white cap. She wore dark stockings and a blue dress edged with white. A watch dangled from a metal brooch pinned over the curve of her left breast.

"Hello," she said. "I'm Rose. I just need to take some readings from you, then it'll be best if you get into bed. It must have been a tiring day for you."

"I'm fine," Julian said. "I'd much rather just sit in the chair for now."

"Very well." She fussed over him, taking his blood pressure and temperature, and making notes on a board she carried. He had fallen in love with her at first sight, the rustle of her dress as she moved, the neatness of her figure, the quick, efficient way she performed her duties. If he'd had a daughter, he would have liked her to be like Rose. She was lucky. To work for an Eliti organisation was a favoured job for many, those not lured away by the promised benefits of a SupaPod. God! (He had no trouble now swearing by Him). He had lived through hell of late. How good it was to find quiet normality once more.

A buzzer sounded in the room. It turned out to be from some small device nurse Rose carried in her pocket. She placed it to her ear. "Yes, I'll tell him, Sister."

She turned to Julian who had collapsed back into the armchair. "You have a visitor," she said. "Are you able to receive a visitor?"

"Who is it?" Julian was suddenly alarmed.

"An important person. Lady Lascelles."

"Who?" Julian, just for a moment, did not recognise the name.

"Pamela Lascelles. She's the owner of this Home – and of everything else around here, for that matter. She would like to see you."

"Ah, of course. You must tell her to come in."

As Jill spoke back into her device, Julian felt some trepidation. Of course, he was only here at all out of the 'kindness' of Commissioner Lady Lascelles.

It was not surprising she should pay him a visit – but why so soon? Tina had already told him about the importance of her Aunt Pamela to her. So perhaps he had misjudged the woman earlier when he had thought of her as 'unpleasant'. As an Eliti, though, she was likely to be patronising to him at the best and, at the worst, dangerous. Tina had spoken differently – that she was, in fact, a friend, a very good and powerful friend, who would be willing to help them.

There was much about this that did not make sense to Julian. He must be on his guard with Pamela – very much on his guard. After the nurse had left, he sat in the chair watching the door, waiting for it to open, his heart thumping in expectation.

* * *

Despite his forebodings, Julian found Pamela to be all smiling concern and courtesy. She swept into the room wearing a full green skirt and sheer blouse, with a patterned silk scarf draped loosely over her shoulders and bosom.

"You must come up to the house," she told him after her first enquiries about his welfare, "as soon as you feel well enough. Rupert is away at the moment, with some of his friends in Scotland, chasing the deer – or whatever it is they do up there."

She laughed, raising a hand heavy with rings to her breast, her fingers resting there playing with the ends of her scarf, a sight which Julian, wary as he was, found strangely erotic. Perhaps she saw the direction of his glance, for her hand fell to her side and she busied herself checking the room and drawing back the curtains more fully.

"Are you sure you're not in pain at the moment?"

"No, not at all unless I try to move suddenly."

"I'll have some books and magazines sent up to you. I'm afraid there're no Screens in the rooms, but there's one in the main lounge downstairs. It's rarely on, however. There's seldom anything worth watching unless you want the SupaPodia feed, and I shouldn't think you do."

She looked at him quite sharply as she said that, and then smiled. "Don't worry, I'm no judge of anything you may have done. My sole purpose is to see you're well looked after until Christine arrives, and we can all get out to the Cape for the Convention. I think we'll be able to make a difference for everyone's benefit, whatever their station."

"When is Tina – Christine – due here?"

"Not long, I think. As soon as St. Augustine's releases her."

269

Everything was suddenly a bit of a blur to Julian. The memories rushed at him – Peter and Marion and how they had died, his escape from the SupaPod, Sandra's sacrifice for him, then Nemesis, the fight at the Control Station, the Major slit open, his body burning. Now he was here, in a perfumed room with a perfumed woman, the scents alien to him; they were making his head swim.

He had a sudden thought, which slid into his mind so abruptly he was surprised he could have forgotten about it. He put it down to the excitement of coming here. He would ask Pamela. She must know.

"Two others – two women – were coming here from St. Augustine's as well," he said shakily, feeling strangely unsure now and quite faint. "Are they here yet?"

"Two others? Women?" Pamela's voice was clipped. "Not that I've heard of. Who are they?"

Julian had the sense left to be cautious. "Oh, just some people I met when I was recovering. I was probably confused and got it wrong."

I wasn't, though, he thought. Tina told me. It seemed to be all decided. So what has gone wrong? Jill had been so hopeful of her release. She had talked of an amnesty. And Boadicea too, he imagined, although he hadn't been able to speak to her. There must be some misunderstanding. They are probably back at St. Augustine's waiting for Boadicea to be well enough to travel. But he was worried. He did not trust Pamela. Tina would be able to sort it out. He trusted Tina. He knew he wouldn't find peace of mind until she was back with him again.

He saw Pamela was looking at him curiously. "You look very tired. I should try to sleep – in the chair, if you wish. Here…." – she fetched a blanket and draped it over his lap: he felt her fingers briefly on his thighs – "…Keep warm. Your injuries were considerable, I'm told. My staff will look after you."

She opened the outer door, then looked back. "Oh, is there anything in particular you wanted to read?"

"Oh, that's kind. Just something light. An adventure story of some sort, perhaps." He felt weak and light-headed. Sleep was heavy on his eyelids. He felt it rushing up to overwhelm him.

"I'll see what I can find."

The door closed with a sharp click. Julian slept. When the nurse returned, she helped him to undress and put him to bed. He remembered nothing of this, only waking up after several hours with the room in darkness and feeling ravenously hungry.

He eat, after his wounds had been redressed, this time by a male nurse with a shiny shaved head. He slept again, and when he awoke there was a paperback book on the bedside table. It had a lurid cover of leaping flames on a black background and was titled, 'Nemesis'. He looked at the blurb on the back. It was hard to focus on the small print.

'....*The woman seeks her revenge on the man who has wronged her. Nemesis may come in many forms, but will it be through love or hate?....*'

Twaddle, thought Julian. He looked at the date of publication: 2033 – the year he was born. Coincidence? A strange coincidence? But surely no more. He began reading, then skimmed ahead, eventually tossing the book to one side. A great deal of violence, some badly written sex scenes. Why would Pamela select such a book for him? Was she trying to frighten him or make a joke of him? Likely so. But why? It was rather disturbing.

He fell asleep again and dreamt. And in that dream he lusted for Pamela. Waking abruptly, he stumbled out of bed and went into the bathroom. Gradually the effects of the dream on his body died away and he became more clear-headed. This must not happen again. He must be strong. His weaknesses must not lead him astray.

But astray from what? What was his purpose? Simply to stay alive? No, he had acted against SupaPodia and he must keep up the fight, whatever the cost to him. There was no other way. Pamela, or Tina herself, must not soften him from his true purpose. In the end, he would overcome all things.

SupaPodia, and all its minions of evil, must be brought down! He would not become one of them himself. He felt like Christ – Tina's Christ – in the desert, being tempted by the devil. The devil presented evil as good, and wrong as right. The devil twisted everything inside out.

Surely, the truth was in Christ. The answer was in Christ!

So Tina was right. She had always been right.

28

As Julian slowly recovered and grew stronger, he spent less and less time in his room, and he began to explore the Convalescent Home where he was lodged. It was much more a retirement home than a nursing or convalescent home, he discovered. The lounge, when he visited it, was full of elderly people, who seemed to have nothing more wrong with them than the fact that they were old. Some sat vacantly in chairs in their own lonely cocoons, while others were seated around tables chatting or playing card games or doing jigsaw puzzles – real old-fashioned people from the old OuterWorld, with whom Julian felt an immediate affinity.

When he had first entered the lounge, hobbling with a stick, a hush fell on the room, and the various sets of eyes were turned questioningly towards him. He had felt constrained to call out, "Hello everyone. I'm a new boy here. Julian is my name", and the curiosity, bordering on suspicion, had immediately fallen away, and he seemed to be accepted after that.

No one, in fact, ever asked him anything other than where he came from (he had replied Cambridge, rather cagily, having once lived there when very young, and not wishing to admit ever having been a denizen of a SupaPod, and particularly not on the staff of one). This was accepted with a mere grunt by most people, although one old lady called Edith, who told him she had lived most of her life in Cambridge – "until the current troubles", she said – had tried to wrest more information from him. Where had he been to school? What job had he done? – questions which he had been able to divert by talking about some feature or other of the old Cambridge he did indeed recall.

Meals were taken in a large open room that occupied the width of the building, with French windows that opened onto sea-facing lawns in front, and on gardens to the rear. It was late autumn, and leaves from the apple trees in the orchard beyond the formal gardens were strewn over the rich grass, the wind catching them and streaming them out so that they jumped and glittered in the pale sunshine. Julian loved to watch the wind straining at the tree tops, hearing their blustering roar, and seeing the long grasses bend before the wind, creating an effect of shivering silver across the lawns. Out to sea, he would watch the white billows foaming in to the shore and hear them crashing against the shingle banks. He recalled having watched the sea from the Upper Deck of the SupaPod. It did not seem possible now that he had once been shut up there, a mere observer of life through glass or Screen, and not able to participate in the real moving, coloured world.

The food was good. Julian thought Pamela must employ an excellent chef. The waiters and waitresses were all of the highest standard too, the men lean and tanned, the women short, petite and dark. Many talked amongst themselves in a tongue that wasn't English: he could not imagine from where they had been recruited, perhaps from a place where there was no SupaPod yet to take them in and lose them in a horror of imposed conformity.

It was clear now to Julian that Pamela and Rupert, although Eliti, for whom the SupaPods represented an ideal solution to the overcrowding and pollution of the earth, did not otherwise conform to the way of life maintained within the buried walls of the SupaPods. The 'culture' of the Podders was for Podders only: the way of life for the Eliti was of the aristocracies who had ruled in earlier ages, and they and their servants were organised by the old hierarchies that otherwise were now banished from the world.

Beauty and perfection of form was created and sustained for human enjoyment; diversity was promoted within the framework of controlling tradition, but was not allowed to run wild. Pamela, Julian knew (he had yet to meet Rupert who was still presumably in Scotland), might want changes in SupaPodia – perhaps she was sincere about this – but she would not want her new eminence as an Eliti altered one iota. So what was the deal Tina had spoken of that Pamela wished to put through her to the High Director? That subject remained largely closed to him, and could only become clearer when Tina arrived here in person. Yet, he could not obtain a date for that, although he had asked Pamela again on one of the few occasions since their first meeting when he had come upon her.

"Soon. Soon," she had replied, somewhat testily he had thought. Then she had turned back to him as if to make amends and asked him how he was recovering.

"Pretty well, thank you."

"Could you make the small journey to the house? I would love to ask you to dinner. It's just that with your injuries…."

"Your house is close by, isn't it?"

"Oh yes. You will have passed it coming here, only half a mile or so up the drive."

"The very modern one made of geometric shapes?"

"That's right. One of Rupert's whims. He once studied architecture – not too successfully, I fear." She laughed, tossing her head and flicking back her hair with her fingers. She's really quite attractive, Julian thought.

"I'm sure I could make it easily. I'm walking further and further. I was on the seashore this morning for a mile or so."

"Really. That's wonderful. Then I'll expect you, say, tomorrow at 7.00 in the evening?"

"Excellent. Thank you." Julian beamed his best smile at her, but later the alarm bells in his brain began ringing. What exactly was it she wished to talk to him about? He felt safe at the Home. In Pamela's own house – his Tina connection or not – he could very well disappear into some horror or other it was not difficult to anticipate. After all, he had killed for Nemesis. Nemesis, he knew, had killed Eliti. The Eliti would not forget or forgive. They would seek revenge. Tina, though, was surely his salvation. Pamela would never dare to move against him, because that could be construed as moving against Tina, and, from that, against the High Director himself.

What should I wear, thought Julian? He had discovered that the Hayling Prospect Convalescent Home had a shop. It was in an outbuilding next to the kitchens at the rear of the building. Julian had first been directed to it when seeking toiletries. Of course, he had nothing at all of his own, only the ill-fitting clothes Tina had organised for him at the convent. He had no money either, indeed had forgotten entirely the concept of money. The OuterWorld he had known before entering SupaPodia had been run largely on barter – another reason why so many had been eager to escape into SupaPodia. Without goods to barter, you could not even gain enough food to live on. A black market run by thugs had developed to control most supply and demand. For many women, and men too, the only value they could provide resided in the wasting value of their own bodies. Julian shuddered as the memories came back. He went to the shop not knowing what to expect.

He was surprised to find that, as soon as he had given his name, the proprietor, a large black man with an infectious smile beamed through very white teeth, told him that for him there would no charge: it would all be to the account of Lady Lascelles. Determining to pay back Pamela one day, Julian had no alternative but to take what he required. Rather reluctantly, he now perused the racks of clothing in the small men's section of Sam's Store (as it was known to everyone).

He selected a blue blazer with the design label of 'Captain's Cabin': it fitted him well. A pair of grey slacks that went with it, he found to be very loose around the waist, such was the weight he had lost since his escape from the SupaPod. Relaxing now into this world of free shopping, he piled up other items – a belt for the trousers, a couple of formal shirts, one white, one with a blue check, socks and underpants, the latter of a silken fabric. A pair of laced-up brown shoes followed: he noticed these had a stamp underneath, 'From the workshops of SupaPod Yangpu', and he nearly put them back. suspecting the slave labour with which they had been produced. Finally, a pair of blue silk pyjamas topped the pile, which he bore back to his room, feeling he had just won a lottery and had more riches now than he had ever known.

Sister Gillian was in the room when he entered, doing a sweep with a clip board in her hand. Nurse Rose followed her, looking worried.

"Everything's fine," said Gillian at length, and Rose's face lit up: this was clearly an inspection of some import for her. The system goes on, thought Julian. Once I was part of the system, and now I am just an observer, a guest, a bit like the Podders were in the SupaPod, but my lot is immeasurably better than theirs. The thought was not pleasurable, and he stood brooding about it while Nurse Rose put away his various items in drawers and wardrobe.

When Rose had left, he collapsed onto the bed, wondering what tomorrow's visitation to Pamela's house would bring. Be careful. Be very careful. He was worried too by the fact that there was still no sign of Jill or Boadicea. Daily, he had looked for them, but there was no whisper of them, and Sister Gillian, whom he had asked – he felt he could not question Pamela again – told him she had no idea about whom he was talking.

Such was the intensity of his feelings created by these matters, and his sense of dread that something was really wrong, that he left the Home and walked to the seashore, his body moving well now that most of his pain had gone. His wounds had healed up faster than he would have dared to hope. A doctor had taken out the last of the stitches from his legs and his right side only a few days ago, and here he was now walking without any aid, scrunching the shingle, the keen air on his face, the sound of the sea crashing in his ears. Indeed, the only pain that he felt now was the continuing ache in his back where Dr. Peter had implanted that faulty second chip. It was only a dull pain, remote in his body, as remote in some ways as the events of which it was a reminder, which would sometimes flare back to him, normally at night disturbing his sleep.

He walked further along the beach than he had previously ventured, entering a wood of evergreens that stretched down to the foreshore, the sounds of the sea now muffled, so that he felt as if he was in an encompassing tent of green, hidden away here and safe. He did not wish to return to the Home; he did not wish to go to Pamela's house; he felt no joy in the anticipation of the Cape; he just wanted his own life back, to be himself, to do what he wished and not what he didn't, to have the whole world stretched before him as a shimmering sheet of peace.

Then he realised the world had never been like that, even in those 'golden days' before this new order of SupaPodia and Eliti had begun. He must make the best of the world as it was. He had been exceedingly lucky. He should have died recently several times over – the hellish descent through the SupaPod pipes, the long escape across country, the battle and the killing. What right did he have to expect to live now at all, let alone in peace? He must take what he could and be grateful for what he had, and not have false expectations of dawns that would never come.

He was Julian Foster: he was alive and he was fed and clothed, and in that fact alone he was very fortunate.

He returned most sombrely to the Home.

* * *

It was nearly 6.45 the next evening went he left the Home to walk to Pamela's house. Rather to his surprise, not having been outside after dark for a long time, he found a total blackness enveloping him as soon as he moved away from the lighted front porch, like a heavy black blanket thrown over his head. The path, however, was lit by lamp posts at intervals, their light just bright enough to show the way. Nurse Rose, who had seemed impressed when he had told her of his invitation to the house of Lady Lascelles, had given him precise instructions. "Follow the lamps on the concrete path; you'll pass through a thickly wooded bit, and then come to an open area on your left where there should be lights showing – that's the barracks where her Ladyship's Guards live – a little further on and you'll see the lights of the house ahead of you. It should only take you fifteen minutes or so."

She had got on with making his bed and bagging up his dirty towels and other washing. He watched her neat bottom in her blue uniform dress bending and straightening, her tanned arms stretching out, smoothing down the white sheets, he longing to hold her and hug her. He didn't want sex in a dirty body-thrusting way, sweating and gasping, he just wanted the comfort of holding a woman again, seeing her head nestled against his chest, his hands lifting her dark hair and smoothing it back behind her ears, allowing him a brief joy to take with him into a future he was dreading.

Sister Gillian, coming suddenly into the room, must have seen the direction of his gaze behind the working Rose, for she said, "Now then, Julian Foster. Be a good gentleman or I'm going to have to give you something out of a big spoon." He had blushed, knowing she had guessed his thoughts, but Rose spun round and gave him a little smile, which made it seem much better.

He had dressed in the best of the clothes he had just acquired, and even splashed onto his cheeks some cologne he had also picked up in the shop. He had no outer coat, and the air was chill, so he hurried along the path with his arms across his chest as if to protect himself from any night monsters that might emerge. He passed the open area Rose had described. A row of lights shone out there into the black void fronting them; perhaps a parade ground, Julian thought, for Pamela's small private army.

He saw the white walls of Pamela's house from a distance, picked out ghostlike by spotlights set in the ground, and followed the path around the house until he came into the gravelled courtyard at the front. Here, he could make out the façade of the house with its sharp angled walls, overhanging upper storeys, and central tower. As he approached the front door, it was opened by a slim young man with dark hair, wearing black trousers and a black waistcoat over a white shirt. He had aquiline features but thickish lips. Julian noted, thinking him perhaps part Asian.

"Dr. Foster?" the young man said in a strange bird-like voice with just a note of query in it.

"Yes, indeed," Julian answered as levelly as he could. He was pleased his title was used.

"Do enter sir. Her Ladyship is expecting you."

A female servant, in a black dress and white apron, was passing as he came into the hall, and she dropped him a curtsy – "Good evening, sir."

"Good evening," said Julian, feeling a sense of unease. It was good to receive such respect and politeness, but it seemed this house was run on lines that might be too formal for him to find relaxing.

The hallway was lined with a grey wallpaper stencilled with white foliage. A light fitting like a glass boat, with high prow and stern, hung from two strands of golden chain. A table of white oak shaped like an artist's palette stood against a wall, as did several small bucket-shaped chairs.

Double-leafed doors at the end of the hall opened, and there was Pamela – Commissioner Lady Lascelles – to greet him, her arms outspread as if welcoming a close friend.

"Julian – it is Julian that you use, isn't it? – you're very welcome."

He stood awkwardly before her, wondering if she knew of his part in the attacks on the Ramsgate SupaPod, but then, of course, she must do, for where else would she think his injuries had come? Why then did she not order his immediate arrest? The chilling thoughts flashed in his brain even as he was shaking her hand with its long, jewelled fingers. Of course, the answer lay with Tina, and with Tina's connection, and with whatever ultimate aim and ambition resided deep within the sleek, rounded temples of Pamela, framed as they were by the silk honey of her immaculately dressed hair.

"I am sorry my husband, Rupert, is not here to welcome you as well," said Pamela. "He is on some hunt or other in the North, which is apparently after wolf and bear now, although I rather imagine he's simply watching rather than doing anything too active." She laughed, showing lines of even, polished teeth. Small coils of gold-spun earrings shook beneath the curls of her hair. "He expects to return soon, though, and then there will be even more trophies about the house."

She is bored with her husband, thought Julian. Remembering the elderly form of the grumbling Rupert seen on that SupaPodia train, he did not find this surprising. He followed her through panelled doors into a huge open hall of a room, its walls hung with many paintings. The room's central space around a massive white-marbled fireplace was filled with a cluster of fine antique furniture that looked too uncomfortable or fragile to use, with the exception of two chaises-longues, upholstered in silver cloth, that were set at right angles to each other, as the ancient Romans might have placed them.

Pamela waved Julian towards one of the chaise-longue while settling herself, half-sitting, half reclining, on the other. She was wearing an ivory-coloured blouse, the sheen of which looked glossy in the electric light, and a flouncy grey skirt, with a froth of petticoats at its hem. Her body seemed to merge comfortably with the silver upholstery of the chaise-longue. Julian, on the other hand, found a sitting, leaning position difficult, so he used his chaise-longue more as he would a chair, his body twisted awkwardly towards Pamela, propping himself in place with his extended left arm.

The dark-skinned servant came over to him bearing a silver salver with a chased-silver bowl upon it, into which he dipped a ladle and poured a measure of a clear liquid into a deep, blue-veined glass. He did the same for Pamela, and then made to depart.

"Sylvester," Pamela called out. "Leave the bowl on the side table."

"Yes, your Ladyship." He placed the silver bowl with its ladle on a delicate-looking table with thin curving legs and a marble top close to Pamela's left hand, and then left. The door closed silently behind him.

"We may wish more," Pamela said, as if by way of explanation.

"What is this drink?" Julian had picked up his glass and swirled its contents suspiciously. He was only too aware of the dangers of inebriation in a situation he did not yet trust.

"It's a punch Rupert and I have long enjoyed," Pamela answered. "Gin, lime, grapefruit, and a few other bits and pieces, topped with champagne. I hope you like it."

"Oh, I'm sure I will." In his nervousness, he added, "I could get tipsy on this, and that would never do…"

"Relax," Pamela said, with a note of exasperation – or was it humour? – in her voice. "You are perfectly safe with me."

Feeling foolish, like an adolescent with an older woman, he sipped cautiously at the drink. It had a cool bouquet; he could taste the citric flavours, delicate yet full too, so his first reaction was that he wanted more. He took a larger sip, then another, seeing Pamela was drinking too. The liquid burst cheerily within him, extending itself from his throat and belly into his arms and his fingertips, his thighs and toes. Comfortable warmth enveloped him. He felt his limbs relaxing, his eyes opening wider, his gaze clearer, his movements more deliberate. If this is getting drunk, he thought, it is the mildest, pleasantest way of doing so. I feel I could drink this stuff all day and still not get my thoughts or my words muddled. At Pamela's invitation, he rose to ladle himself some more, refilling her glass too.

He talked – inconsequential things at first, about where he had lived before SupaPodia, his teaching work, his love of the sea and the land, of nature, the clumps of twisted thorn bushes on the skyline of the Downs, the flights of birds settling to their roosts at dusk. Pamela listened, her body spread out languidly on the chaise longue, one foot touching the carpet, her glass balanced, it seemed, against the very point of her right breast. He thought he could see the outline of the nipple through the thin silk of her blouse.

He asked her about the Convalescent Home; what had motivated her to open it and what sort of clientele did it usually cater for?

"Oh, Eliti who have fallen on hard times and OuterWorlders from the upper classes who need support."

"Not the Podders themselves then?"

"Of course not, Julian. They have the best health care of all." She seemed genuinely shocked at the suggestion.

But Julian thought: does she really believe that? He remembered the rows of beds he had seen on the Lower Levels and their silent occupants, and of being told by Peter what would happen to them. Does she know anything of that, he wondered? – trying to look into her face, and only seeing inscrutability. One of her hands rested lightly in her lap.

Sylvester appeared on silent feet.

"Dinner is served, your Ladyship."

"Thank you, Sylvester. We shall eat here and not at table."

"Very well, your Ladyship."

Pamela stretched and yawned, thrusting out her arms. "I hope you don't mind. I'm too comfortable to get up and sit at formal table. How I hate those hard-backed chairs. Rupert and I often ask our guests to dine informally, à l'ancienne – in the old way, don't you know. The servants will bring the dishes to us on a low table, and we reach for them from the chaise. If you like, a servant may feed you…"

"No. No," said Julian hastily. He could not imagine having someone stuffing his mouth with food as if he was a nestling with a parent bird. "I will manage with you. It will be something different, I think, something fun."

Pamela's eyes gave out a sparkle and her pink-lipped mouth curved into a smile. "Yes, fun. I would like you to have fun. I doubt you have had much of it of late."

Caution, thought Julian. What does she know of me? What does she really think? He tried to keep his vision clear by thinking of Tina, to have her face before him, to see her grave, wise eyes filling his.

The food arrived – a line of uniformed servants, girls and boys, some very young indeed, bearing various pots and dishes, with ladles, glasses, spoons and napkins, all set down on a small table between their couches, its top no more than a foot above the flower-patterned carpet.

It was indeed pleasant to eat like this, Julian agreed. A servant would help him select food from the many bowls, and place it on a dish of black earthenware held out for him. When he wanted more, the food was held up for him to select. He took some white wine from a crystal carafe, which complimented excellently the meat (was it lamb?) and vegetables he was eating. Fruit and cheese followed, selected for him now by a young girl servant in a white, pleated chiffon skirt, her top bare but for two loose straps dangling from a halter neck, revealing rather than concealing her bud-like breasts. Julian saw Pamela was being helped by Sylvester himself, although one giant of a male servant wearing a gold fringed tunic also assisted.

In this unconventional setting, Julian found the conversation rather stilted. Pamela had been telling him about a play she had seen at a Greek-style theatre, hollowed out of the Sussex Downs at a place Julian did not recognise. When he asked what the play had been, she gave him a title entirely unknown to him. They moved on to talk of history. The ancient Greek and Roman worlds were favoured by Pamela, it seemed, subjects which Julian could certainly discourse on as well: those many years back, he had taught the history of the ancient world.

At last the food was eaten and taken away. The wine carafes and the silver bowl with the punch remained on the low table before them.

"More to drink, Julian?" Pamela asked. "I'd like you to join me in a toast."

She signalled to the white clad girl to fill his glass from the bowl. Julian was going to protest, but then thought, why not? I am far from tipsy. I can take more. The girl leant right forward so he could see her small pointed breasts. He felt a great desire to take them in his hands. Looking up, he saw Pamela's eyes boring into his. The giant in the tunic had poured wine for her. She raised her beaker, an action which Julian clumsily tried to match.

"To SupaPodia and the New Order," she said. "May the vision not fail."

Julian hesitated. Seeing his unease, Pamela added. "Where the vision is imperfect, we can drink to it being made whole."

He thought: that is true, that is what I believe. I can drink to that.

He steadied his glass. "To a more perfect world," he said, and all at once a line of falling faces tumbled before him, of Peter and Marion and Sandra…. and….and the Major, and faces he did not know, but whose poor tortured bodies he had seen, with the wires pulsing from them, and he felt sick at his own betrayal. He spilt his drink before he could place it to his lips, and in sudden despair dropped the glass cup onto the table where it split into glistening shards. The girl in white jumped forward from the shadows behind him to mop up the mess.

Pamela watched him, her mouth set in a sardonic smile, her own beaker raised to her lips.

"My toast. To the way we do things now. May it never end."

Julian sat, full of horror, knowing now there was no change in Pamela or any of the Eliti, or ever would be. Tina would be coming here to convert her, to convert the world of SupaPodia, but it would be a mission of the impossible. She must be made to realise that.

"You know you can have anything you wish here, Julian, don't you?" Pamela's voice throbbed at him through the mists of alcohol. How he wished he had not drunk that clear, deceptive poison again.

The girl had finished picking up the glass and mopping the table. The wet cloth she had used was in her hand. Her exertions had pushed aside the straps covering her breasts. Her nipples were small and hard, like pink marbles.

"If you wish her, you can have her. I'm sure you would like to." Pamela's voice sounded deep and husky. He looked at her. One of her hands, the wrist ringed with gold bands, rested high on the thigh of her giant servant. Panic seized him. Oh God, what nightmare world have I been stupid enough to come into?

"You can have her, or another, or is it as boy you want? No I don't think that's your predilection. Would you like to do it here in front of me, would that excite you? Or would you like me….?

"NO!" he yelled, the blood rushing in his ears. He rose to his feet, pushing against the girl so that she fell forward over the table, revealing her naked bottom.

"Where are you going?" laughed Pamela. "You can't leave now. You'll be arrested."

"Then arrest me!" he yelled. "You degenerate. You filthy old woman."

"I can get you anything you want," continued Pamela smoothly. He saw she was rubbing the giant under his tunic now. The giant stood there impassively like a statue, without thought, without feeling – a living toy.

"All I want from you…," said Julian, surprised by how suddenly his mind retreated from the vileness before him, his panic, his fear, his anger subsiding. He knew evil now, and he knew truth. The two would not mix. They did not make a drink you could savour, then chuck the dregs away. It was one or the other, and he knew which he chose. The discovery gave him strength. He was no longer frightened of Pamela.

"…All I want from you," he repeated, trying to penetrate the ghastly veneer of her face, seeing her claw-like hand now sawing at the exposed uprightness of the slave, the girl beside him too, still poised, bent-forward, her white bottom raised. "Is a world without you and all your kind, and that *we are going to get*!"

"And so think you," laughed Pamela. She had raised her dress and was beckoning the serving girl forward, crawling on hands and knees. He saw the girl had cut herself on one of the glass pieces; blood was splashed upon her white skirt.

He went to the door and out into the hall. No one tried to stop him. Indeed, there was no one about. He opened the front door. A chilled breeze met him. He shivered, although his whole body felt on fire.

As he prepared to step away, a voice – Pamela's voice, high, demented – screamed out.

"If we are damned, so are you. See you in hell, little man!"

He went out into the night.

* * *

It was pitch black. The spotlights lighting the house and the path beyond had been switched off. Had Pamela done this with her own hand, Julian wondered? – throwing some master switch to cut him from out of light into darkness. He felt frightened by what had taken place, despite his previous defiance. What would happen to him now? As importantly, if not more so, what would happen to Tina, who would be coming here to form one of this triumvirate, whose purpose was to gain better conditions for the SupaPods?

As he stumbled along trying to remember the line of the path, with no moon or any star in the black wind-stirred canopy above him, the response of Pamela came quicker than anything he might have feared. With a sudden rush of light, hand-held flares sizzling like fireworks, a patrol of her Guard swept down upon him, five or six of them in combat suits with their automatic weapons pointing forward at stomach height.

"Come with us," their lieutenant said. She wore a cloak across her shoulders and a high-peaked cap. "If you try to run away, you will be shot."

Looking at the deep wells of blackness beyond the hissing flares, he thought if I make a dash for it, I might just about get away – but what then? Where would I go? Everything I have now is at the Convalescent Home: I have found kindness there and new purpose. If I try to escape, they will probably not allow me back again. All that I have built up would be lost and I would have let Tina down. Yet, everything now is changed. I know there can be no trust in Pamela any longer. She may just have been drunk, or acting out a part to humiliate me, but she has revealed herself in her true colours. Will Tina believe me, though? She may think I am making it up to disguise my own weakness when tempted. So, I must do what they want. I have no other choice, anyhow.

The slim chance to make a break for it had disappeared as the female soldiers surrounded him, some even prodding him with the barrels of their weapons. They marched him back to their barracks, he limping and beaten, the strength that the alcohol had given him now wasted, his well-being sucked from him as if from a punctured balloon.

He was taken through a wide gateway and into a brightly-lit office where he was photographed by a corporal, who was wearing a camouflage-patterned skirt. He was then left alone in a small adjacent room with whitewashed walls and a wooden bench. He sat down.

After what seemed an age, there was a rattling of keys and the Guard's lieutenant who had captured him entered. "Come with me," she said. "There are some friends of yours here who are asking about you."

Greatly wondering, he followed the lieutenant down a long stone passage. He could perhaps have put some of his recent military training into use; attacked her from behind and taken her keys, then sought a way out, perhaps using her as a hostage – but he did not get beyond a flicker of thought of such an action. It would be even more hopeless now than it had been before. In any event, the lieutenant looked tough and fit enough to sling him over her shoulder and stamp on his neck if he tried.

The lieutenant unlocked a door. It was low and he had to bend his head to go inside. The lieutenant followed him. The room was dimly lit and it stank. Two faces stared at him startled from bunk beds, one above the other. He recognised them at once. They were Captain Jill Bradwell, whose life he had saved, and Carol, his Boadicea.

"What on earth are *you* doing here?!" he exclaimed, realising in that moment the foolishness of his words – but too late now.

They struggled up in their bunks and gazed at him with fear in their eyes. They each wore a sleeveless white garment. Julian could see that Boadicea had only one arm; the skin around her stump looked pink and raw.

"Who are you?" said Captain Bradwell.

"We don't know you," said Boadicea. Then she began to cough. She coughed for some time.

"That's all I needed," said the lieutenant. "The final proof."

"The final proof of what?" shouted Julian, knowing he had been taken in. "What is going to happen to these women?"

"Don't worry, they won't be executed but will be sent to our Correction Camp." The lieutenant added, "They would probably prefer to be shot."

"I'm sorry," Julian said to his former comrades. "I had no idea. I thought there was a truce, an amnesty, and you were to be set free to go where you wished."

"We were," Jill said. "But we were betrayed."

"Don't you give up!" Boadicea yelled out suddenly at Julian. "Long live Nemesis! Death to the SupaPods!"

The lieutenant was ushering Julian out of the room. "Correction is too good for them," she said darkly. "Now, there is one more person for you to see. You will know him."

"*Him*," thought Julian. I thought everyone here was female. Everything around me of late has been female. Nurturing female, self-sacrificing female, holier than thou female, aggressive female, manipulative female, rapacious, sexually insatiable female. It will be good to be in the company of a man again. But which man?

They walked several more corridors and at last came to a green door with the notice on it, 'Guard Commander."

Surely not, thought Julian. Pamela would have a woman in charge of her Guard, wouldn't she? Where would she find a man to command this high-stepping, lipsticked lot?

The lieutenant knocked on the door and a deep voice from inside said "Enter."

With her hand in the small of his back, the Guard pushed him inside. The door slammed to. Julian stood alone in the room – alone but for a man dressed all in black seated behind a desk. He was a large man, his two arms outstretched on the desktop, his fists bunched.

"It's so good to see you again," he said. His tone and rock-like expression belied the statement.

Julian made out the form and the face of the Beast. His head swam and he sat down on a round stool beside the desk. Was there to be no end to these sudden shocks?

"How in fuck's name did *you* get here?" was all he could think to say.

The Beast had lit a cheroot. Smoke circled in delicate white coils above his head. He had not offered one to Julian. He was in an expansive mood, however.

"You want to know why I'm commanding a bunch of women and my boss is a woman? It's because I'm being paid for it, and paid very well too. Nemesis was always going to fail. The Major was an idiot. He died an idiot. If your life is soldiering, you don't serve idiots."

"Nor," he added, dropping the burning end of the cheroot to the concrete floor and grinding it out with his boot, "do you work for any great ideals or purpose. Money is the decider; whatever one side or other is prepared to pay you, or what loot you can get when you smash up enough people and their property. I horrify you perhaps."

"No," said Julian glumly. "I've learnt of late not to be shocked by anything. There is no moral purpose left anywhere."

"You're probably right there," agreed the Beast. He lit another cheroot taken from a box on the desk. "These are good. Mexican, I believe. They were loot from an Eliti stores broken open by rioting Podders. We killed the Podders and took what they had looted."

"Who were you working for then?" Julian was not really interested. He felt so low that he wouldn't have resisted if he was be taken out and shot. But that didn't seem about to happen.

"For Nemesis, of course."

"I thought Nemesis was fighting for the Podders, not against them."

"With a gun in your hands, and the knowledge to use it well, you can swap and change about, particularly when people see that violence gets things done."

"But that's immoral."

"Jeez, Julian. It is Julian, isn't it? I hadn't put you down as a wanker. What planet are you on?"

Julian was being stirred out of his despondency. He was growing crosser. "What planet are *you* on?"

"The planet that has the power. That's what mercenaries go for. The people who are winning and have the money. We don't want to be killed for lost causes."

"So why did you fight for Nemesis?"

"Because I was paid a lot. It was worth the risk."

"So how did you escape after our battle and change sides?"

"I had my contacts. I knew the Eliti were arming themselves and wanted experienced soldiers to run their Guard outfits. Lady Lascelles took me on to train her girls."

"Why use women when you could get men?"

"Ah, you see, you couldn't. It's the girls who want to join the military these days. And they're good too, once you've got some training into them. Good enough for anti-terrorist operations, anyhow. I wouldn't want to go into a real war with them, but you see there aren't any wars like that any longer. The days of long drawn out, bloody, foot-slogging campaigns where men's strength and endurance were needed are long gone. It's cut and thrust stuff now, plus the old art of hand to hand, cold-blooded killing."

"And women are good at that?"

"They're more ruthless than men.

"I can't believe that."

"Believe what you want." He inhaled the cheroot, eyes raised to the ceiling.

"What are you going to do with me?"

The Beast chuckled. "Do with you? I'm not going to do anything with you. You're protected property. Lady Lascelles orders. She just wanted me to frighten you a bit. She's like that, a pussy cat really. Well pussy anyhow."

"You're as disgusting as she is," said Julian, his courage returning.

The Beast's expression didn't change. He just sat looking at Julian with a steady gaze, until it was Julian who had to look away.

"You wear your heart too much on your sleeve, to use an old expression," he said at length. You ought to be more canny. My advice to you is to feel which way the wind is blowing and go with it. You obviously have something that the Lady wants, or you wouldn't be here now. So, think. Think what that might be and act accordingly."

"And what about you? What are you going to do?"

He stood up. He looked huge in his baggy, black combat trousers and his black tee-shirt, its neck tight under his chin. A khaki beret lay on the desk beside him. "I've trained the Lady's Guard to the best of my ability. And it's a good unit now. They may be females but they know their stuff, as good as men. I'm proud of them. The Lady's got other plans for me. That's all I'm saying. You may hear more."

He held his hand out and Julian took it. The grip was like a vice on his fingers.

"They'll be an escort outside to take you back to the Home. We'll meet again, I'm sure."

"What about the Nemesis women who are here in your cells? They were very gallant, as you well know."

"Yes, I'm sorry about them. But they're out of my control. The Lady wants them punished."

"You're a coward then. They helped to save your life."

The amiable expression on the Beast's face vanished in a flash. "You know nothing," he said. "You're playing with shit. Get out now before I change my mind."

"I'm pleased to have talked with you," said Julian daringly, "but I can't say it's been a pleasure."

"And now you do disappoint me," he said. "Don't say I didn't try to help you."

There was a crash of boots outside, a knock on the door, and an escort of three Guard girls awaiting him.

When they were outside the barracks, Julian saw that dawn was breaking. A grey light in the sky was picking out the white breakers of a sea still deep in night. The winter trees stood along the shore like giants with crooked black limbs. He tramped between the smartly marching girls. At the Home, Sister Gillian awaited him.

"Where have you been all night?" she scolded.

"Life is hidden by shadows," he answered. "And nothing is clear. Neither coming by day or by night."

"I think you need your breakfast and some of your medicine," she said, shaking her head.

Julian was not going to argue with that.

29

Pamela brought Tina to see Julian at the Home some days later, just as if nothing had ever passed between them. Pamela was dressed in a light green trouser suit which billowed out around the upper legs as if blown up with a pump (perhaps the latest Eliti fashion, he thought). Tina stood beside her in a plain skirt and blouse, smiling down at him in that calm way he remembered so well. He had been reading in a canvas chair in the garden, enjoying the sunshine of an unseasonably warm day: he had had no expectation of either woman's arrival.

"Tina!" he exclaimed on first catching sight of her. "How marvellous to see you again!"

Tina did not answer in words, but her smile showed the warmness of her thoughts. She kissed him on the cheek, like a garden bird pecking at a dangling fruit. Pamela was also smiling. The whole world was suddenly smiling, thought Julian.

How did you get here? he asked.

"Pamela arranged transport. A lovely old coach with bunks, all to myself. I was very comfortable."

Good old Pamela, he thought, looking in her face now for the first time since that dreadful night. Her features were relaxed, cheek bones sharply moulded as if by a sculptor's hands, lipstick curling her mouth upwards and holding it in an inscrutable smile.

"How are you coming on?" she asked him in a voice that was innocent of any complaint between them. Indeed, the memory of what had happened that night, recalled now by Julian in the warm daylight, was losing its reality, becoming a mere dream, at worst a fevered nightmare. Had it ever really happened? Yes, of course it had: the Beast in black and those poor women, mutilated Boadicea and the brave Captain Jill, now consigned at Pamela's orders to some ghastly Camp. And, further back in his mind, the memory of that girl's bare backside and the jewelled arm – that very green-clothed arm he could see now – pumping rhythmically up and down. Those awful obscenities still raised themselves to fill his inner vision.

Yet he forced himself to smile back at her. "Very well, Lady Lascelles, thank you." He would play the game in the detached, non-emotional way that the Beast had recommended to him. He had no energy left for a fight. Tina could take the strain now. It was Tina who would lead the way with her father to reconcile the world between truth and evil. From now on he would simply be a follower, lucky – oh so lucky – to have survived to be in her company at all.

Tina had clearly been surprised by his use of 'Lady Lascelles'. When they were alone after Pamela had left to attend to a matter brought to her attention by Sister Gillian, she asked him, "Why are you referring to her title like that? Call her Pamela. It's what she would want. She has no pretensions about her position."

"She's evil," Julian hissed in her ear. "She's a wicked woman."

Tina was shocked. "Of course she's not. Where do you get that idea from?" She hesitated. "Are you…Are you still on some medication?"

"No, I'm not! I can't tell you now – there are ears everywhere – but you must believe me."

"Julian, you're a lovely, brave man, but I think you're a little paranoiac. Pamela is the one person who will help us. She is endangering her own reputation with her fellow Eliti by doing so. Far from being evil, she is committed to goodness, even if she doesn't share my faith. She has seen the wrongs that infect SupaPodia and wants to help improve things for everyone."

"She has her own military Guard unit and she keeps prisoners."

Julian had led Tina away from the walls of the Home in case they held microphones that could pick up their conversation. He was suspicious of everything now, paranoic perhaps, as Tina had suggested, but with good reason.

"I find that very hard to believe," Tina said. "How do you know it?"

"Because I was taken by the Guard to see them – the prisoners."

Julian didn't want to give Tina any more details. This was not the place or the time. He looked around him to make sure they were alone.

Tina gazed at him wonderingly. She doesn't believe me, Julian thought. She thinks I'm still ill, semi-deranged, and making this up. He recalled the sexual obscenities Pamela had put on show. He could never tell Tina about those.

"Perhaps you've picked up some story or other about Pamela," said Tina in a consoling voice. "I know she's been no angel in some of the things she's done; that's one reason, I'm sure, why she's been atoning with good works of late. But her heart is good and her intellect incisive. She knows SupaPodia can only survive if there is more democracy in the way it's run. There is a great need for change. She realises that."

"Hush," whispered Julian urgently, seeing Pamela emerging again from the front door. "You see what a fine view of the sea I have from here." He flapped his arms out as if embracing sea and sky. "I'm very fortunate to be able to enjoy it."

"Indeed you are," said Pamela, overhearing the last as he had intended. "But now you – all of us – must be on the move. The time has come."

Tina looked at her expectantly while fear stabbed at Julian once more.

"I've just been confirming dates and times. My staff relayed a call to me here. Owing to recent troubles, the SupaPodia Convention has had to be brought forward by a few weeks. Our flight to the Cape – it'll be by one of SupaPodia's executive airships – will leave in two days. We'll fly by Istanbul and Nairobi. The airships are slow, but they're much more comfortable than the cramped airjets. We should be in the Cape a week or so from today – just in time to make the new Convention date."

Pamela put out a hand to touch Tina's shoulder. "Your father, my dear, has sent a message to say that he is looking forward so very much to seeing you again. He is extremely busy at present, otherwise I'm sure he would tell you so himself. But at the Cape, you will have – we will all have – as much time as we wish with him. Our views will be very important to him."

Things moved fast for Julian after that. He was officially discharged from Hayling Prospect Convalescent Home, much to Nurse Rose's obvious distress, which, despite her professionalism, showed on her face. Julian found it a wonder that a lovely young girl like her had taken such a sentimental interest in him. Sister Gillian offered him more practical advice, however.

"Keep the bandage supports on your legs for a while yet. Do some exercises, like this…." – she began kicking up and down her own plump, black-stockinged leg in a way that Julian found vaguely obscene – "….so you can build the muscles up. If you do this regularly and by degrees, you should get full movement back."

"Thank you, sister." He leant over and kissed her forehead, causing her to bustle out of the room, her face reddened, muttering, "Well I never…"

He selected a much fuller wardrobe from the shop, thinking to pick out some thin shirts and trousers of combed linen, as he had learnt it would be high summer in the Cape, noted for its blistering temperatures. He also ordered a suitcase, which came the next day: it was a commodious one with little wheels on its base, so that he could bowl it along easily and spin it like a top. A label on it said it had been made in a SupaPodia workshop in Algeria. No wonder the OuterWorlders are so poor now, he thought, if small industries like that are being taken into the SupaPods. The SupaPods, the OuterWorld, the lands of the Eliti were becoming confused in his brain, hard to separate out.

He hoped some clarity of vision would return to him in the Cape should he be required to speak at a committee meeting, or even to the High Director himself. He was placing his trust in Tina, that the influence she would have on her father would be instrumental in bringing about the great changes needed. Pamela, as a Commissioner and – so he understood – a personal friend too of the High Director, had clearly, by her contacts, been able to smooth a way through the complex bureaucracies of SupaPodia International, so that the necessary meetings could take place. His own position in these dealings was fortuitous; yet, it was his testimony above all, supported by Tina, that could be vital.

The High Director must have been entirely unaware of the deleterious practices that had been going on worldwide in his organisation. Perhaps he still was, despite the revolts breaking out. Well, he would soon learn. The Convention was the opportunity for his education – and the education and enlightenment as well of the many senior Commissioners and other officials who would be present; indeed, of the entire Eliti class, many of whom would have sent representatives.

But what of Pamela? After that terrible evening at her house, he had every reason not to trust her. What was her true motivation in all this? He suspected she had an agenda of her own. But what was that?

Then, with a sudden flash of insight, it came to him – the possibility, if not yet the certainty -

Pamela wanted to be High Director herself!

Tina was staying at Pamela's house, so Julian had little opportunity of seeing her again before they went away. They were all going to travel together to the AirshipPort at Bromley in LondonSouth. Rupert, flush from the Scottish moors and forests of his friend, Lord Cairngorm, who had found his way into the ranks of the Eliti as a wealthy manipulator of the international pharmaceutical markets, had returned home just in time to accompany his wife to the Cape. He was a bit disgruntled by this, as SupaPodia affairs bored him. Tina had told Julian these things on the one occasion when he did meet her for a brief walk by the sea.

"We'll have plenty of opportunity to talk on the voyage," she had said. "I've got to give my time for the moment to Aunt Pamela. She's been so good to me."

She was wearing a straight skirt and a red woollen top, her nun's habit abandoned for the present, in case – as she said – "it antagonises people who need to be brought over to our side."

"You look very nice," Julian said.

And, with her shining blonde hair, which had grown almost to her shoulders, her neat figure no longer wrapped bulkily in grey, and her graceful walk, she did seem so most certainly. Julian, in rapture at the peace she always brought him, thought that even the seabirds were swooping low to see her.

He wanted to tell her what he knew about Pamela – how she had tried to compromise him by having him caught up in her vileness; how she maintained a punishment camp somewhere close to where they now walked by this sunlit sea, to which two women Tina had helped, then been promised clemency, had been consigned; how, very likely, she had her own ambitions for the highest position SupaPodia International had to offer – but he knew that now was not the time to speak of any of these things. What good would it do at present? It would likely destroy Tina's happiness, her belief that things were progressing in the love of the God she worshipped. And it would endanger their own relationship, as she would find it difficult to believe him, thinking him unbalanced in his mind and deliberately obstructive – 'paranoic', she had called him earlier.

He would tell her later, of course – *he had to* – on the airship voyage, when they would talk as she had suggested. There was nothing either of them could do for the moment, anyhow. It was what was said and agreed at the Cape that would be decisive. There, the High Director held the power. It was before him that Julian must tell what he knew, and all that he suspected, and then the truth of it could be judged.

All will evolve, he thought. The evil will drain out. The guilty will fall and be punished. Be patient. Perhaps believe in Tina's Lord who – if he remembered rightly – sees everything that happens, every sparrow that falls, and will ensure that in the end good prevails. He had to believe the struggle was ending and that they were on a path that would bring justice back to the earth, with peace.

So Julian thought, walking by the boundless ocean with the gulls screaming about him, little knowing that it was the ocean itself that would soon show the power of God – to end all things that were bad for His creation.

30

From the airship, the land was spread out below in a patchwork of yellows, greens, and browns, part-veiled by long tendrils of clouds, as if the lower air had been furrowed into white by some great airborne plough. Looking from the glass-walled gondola which projected beneath the fat cigar-shape of the airship, like a silver-sided bubble about to drop away and splash down to earth, Julian thought the world seemed a place of dreams, an unspoilt paradise, with little sign of human blight – the yellow smoke of industrialisation or sprawling ruined cities or graveyards of waste, or indeed of anything else that might blur this perfect outer vision. From such a high distance, it seemed easy to believe that humankind was now stowed away beneath that earthly face in utopian fulfilment and peace? Perhaps, then, he had misunderstood SupaPodia. Perhaps he should allow it more time to eradicate its own errors and come to a full maturity. It was tempting to think such thoughts, gazing out with his chin pressed against the glass, with Tina beside him reading from a book (the 'Life of Saint Cuthbert', he had glimpsed from its gold-blocked title), but, no, the rush of horrors witnessed returned to him and he looked away, his stomach constricting, his head spinning.

Sensing his discomfort, Tina looked up from her reading and smiled at him. "You don't like heights, do you? Why don't you lie down? It's an hour or so yet before dinner."

It had been like this for him the whole six days of the journey – a mixture of relaxation and hope alternating with fear and dread, evenings in the restaurant with Pamela and Rupert, bored stiff by their dull, self-obsessed conversation, which rarely admitted any comment from him (indeed, he was positively ignored); board games played with Tina and others during the day; watching SupaPodia News on the big Screens that enveloped the living areas, pumping out tedious drivel about the happy SupaPodia world, as if nothing was wrong anywhere, but all endless bliss – the exact opposite of the realities he had witnessed.

When then would this pretence end? What could any of them put to the forthcoming Convention that would change things? What was Tina planning, or, for that matter, Pamela? Nothing of any import had yet been said. For some reason, he was reluctant to remind Tina of the urgency of their situation or acquaint her with the truths that he had bottled up inside him. Perhaps he did not really want this drifting delusion to end. Yet end it must as soon as they reached the Cape tomorrow – the Africa which held the home of the High Director himself.

He had expected Pamela to come up with a plan, even if a false plan that served her own ambitions rather than the interests of Tina and himself. But there had been no inner meetings, no discussion, as he had been led to expect there would be, only languid talk about the Eliti estates, the game hunting, the greatest artists and jewellers and silversmiths whose works were in demand, the new colleges of SupaPodia that might take in a small percentage of bright Podders too; nothing at all of insurrection and revolt, of brutal murder, repression and looming technological failure, set soon to engulf SupaPodia, with the urgent need by the organisation for self-examination, assessment, and renewal.

And what was Tina doing? She was sitting reading in apparent contentment and peace. What of her own expectations of SupaPodia, her own wish for change based on her most holy books? Had she forgotten everything she had learnt and spoken with him about?

He retired to his cabin. It was scarcely bigger than the Pod he had once occupied – it seemed a long time ago – a place where there had been no real time, only pretend time, while the real OuterWorld still raced on increasingly out of control. He lay back on his bed and switched on the Screen: the female presenter was talking about the Cape Convention. Pictures of delegates arriving from all over SupaPodia International were being shown – Brazilians, Inuits, Chinese, Punjabis, Mohawks, Icelanders, Iranians, Scots, Cossacks, Monglians – plus many other peoples Julian did not recognise: they were seen being received from a variety of airborne machines, ships, and landtrains.

The High Director appeared on Screen, seated on what looked to be a great marble chair (Julian had never seen an image of him before: he thought this one must have been especially authorised and released to the world). He was wrapped in a long, maroon-coloured robe, with what seemed to be a plain black suit underneath, and had a feathered flat hat, like an overlarge beret, perched centrally on his head. His face was fleshy, set in a smile of beneficence, yet the narrowed eyes did not seem to match the full lips and cheeks, suggesting someone who was either ill at ease or suffered from constant pain. He looked, Julian thought, a little like an overworked academic he had once known at university, whose crowning as vice-chancellor had been unexpected and unwanted, by himself and by others.

To Julian's astonishment, the announcer now declared, "A great and pleasurable surprise awaits our Lord and High Director. Even as I speak, his daughter, long separated from him, is speeding towards him. Her name is Christine – a name that will soon be on everyone's lips. We send them all the love of SupaPodia that they will be able to find new happiness together. Christine, we know, has acknowledged her former wrongdoings, and our hope is that she will be made welcome into the international family of SupaPodia."

Julian's mouth dropped open in astonishment. This was not what Tina had said at all. A picture of her appeared next. She was dressed in the red top and straight dark-coloured skirt that she had worn at Hayling before coming away, and which she had worn too at times on the airship. There was no background to the picture, but it must have been taken very recently. But how? And by whom? She was looking away from the camera; her face was calm but unsmiling. So perhaps she had not known she was being photographed. So who had done this?

A few minutes later, as he lay on the bed puzzling over this, there came a knock on his cabin door. He started. It must be one of the crew who serviced the cabins. "Come in," he yelled, sitting up

But it was Tina's blonde head that pushed round the door. "Am I disturbing you?"

"No, of course not. Delighted to see you." It was the first time on the voyage she had talked to him alone.

"You saw the pictures?" she said, indicating his Screen that was still on.

"Yes. I'm puzzled. Why have you left me alone to be puzzled?" He said the last querulously. He had been disappointed that Tina had seemed to be ignoring him, contrary to what she had promised.

"I'm sorry," she said in a low voice. "I've had several talks with Pamela and we've only just decided on a course of action."

"Really. I thought it was you and me against SupaPodia, not Pamela whom I don't trust. And neither would you if you knew what I do – and which I've been waiting to tell you about."

"Shush!" she whispered urgently. "Walls have ears."

He had not thought of that. A feeling of panic returned like sparking electricity setting his nervous system jangling. Had he done, or said anything here, or anywhere on the airship, that might have been observed or listened to? No, he was sure he hadn't. Was that then why Tina hadn't been able to talk to him?

"It was a good picture of you," he said loudly. He knew now the game he had to play.

"Yes. Taken remotely here."

"Good God. What technology."

She had come half into the room and pushed a piece of paper into his hand. "Read it. Eat it." She mouthed the words. Then aloud and brightly, "See you later for Monopoly." And she had gone.

He left the bed and went into his small wash room. Holding the piece of paper close to his chest while hunched over on the toilet seat, he read, 'After dinner. Lower Spar 2A.' That was all. He put the paper in his mouth and chewed it until it was gone. Then he pissed and pulled the chain. Would they be watching that too? The thought made him want to laugh. Who then was observing him through cameras? Was it some security operative of SupaPodia or was it perhaps Pamela herself, or even her whisky-swilling, red-faced paunch of a husband? When would anything become clear in the nightmare that was SupaPodia?

Dinner in the gondola that evening was long and languid. Julian, seated at a table with Pamela and Rupert, grew more and more impatient as the various courses were delivered and consumed, with Rupert eating twice as much as anyone else and swilling constantly from his own bottle of red wine. At last, after coffee and cheese, the twenty or so fellow passengers were breaking up and going into the lounge, and only Rupert was left with the liqueur he had insisted on. It stood deep red, like blood, in a tall waisted glass.

"Joining me, old boy?" he said to Julian.

"I'm afraid not. Early night for me, I think."

"What by yourself? What life is that? You need to get yourself a woman like my Pamela."

Tina and Pamela had risen. Julian saw Pamela give a look of sheer disgust at her husband. There was no secret game being played out between them. Pamela clearly loathed her husband. Did Rupert know of his wife's own squalid behaviour, he wondered?

"Good luck with the nun then," said Rupert chortling. Although Rupert had behaved like a pig throughout the voyage, this marked a new low from him, and in Tina's blushing presence too. He was tempted to challenge him – but to what? A thumping (not practical) or an apology (unlikely, as the bastard was too drunk for that) So, once again, cursing himself, he said nothing, longing to break free from the chains that bound him here. For a moment, he even yearned for the freedoms and action of Nemesis.

He looked meaningfully at Tina. She inclined her head, calling out "Good night", and walked away with Pamela, looking lovely in a long powder-blue gown. She really is adorable, he thought. What a shame she has given herself to her God when she would make any man very happy. He had to accept, though, that, if Tina was ever moved to take an unredeemed soul of pulsing blood to her bosom, instead of the sanctified white bones of a saint, it would hardly be he, but some far more youthful man, whose halo was much brighter than his.

He had walked on the airship's promenade decks before. They ran at various heights within the curving sides of the fuselage, constructed from aluminium platforms within the network of girders that formed the airship's structure. High sides to the decks, made of blackened cork-faced panels, prevented any chance of promenaders pitching down into the bowels of the airship. However, he had never ventured as far as one of the Outer Spars: these were much narrower, lower gangways that ran out into the projecting wings at the airship's stern. Used most often by the crew, they were not barred to passengers, but only those determined to take their desire for exercise to the remotest parts of the airship would bother to enter them. One such clearly was Tina: perhaps it was a place she had used to separate herself from the others for periods of private meditation. He wished she had told him about it earlier.

Julian found Lower Spar 2A easily enough on the starboard side, clearly marked by a sign. It was a narrow passageway rather than a deck, the metal floor of which sloped down into a series of small chambers, surrounded by a lattice-work of thin girders upon which the inner surface of the airship's skin was stretched. The furthest chamber was '2A': the passageway ended there. A low metal bench ran around the chamber. On this he found Tina waiting, her arms folded. She had changed the blue dress for a plain woollen top and trousers.

"Can we be overheard here?" he mouthed at her.

"No." Her answer was abrupt. He thought she looked tense.

"How are you so sure?"

"Pamela told me."

"*Pamela told you!* But she's the one we've got to be careful of."

"Oh, Julian, why do you keep saying that?" Tina sighed, looking exasperated. "Pamela's our friend and ally."

"She's a dangerous Eliti."

"No, she's not. She wants a way out of this current trouble within SupaPodia. She knows I'm the one to help achieve it."

"Tina, you're a lovely trusting girl, but I fear you're making a very bad misjudgement."

Tina sighed, looking annoyed. "Why do you say that?"

"I know some things you don't."

"Well, tell me then."

"I can't – not yet. I've wanted to for ages, waiting for the chance to do so. But now – from what you've told me yourself – I just don't trust anyone or anything, anywhere on this damned airship. We'll have to talk at the Cape, somehow or other. All I'm asking you for the present is to be as wary of Pamela as of anyone else."

There was silence. Tina shuffled her feet. She looked upset. He wanted to held her and comfort her, but he didn't dare. He thought she looked unwell; her face was very pale.

"I have Pamela's permission to let you know about the plan that we've made," she said. "So we can do that now, if you like. It's what I intended for our meeting here."

"Please go ahead," Julian said a bit snootily. "It won't matter then if Pamela happens to listen in."

"Julian, you don't understand!" He could see tears of frustration in her eyes. "It's not she who would be listening in, but others. That's why she told me this place is safe from them."

"Well, go on." Julian didn't know what to think anymore, but he recalled Pamela's evil, and Jill and Boadicea locked away in purgatory, and the Beast too recruited by her to do her will. A dangerous enemy she made, but perhaps there were others greater. His head had begun swimming in great ballooning circles.

Tina took a deep breath, steadying herself. "Pamela thinks some Eliti might be out to stop any bad reports being made that could affect SupaPodia's current programme. There is so much investment at stake, so many Eliti finances bound up in it, as well as large land deals, that any changes could be catastrophic for some, even throwing them out of the Eliti ranks altogether. Hence the opposition. Any Commissioner supporting new radical policy changes, such as Pamela, might be removed from office by the malcontents. And there could even be a call for a new High Director, if it's thought he's being influenced by moderates."

So SupaPodia is as full of rivalry as anything in the old OuterWorld, Julian thought, trying to get his head around what Tina had said. Was Pamela then playing some sort of double game, having to appear to be hard line to have any hope of putting her more liberal policies through? If that was true, then his intervention with Tina might make things much worse for her, rather than better.

But could he believe what Pamela said? He had seen her at first hand. What he had witnessed was surely not some act to deceive him while creating camouflage for herself. The circles made by his spinning head intensified, and he put both hands to his temples as if to steady it. Only the High Director, Tina's own flesh and blood, could decide these matters. While this HD was in place, they had a chance of reform. If he was replaced by someone much more inflexible, then their cause – and the cause of all the other discontents amongst the Podders and the OuterWorlders – would be harmed. At the very least, it would lead to an endless round of violence and repression. At the worst, all hope of a new liberated world would die.

"What's the plan then?" Julian asked eventually, seeing Tina looking at him with concern in her face. "What have you and Pamela got organised so that our cause can be presented at the Convention?"

Whatever that plan is, he thought, I will have to 'think double' – whether this is true to Tina and myself or a ploy by Pamela to get what she really wants. He hadn't forgotten his suspicion earlier that she might want to take over as High Director. Only then things had appeared much clearer to him.

"She's going to work our cause through various sub-committees," Tina replied, "and then get together a concerted resolution to put before the main Convention assembly. Our chief hope of altering SupaPodia policy would next be through my meeting with my father. He will listen to me, I know. I want you to be present as well."

"Yes, of course, but…but I'm worried."

"Worried of what in particular?" She stood up. There was more colour in her face now.

"It should be obvious!" Julian exclaimed. It was he who was irritated now. "I've been a rebel in arms against SupaPodia. I've killed their people. I could be arrested, tortured, and executed."

"No!" Tina cried. "That's not going to happen. Not with Pamela's protection. You see, she's very close to my father, she's been…"

"His mistress. His shag on the side!"

"How can you speak to me like that!" Tina's face had gone bright red and she had sunk back onto the metal bench.

"I'm sorry to hurt you," Julian said in his gentlest voice, "but it's true. We have to face reality. I don't, and can't, trust Pamela. I think she wants to overthrow your father, not help him to find any new way. She's evil. She believes in SupaPodia entirely."

So much for his double thinking! It hadn't lasted long. He had declared himself to Tina now, and he suddenly did not seem to care that what he was saying might be picked up by Pamela herself. Only he did not want to implicate Tina. Neither did he wish to upset her.

However, Tina's head was down on her knees and he could see her shoulders shaking. He lifted up her face gently. It was wet with tears. "I had such hopes," she wailed. "Of meeting my father and putting things right, letting God's power work on the evil to destroy it. To have a new dawn for SupaPodia and all the world."

"Wonderful ideas," he whispered, holding her close. "Perhaps they can work out. But we have to be careful and not be too trusting – of anyone. We have to go on. There's no way back."

She raised her head, sniffing, wiping her eyes. "I'm sorry," she said, "for my weakness. A poor Christian I am if my resolve is so easily broken."

Then the light came back into her eyes. "You are right, though. We have to be careful. *I* must be careful, but we will go on and we will succeed. It's God's will, through Jesus Christ his Son, whom I worship and adore." She was fingering a small golden crucifix at her neck.

"I would give much to have your faith," Julian said.

"But you can!" She jumped excitedly to your feet. "You can! Say after me…"

Extraordinarily Julian found himself kneeling on the metal planks before her.

"I believe in God the Father almighty…"

"I believe in God the Father almighty," he repeated dutifully.

"….I believe in Jesus Christ, his only Son, our Lord...conceived by the power of the Holy Spirit and born of the Virgin Mary…"

He followed the words again, feeling compelled to do so, enjoying the sound they made in his mind.

"….He will come again to judge the living and the dead….I believe in the Holy Spirit…the forgiveness of sins…the resurrection of the body and the life everlasting. Amen."

"Amen."

Julian still knelt, his knees hurting from the grooved metal pressing into them. He did not quite know what had happened, but for the first time for a very long time he felt truly at peace. Everything had slowed down. He saw Tina's face swim towards him as if in slow motion. She smiled, and her smile held a radiance that burst like a sun upon him, the yellow light drifting outwards like vapour into a cosmos of a billion other stars, as if he stood at the very heart of creation seeing everything newly born.

"What has happened?" he said weakly.

"I don't know." Tina's face was full of joy. "You must tell me."

"I don't want to lose you." He felt so weak he knew tears were not far away.

"Of course, you won't lose me. Or anything, or anyone else you have belief in. For you have given of yourself now and God has received you."

"Has He?"

Tina smiled. "You will know yourself. You won't need me to reassure you."

"No," said Julian thoughtfully. "I don't think I do. It's strange, but I do not feel any fear now. Whatever is to happen will become clear, and it will be right, as if a power far greater than me is showing me the way."

"And I will follow that way with you," she said taking his hand. He thought her hand had a quality beyond mere flesh; it seemed to tingle with power. Why has it taken me so long to understand this power? Yet, not too late. I have been blind but I have found truth when I have most need of it.

Pamela and her wiles, Rupert, the Eliti, SupaPodia seemed suddenly of little consequence, just rocks and boulders that he could move and arrange as were best demanded.

"Come," said Tina, leading him from the chamber and out of Lower Spar 2A. "You'll need to rest now. Go to your cabin. I'll see you at breakfast before we disembark. God be with you."

"Yes," said Julian. "Thank you." For some reason, he felt unable to return the blessing, and for a moment was fearful that his conversion – if that's what it was – had not been genuine, but one more of wishful thinking than conviction.

Tina was smiling at him, seeing the sudden worry in his eyes."

"Julian, receiving God is not easy. The devil will still be with you on your shoulder, whispering to you, giving you doubts. But you are immensely stronger than you were ten minutes ago. So go from there, one step at a time."

"Yes," he agreed, laughing now, clanging his feet on the metal walkways. "One step at a time."

He said goodbye to Tina, letting her walk ahead of him and he lingered for a while where the promenade deck was broader, leaning against its high panelled side, his head in a whirl. Coming towards him was a crew member. He wore the blue and white uniform of the crew, but there was something recognisable about the shape and bulk of the figure. As it came closer, the blue and white seemed to turn into black, and he knew who it was – the Beast. Unmistakably, the Beast. The Beast passed him without a word, looking away from him, while Julian clung to the top of the panelling, his legs so suddenly weak they were unable to support him.

Eventually he found his way back to his cabin, relieved to find everything as he had left it. He slept. Somewhere amongst his sleep a voice said to him, "Who do you believe in most, God or the devil?" And he repeated over and over again, "I believe in God the Father almighty…" until morning came up with a rush, and, looking from his cabin porthole, he saw the rocky, scrub-covered summit of Table Mountain floating by close beneath them, with a few people at its edge gazing upwards and waving.

And so they descended slowly and magnificently, an elongated silver ball suspended in a bright blue sky, to the Airship Port of SupaPodia's biggest investment in Africa – Robben Island SupaPods Nos. 48-54, with the Convention Centre, pleasure ground, and hotel complex of adjacent Mandela Park.

31

The Cape was a riot of heat and colour. Banks of red, yellow, and purple flowers were piled high beside the broad paved way from the AirshipPort to the Mandela Hotel. The sun blazed above the flat, brown acropolis of Table Mountain. Julian could almost see the yellow columns of sunlight bearing down on him, as if the earth was framed by a portico of fire. He sweated in the heavy heat as he was borne along in a litter carried by four burly black men. Their white tee-shirts were stamped 'Robben SupaPod No.53', so he thought they were probably Podders selected to serve the Eliti for the period of the Convention. Other faces, of differing shades from light brown to black, both men and women, bobbed and swayed above the flowers, white teeth gleaming, arms and shoulders festooned in bright fabrics, so they made an ever-moving fairyland of colour. How could they bear the heat? he wondered, but it seemed to have no effect on their prancing jollity. Some blew on long instruments, pointed upwards against the sky like the spikes of giant porcupines, producing a high-pitched fog horn of a sound that never ceased, making him want to clasp his hands to his ears.

His bedroom, high in the sumptuous tower of the Mandela Hotel was the most luxurious he had ever been in. Not only was the room enormous, with a vast emperor-sized bed, of dimensions it would have been possible to land a helidrone on, but it had an outer glass-fronted balcony that gave sweeping views over the bay. Across the shining waters, he could see the buildings of the Robben Island SupaPods, linked to the shore by the slender girders of parallel bridges, upon which the bulbous silver wagons of their servicing trains were in constant movement.

Tina's room was off the same corridor as his, which was convenient as it meant he could arrange to go down to meals with her. Thankfully, the room of Pamela and Rupert (assuming they shared the same room) was buried away elsewhere in the building, perhaps, Julian thought, on the uppermost penthouse floors where the most luxurious suites for SupaPodia's senior delegates were situated. Julian had not seen either of that dreadful couple since entering the hotel.

He attended one welcoming function, in a vast marble-walled ballroom, where crowds of exotically-clad delegates mingled, sipping drinks off trays brought by lithesome girls in pelmet skirts, while addressed by a huge African, wearing the leopard skins of some warrior chief or other. He delivered an oration about the need to preserve individuality amongst the human species while at the same time moving to suppress it by a necessary conformity – at least that is how Julian, cynically, interpreted his words. Judging by this man's pot belly, which swelled out in front of him as far as the business end of the replica tribal spear with which he emphasised his words, he was unlikely to have spent too much time in a SupaPod himself, but must be one of the local Eliti with territories perhaps extending from the Buffalo to the Crocodile Rivers (Julian's knowledge of Southern African geography was admittedly rather hazy).

The alcohol was very strong, or he was very weary, for it had a bad effect on him, and Tina had had to help steer him back to his room, where she sat with him while, sprawled across a zebra-striped sofa, he slowly recovered.

"The Beast is here," he said, as reality returned to him together with a thudding headache. He made signals with his hand for Tina to draw the curtains close together to shut out the evening light. Any light, even that of the sub-tropical dusk, seemed too much for him to bear at present.

"It serves you right," Tina said, pulling at the curtains. She looked cool and composed in her long blue gown. "I thought you'd learnt more sense."

"I have." He thought she was referring to his conversion, the memory of which caused him some stabs of embarrassment; he did not know why, because he had felt most sincere at the time.

She looked at him steadily, her clear eyes on his, her small mouth pursed, pensive. "You're not back-sliding are you? The devil has his ways of putting doubt into your mind. If you are truly committed, then God will receive you fully, and the doubts will go away."

"I am committed."

"Good." She smiled at him, taking his hands. "Then we must move to having you baptised. You haven't been baptised, have you?"

"No, I don't think so."

"We will have to find you a priest of the old order. Or I can do it. I am qualified."

"When?" he asked.

"When you are ready."

"When I've stopped drinking?" He was trying to make a joke.

"It's because you are drinking that I know you are not yet ready."

"Oh, come on, Tina, cannot a man have pleasure and still believe in God?"

"Yes, of course he can. But pleasure should come from God, not from a hand-maiden bearing a cup, undressed by you with lustful eyes."

"Oh, Tina, you see right through me."

"You are a good man, Julian. Your faults are few, your strengths great."

These words brought sudden tears to his eyes. He closed them so she would not see, and he slept.

When he awoke, she was still there, reading from a book. "What is this beast you speak of?" was the first thing she said to him.

"Beast? Did I? Oh, yes, so I did. A haunting perhaps. No, a real sighting, I'm sure."

"What do you mean?" She sat opposite him, leaning forward.

"The Beast is a man I knew, who served with Nemesis. I have seen him since. He works for Pamela. He was on the airship."

"If that is true, perhaps he is just a servant. Why do you call him the Beast?"

"That was his own name for himself. He has been a professional soldier. He survives everything. He is never killed."

"Are you sure it is he you saw? Or was it a dream?"

"No, he is real. And he will be with Pamela somewhere directing whatever evil thing it is she wishes to do."

"Julian," Tina laughed, "that is not true. You must rid yourself of those notions."

"Is there not a beast in your Book?" Julian asked abruptly. The vaguest memory of something that had happened when he was very young: had surfaced in his mind. Mr. Hibberd, the verger at the church in the village, had tried to scare the small boys one day when they were making a noise banging on the heating pipes. "The beast will come for you boys, as it says in the good Book. It doesn't like ill-behaved boys and it will drag you away and devour you."

"Revelations speaks of a beast," said Tina thoughtfully. "It had great powers and some foolish people worshipped it."

"Was the beast not powerful in war?"

Tina looked startled. "I'm not sure. I'll have to find the passage."

She picked up the Bible she had been reading and opened it, turning the pages. After a while she looked up. "I'll read this to you, but I don't want you to think I attach any importance to it. I am sure it is purely coincidental. We shall probably never see or hear of your beast again."

She read:

"*Who is like unto the beast? Who is able to make war with him? It was given unto him to make war with the saints, and to overcome them: and power was given him over all kindreds, and tongues, and nations*".

There was a long silence after she had finished. She carefully put her book away in the pocket of her gown.

"Nothing more?" Julian asked at last.

"Not unless your beast has the number 666 tattooed on his head."

"No, I haven't seen that. Why? What does that mean?"

She laughed, a little uncertainly. "'Revelations' says it is the number given to the beast. It is normally interpreted as an evil number: the devil's number."

"Well there are enough candidates, both within and without SupaPodia, to have the number tattooed all over them."

Tina looked serious now, staring down at the floor. She got up to pull back the curtains, and peered out at a blood red sunset flooding Table Bay. The crimson of the horizon was so intense that the colour seemed to fill the room.

"I know what you're going to say, Julian. So please don't say it. I – we – have to work with Pamela, otherwise there is no way forward, and then, if I'm frank, we could all be in danger."

"She knows what she's doing," he said in a flat tone.

"Yes, but so do we. And I hold the trump card – my father."

"While he lives."

"What?! Why do you say that?" Tina's usual composure was upset.

"Tina, the last thing I want is to worry you or frighten you, but you must face the facts."

"And what are those facts?"

"I've tried to tell you some things already. But others I haven't told you, as it did not seem safe to do so. Here, though? Are we safe in this hotel? I don't know. There could be bugs anywhere. They have the technology for it. But, let's take a chance, shall we? You need to know what Pamela is capable of."

He saw her raise her hand as if to stop him, but he plunged on. "Before you came to Hayling, she entertained me one evening at her home, just she and her servants there, and…and… – it's hard to tell you this – …she tried to compromise me sexually in a most disgusting way."

"Oh that!" Tina exclaimed much to Julian's surprise. "Pamela told me all about that; how you both had had too much to drink and you made a pass at her. She found it funny; she was laughing when she told me about it."

"Is that what she told you?" Julian said bitterly. "And you believed her?"

"Now come on, Julian." Tina had left the window and was taking small steps up and down the room. "You may not think me a woman of the world, but I know how mistakes can be easily made through the devil's alcohol. I'm not blaming you, I'm not blaming Pamela – she was probably as silly as you – but the fact is that nothing happened, did it? So it's a clean slate and we can forget about it. She has no hard feelings or the slightest desire to do anything but forget the whole thing."

"She said that?"

"Yes, in so many words."

"How very noble of her," Julian chuckled sarcastically. He knew it was useless to say any more. There was no way he wished to describe to Tina the obscenities he had witnessed, or Pamela's vile language to him.

Tina stood beside Julian as he sat up on the sofa, placing a hand on his shoulder. "You're probably going to raise this next, so I have to tell you I *do* know about Pamela's armed Guard. She assures me she only formed it for the protection of the people on her estates, given the recent murders of some local Eliti. She says she's placed her Guard in the hands of a professional ex-soldier, whom she declares is very good and gives the recruits – women mostly, I understand – a lot of drill. That is probably the man you've called the Beast; perhaps he just seems like that to his recruits! Pamela says he's done much good by distributing food parcels to some of the poorer OuterWorlders, and by organising work for them as well in the renovation of the buildings she's using as a barracks."

"She keeps a prison at those barracks!" Julian broke in. "And you know whom I saw there? The two women you were helping at the nunnery, one of whom has lost her arm."

"Yes, I know that too. Pamela said she's keeping them there under expert care – care she's organised and paid for, by the way – until they've recovered enough to go on to her Convalescent Home for rehabilitation. To be honest, I would have liked them to stay longer at St. Augustine's, but it wasn't possible, so Pamela has done us a favour."

"It was nothing like that!" Julian shouted. They were ill, kept in stinking conditions, and frightened out of their minds."

"Julian." Tina took his hands in hers and pulled him to his feet. "I know you are passionate. I know how much you've suffered. I know you have witnessed things that trouble you, and, I admit, there may be grounds for worry about some of them, but Pamela – who has her faults; I will admit that too – is someone who is on our side and is prepared to help us. She would not give me her support if that were not true. What would be her purpose?"

"I don't believe Pamela is interested in reforming SupaPodia," Julian said in a dead tone. He felt played out and exhausted. "I think she wants to get more power for herself. She might even be contemplating getting rid of your father."

"How would she do that? His reputation is high and his Inner Command all support him."

"How do you know that? Who's told you it's true?"

"Well, Pamela has, of course. She's told me as well that she's already had several meetings with delegates who will be useful to our cause"

"Don't you think she might be leading you on?"

"No, I don't. Now, that's enough! I'm going to my room, and I'll ask you to have a think about everything I've told you. God will go from you if you remain as obdurate as you seem at present."

"You threaten me with God?"

She held her arms wide and embraced him. He felt such love for her then, to hold and protect her, to help her towards the God she had revealed to him, to do all and everything to please her, and not to upset her, for she was the only thread of life he had left, and he was frightened that it might snap and he would lose her.

"Julian, please don't quarrel with me." Her small mouth was turned up to him. Her eyes were moist.

He kissed her quickly on the cheek. "That's the last thing I want. We'll find a way through. With God's help, we shall overcome and we shall win."

"That's more like it," she said, sighing.

"And you know where that '666' will be found?"

"No, where?" She looked worried again.

"This is a joke, right. I imagine it's tattooed on dear Pamela's bottom."

She looked shocked for a moment, and then she laughed. Every time the laughter looked set to end, she began giggling again – most un-nunlike, Julian thought

He said to himself: Thank God – and God, I do really mean this – how pleased I am to have got her back. Yet – and another shadow passed over him – there's a good chance Pamela does have that number stamped on her skin somewhere, or perhaps she's tattooed it with her own hands onto the Beast's most upright part. Another joke, but this one he couldn't laugh at.

He had passed through many dangers, but these were mere foothills to the mountain of peril that now lay ahead.

32

Julian sat in the grand auditorium of the Convention Centre. It curved in a half circle around the stage like an ancient Greek theatre, the seats being tiered steeply up so that not even the large woman in front of him, with a tall headdress made up of swathes of shiny yellow and green cloth, could obstruct his view of the stage. Here, sat members of the High Director's Executive Committee, a row of men and women's swarthy faces – or were they just well-tanned? – with the occasional blob of a paler face amongst them. A high podium at the centre of the stage, adorned with the SupaPodia crest, awaited the presence of the High Director himself.

A flourish of trumpets announced the High Director's imminent arrival onto the stage. Ahead of him, walked a black child in an orange tunic carrying a small tasselled cushion upon which lay a golden orb – perhaps, Julian wondered, representing the power of SupaPodia throughout the globe? – and then the High Director himself appeared with a woman by his side. Julian could see Tina next to him leaning forward tensely, her face briefly showing a mixture of curiosity and sadness, before her habitual placid expression was resumed.

The woman was Lucinda – Joshua Pomeroy-Collyer's current mistress, his consort, and the real power at his side (or so his Inner Command reluctantly accepted). She was dressed in a long gown of shimmering silver, with a bodice that was split open almost to her navel, the orbs of her breasts swaying freely as she walked, the nipples exposed by her movement, though covered by silver caps. Although such a dress was evidently high fashion now amongst high-born Eliti women (Julian had viewed one or two rather less dramatic examples at the welcoming function), he could not help thinking it made Lucinda looked like a high-stepping courtesan out of some billionaires' brothel. What could have possessed the High Director to allow her to appear like this? Tina was clearly having similar thoughts, as her mouth tightened and her fingers begin to drum on the arm rest separating her from Julian.

The High Director wore a long cloak, the silver and gold of its embroidery glinting under the spotlights. Julian could make out a jumbled decoration of dragons, griffins and flying horses, all interspersed by stars, giving him the appearance of some wizard out of a story book. Why this form of dress had been chosen for him – or perhaps by him – seemed as incongruous as his consort's apparel? However, none of the audience seemed at all concerned by their joint appearances, and were all standing and applauding, including the Executive Council members ranged on the stage. Tina and Julian were obliged to rise too or they would have stood out in a way that might be misconstrued. Tina's small white hands, however, flapped against each other with little enthusiasm.

When the audience were seated once more and the High Director began his speech from the podium, Julian was surprised to hear a voice that was thin and reedy, not at all the full confident tones that he might have expected from one so eminent. His oration, though, was full of the glorification of SupaPodia; how the number of SupaPods had now reached 100,000 (this magic six figure number having been achieved by a SupaPod drilled into a mountain in Kurdistan), how there was no continent of the world or old nation state that did not now have access to SupaPodia; how the number of people world-wide who were benefitting from SupaPodia, either within or without the SupaPods, could be estimated at close to a billion. Julian wondered how that last figure had been arrived at. Did it include, for instance, all the semi-slave labour working in the OuterWorld to feed and equip SupaPodia? And what about the other seven or eight billion of the world population?

The High Director went on to admit that recently there had been one or two regrettable 'anxieties' affecting SupaPodia, but these were now largely resolved. Some considerable additional sums were to be spent on improving local Guard forces. This last statement received a cheer from the audience. Julian, however, was disappointed by the brevity and vagueness of the comments, which must have been intended as a reference to the recent outbreaks of terrorist violence within the SupaPodia empire, of which he, of course, had been a compelling witness and, indeed, participant. If that was all the High Director had to say about those events, thinking there was no longer any danger, then the present purpose of Tina and himself for reform was hardly boosted. But then, he supposed, any progress would only be made in secret conclave, to be spearheaded, if Tina was right, by Commissioner Lascelles.

At that moment, Julian caught sight of Pamela in the audience, seated with Rupert whose head was bent forward as if he might be sleeping off an excess from the previous night. She was in a row at a lower level to Julian's right, much of her face being hidden by the broad brim of her rakishly-tilted hat. While he was looking at her, he saw her turn her head towards him as if she was in tune with his thoughts. She immediately looked away, so perhaps it was just his over-active imagination at work. Tina did not seem to have noticed; she was now sitting impassively beside him once more, any inner tensions only revealed by the curl of her fingertips.

The High Director had now moved on to the vexed question of climate change. He said that the many rumours circulating about rises in the level of the oceans, consequent upon a supposed melting of ice at the polar caps, were demonstrably false, and represented an attempt by rebellious elements in the OuterWorld to discredit SupaPodia – insidious fake propaganda that SupaPodia Intelligence would be moving to eliminate. SupaPodia's own scientists at bases at both poles had sent proof that the very opposite was the truth – that, if anything, the globe was growing colder rather than hotter. So there was absolutely nothing for the SupaPods constructed at the sea's edge to worry about; they were *not about to be inundated*. He summoned up extra vocal force to utter those last words, and a roar of applause followed from his audience.

As this statement marked the end of the High Director's address, the volume of applause increased to a crescendo, the clapping and whistling, the banging of benches and the stamping of feet, merging into a general din that went on and on for a very long time. The High Director acknowledged the applause with both arms raised, while members off his Executive Council rose individually to congratulate him. Then he left the stage with Lucinda beside him, his hand on her bare upper arm, his fingers inches from one of the jiggling, silver-tipped breasts.

There followed a series of motions from the Convention Convener, an Oriental gentleman in a black suit and white bow tie, who pranced upon the stage like the compère of a variety show, and whose voice, unlike the High Director's, was loud and commanding. To each motion, which was presented by its number (Julian and Tina did not have any key to these numbers, although others clearly did), delegates proclaimed a baying 'Aye', flowed by applause, in which Julian could see both Pamela and Rupert joining. After the final motion, which was greeted with even greater applause, the Convener proclaimed: "Thank you, Convention. Thank you. The Convention is now adjourned. Refreshments are being served...."

Julian heard no more owing to the rush of the delegates making for the exits. Tina took his hand. "Wait," she said in a tired voice. "Pamela said she'll come over to us at the end of the session."

And, after several minutes, while the tide of delegates receded about them, Pamela did indeed appear, without Rupert whom Julian had seen being borne off by a group of leather-jacketed young men – to what event he could not imagine.

"Well, my darlings," proclaimed Pamela, her colour high, her honey-coloured hair coiffed elegantly. "What did you think of that?"

Julian did not answer. He found it hard now to talk to her at all, not knowing what thoughts were filling that evil head, what plans for his own fate were even now being formulated within it. Tina, however, clearly made an effort to be cheery.

"I didn't understand too much to be honest!"

"Well, you wouldn't. It was all routine. The difficult part comes next."

Ignoring Julian completely, she took Tina to one side, talking into her delicate ear, her rouged mouth opening and shutting, pursing, then splitting into a thin smile. Julian wondered what lies were being delivered.

When Pamela had left, Tina returned to him. "There's been progress," she said. "Pamela will be having a meeting with members of the Executive Council who are also on the Inner Command, and they are said to be receptive to change. There will be discussions that follow with the High Director." She paused for a moment, her eyes bright. "And I am very lucky, for I will be seeing my father tonight."

Julian reached out and held her by the shoulders. "That's wonderful!" He was genuinely pleased for her. But, then, why shouldn't he be? Only out of the trail of doubt and fear that never left him now. He, who had fled from a SupaPod and had made war on SupaPodia, was he to meet the High Director too? No amnesty had ever been confirmed. Would he not be arrested immediately afterwards, as soon as they had his confessions out of his own mouth?

"You will come with me as well," she said. "My father will want to hear your experiences directly from you."

The fear was flooding into him again. He must be mindful of his recent conversion; he must keep his mind on that higher power – higher even than the High Director – which watched over them all.

They had a drink in a bar. It was the quietest bar of the many in the Convention Centre that Julian could find. Most were very rowdy, with young men and women who seemed to have no part in the Convention but were probably just Eliti hangers-on – the sons and daughters of delegates and their friends, a noisy, swearing, laughing crowd in various types of dress and undress. The leather-jacketed youths who had borne off Rupert were in one bar that Julian peeped into and hurriedly withdrew from, his face showing his shock. So that was Rupert's predilection! No wonder Pamela took her pleasures elsewhere. At last, Julian was able to escort Tina to a quiet space hung with a sign, SAFARI: it was set with tables raised on antelope legs, its walls and ceiling bearing large images of wild animals, its floor covered by striped zebra skins.

"Dreadful," sighed Tina. She was perhaps referring to the cut off antelope legs that supported the table tops, but nonetheless she sank gratefully into a bucket-shaped chair.

He ordered her coffee, and a beer for himself. The beer came in a tall frosted bottle labelled 'Lion': it tasted like nectar to Julian. He ordered another. There was nothing to pay. The room number at the Mandela was all that was required by the waiter, who wore a loose safari-type suit.

Later, pushing through a scrum of delegates and their youthful adherents blocking the steps outside, a number of whom had flung off their clothes and were splashing naked, or near naked, in the fountains jetting high in the forecourt, Tina and Julian made their way on foot back to the Mandela. They both retired to their separate rooms.

"I'll call for you at 4 o'clock," she said. "It's when Pamela said to be ready. She'll be taking us to the High Director's headquarters." He thought it was strange the way she referred to her father in this formal manner, as if he was someone so remote from her now she could not think of him as her own flesh and blood.

"What should I wear, do you think?"

"A smart jacket and trousers. A new suit, perhaps Do you have one? If not, you have time to get a tailor up to measure you. They'll finish it in next to no time."

"Right, I might do that." He was not paying, so why not? At least it would be something to occupy himself with in the meantime. He put in a call and requested a tailor. A little black man with a head of curly white hair arrived almost at once. His tape measure whizzed over all the salient parts of Julian's body. When he produced a cloth block of colours and patterns, Julian chose a striped charcoal made of a lightweight material.

"Good choice, baas." It won't crumple or crease. Stains you can wipe away."

"There won't be any stains."

"Of course not, baasie. Ready in two hours." He held up two fingers. His fingers were gnarled and calloused; presumably he did not do the cutting and stitching himself.

Julian picked up the control to his Screen and flicked through the channels. There was little showing of any interest. A news programme, however, was covering the Convention. A female reporter in a green dress with a bare midriff stood in the forecourt Julian had just left. The fountains sprayed their water high behind her, and occasionally the breast or bottom of one of the frolicking bathers loomed in and out of view. The reporter kept turning her head as she talked, "Some delegates – as you can see – are refreshing themselves after the very warm welcome given to Joshua Pomeroy-Collyer, High Director of SupaPodia. The Convention was in unanimous approval of the plans for SupaPodia drawn up by their High Director, despite a notification received by Channel Mandela that there has been some dissent amongst several delegates."

The camera panned away from the reporter to focus on a naked couple streaming with water bent over a fountain basin, spectators urging them on.

"All, though, seems pretty cool at the moment." The reporter laughed, and the shot dissolved into one of lions roaring, giraffes swaying, zebras running, the azure sea foaming over sun-seared rocks, 'News from Channel Mandela – AFRICA.'

Ignoring another programme entitled 'TransWedding. Could it be you?', Julian switched off the Screen and lay back on the bed. He slept, awakened at length by a knock on the door. It was the tailor with the completed suit. He tried it on. The fit was perfect.

"Marvellous. Thank you," he said to the smiling tailor.

But the tailor did not want to leave. He held his hands forward, cupped.

"But you'll be paid, won't you?"

"Yes, baas, SupaPodia Clothing, but not me. Wife, three children, baasie, please."

"But I don't have money. Does anyone these days?" Julian looked around at his possessions. He picked up the timepiece he had brought away on his wrist from the SupaPod, with its useless segments of coloured time. Was there a greater symbol of SupaPod's divorcement from the real needs of mankind than this?

The tailor, though, was very pleased to receive it. "Thank you, baasie. We eat now." A last sight of his smiling face, and then he was gone.

Julian sighed, and sat in a chair in his new suit. He fell asleep again. The next knock at the outer door was Tina's. When he opened it, he could see at once that she was upset.

"What's wrong?"

"Oh, Julian. My meeting – our meeting – with my father has had to be postponed."

"But why?"

"He's had to go away. Back to his palace. The story is that there's been a move against him, and he's returning to his palace to sort things out."

"Surely not. How do you know?"

"It's on the news," said Tina, flinging out an arm towards the Screen.

"Is it? It wasn't just now."

"Pamela's confirmed it." She looked about to burst into tears.

"Come in, won't you?" He reached out for her arm.

He sat her in the same chair he had just been sleeping in. "Would you like a drink?"

"Have you got tea?" Her voice was a little shaky, but the Tina he knew was coming back. Her face was pale, her blonde hair plastered to her head, the ends dripping onto the shoulders of her white blouse. She saw the direction of his glance. "I was washing my hair when I heard. Do you have a towel I could use?"

"Of course." She followed him into the bathroom, and he watched her as she rubbed vigorously at her head. Perhaps by that action she hoped to remove the bad news too. Yet it still stood there between them, unresolved.

He made the tea. She had re-seated herself in the chair. Her blue skirt cut prettily across her knees. She held the cup against her chest, her back straight. He thought: I have never loved her as much as I do now. I will protect her to the end, whatever happens, whatever the cost.

"What's the plan then?" he asked.

"We're to go up country to the High Director's palace. Pamela will come with us. We'll have our meeting there. Pamela says it is a better plan, anyhow, away from the mob of delegates, as she calls them. It'll be easier to resolve matters when my father's back in his own place, on his own land. It's his real working headquarters, not the Cape."

Julian hesitated, as he did not wish to upset Tina any further, but he had to ask. "Are you sure of Pamela? What is this move against your father? Who's behind it?"

"Oh, not Pamela, for sure. She's been a dear. I know you don't trust her, but I do. The opposition comes mainly from some of the South American

SupaPods where they've had a lot of violence. They blame my father for it. I don't know why. It can't be his fault personally, but perhaps of the whole system. That is the point I have to make to him."

Julian was far from convinced. He suspected Pamela in this, out for her own advantage – yet he couldn't tell Tina that. After all, there had been terrible violence in Britain too – as he knew so well: he had been part of it! Could UK Commissioners also be stirring up trouble against the High Director, seeking greater assurances of their safety and for far better defence forces? One of those Commissioners, of course, could be Pamela herself. But he had no alternative but to go along with what Tina was telling him. Suddenly the image of the Beast came into his mind. What was *he* doing here? Was the Beast under Pamela's orders?

"How are we to get to the High Director's palace? he asked. "Is it a long journey?"

"By helidrone. Pamela's organising it."

So I'm back under the control of Pamela, Julian thought. And then he realised he had never left her control – not at Hayling, not here now, not since he had been under the command of the Major fighting for Nemesis. What future purpose did Pamela – did SupaPodia – have then for him? Why did they not just get rid of him, as they had done so many others, back into the deepest bowels of a SupaPod or to a Correction Camp?

"Pamela says the flight will be tonight. We're to have dinner and then meet her with our possessions in the hotel lobby at 8.00."

"And I had this suit made too." Julian was trying to raise a smile, but Tina took him seriously.

"You can wear it when you're there. I'm sure there will be formal occasions at the palace."

Julian thought: My life is like a story book now. I have no idea what each fresh page will bring to me. Or I am like a surfer riding the waves, sinking then rising, spinning and turning, never knowing when a wave might crash over me and drown me.

He did not wish to spell out his doubts to Tina any more. What would be, would be. He would remain strong until the end – if end there was – and he would protect Tina, and defend her beliefs – which he recalled hastily were now his beliefs too – to the utmost of his strength.

He raised his cup of tea to her and she raised her own cup in response. "To the future," he toasted. "To your father and to success. We shall not be beaten. We have come too far for that."

She looked at him gravely, her eyes steady above the rim of her cup, and then she drank.

"God bless you, Julian," she said.

* * *

Julian had never travelled in a helidrone before, and nor, judging by her awkward posture in the small glass bubble, had Tina. She sat wedged against the sides of her enveloping rubber seat with an expression on her face that showed a grim determination to comply and not to complain. It could not be any fear of being suddenly violently ejected into the thinning air of eternity that affected Tina; her belief in a protecting deity was so strong she would accept whatever fate He (or She or It) planned for her with her habitual equanimity. No, Julian thought, observing her with curiosity, it must be sensations of vertigo that were affecting her, although she had given no indication of this complaint in the airship; indeed it had been he who had felt uneasy. Seating himself beside Tina, he could sympathise with her as he too experienced a dislike of the enclosing embrace of the seat and the exposed, vulnerable feeling the glass sides of the helidrone gave him: it was like sitting without visible support in the open air.

In front of him, Pamela, however, appeared to have no such ill feelings. She was chattering away happily, as if to herself, about the great vistas of Africa they were about to witness as they flew north at low altitude to the High Director's palace complex. Perhaps, though, it was the absence of Rupert, who was to follow in a later helidrone, that had brought on her relaxed gaiety; the cruel, scheming Pamela whom Julian had witnessed, and of whom he was so suspicious, was replaced now by a woman of light-hearted gaiety, as if she was the hostess of the helidrone, welcoming them to the most pleasurable experience of their lifetimes.

The point, though – as Julian now noted with a thud of his heart – was that there was no hostess, nor any crew, not even a pilot. The helidrone would be flown by ground control. Some person, even at this moment, had its hand on a lever that would set the engines whirring and project them upwards. If that hand spilt its coffee, or reached out to touch the gleaming hair of its assistant, or was distracted by some alarm going off, then they might be dashed violently sideways, or upwards, or, worse of all, downwards.

As it was, a calm voice, female and educated, broke in to the cabin out of some speaker or other, stating, "Engines starting…Prepare for take-off… Taking off now." Looking out, Julian saw the blades on the two stubby wings begin to turn until they became two circular blurs, and above the bubble where they sat he imagined the main blades were doing the same. There was little sound, just a high-pitched whine which rose in volume as they left the ground. The nose dipped a little, enough to make Julian start and clench his knees, and then they were flying forward, but gaining height so that they passed low over the crest of Table Mountain – as they had done in the airship – and the wrinkled sea opened out all about them.

To begin with, they followed the coast. Julian could see the upper works of a SupaPod right below them, with hands waving at them from its roof deck. Poor sods, Julian thought, are they Lilacs or Podders seeking some sunshine and fresh air before another long period of incarceration in the bowels below? The hideous reality of SupaPodia was illustrated to him – as if he needed any further example – by the straggle of a ruined town that had once stretched up to the coastline, lying now roofless and derelict, the railway lines running through these ruins to the SupaPod the only objects that looked bright and in order. The open grassland changed suddenly to a geometrical order of vast, squared fields, each with a long red-roofed shed beside it, and rows of black ants in the fields bent over working. All about, ribbons of smoke were rising – or were they perhaps the jets of water pumps irrigating the fields? Orchards passed beneath them, with perfect lines of dark-canopied trees, like great gaming boards where the counters were blocks of workers picking, then bearing the fruit to wagons pulled by…were they camels? Julian blinked his eyes; he could not see for sure. The helidrone buzzed on like a glass bee.

It was a long flight without any sustenance other than for a packet of raisins and one of biscuits, and a small plastic bottle of some thick fruity liquid in a pocket of the seat-back in front. Julian did not touch the liquid, realising anxiously that his bladder had already begun to ache. How much longer would the flight take? He nudged Pamela's shoulder, and, leaning forward as far as the straps on his seat allowed, yelled into her ear. "How long to touch down?" Pamela, however, did not answer: she may not even have heard. It was the flight controller – wherever she was – who intoned straightaway "67 minutes, if no head winds."

So all that we say is overheard, thought Julian, just like the SupaPods. What things had he said? Nothing much, just some laughter and a riposte or two to Pamela's jokes, and the calling out of an enquiry to Tina as to how she was doing. Nothing to hang him with. All his old suspicions and neuroses were returning. When this was over, he had to get away forever from SupaPodia and its pervading influence, even if it meant finding a cave to live in – somewhere, anywhere. Like one of the old hermits, he sought peace and seclusion and an end to fear, when he could meditate on the true meaning of existence and strike up a dialogue with that freshly-revealed God, who was his to worship now.

They were following the coast, buzzing low, so that grazing animals were disturbed by them and the occasional human too; some fishermen with their blue-hulled boat were trying to push it out through the booming surf. A beached liner with many decks lay on its side on the narrow beach of a rocky peninsula, its rusting steel oozing streams of dark water into the sea. Seagulls swooped upon its rails, hanging there like the souls of those forced to jump into the black, engulfing waves. Rising higher, they passed close to what had probably once been a great seaport, but now was the home to at least two SupaPods (Julian could see their portals on artificial islands in the bay, their roofs clearly marked with huge silver figures, '31' and '32').

They flew inland, rising higher in places flying between mountains rather than over them. Walls of brown rock and loose, tumbling screes, covered with bushes and stunted umbrella trees, passed close to them. At one point, a mountain goat stood transfixed on a ledge, its gaze level with Julian's own, only feet away. Julian shut his eyes and refused to look out further. He hoped the controller's grip on her toggle switch was secure, or was the flight controlled entirely by computer, safe unless there was a glitch in the software? He did not know. He could only pray. His bladder was by now painfully sore.

At last, they were descending. They were following the black strip of a road; a plain opened out, more mountains, their stark flat tops rushing by. Their speed must be considerable. "How fast?" he called out. "523 knots", came back the immediate response. Hell! He had not realised they were moving so quickly. The helidrone must have additional jet power. Its blades alone would surely not propel it so fast.

They were much lower. "Jet power off," the disembodied voice said. So, he had been right. "Passengers: prepare for landing." A green area was below them, studded with buildings, mostly rectangular in shape, their purpose clearly utilitarian. They were surrounded by several rows of fencing: Julian could see the coiled wire catching the sunlight. They hovered now above a series of ledges carved out of a mountain side, each ledge filled with white-walled buildings, some with towers at their corners, others enclosing courtyards full of flowering plants. A blue swimming pool with a transluscent roof filled one court. Next came gardens and orchards, and then a huge stone and red-brick house, its walls covered with purple trailing vines. They were close to the ground now, dust swirling up – grey-green grass, then perfect emerald grass marked with white lines like a sports field, a great 'P' at its centre – and they were down.

Looking out of the bubble, Julian could see a line of yellow-clothed servants, women and men, coming towards them, bearing silver trays on their heads, filled with bottles, jugs and flowers. A vehicle, a type of small, four-wheeled lorry, crept behind them; its load was a square white kiosk with a pointed roof, like a small pagoda.

Pamela had released herself from her seat and was half-standing, her body turned to Julian. "That's the piss wagon," she said. "I need it even if you don't." It seemed a bizarre introduction to the High Director's palace, even if a most necessary one.

Stepping down from the helidrone (Julian had the grace to call out "Thank you" to which the unknown flight controller responded with a girlish trill, "My pleasure"), the three of them stood looking around. The line of advancing yellow servants was still a little way off. The great house stood at the far side of the green sward, with its high towers and pinnacles, its gilded roofs, and its fantastic porticoed front, from which a line of stone columns continued towards the lower terrace cut into the mountain behind, where they became two lines forming a covered way. Above, the mountain swept skywards, cut by terraces that were each full of golden buildings, some with white smoke eddying up softly into the clear, blue sky. Fountains played, flowers bloomed, trees waved and shook, everywhere was a harmony of shape and form, of nature and building. Looking away to his right, Julian saw the sharply defined form of another smaller mountain, its flat summit ornamented with a white circular dome, surrounded, he thought, by more columns: the distance was too great to see clearly.

Tina, standing quietly absorbed by the view, said she didn't need the lorry-born loo, but Julian followed Pamela to it: there were two cubicles side by side. A bird was calling somewhere close by – a high croaking sound – and the jabber of the servants could be heard, now pressing flowers, food and drink on Tina, whom they had left alone. In his cubicle, Julian most gratefully relieved himself. Through the plastic walling he could hear Pamela doing the same. Her piss stream sounded like a hippopotamus draining itself. The thought made him chuckle. He was still grinning about it when he emerged. Pamela appeared beside him smoothing down her skirt. "You seem in a good mood," she said.

"Yes," he replied. "Relief", and she laughed too at that, but he could see in her eyes the coldness returning, and he remembered and he feared.

Rejoining Tina, Julian and Pamela were confronted by the smiling black faces of the servants who, bearing their salvers, moved to surround all three of them, chanting a song of welcome and dancing to its rhythm as they whirled about, placing garlands of bright red flowers over their heads – like nooses about our necks, a now sombre Julian reflected. The helidrone, attended by a mechanic – he must have come out in the toilet wagon – stood on the grass like a round-bodied insect with wings and tail. Julian could make out the jet funnel projecting from underneath like a red phallus. The air around vibrated with heat. He suddenly had a vision of Pamela seated astride it with her skirt pulled up, her white thighs pressed hard against the red metal. Surely that would satisfy even her!

He looked away troubled. Was he going mad to have such thoughts? Two servants were pressing glasses of sparkling wine on him: he drank one, then drank another. He helped himself to some grapes and then to a bread roll filled with cooked meat that had a perfumed, gamey flavour. He did not like it and spat it out. A servant immediately picked up the mess while another offered him a tray of iced cakes, of which he took a handful, feeling hungry.

Their immediate needs met, a tall male servant, whose yellow uniform was ornamented with gold braid and epaulette, ushered them towards the house. It was a long trek over the grass. Why could not the helidrone have landed closer? thought Julian, suddenly tired and irritable. The controller, who had guided their flight within feet of mountain sides, should surely have been able to set it down by the house walls, or even in one of those inner courtyards, and then there would have been no need for all this pantomime with refreshments and portable toilets. He was certain there would be a good reason why not, but this SupaPodia world was never going to be one he understood.

They entered the house by a very modest side door, and found themselves in a long passageway, plainly decorated with differing shades of greys and blues. The many servants had now left them, and only the head servant led their small column along the passage. They came into a hallway that was panelled in a yellowish-brown wood, pleasing to Julian's eyes. Deep chairs stood on the thickly-carpeted floor, beside low tables piled with magazines. A complete tree, branchless but for its round dark-green top, occupied one end of the hall, rising into the open roof timbers from a massive bronze cauldron. Pictures attached to the wall panelling were all of English country scenes, as perhaps they had once been – a village street with thatched cottages and hollyhocks in the gardens, a view of the open Downs with a windmill and a shepherd's flock, a glade in a wood with a gypsy caravan and children playing. All very nice and sentimental, thought Julian, still peevish, but nothing much to do with a SupaPod – the long plain corridors, the deep shafts, the endless rows of accommodation Pods, filled with drooling, shambling orange-clad residents. The High Director was clearly a man who sought to escape from the very idea of the things he had helped to create and perpetuate.

They had seated themselves. The head servant had left. Pamela sat forward, expectant, her eyes alert. Tina had reverted to her habitual inscrutable pose. Julian looked at her. Of course, she would be keyed up inside, her blood racing. The moment had come when she would meet her father again after many long years. She must be wondering how he would react to her.

The servant returned. He called out, "Lady Lascelles, please," and she, with an apologetic back glance at them, was led away. Minutes passed, five minutes, ten minutes, half an hour. Other servants arrived with their silver trays and white-toothed smiles. Julian helped himself to more cake and another of the rolls, this one full of cheese. He munched at it. It tasted good. Tina did not take anything. She did not want to talk. Only the sound of Julian's eating stirred the room.

Pamela did not return. But the head servant did. "Miss Christine," he said, reading from a piece of paper. "Would you follow me, please." He sounded an educated man. His English accent was very good.

"Good luck," said Julian, rising to his feet and giving her a hug. "I hope it goes well and makes you happy." She looked pale. He could sense her inner worries through the calm façade she pretended.

She pleased him by taking both his hands in hers. "It *will* go well. For both of us. My father will like you, I know, and understand what you have been forced to do." She disappeared through the far door, and he was left alone.

He felt suddenly scared. Was he ever going to see Tina again? Or would the opportunity be taken to get rid of him now? He had had the luck of a survivor so far. That luck might be about to run out. He had imagined all three of them bearding the High Director in his den, setting out to him – a fair-minded man – what he clearly didn't know – the brutal realities of his own organisation. He had not expected them to be split up in this way. Yet there might well be another turn, another twist and all would become clear. Tina was his safeguard. The High Director would not betray the trust of his own daughter now that he had so recently re-found her.

Yet, Julian admitted he did not know for sure. He sat biting at his nails. What was his plan? What would he say? He found he did not know that either. But he felt his instincts would guide him when the time came.

The time *had* come. Another servant, a woman in a braided yellow uniform, appeared at the door. "Dr. Foster," she said with a smile. She had a pleasant Asian face. Surely she could not be the messenger of a tyrant. He tried to get up, but his knees at first would not work. He stumbled out of the chair and nearly collided with her. She smiled again at him.

"I'm taking you to Mr. Pomeroy-Collyer," she said in a sing-song voice. They were in a passage beyond the hall now. A stag's head stared down from a wall. "Just a word of advice, sir. Please do not speak to him until he has first spoken to you."

"Of course," he murmured. The carpet they were treading seemed like thick grass. Did criminals mounting the scaffold feel like this, their legs not wanting to work, as if they knew their human purpose would soon be extinguished?

The passage widened into another, smaller hall. A tabletop bore the bronze statue of a mounted knight in full armour, lance extended. At the end of the hall were huge double doors.

The messenger knocked on one leaf of the doors, craning her head forward against the wood. Surely, Julian thought, the knock could not penetrate that thick oak. Then the messenger stood back, pushing open the door with one arm.

"Please enter, sir," she said.

* * *

Julian came into the room as if through a mist, an effect he often experienced when he was tense and nervous. He had to blink his eyes a few times before he could make out the shape of the room, with its tables and chairs, and its bookshelves filled with volumes all in similar red and gold bindings. But there to greet him was the High Director, arm outstretched, dressed much more conservatively now than at the Convention – in a fawn-coloured, collarless jacket over a pink shirt, and tight brown trousers stuffed into high boots. The High Director's face was fleshy and pink, with fluffs of white hair on his cheek bones and a spray of greyer hair too about his chin It was as if the act of shaving was too much for him or for his barber to complete.

Julian reached forward to take the High Director's hand. "Very pleased to meet you, sir."

"And I, you." His voice sounded much firmer than the thin piping tones Julian remembered from the Convention. His opinion then had been that he was a rather weedy, insignificant figure, although he had found it hard to sustain that view in the knowledge of the powerful position he held. Yet powerful men could be sensitive and sycophantic as well as forceful and cruel; look at the Emperor Nero, for instance, a tyrant who aspired to great art or Hitler who was sentimental about animals while killing millions of human beings.

The immediate blur about the room had now dissolved to reveal to a surprised Julian that both Pamela and – the Lord be praised! – Tina were also present, looking up at him from chairs. Tina was smiling and looked relaxed and happy now, he was pleased to note, but Pamela still had a twisted half-smile on her face that perhaps spoke of secret thoughts, of what exact nature he could not imagine. Yes, she was the one Julian feared, rather than the homely-looking Joshua, lord though he was of the SupaPodia world.

"Pleased take a seat," said Joshua, waving a hand towards a vast leather chair into which Julian settled back, feeling his feet were now higher than his head, an uncomfortable sensation. Joshua took up a central position in a small wicker chair with wide, flat wooden arms, upon which various books and documents were piled. It was clearly a favourite 'working chair' of his.

"Now," he said, looking over his audience with a benevolent smile, "this has been a joyful day for me, a most joyful day…" – his gaze lingered on Tina – "….with my lovely daughter returned to me in the presence of a very good friend…" – his smile was transferred to Pamela – "…and now I have a visit from one of our employees in my favourite land of far off England. Julian, isn't it…?"

"Dr. Julian Foster, sir," said Julian hastily. He had expected the High Director to have his record in front of him – his recruitment, his service, his betrayal, his escape, his armed rebellion….enough to hang him several times over.

"Ah, yes. I shall just call you Julian, if I may. We only use first names here. I am Joshua."

"Right, sir. I mean, Joshua. Thank you." Julian was becoming a little flustered. He had not expected this smooth urbanity.

"And you were with SupaPod No. 16 Ramsgate, were you not, when you bumped into Christine?"

That was a strange way of putting it, thought Julian – chums and mates bumping into each other. He recalled the Podders he had seen being admitted to the SupaPod, the long lines of displaced people, with all their hopes of a new secure life, going cheerfully down to their doom – to their interment for ever, for that's what it amounted to. And the newly recruited Lilacs, not knowing what the hell was expected of them, and the disillusionment when the reality became clearer. Had he *bumped* into Tina then? Or had she bumped into him? And what of Peter or Marion or Stanley, or any of the others? Had they all been bumping around together? No, they had just been there, a small part – a very small part – of the forced artificial world of SupaPodia with its hidden evils. Stanley had been evil, as had Marion, but Peter had been brave and good. And Tina? Well, she had been something exceptional. He was very glad to have bumped into her.

"That's right," he called out, seeing Joshua had paused, expecting an answer. "We were both entrants at the same time."

He looked across at Tina, who was smiling and nodding, clearly encouraging him in what he was saying. What had she told her father, he wondered? Had he forgiven her for her activities in supporting superstition within one of his all-knowing, all-rational SupaPods, offering a superior deity – a superior obedience – to that of SupaPodia itself?

"And what are your plans now?" Joshua suddenly shot out the question, taking Julian by surprise. He was surprised because he had no plans. His intent had been to reform SupaPodia, destroy it, if necessary. If he couldn't fulfil that aim, what could he do?

"To take up teaching again," he said uncertainly, struggling for an answer.

"But not in a SupaPod? I understand you don't like the life there. I could make use of you here. You wouldn't have to go underground."

"Really, sir! That would be interesting. What sort of job would that be?"

"The Eliti need good teachers for their offspring. Little bastards, a lot of them – the kids, that is. They need the firm hand of a teacher who's got experience and is not soft with them. Does that sound like you?"

Julian did not know what to say. He saw the smile was still on Tina's face, so had this idea already been discussed with her? Did she approve? "I'd like to know more, er..Joshua. Where would I teach, for instance?"

"Why, here at the palace, of course. Lots of Eliti sprogs come here for their coming-out, as it were. They need a final polish, gaining knowledge, for instance, of the world before SupaPodia, the OuterWorld before the new dawn, that sort of thing."

"So you'd want me to teach propaganda." The words were out before Julian could stop them. He saw Tina's face fall while Pamela's lifted her eyes hard on him.

Joshua's tone did not alter. He was the avuncular uncle, doing good deeds, used to recalcitrant children about him. Julian was a child who might be corrected by being offered a new opportunity, He could take it or leave it. The uncle did not really care.

"You can call it what you like," he said. "It's what I can offer you. A teaching post here is much sought after. SupaPodia pays well – very well. You'd have your own rooms, a great deal of time off, and the opportunity for travel. The Eliti are likely to invite you back to their own estates – that's what usually happens. It'll be the life of Riley, as we once used to say. I don't know who Riley was, mind you."

Julian had to admit it sounded very fine. He would be joining the world of the Eliti. But would that not be a betrayal of everything he had fought for, of his conscience, his beliefs? How would that help even one denizen of those underground chambers, the poor Podders to whom he had wanted to teach truth?

"What do you think, Tina?" he asked her, his brain in a whirl, using the intimate form of her name in front of her father, to whom she was clearly plain Christine.

"I think it's a great opportunity for you," she said. "The very best you could hope for."

"And what will you be doing?" he asked daringly, for what right did he have to put such a question to Tina, unless there was the presumption of some attachment between them.

"I've told my father I'm going to stay here too," she said a little guardedly, looking up at Joshua as if to judge his reaction. The High Director was waving his hands as if conducting her words. The kindly smile lingered on his face. Was he on some drug or other, Julian wondered, suspicious again?

"I want her to be with me now," Joshua said, apparently unabashed by his personal needs being discussed in front of a complete stranger. Did he even know what Julian had been involved with? "She'll bring solace to me as I grow older. She can set up her own nunnery – or whatever it is those places or called – or an abbey even, or a stack of abbeys, provided she sticks to spreading her word to the Eliti. I don't want it in the SupaPods any longer, though, if it's going to encourage further dissension."

"What about the OuterWorld then?" Julian asked, looking at Tina. "You taught your religion there before."

She had resumed her placid expression, her hands in her lap. She said calmly, "And I will teach the World of God there again, until all of these three worlds are reconciled in God's love."

"Quite," said Joshua, clearing his throat. "Providing it does no harm, certainly."

He got to his feet, spilling a book or two onto the carpet from the arm of his chair. "Now, if you'll excuse me. I have another meeting outside somewhere. Where is it, Pamela?"

"In the Tudor Hall," Pamela replied in a sharp voice. She had sat with her face turned away during the previous conversation. Julian could see she did not approve.

"Ah, of course. In fifteen minutes then? Good."

"Well, my boy…" he said as he passed Julian's chair. Julian was struggling unsuccessfully to raise himself. Boy, indeed! he thought, I'm only a little younger than him. "…You'll have to let me know what you decide. Don't be too long about it, though. If I'm honest, I'm sticking my neck out a bit for you. There're others who wouldn't be so generous."

Julian saw Joshua look at Pamela, and he knew who was one of those 'others'. The thought sent a chill through him. The two of them left the room together.

For the half minute or so before the servant reappeared to escort them away, Julian was alone with Tina in this den at the heart of SupaPodia.

"Aren't you abandoning all your principles, Tina?" he asked.

"No. There is more than one way to God and the business of God. I can't go where the way is blocked."

"Well, that must apply to me as well."

"I think so, Julian. You'll probably be happy here, at the heart of things."

"I hope so, Tina."

But he knew he wouldn't be. It wasn't right. Yet, if he took this path, fully aware of what he was doing, couldn't he in time, by some circuitous route or other, reach a truer destination for himself, more in keeping with the principles he sought to fulfil? He would hope to change SupaPodia by his reasoned judgements from the inside rather than his destructive actions from the outside. It was surely worth a try.

33

For a few days Julian did not see the High Director again, although he met Tina frequently, as well as Pamela, although it was obvious Pamela did not wish him around now. Probably her plans for him with the High Director had not worked out.

Julian had been allotted a room high in a tower at a corner of the main house. He thought this tower must be reserved for visitors because he knew Tina was on the floor below and Pamela, whom he had passed once on a lower landing, was somewhere close by as well. Everything Julian needed was provided, quicker, smarter and more efficiently even than at the Mandela Hotel, and certainly much better than the clumsy, impersonal system of delivery shoots in a SupaPod. His laundry was done each day; new clothes were provided from a catalogue in the room, and fitted, as at the Mandela, by a personal tailor. Meals could be taken either in his room, at a table with wide views from the large curving window over the sweeping Ingogo plain, with its long swaying grass sprinkled with the pinks and whites of the cosmos flower and the bright red clumps of aloe, or in the private restaurant on the tower's ground floor. Here he would generally see Tina each day, and occasionally Pamela, who was normally leaving as he entered. She gave him some unfriendly looks, although she was unfailingly courteous. He was not so concerned about her now, since he seemed to have the High Director's support. He hoped her sour face was down to her own plans going awry and not on account of him as such. He had no desire to be her particular enemy.

By the third day, he had made up his mind; he would take up Joshua's offer. He told this to Tina when he found her at breakfast. He thought she looked particularly beautiful this morning sitting at the table, looking out over the green lawns at the front of the house, which were being watered by yellow-clad servants. Her hair was tied up at the back with a blue ribbon, her neck and upper chest bare, showing a hint of cleavage, her blouse light yellow and her skirt full and floral-patterned. He thought she looked like a girl in one of those weather houses, just emerged into the morning sunshine.

"I'm pleased," she said when he told her his decision. "I'm sure it's right for you. A way forward."

"And what about your plans? Any advances?"

"Pamela's helping me with setting up a small mission station nearby at Mount Pleasant."

"Pamela is!"

"Yes, Pamela. She's always had my interests at heart. She wants to help me." Tina's small chin was tilted up obstinately.

"I think you're wasting your time."

"Oh, Julian. I hoped I had converted you."

"Times and circumstances change," Julian said. "I *do* still believe. I just don't think you're going about things in a sensible way."

"There is only one way to God."

"Come on, Tina. You know that's a platitude. You have to be practical."

Her cheeks went red and Julian was sorry to have upset her. After a while she said, "So you're not ready for baptism yet?"

"No. I don't believe so."

"God will tell you when you're ready," she said, "and it will be at a time when you call upon Him and feel Him close to you, even if you forget Him now." She rose and excused herself.

Julian was to remember her words, for, of course, as ever she was right.

The Asian servant to the High Director – Julian thought she must be his secretary -obtained him another appointment to speak with him. It was to take place in Joshua's private quarters – an inner series of rooms and courtyards – at 3.00 that afternoon. He was told to dress informally, casually even, as it would be the High Director's 'down-time', so he wore a light tee-shirt and shorts, with only flip-flops on his feet. The secretary served again as a guide. She was dressed in a yellow silk sari, arranged in such an elaborate way that it was pulled up to cover her head as well; only her large dark eyes and beaked nose peeked out while her shapely body rustled lusciously as she walked.

At corners of the passages stood sentinel guards, dressed in baggy embroidered shirts and trousers, each carrying a broad-bladed weapon set on a long shaft. The High Director clearly liked to be surrounded by ceremony, thought Julian, passing by the guards, each of whom saluted with his free arm held across his chest. I wouldn't wish to have one of those axes swung at me, though.

They came through a series of extravagantly furnished rooms – a dining room with a huge central mahogany table set for a grand banquet, a lounge with modern chairs and sofas, a music room with a grand piano and a harp, and incongruously, in a corner, a set of steel drums – and then at last through a wide doorway into a courtyard open to the sky, surrounded by the walls and towers of the palace and overlooked by the terraces of the Inkwelo mountain. Staring up, Julian thought these terraces, festooned with a luxuriance of trailing plants and vines, must resemble the legendary hanging gardens of Babylon. His gaze fell to take in a swimming pool before him with sinuous curving sides. It filled much of the courtyard, and was overlooked by a jacaranda tree in full purple blossom, the trunk of the tree appearing to grow out of the blue and white Moorish tiles that paved the surrounds of the pool. In the shade of the jacaranda, a sun lounger bore the recumbent form of the High Director, naked but for a white towel thrown over his middle.

If these sights were not remarkable enough to Julian's questing eyes, dazzled as he was by the bright sunlight that seared the courtyard beyond the jacaranda's shade, the sight of a woman floating languidly on her back in the pool, only the ripples made by her hands and feet providing any cover to her nakedness, brought him up short in his tracks. Surely he should not be here at this time. Should not the secretary have announced him first, allowing the High Director and his companion time to make themselves presentable? But no, the secretary in her lovely sari had gone over to the High Director and was talking to him: he had sat up in his lounger to listen, an action that had caused the towel to slip to one side. Julian abruptly turned his gaze away. When he dared to look back, he saw the secretary was waving him over, while she, bending low, retreated from the courtyard, disappearing into the interior darkness.

Julian almost wished he could do the same, but he remembered why he had come and the opportunity it was to provide, and he girded himself to face Joshua, whether he and his companion be naked or not. Joshua, in fact, had risen now and slipped on a pair of duck-white linen breeches. He held out a hand. "Very good to see you. Something tells me you've made a decision on my offer."

"Yes, sir. I would like to accept." Despite the considerable informality of this meeting, Julian still found it difficult to use the High Director's christian name.

"And you feel you can give the pupils who will come to you here the right sort of education?"

"Yes, sir."

"Please call me Joshua." He smiled through his thin beard. A thick mat of dark hair covered his chest, too close to Julian for him to feel comfortable. There was something about hairy men that repelled him.

"Yes, of course. Thank you, Joshua." He was standing full in the hot sun. Despite his light clothing, he felt his head beginning to swim.

"Come, lie in the shade with me." Joshua reached out and dragged another sun lounger beside his. Julian sat down on its edge gratefully, then extended his body so that his head was against a towel left draped over the sloping back. The towel smelt of a deep, exotic perfume, and he realised that its last user was the lady in the pool, who might be returning for it at any moment. For some unaccountable reason this sent him into a mild panic. The unconventionality of the situation had momentarily disturbed him. He felt out of his depth as surely as if he was plunged in the pool, struggling to swim.

Nonetheless he managed to ask, "What subjects will be required? "English literature, history and geography, I could teach."

"Yes, yes, that would do fine. I have another teacher in mind for the sciences, so you would fit in well, indeed plug a gap, so to speak." Joshua chuckled, stroking the hair on his chest with one hand. Julian looked away.

"What periods of history are you most familiar with?" Joshua asked after a pause when he had seemed abstracted, watching the black head of a now swimming Lucinda as it tracked slowly across the pool.

"Oh, all periods really, of British history, at least. I have taught prehistory, the Roman period, early medieval, high medieval, Tudor, Stuart, the Civil War, the Glorious Revolution, the Ages of Imperialism, 20th Century Militarism, Diversification and Multi-Culturalism, the Ages of Austerity and Decay – that is, both pre and post Brexit – right up to the advent of SupaPodianism."

"Excellent. And which do you prefer?"

"My heart has always been with the Romans."

"Really. Why is that?" Joshua, lying on his side, was turned towards Julian. His balding head was growing pink with the sun, despite the shade of the jacaranda. He should be wearing a hat, Julian thought. He felt the sun pricking at his own bare legs.

"I'm not sure." Julian was finding it hard to think. A disturbance in the water showed that the pool's occupant might be preparing to get out. "Something about the system of Rome and their power to control appeals to me."

"Yes, indeed. But they suffered many rebellions."

"The Romans knew how to rule. They had order in society," Julian said stubbornly.

"The ordinary people suffered appallingly. Most were slaves. There was none of the welfare that a SupaPod today would give them. How very far we have advanced. I hope you will be saying that in your lectures, Dr. Foster."

Julian was shocked. Joshua's manner had changed decidedly. "Of course, sir. Of course, I will. I will teach the beneficence of SupaPodia."

"Why then did you seek to overthrow it?" asked Joshua icily.

Julian's heart was racing. Ever these ups and downs, changes coming as quickly as wind-swept clouds that suddenly block out the sun. No point in pretending. "I didn't, sir. I wanted to root out corruption for the greater good, not to damage your organisation."

Joshua stared at Julian for a long time, his chin in his hand, looking out from the sun lounger like a mad Roman emperor from his couch; Julian saw the likeness at once, as the now familiar stabs of fear began to strike him in the bowels and the limbs.

Then, to his surprise, Joshua burst out laughing. "Well done. You stand up well for yourself when tested. I *can* use you. We will talk further. Now I must take my ease with my wife and that I cannot share with you, I fear."

Julian, bemused, scrambled to his feet. "Of course, sir."

The woman was out of the pool, standing stark naked shaking out her long, black tresses. Water drops flew from her like small silver arrows. She smiled at Julian's discomfiture, seeing him desperately trying to look away.

"Does he want to swim?" she said. She held her arms across her body like Venus trying to disguise her charms.

"No, my love. Dr. Foster is leaving us now."

"Prepare me a synopsis for a course on British militarism," Joshua suddenly shot out, turning to the astonished Julian, who was standing frozen on the blue and white tiling. "I am particularly interested in the campaign of my forebear, Sir George Pomeroy-Colley. Perhaps you can find something out about him too. He died in 1881, by the old calendar, in a battle on that mountain there – Amajuba".

He raised his hand to indicate the distant flat-topped mountain, the nearest point of which was surmounted by the white dome of the rotunda that was his particular 'place of peace'. Julian, forcing his eyes upwards and away from Lucinda's gleaming body, thought it looked like an acropolis of light above this dark city beneath.

"Yes, sir, I will," Julian moved towards the courtyard exit, thinking I have never heard of this man Colley, yet I must make some enquiries. Tina will help me. She will be able to find out more about her father's interests and what exactly he wishes to know.

He turned back to the courtyard just before disappearing inside, seeing the naked Lucinda now standing over Joshua, her breasts flattened against his hairy chest, and he reaching up to her. He wondered what Tina would make of these other of her father's interests, so blatantly pursued – but it was probably best that she never knew.

And so he wandered back alone into the palace, lost now, until at last a yellow-clad servant found him and took him to his quarters – before a guard with his broad axe could seize him and chop off his head.

* * *

It was several days before Julian saw Tina next. She had left no message for him, but she was clearly away, perhaps with Pamela, for there was no sign of her either, nor of Rupert who must be with them as well, if sober enough. Julian concluded that their absence was involved with the setting up of the new mission station in the nearby settlement of Mount Pleasant: Tina had told him her 'aunt', as she still liked to call Pamela, was helping her materially with the mission. What could be Pamela's purpose in that, pondered an increasingly fearful Julian? He imagined it was just to keep Tina on her side and to prevent her seeing through to her own great ambition, which Julian had the gravest suspicion was the capture for herself of the crown of SupaPodia. How was that to be achieved? Julian wondered. By fair means: convincing SupaPodia's Executive Committee of the waywardness of the present High Director? – or foul: a palace coup through violence, to be achieved how and by whom? Julian recalled again his strange sighting of the Beast on the airship. He had not set eyes on him since. Where then had that evil force gone to ground? If anyone could organise a coup, and put it into effect, Julian knew it would be the Beast.

Julian filled in his time by walking in the palace grounds, chatting with the amiable gardeners in their yellow work suits, who worked in long rows digging, planting, and pruning. He also inspected the outer perimeters of the palace estates, with their triple lines of fences topped with coiled razor wire, watching the soldiers who patrolled outside, not here in fancy, old-fashioned costumes bearing medieval axes, but in grey camouflage uniforms carrying short, stubby plastic-cased weapons, the workings of which flashed with red and white lights.

From that first aerial view of the palace he had obtained as the helidrone had swooped in, Julian had gained the impression of palace gardens that merged seamlessly with the wilder landscape beyond, but his much closer-up ground inspection showed that the High Director was guarded even beyond the perimeter fences by further widths of wire, minefields, and regularly-spaced sentry posts, as well as by frequent mobile patrols. No wonder the way in and out for visitors was by helidrone only. A number of these had come and gone as he walked and watched, landing at various points on the lawns. Probably the servants had another way into the palace complex, the same entrance as would be used for all the necessary supplies and servicing, which must be on the far side of the Inkwelo mountain, out of sight of the palace itself.

As he walked through a geometrically laid out shrubbery, where smiling gardeners with shears were cutting back bushes still aflame with blossom, and weeding the path borders using what looked like old table knives, he looked up at the other mountain with the sliced-off flat top lying beyond the Inkwelo, which the High Director had told him was called Amajuba. Joshua had rambled on about a general called Colley who had been killed there, presumably with his army, and told him to research the history of that battle. It made a project for him which he would attend to this evening.

What sources could he find? Did the High Director have a library he could use? He would ask around. Or was he expected to get his results from the Screen in his room? He was doubtful of what the Screen could tell him. Most of its historic information was severely edited by SupaPodia Academia, whose main function, Julian knew from his university days long before his SupaPodia adventure began, was to rewrite the history of the world in SupaPodia's own terms: they even used the abbreviation bSP for the unenlightened period before SupaPodia, which, of course, consisted of most of the history of mankind. The period of SupaPodia, since its blessed founding by Sir Dickie Randsom, was denoted by the academic purists of SupaPodia simply as SP, yet these designations had yet to catch on with the Eliti or indeed the wider OuterWorld.

As the Amajuba summit was a fair distance from the Inkwelo mountain, Julian wondered how the High Director reached it in order to indulge in one of his peaceful reveries. It would seem to involve too long a tramp from his palace, along paths that must be difficult to patrol securely. Joshua did not appear to employ a personal bodyguard. Perhaps he would dare to ask Joshua when he saw him next. He might even persuade him to take him there. But first, he must do what he had been asked, and research this man, General Colley, about whom Joshua seemed to have some sort of fixation.

The Asian secretary was the person who helped him. It was almost as if she was expecting his enquiry because, as he wandered the palace's corridors, aimless, hoping for some inspiration for his enquiries, she appeared suddenly beside him in her yellow sari.

"You are looking for the library, I think?" Her voice was low and sultry. On her head she wore a round cap, from which several strands of jewels cascaded onto her brow. From her long, shining black hair to her diminutive brown toes peeking out from the hem of her sari, Julian thought her perfection. He desired her. Desperately, he tried to overcome this sudden lust. He was searching for books, not sexual adventure – not here, anyhow, with one of the High Director's own servants.

"Is Joshua available? Can I ask him my requirements?"

"No, my master is away at present. He is with his daughter, Christine, and Lady Lascelles." As she spoke, she emphasised her words by movements of her slender hands, her finger nails like small moons in the filtered light through the half-shuttered windows.

"Oh." Julian was quite shocked. Tina had not told him of her father accompanying Pamela and herself to the mission station. So why was the High Director involved? Perhaps he just wanted the chance to be with his daughter. Julian, nevertheless, found the news rather disturbing.

"My master told me you might wish to use the library. He told me to help you when you asked."

"Really. Well, that's good." Julian did not quite know what to say. He felt clumsy and awkward beside this enchanting woman.

To Julian's surprise, because he had expected Joshua's library to be in his study where he had first met him, she led him to a part of the palace new to him – along corridors, up flights of stone steps, past many bronze busts set on table tops of men he did not recognise, past hunting trophies, snarling lions and rhino heads, past enormous paintings of battle scenes, and rifles, muskets and bayonets arranged on walls like stars, until at last they entered a broad room with wooden shelving raised ceiling high, the shelves filled with row after row of tightly-packed books.

She looked at him expectantly, her rouged lips slightly apart, her large dark eyes pools of mystery, as mysterious as anything else in this place of dreams.

"What is your name?" he asked.

"Shanaya," she said, her eyes cast down. This was strange. She was confident the one minute, then shy of him the next.

"Well, Shanaya. Did your boss tell you what I am looking for?"

"Boss?" She looked puzzled. "I do not know what that is."

"Boss, Master, the High Director, Mr. Joshua," he said in a rush, for some reason a little irritated now. "You seem to know everything I'm doing. Did he not tell you?"

"Ah." Her face lit up. "The books you wish. I will show you."

She led him to the shelving in the far corner of the library near a shaded window. The white blind looked as if it would burst open with the yellow sunlight of the day outside. He felt the heat on his back as he bent to look at the shelves. 'Victorian Military Campaigns'; 'Queen Victoria's Little Wars'; 'The Transvaal War'; 'The First Boer War' – he read off the titles. They were all old books but kept in good condition, some not re-bound and still with their dust jackets. He pulled out one of the volumes and checked the index. Yes, the name 'Colley' was included. He looked at more titles: 'A Narrative of the Boer War'; 'With the Boers in the Transvaal; 'The Battle of Majuba Hill' – that was the battle in question. He would read that one first.

Then, his eye was caught by a further title: 'The Life of Sir George Pomeroy-Colley'. He pulled out the volume and opened it. A picture of the long-deceased general was at the front. He had a beard and a balding forehead, with a dreamy lost look about his eyes. So this was the man whom Joshua had said was one of his ancestors – certainly his name was very like the High Director's – the general who had died with his troops on that nearby mountain top.

"Can I take these back to my room?" he asked, indicating the two books he had pulled from the shelves.

"Of course," she smiled. "Do you wish more? We can carry more."

"I'll take another two then," he said, returning to the shelves. "They should do me for now."

She held the four books against her breast, her arms wrapped round them, as if they were the most precious burden.

"Are you alright carrying those? Give me a couple of them if you like."

"No. It is my job."

He shrugged his shoulders. What else is her job, he wondered? Dare he? No, that would be madness.

He followed her back through the long passages, up and down steps, until they came to the base of the tower where his room was.

"Shanaya." He touched her arm. She turned to him. "I can take the books from now on," he said.

She smiled. The jewels on her brow rattled lightly as she tilted her head. "I can help you read too," she said. And he knew what she meant.

He yearned for her now, but heard himself say, "No. That would not be right. What would your boss say?"

"My boss. He will not know. Or anyone else. Just you and me. Our secret I will bring sweetness to you for you have suffered. I can see that."

"I am twice your age. I don't know…"

"Shhh." She placed a finger against his lips, which he immediately took into his mouth. She said, "You have many worries, I know, but that will not be one of them. You are a teacher but I will be *your* teacher now."

And so it was done.

* * *

When Julian awoke, he was alone in bed with the dawn light already touching at the windows, the palace birds beginning to scream their dawn chorus. Shanaya had gone. Had she been just a dream, a wonderful dream? Then he saw the books set out neatly on his side table, as he knew he had never placed them. The far side of his bed, too, was still indented where she had lain, and he smelt her perfume on the sheets and on his arms and chest where he had held her. On the pillow were two long strands of black hair. He picked them up and wound them on his fingers. Could he remember? Dare he remember? Would she come to him again?

He dozed, and was awakened by a knocking on his door. He leaped out of bed stark naked? Had Shanaya returned? He had the sense to pull on a bath robe, which was just as well because he found it was Tina at the door. Her face was alight. He had never seen her smile brighter.

"Well you are a lazybones! Can I come in? I have something to tell you."

He let her in and made her a cup of tea while he went to the bathroom, and washed and dressed. When he returned, she was sitting in the armchair by the window looking at a magazine produced by SupaPodia South Africa – an edition on the country's wild life and the new game parks set up by various hunting Eliti.

"Horrible," she shuddered.

"What is?" He was disappointed to see her earlier happy smile had disappeared.

"The fact that people kill God's creatures for fun."

"That's the Eliti for you," he said. He shared her view absolutely. "No desire for anything but their own base gratification."

"Oh, that's a bit strong, Julian. You shouldn't generalise in that way. Evil runs throughout all classes of society. I expect many Podders would hunt and kill, if they could. And OuterWorlders too."

"But the OuterWorlders would hunt for food, Tina, to feed themselves, as would the Podders if they were able to escape the SupaPods. The Eliti, though, do it just for the pleasure, and perhaps the status they think it gives them."

"Mmm, perhaps," she mused, her lips pursed. She looked beguilingly sweet. He hated to argue with her about anything.

"Anyway," she said. My Aunt Pamela is an Eliti and she doesn't hunt."

"Not animals perhaps, but human beings for sure."

"Oh, Julian!" Tina cried, he knew only in mock exasperation. "Not all that again. Come, let me tell you what my father's promised us – all of us."

He couldn't imagine. They had clearly been hatching something or other while away together.

"First," said Tina, and he was pleased to see the excitement back in her eyes, "my father's going to help fund the mission at Mount Pleasant. It's such a beautiful place, up against that mountain, what's it called?"

"Amajuba," guessed Julian.

"Yes, that's right. I haven't managed to covert him to the truth of God, but he's quite in favour of me spreading my beliefs Outside, providing I no longer take a mission directly into his SupaPods. He says he can't believe in God. but, if he did, it would certainly be my God! Christian morality he likes – morality without the superstition, he calls it. That's our compromise for now. I can accept his help on that basis and he's prepared to support me in the OuterWorld. That has to be enough for me for the present. In time, I think I can take the faith back again Inside – but I haven't told him that." She clutched at Julian's arm. "Do you think I'm bad?"

"No. You could never be bad, dear Tina. I'm so happy to see the joy in you. Just be careful. The world of SupaPodia can change suddenly."

"What do you mean?"

"Your father won't be the High Director for ever. Other people may have different ideas."

Her smile did not fade at his last words. "That's a chance I'm prepared to take."

She told him about what else had been decided. "My father has asked us all to go with him to his special place, on that mountain of…What's it called again?"

"Amajuba."

"Yes, that's right. It's rare for him to allow anyone to go there. He's normally alone, perhaps with a servant or two. He likes to meditate there: he says it gives him the strength for the decisions he must make for the benefit of SupaPodia – for the future of the world"

"You don't really believe in that, do you; I mean that SupaPodia is a good thing?"

"With reform, it wouldn't be all bad," she said guardedly. The concept is enormous, the vision utopian. But the practice, I agree, is far from perfect."

"The practice is corrupt," said Julian sharply. "SupaPods are places of evil, as I have witnessed myself. It's what I fought for, what others have died for. I thought you agreed. Isn't that why we're here, to try and reform the whole ethos and practice of SupaPodia?"

She took his hands in hers. "I do agree with much of what you say, Julian, and I would like there to be great change, not least in allowing the message and the spirit of Christ into the SupaPods. But I believe my father as well when he says he will move to root out the wrong and bring a better, more fulfilling life to the Podders, and to all those who work hard in the OW to support them. He won't allow Christ to be worshipped Inside yet, but isn't it wonderful that he will help me in keeping Him alive for people Outside. I think I have moved my father, Julian, and I may convert him yet – quite soon too." Her face was lit once more with joy.

"Tina," he said. "Sweet, good Tina. Be careful. Take one small step at a time. How I hope you are right! Yet, I fear, as I am full of doubt."

Her face was so close to his that he thought she would kiss him. But she drew away. "We will not discuss this anymore," she said, still smiling. "We will work together, though, as I know we both wish the same thing, albeit our perceptions, and our ways, may be different at times."

"Yes, that's fairly said, Tina." He did not wish to argue anymore, either. He changed the subject. "How's this trip to Amajuba going to be organised?"

"We're going to have a banquet there!" Tina suddenly sounded like a small girl excited about a party. "We'll be served like lords – lords and duchesses. And there'll be an orchestra to play music to us. And a grand firework display as it gets dark."

"Who's going? I mean, who are the other guests?"

"Well, you and me, and Pamela and Rupert, and my father's friend, Lucinda. And probably one or two others. He mentioned his secretary…"

"Shanaya!"

"Is that her name?" She looked at him curiously. "You know her?"

"Yes, she's been helping me with a little bit of research. Anyone else?"

"I'm not sure. Probably not. He said he wanted to keep it intimate. Julian, what an honour it is."

"He's your father, Tina. He'll want to please you."

"I meant really an honour for *you*. Instead of being angry with you, he's raising you up to his inner circle."

"Yes, I suppose he is." Julian had not thought of it that way. "I wonder why."

The last he said to himself softly, but Tina had heard. "Because he likes you and because he wants to please me."

"I think more the latter."

"I don't think that's true. He told me he admired you."

"*Admired* me!"

"Yes, for the way you have persevered and fought for what you believe in. He is a great respecter of courage – of the martial virtues, if you like."

Julian did not reply. He thought, yes, that may be true – but he is odd too, very odd, and his mood changes like the wind. I do not feel safe with him. He remembered he had to read up on Joshua's own hero, or was he an anti-hero? – Sir George Pomeroy-Colley. The books were lined up by his bed, as Shanaya had left them.

"How do we get up there? he asked. "I mean to the top of Amajuba. It looks a steep climb."

"My father *does* walk it occasionally." Tina's hands were clasped before her chest as if she was about to pray. "But there are security considerations and the distance is too far really, let alone for all the stuff that will need to be taken up for the meal, and the orchestra and the servants! So he says we'll be taken up by the helidrone he often uses."

"I see. And when is this going to take place?"

"Tomorrow," she said excitedly. Tomorrow afternoon. It will mean formal dress."

"I don't have any."

"I thought you had a suit made at the Cape."

"Oh, yes, so I did. It'll be all crumpled up somewhere in my bag. We weren't able to bring much with us, were we?"

"But I'm sure the servants will have pressed it and it will be ready for you to wear."

Tina swung open his wardrobe door and searched along the rail. "No, there's nothing here. Don't worry, I'll find out about it for you."

"Thanks. That'll be one worry less."

"It'll be the event of the season," Tina said, her excitement still in her face. "The Eliti will be so jealous."

"Tina! You do surprise me. I thought you believed in Christian simplicity and modesty."

"Even Christians can occasionally splash out a bit." She jutted out her chin, as if to defy herself as much as him. "It will be the one and only time. Afterwards, my true work begins."

"And what does dear Pamela think of all this?"

"Oh, she's excited too. Very excited. She's having a gown flown up from the Cape."

"And one for Rupert too?"

"Oh, Julian. You can be so dry. I think I should go now. Pamela will be looking for me."

"You are not at her beck and call."

"No, Julian, I'm not."

"Watch her. I don't trust her."

"Julian, I won't let you upset me. Pamela is a friend – to me and to you. She speaks very highly of you."

I bet she does, thought Julian after Tina had left. He sensed there was something afoot. Pamela might be about to make her move. He would be watching her. He would be ready for her. In the meantime, he must get to grips with this General Colley who had gone to that same place of Amajuba two hundred years ago, and apparently been unlucky enough to have died there.

He put on some music from his Screen. He wanted to study his books, but found he was too tired to do so. They could wait until later. He fell asleep. The music came to its final chord and there was silence in the room. Julian slept on dreaming of Shanaya. For much of the day he slept. The red light of the sun dipped across the turret window, outlining the mountain peaks with fire.

34

'So General Colley with his party of 350 men, made up from three separate regiments of his force, came to the top of the mountain of Amajuba. It was still dark, and the men were dispersed in ones and twos around the perimeter of the summit plateau, a reserve being left in a hollow at the centre.'

Early the next morning Julian read from one of his books and made a note in pencil on a pad he had found in a drawer by his bed. Each page of the pad was stamped with a crest, showing a lion's head above a crossed spear and rifle, and the words underneath – 'SupaPodia – High Director: Inkwelo Palace'.

'The Boers began firing at first light and the British troops found themselves increasingly pinned down by very accurate shooting, the rough sangars of loose rocks they had tried to build providing little cover.'

Julian cross-referenced this account with another. He was amazed by the incompetence shown by the General, who had neglected to give his troops the order to dig in, although picks and shovels had been carried for that purpose. Some of his officers had become anxious.

'Lieutenant Hamilton, at considerable personal risk, ran back to report to Colley on no less than three separate occasions that the Boers were gaining a foothold on the mountain, moving across the terraces below the summit rim unseen from above. On the third occasion he was told he could not disturb the General because he was asleep.'

This is incredible, thought Julian, engrossed in the story of this distant battle, his four accounts open before him, weighed down by various objects – a

Chinese black-lacquered vase complete with orchid, an alabaster toothbrush holder, an ivory shoe horn, and a copy of SupaPodia International's 'Complete Directory of Office Holders' – plunging between each of them to see if these extraordinary details were confirmed by all.

> *'A sudden great crash of firing indicated that the Boer skirmishing line had reached the mountain crest. A cry for reinforcements was raised. Men were hustled forward by their officers, some being most reluctant to move. Fire was now sweeping the central hollow from both flanks. General Colley was on his feet, his revolver in his hand. "Stand firm, men," he was heard to call out.'*

Peering from the tower window of his room, and craning his head to the left, Julian could just make out the flat summit of Amajuba. From this angle, it looked like a volcano with its top sliced off flat. So everything he was now reading about had happened up there close to the clouds two hundred years ago. There, men's lives had been wasted for no practical purpose whatsoever. It had been a battle not worth the fighting, so badly directed by the General – this absurd Sir George Pomeroy-Colley K.C.S.I – he might just as well have ordered his men to shoot themselves. The Boers, avenging ancient wrongs – a force of mere amateur soldiers – had swept aside the British army like a tide scouring the shore. How on earth could Joshua – High Director of SupaPodia – find anything redeeming about Colley? What was he – Julian – expected to say to him when questioned about his study of the battle? Was this some sort of test? Was it best to give him the truth of what he thought or some pretence or other of what he might be expecting to hear?

Today would surely be the day he must make that decision, the day perhaps – he thought, with the familiar quivering of his insides – of many other decisions too, when the whole edifice of doubletalk and subterfuge that he felt built up about him might well come tumbling down – a day of destiny indeed.

> *'With a cry of horror, the whole line broke and men ran back, seeking the way by which they had come up the mountain, leaping over the crest and tumbling down from rock to rock to save themselves from the heavy fire still aimed at them. Only the General now faced the enemy. Almost immediately, he was shot in the head and fell back dead.'*

At least Colley had not been a coward, thought Julian. He had died a soldier's death, which was perhaps just as well, for what would have happened to him if he had lived on? He would likely have met with such scorn that his life would have become impossible. Probably he would have had to resign and take up some other occupation. And what could that have been? He would have been forced out entirely from the world he had known – the world of patronage and elitism – and there would have been no place for him either with ordinary people, nor any 19th century SupaPod in which to hide himself away. His mind might well have become unhinged. Perhaps he was already half way to madness before the battle. The accounts said he scarcely ever slept.

Julian was depressed by the whole story, not knowing why he had been required to read it. He swept the books aside and got washed and dressed. Then he descended for a late breakfast, finding he was alone in the small guest dining room; there was no Tina and, thankfully, no Pamela or Rupert either. In the corridor he passed Shanaya, but she looked away from him.

He felt suddenly very alone and frightened.

* * *

"Where have you been?" cried Tina, when Julian opened his door to her knock. "You weren't at breakfast. No one seems to have seen you for a while. Are you alright?"

"Yes, of course. I was busy earlier on." Julian found he did not want to tell Tina about his research for the High Director, nor the fears he had felt afterwards.

"Are you ready for the party? We'll be leaving in an hour."

"Of course."

He was surprised he hadn't been told the departure time earlier. He was also surprised that he didn't really seem to care. He realised it was likely he was going through a bad bout of depression. Quite honestly, he was not bothered if he went to this party or not. What was going to happen could happen without him. Life was closing down about him to a mere sliver of light. He wanted extinction to find him in his bed, not on a distant mountain top where so many bad, unpredictable things had happened that long time ago.

"You're not going like that, are you?" Tina said, scrutinising him.

Julian looked down at himself. This morning he had pulled on an old pair of baggy trousers and a crumpled shirt that was in need of washing. His feet were in flip-flops.

"Put on some smarter clothes. You've got something, surely."

She went over to his wardrobe, and pulled out a pair of fawn-coloured slacks and a white shirt with epaulets that he hadn't worn yet, although ordered and delivered to him several days back.

Tina, he noticed, looked as fresh as a daisy, with her hair swept back into a pony tail. She wore a loose pink dress that covered her like a tent, hiding her figure.

"These will do nicely", she said. "Wear them to travel to the top of the mountain, then it'll be your Cape suit you should put on for the party itself. I've arranged for it to be ready for you, along with everything else you'll need – shirt, socks, shoes, necktie, even cufflinks

"Ready where?"

"On the top of the mountain, of course. We'll be able to change before the 'do'. My father has every facility up there, including rest-rooms."

"We're going by helidrone, aren't we?" The mists of his depression were dispersing. Things were coming back into focus. As Tina had said, this should be quite an occasion. Yet, why was he still so fearful?

"Yes. We'll be squeezed in pretty tight and it'll be hot and sweaty, hence the need to change later." She giggled. "A girl doesn't like her best dress spoiled."

Looking at Tina's smiling face, a bloom of pink on her fresh cheeks, Julian thought she has certainly changed from her former serenity as a nun. Was she then turning into a new Tina – perhaps the real Tina – much happier now she had made a loving connection with her long-lost father? But, whatever the changes in her, he was certain she retained all her beliefs and principles, the beliefs which she had put so assuredly before him to help him towards his own conversion, however much that trembled at times. Like any other young woman, she was probably just excited by this glamorous new lifestyle she was so suddenly part of, by its opulence, its luxury and splendour, determined to enjoy it to the most before returning to the much simpler, modest life that her deepest convictions demanded. Neither, most likely, did she wish to spoil the pleasure her father clearly sought to bring to her, a father of whose eventual redemption she was still hopeful.

They assembled on the front lawns. They were quite a crowd – members of the Eliti, servants, music-players with their instruments, caterers, florists…. There was no sign yet of the High Director, however. Julian expected he would only arrive when all was set up and his guests in place. Several helidrones stood on the grass awaiting their loads, some of people, some of supplies. More helidrones arrived even as they were waiting, swooping in, their blades whirling, one the largest helidrone Julian had ever seen, with its cargo doors wide open. This last one had a pilot, but most were without even a single crew member. Where were they controlled from? Julian wondered once again. From a bunker at the palace, or from some control room which could be anywhere? So many aspects of SupaPodia were disturbing, as he knew so little about them.

Could such a powerful organisation, controlled so secretly, ever be brought down? He had met its High Director, amiable enough, yet probably sharp and ruthless too under that eccentric exterior: it seemed hard to imagine him holding all those secrets in his head. Not for the first time, he found himself wondering who really master-minded SupaPodia. He felt sure Pamela, Lady Lascelles knew.

Julian suddenly caught sight of Pamela standing at the edge of the crowd with Rupert beside her. Rupert was red-faced and seemed unsteady on his feet: he must have been at the sauce already, thought Julian. Tina left his side to go and talk with Pamela, but he did not feel inclined to accompany her. He stepped back and brushed against someone behind him, turning to apologise and finding it was Shanaya, gorgeously dressed in jade coloured silk, rather than the habitual yellow she wore as a palace servant.

Whatever had been troubling Shanaya earlier when she had not met his gaze in the corridor seemed to have been lifted, for she returned his greeting now with a warm smile. Is it true, thought Julian, that I have made love to this most beautiful woman?

She placed a hand on his wrist, causing him an explosion of sensation as if fire was filling his finger tips. Her fingers were long, the nails painted the same jade green as her sari; golden bracelets jangled about her wrists. He longed to hold her and kiss her.

"Today we go to the mountain. Are you looking forward to it?" Her voice held a delightful cadence.

"Very much. Can I see you afterwards?"

"For why?" she smiled at him teasingly, then whispered close to his ear. "Of course, I would wish that too."

Excitement surged in him. Had a woman ever so erotically charged him? This land, this place, was surely paradise. Then he saw Pamela's head turn from Tina to look at him, and he realised he was a fool. Even in paradise, the devil keeps his serpents about him, and he knew he must be on his guard. The premonition that had disturbed his morning – that something terrible was about to happen – had returned to him.

The helidrones carrying the servants and their equipment began to take off. Then Julian was ushered towards a helidrone, which was just a small bubble of glass with four rotors above. Here he was seated and strapped in with Tina on one side and Shanaya on the other – a bubble of love, he thought, knowing he was growing increasingly hysterical, but unable to steady himself. They took off and climbed above the palace buildings. Was that the courtyard with the blue pool down there? Was a naked Lucinda at this very moment embracing its waters? Hardly likely, as she too must be on her way to the mountain top.

As they soared over the green shoulder of Inkwelo, he felt it was he who was flying, supporting the two women on his wings. He could soar like Icarus, and he could fall too. A sudden terrible vertigo seized him, and he grabbed at the legs of the women as if to support his body which would otherwise tumble away.

"Are you alright?" They spoke almost in unison.

There was a sheen of sweat on Julian's forehead. "Yes, of course. I'm sorry. I felt I was falling." He made himself sit up straight, his gaze fixed glassily ahead.

Tina placed her hand on his arm. "Feeling better?"

"Yes, thank you."

He wondered what Shanaya thought. He must get a grip on himself.

They had ascended now to the upper rim of Amajuba and were passing over the domed roof of the High Director's columned rotunda. Julian saw high brown pinnacles of rock rising out of the parched yellow grass, then a greener area below a ridge of rock, and here they descended vertically in slow spirals until the helidrone's landing feet touched the ground, and they were down. The whirr of the rotors died away. Other helidrones were close to them; a large one with a pilot at the controls was at this moment taking off, its bulbous belly dipping as it set a course towards the south, passing low above the flat summit plateau of the Inkwelo.

"Are you sure you're alright?" asked Tina anxiously as they crossed the grass, the sun beating hotly upon them.

"Yes, thank you." He replied as calmly as he could. He did not want to indicate to Tina the confusion of thoughts that jumbled his mind, nor the fear which pervaded him. "Just a touch of vertigo. Not surprising really." He waved a hand towards the glass-sided helidrone that had brought them. It had taken off again and was buzzing over their heads. With the sun's rays gleaming upon it, it seemed almost without form.

Tina was now being led away by Shanaya, while Julian was intercepted by a male servant with a black bushy beard, dressed in a short green tunic. "Dr. Foster? Your clothes, sir. Please follow me."

From the exterior white columns of the circular rotunda built on the crest of the mountain, a path formed of flagstones led to a small flat-roofed building, which proved to be a rest-room for visitors. Its walls were faced with the brown stone of the mountain and the roof piled with boulders, so as to blend the building more with its surroundings. Beyond, the level mountain top stretched away to the rocky ridge which Julian had seen from the air. Across this tract of long, waving grass, he could see a blur of white – of what exactly he could not make out.

Ahead of him on the path, he saw Tina following Shanaya into a door at the right end of the rest room building: he followed the black-bearded servant into a similar door at the opposite end, grateful to find straightaway a urinal into which he was able to empty his nerve-stretched bladder. The servant then took him to a small dressing cubicle, where his formal party clothes, beneath plastic covers, awaited him.

"When you are ready, sir, you will find me outside. I will then take you to join the company."

It all sounded forbiddingly formal. Julian's heart sunk further. He did not feel right about this day. At the very least, he suspected it would prove something of an ordeal. At the worst…. He did not know in what form 'worst' might come.

There was a surprise for him: the clothes turned out not to be the dark suit he had had made in the Cape, but a white linen jacket to be worn over a pink, collarless shirt, and narrow dark trousers, with chunky black shoes that were more like low boots. Julian surveyed himself in a long glass. He did not look too bad, he thought, these new clothes much more suitable for an event outdoors in this hot, sunny weather than that dark suit. Someone had clearly made a decision on his behalf, which he wasn't going to argue about now since everything fitted him so perfectly. They must have got his measurements from that Cape tailor, or possibly even – quite a frightening thought, this – from SupaPodia's staff database. He felt quite fit, his face was lean and tanned, and he had retained a stubble of greying beard about his jaw. His legs still pained him a little, the result of the battle injuries he had sustained, and he experienced the occasional awkward jolt in his spine from the aborted second implant, but these were afflictions he could live with; their origins now seemed a long way from him.

He emerged from the cubicle. The servant was waiting, squatting on his heels on the red-tiled floor. Julian could see him looking him over, judging if he was fit to go into the presence of the High Director. He evidently passed the inspection, for the next moment he was out in the open and in the heavy heat again, following the servant towards the white columns of the rotunda. As he passed between them and through the entrance into the shaded interior, he saw he was treading on a floor of inlaid coloured marble. A string orchestra was playing. Some ladies in long dresses were sipping from glasses. Amongst them, he saw Pamela. She was in a golden-coloured gown, her back bare, her breasts scarcely covered, a spray of diamonds flashing at her throat, kept in place by a black band about her neck. She was looking away from him, talking to another woman – Shanaya, he realised, with a burst of suspicion. Shanaya's head was turned away as well. Now why should Pamela wish to speak with Shanaya? He had thought she was only a servant – a secretary – but might she not have a much greater role in Pamela's scheming? He realised how in his weakness he had been playing with fire.

Julian felt sweat trickling down the small of his back. Tina had not appeared yet. He hoped she was alright. Had Shanaya left her at the changing room? Surely she would need an escort to the colonnaded rotunda. Clasping a long glass taken from a servant, which turned out to be of most welcome chilled lager, he went to the front steps of the rotunda, and, peering between the columns, spied Tina at that very moment coming towards him over the shimmering, sun-seared flagstones. She was on the arm of a man, a man wearing a long embroidered tunic – yes, of course, it was her father, Joshua: he could make out his round bearded face now, and with another man beside them, who reeled away from them from time to time and then lurched back; that must be Rupert, Pamela's husband, clearly already with three sheets spread to the wind.

The violin music was rising to a pitch that irritated, rather than soothed, Julian. He seized another glass from a passing servant, and found this was not lager but some sweet concoction that slid smoothly down his throat and then burst into fire. He was still coughing when the High Director, with Tina and Rupert beside him, came up the steps into the rotunda. He saw that the ladies and their servants were all curtsying, the men bowing, and he made a hurried attempt to do so too, but the coughing fit went on. Tina, lovely with her hair pinned up, and now in a figure-hugging gown of soft blue silk, glided up beside him, and patted him on the back. "Why, whatever's wrong, Julian? Did it go down the wrong way?"

352

"Something like that," he said, straightening up, seeing Rupert's face on him too, creased into a sneer.

"Really, old boy, you should hold your liquor better", slurred Rupert, before staggering on behind the High Director, acknowledging with a wave of his podgy white hand the curtsies and bows, as if they were meant for him too.

Joshua seated himself on a high marble seat set against the far curving wall of the rotunda facing the entrance, motioning to Lucinda, whom Julian had not noticed up to now, to leave her female entourage and sit beside him. To Julian's heated mind, the two seated side by side were like the Emperor Justinian with his empress prostitute, Theodora. Lucinda was certainly playing her part in this historical fantasy. Her silver gown was split high to both thighs and cut so low at the front her breasts were completely exposed, although veiled by a panel of gauze.

Higher up on the wall behind the High Director's throne – for that was the best way to interpret it –was a niche in which stood the bust of a man. A wreath of dark green laurel, with a centre of bright red protea flowers, had been placed over the stone shoulders. As Julian stared upwards at it, he realised with a start that Joshua's eyes were focussed on him and that he was being summoned forward.

He gave the High Director an awkward half-bow, not certain if this was required, which he then repeated to the cold-eyed Lucinda next to him, whom he was sure expected it.

"Ah, teacher Julian," drawled Joshua, "Have you read my books? Are you ready to discuss this great man with me?" He had flung his hand upwards, pointing at the niche above his head.

Julian realised now whom the bust depicted: Sir George Pomeroy-Colley, the disastrous commander of British troops who had died here two centuries before.

"Of course, sir," he said. He did not feel it would be proper to use the High Director's first name in this formal assemblage.

Joshua was rising to his feet, servants scuttling forward to assist him. He brushed them away with a sweep of his hand.

"Christine," he said to his daughter. "Please sit in my place and talk to Lucinda. I have some things to show your teacher man, Dr. Foster."

He turned to the company, amongst whom were further smartly-clad new arrivals, probably, Julian thought, other guests from the palace, some perhaps even his future colleagues. He had no chance to meet them, however, because Joshua had taken him by the arm, calling out to those close enough to hear him, "Dr. Foster and I must address some matters about which I consulted him earlier, but we will be returning in order to dine: we shall not be leaving you for long. In the meantime, please enjoy yourselves."

He signalled to the conductor and the musicians struck up again – a cheerful polka. "Please dance, good people," Joshua called over his shoulder.

As Julian left the rotunda with Joshua, a crowd of servants who still hovered about them were soon dispersed by a wave of the High Director's hand, like the swatting of flies. Julian gazed back and saw Tina looking lost and lonely high on the marble seat beside Lucinda's clearly bored and yawning figure, and the fury on Pamela's face. If anyone should have been placed on that throne, her face said to Julian, it is me – but watch out for yourselves, all you grovellers and sycophants, I am coming, and very soon too, sooner than you will ever realise.

They descended the marble steps of the rotunda's plinth, and took a stone-paved path that led out onto the open summit of Amajuba mountain. Perhaps it was a flicker in the light striking Julian's eyes, or perhaps it was the premonition that had stalked him all day, but something made him look down the steep craggy slope to his right where a small detached hill stuck up like a cone. Beneath this hill, moving from rock to rock amidst a scree of fallen boulders, moving precisely and with purpose until disappearing out of sight to Julian's left, he knew there had been a shape, a black shape – for one moment he had seen it clearly, but then just as a dark smudge, until with its vanishing he was not quite sure he had seen it at all. Yet, if what he had glimpsed was real, and not contrived by his brain out of some trick of light, he knew what that shape – that figure – was. It was the Beast – the Beast he had last seen, or thought he had seen, on the airship coming into the Cape. Now what would he be doing here skulking amongst the rocks below? All at once, Julian's great sense of foreboding returned.

He was lagging behind Joshua, who turned back to him. "Why don't you keep up with me?" he demanded.

"I'm sorry, sir. I'm just a little weighed down by the heat."

"You'll soon get used to it, like me."

"Of course."

But he knew that was unlikely, for everything seemed to be gathering pace to an inevitability that must spell out 'the end'. He did not know in what way that end would come. Perhaps it was just his fear speaking out to him. Perhaps the Beast was a contrivance of his mind and would not reappear. But, if he did, Julian knew he must spell out death.

Surely death would not come here in this bright sunlight, with the music playing and the ladies in their flowing coloured dresses, holding wine cups to their breasts. His imagination was too much aflame, too tortured, too gross. In any event, he had to play out this game with the High Director – with SupaPodia itself – to the very end. There was no other option left to him.

Julian followed Joshua over the rock-strewn ground. A path had been cut here at some time, making the way clear. Julian's hands and legs brushed against grass heads on either side. The sun was a yellow furnace in a clear blue sky, the heat like bars of lead pressing down upon his shoulders.

Joshua turned back to Julian occasionally, as if to make sure he was still there. He looked cool and unruffled in his tunic, his bare legs and sandalled feet swishing rhythmically through the grass, while Julian plodded and stumbled behind him. He was boiling in his linen jacket, the sweat soaking the pink shirt, annoyed by this sudden effort demanded of him – and for what purpose? He had been invited to a party, where he had expected to lounge and sip cool liquids, and watch beautiful women vying with each other like coloured birds. So why this? Why was the High Director luring him away? Was it to have him shot? And was that indeed the Beast he had seen climbing the hill, or had it been his fearful imagination, or perhaps a black floater drifting before his eyes? Yet his gaze surely was unblemished now. Watching Joshua's back moving on in the sunlight, his sight was so clear he could make out the detail of the embroidery covering his tunic in horizontal bands, the stitching of squares and chevrons picked out in red and grey and black.

The white blur that Julian had seen earlier from beside the rest-room building was coming closer and taking shape. He could see now it was a stone, a shaped stone, the headstone of a grave. They reached it at last. It lay just below a rocky ridge about six feet high, its crest brushed with grass, beyond which Julian could see nothing but the burning sky. He read, 'Sir George Pomeroy-Colley, slain here by the forces of darkness, 27th February 1881. A Hero of the People. His Memory is Eternal. Erected by SupaPodia International on the bicentennial of his death, 2081'.

Joshua stood before the grave, his head bowed, and Julian thought he should do likewise. A light wind ruffled the grass. A flying insect landed briefly on the stone, then flew away. The grave was outlined with myrtle cut low to the ground, its mound raised with reddish soil sprinkled with quartz that shone like diamonds.

Joshua raised his head. "This is the very spot where he was killed," he said solemnly. "He was shot down by the Racists when left alone by cowards who deserted him."

Julian's head buzzed a little at that. It was not the story he had read. But he did not say anything.

Joshua continued, "He was not buried here originally, but with others below who were slain in that war. I had his body exhumed and brought up here so that he might lie on his place of sacrifice."

Julian did not know what to say. "Quite right," he managed at last, adding, "He was a brave man."

"He was that," said Joshua, suddenly seizing Julian by the arm. "Now sit here..." – he indicated a low stone bench a little distance from the grave – "...and tell me what you have learnt, as I asked you. You are a historian. This will be a test for you, so I can judge your capabilities for my school of history. I am sure you will be able to sum up the heroism of our most distinguished forebear."

Julian could not speak for a long time. He sat as if in thought, while Joshua waited beside him speculatively, fingering the hair on his chin. Julian was indeed thinking hard, but it was more along the lines of how do I get out of this situation? I do not wish to offend the High Director and I do not wish to endanger my new job, but what can I say about this General Colley other than that he was a bad commander who led his troops to disaster? He was undoubtedly brave, and many of his troops did turn and run, but that hardly exonerates him.

Julian longed to be out of the sun. He felt the skin of his face pricking, knowing he was being burnt. His armpits were wet with sweat; the stains would probably be spreading onto his jacket. God! this was mad. How had he come from madness into hope to find yet more madness, the whole world madder than before and consumed with lies?

At last he said carefully, "He was unlucky, I think. A difficult situation at a time when the military systems were changing. Mass rifle fire confronting British troops who still thought of fighting in line on direct orders, when their enemy – the Boers – were natural guerrilla fighters, trained in hunting from birth, using fire and movement, and superb shots...."

"What!" Joshua exploded, sending a shudder through Julian. "You repeat those old lies to me! You *do* disappoint me. Here, come with me!"

He pulled a frightened Julian from the bench and dragged him up onto the ridge above the grave, so that Julian could see the grassy slopes falling away to a line of rock that must mark the very edge of Amajuba. Beyond, the grey green land stretched out far below, with the bright snake of a river coiling upon it.

"Here!" Joshua shouted, punching Julian in the upper arm, then flinging out his own arms, so that Julian had a momentary crazed image of him as Moses on his mountain receiving the tablets from God. "Here, the Racists advanced and Colley's men died, before the rest ran back. Only Sir George stood up and received their bullets like a martyr, a sacrifice to a world of humanity over one of evil. Of everything I have done during my term as High Director, I am most proud of instilling the values of that martyrdom into SupaPodia – freedom from racism and freedom from the bigotry of superstition."

"Of course, I see that now," said Julian meekly, pretending contrition, fearing a mind that was unhinged. Despite his own confusions, even he could see those hinges bursting wide. "I'm sorry I got it wrong before. Please forgive me." He attempted a joke. "That's the trouble with book learning. You have to come out and see where things happened on the ground to understand."

"Indeed," said Joshua heavily. He took Julian by the arm again. "You are probably a good man," he said conciliatorily, "but you have much to learn. Whether you will suit me now, I don't know. We will have to see."

"Oh my God," Julian was thinking. And this perhaps was a genuine prayer. What have I gone and done now? Why couldn't I have understood this Wonderland better and just gone along with it. For that's what I've become – Julian in Wonderland and this mad man is the Red Queen.

Again a blur out of the corner of his eye, and a black dot of movement far below where a ledge in the hillside jutted out, a figure moving from rock to rock and bush to bush, then climbing higher. The Beast again? It had disappeared once more from sight.

"There's someone down there," he called out to Joshua, but the High Director had turned away, laughing.

"Now I *know* you're useless. Imagining things too, not only out of history but in the present as well. There can't be anything living anywhere around this mountain, as it's all 100% security controlled, ringed with steel and wire and set with mines. No one could get through, even if they wanted to – not even one of those terrorists against SupaPodia whom you supported. Oh, yes, I know your past! If it wasn't for my Christine, you wouldn't be here now, that I can tell you!"

Julian's world was suddenly rushing away, sucked from him as if into a black hole, so that he felt he must prop himself on these firm rocks holding onto the sky for support, or he would slip inexorably below the ground. He still had consciousness left to argue, though, trying to follow a path of reason through another's paranoia.

"If you think that about me, how are you able to come out here alone with me when I might attack you?"

Joshua laughed again. "You give yourself an air of importance that, I assure you, you don't possess. If I walk with snakes, I will see that their fangs are drawn first. You would do me no harm, for you seek my favour first and foremost. You will not rebel again, because you know now SupaPodia *is* the world and there is no other. I can make you and I can break you, and there's nothing you, or anyone else, can do to alter that fact."

There it was again, the blur of black: he saw it move forward, then drop down parallel with them across the grass. They were almost back to the rotunda now, their feet meeting the hardness of the paving stones, hearing the music sounding between the columns, the conversation clinking like bird song high on the air.

One last look back, and, yes, the Beast was there, unmistakably, standing up straight and challenging, encased in black, his visored helmet pulled low, a stub of a weapon pointing forward between his hands.

"Look!" he called out to Joshua, and he, suddenly startled, swung on his heel and stared.

"Look at what? There's nothing there!"

And there was not now. Only the long sunlight shining across the grassy plateau and the white of the grave like a distant eye.

"You're mad," said Joshua, clearly cross, then suspicious. "Unless you're trying to set me up with something? Well it won't work. After today, I want you *out*. I don't care where you go, only you will leave my daughter alone. Best, I think, that you had been killed when we had the chance to do that, just as Commissioner Lascelles has said."

So he had been right. Pamela had been out to get rid of him. What else had she been up to? To get rid of the High Director too? Suddenly her course of evil leaped out at him clearly.

Tina saw the two of them come back up the steps into the rotunda where the servants were circling with plates of food and the orchestra was striking up a lively new dance tune. She realised from their faces that something was very wrong. Julian was looking round wildly for Pamela. Ah, there she was, leaning back nonchalantly against a wall talking with Shanaya: they both had glasses of wine in their hands. The High Director went directly to his throne, now vacated by Tina who stood to one side. He sat down, looking angry, and called for a drink. Rupert, carrying a bottle, reeled over towards him.

The world like this stood still, frozen, only the music played and the wind breathed and the sunlight sent out its dark shadows from the columns of the rotunda. Along the line of one shadow came the Beast, out of the glaring vortex of the sun as killers are taught to attack.

The scene re-started, moving into motion. Julian saw Pamela's hand rise and point: the signal. She fell to the floor, taking Shanaya with her. Out of the shadow, stepped the Beast, all black, weapon raised. His first shots hit the High Director, who fell back slumped in his stone chair. Rupert, hit also, collapsed beside him. A screaming Tina flung herself across her father and took a bullet in her body, as did Julian too, dashing forward, trying to protect her.

It all happened so quickly, the musicians were still playing.

* * *

Pamela commanded the helidrones. She had on a headphone set and was giving orders. Shanaya was her aide. Their lovely dresses were splashed with blood. Rupert had been shot in the neck and his blood had sprayed out like a fountain. The Beast had gone. No one saw the assassin again. He had disappeared into the mountains.

A helidrone took Joshua's body back to his palace, where it lay in state in his great baronial hall. Lucinda tended to the washing and dressing of the body. She must have really loved him because she knelt beside him all night and begged to be killed, so as to join him in death. But no Beast came to oblige her, and in the end she was taken away, to where exactly is not known.

Commissioner Pamela Lady Lascelles was installed unopposed as the new High Director, her appointment, temporary at first, confirmed at an Extraordinary SupaPodia Executive Committee meeting held a month later in Addis Ababa. A SupaPodia investigation into the killings found that an unknown terrorist was responsible, from some dissident group as yet unidentified, but likely to be from Europe or possibly South America. SupaPodia's Intelligence and Security Services were still investigating. A massive increase in security around the whole SupaPodia empire and its affiliated Eliti estates was authorised, costing a multiple amount, which could only be raised by taxing the OuterWorld further. Any militant resistance to these measures was crushed by uncompromising new powers adopted by the new High Director as soon as she was fully installed, and sanctioned by her Inner Command.

Christine Munro and Dr. Julian Foster, both badly injured, said to have been guests of the murdered High Director (his relationship to Ms Munro was not made publicly known) were flown, on Lady Lascelles's immediate orders, by helidrone to a hospital in the Cape, where they received emergency surgery. The lives of both were saved. On the accession of Commissioner Lascelles to the High Directorship, she ordered them to be conveyed by medical airship to her own hospital in Hayling, SouthBritain for longer term recuperation.

Rupert Lord Lascelles, whose death trying to save the life of Joshua Pomeroy-Collyer was commended by the Executive Committee (he was posthumously awarded the most prestigious Star of Sacrifice) was buried in the Eliti Burial Ground at the Cape, close to Joshua's own final resting place. Both graves were much visited by denizens of the city and tended by working parties of Podders from the Robben Island SupaPods, being decorated daily with fresh flowers grown in the SupaPods' own sea-platform gardens.

35

Julian found Tina praying on the beach, fallen to her knees on the shingle, her arms held out before her. She was dressed in a blue-checked hospital shift with a blanket over her shoulders, as the spring sunlight was weak and the air chilled. Her face had thinned and her hair grown long and straggly during the many months of pain. Her wound had been a glancing one in her right side, breaking ribs, penetrating muscles, but most fortunately not destroying any internal organ. Julian had been similarly fortunate. His wound had been to his right leg, the one badly damaged previously. An artery had been severed, but his life saved by one of the musicians, a violin player, who had pinched the pulsing blood vessel closed until the ambulance helidrone had appeared with a medico who had then taken over.

Pamela had organised their transport back to Hayling and their care at the Convalescent Home on her own estates. It was the realisation of her betrayal that nearly destroyed Tina in the immediate aftermath of the attack, rather than her wound. Julian, weak from loss of blood, had fallen into unconsciousness, so his own sense of the combined treacheries of Pamela and Shanaya did not affect him until later. His life was saved by transfusions at the Cape hospital, the blood coming from supplies donated by Podders. Remembering what he had witnessed at the Ramsgate SupaPod, Julian realised that those donations were likely to have been made without the Podders' direct permission or even knowledge.

The evils of SupaPodia were now consuming Julian again; they had never really gone away. How could they after what he had witnessed? When he learnt of Pamela's elevation to High Director, just as he had predicted, he put his head down and he wept. He wouldn't speak to anyone for days. His foolish hopes for SupaPodia's redemption seemed now just so much hot air blown away by fierce winds.

The staff of the Home had changed. No longer was the comforting Sister Gillian there or the lovely Nurse Rose The changes seemed to have happened recently, probably, Julian thought, on Pamela's direct orders. She had wanted Julian and Tina to recover – or presumably so – for otherwise she could surely have contrived their deaths in one of many ways. Perhaps it was her perverted sense of power over them, like a cat playing with a mouse, which decided her that they should live on in the SupaPodia system, once again holding them tight. This time there would be no circumstances for escape. Pamela's own new position probably demanded that she make an exhibition of them. Capital punishment through the judicial system was firmly abolished in SupaPodia. Yet, as Julian well knew, people 'disappeared' in a large number of other unpleasant ways.

The new staff at the Convalescent Home – it did not deserve such a title now – were poorly trained and had little medical knowledge. Julian learnt they came from the nearby SupaPodia Work Camp, or Correction Camp as it had previously been known, to which he recalled Jill and Carol (Boadicea) had been consigned after their own betrayal There was no sign of either of these two at the Home, however, although he had looked out for them. Perhaps they had long since been moved on to a worse fate.

All Julian's earlier optimism had gone, shut off by the latest horrors he had witnessed. The Beast! He had seen the Beast and had known he was coming. He should have done much more to warn Tina – and others – of this evil presence amongst them. And Shanaya, with whom he had lain and whom he had briefly, and so foolishly, loved, he should have realised that no young woman would welcome the sexual attentions of an elderly Lothario such as he unless she held some other purpose, probably under another's direction. His lusts had deluded him, and he was a victim of his own stupidity – so he could only blame himself.

Tina, however, had believed in her Aunt Pamela entirely, not only entrusting herself to her but her faith also. Pamela's perfidy surely ranked in its terribleness with that of Judas. Every Christian eats and drinks of the body of Christ, so Tina had been most grievously affected by the betrayal of one who had shared the food of life with her, together with her innermost thoughts.

At the Home, they did at least have the space and time to recover, however inadequate the conditions there. There was still a community present, as before, mainly of the elderly, who seemed happy enough to see out their days in the place; they were probably the lucky ones. Tina was in one wing of the Home, Julian in another; not in private rooms now but communal wards. As he grew stronger (the long airship journey had threatened his small fund of remaining resistance), he began to walk outside, finding that the Home was now ringed off with a high steel fence, so there was no access any longer to the areas of the women's barracks or to Pamela's grand house. He wondered who lived there now. Of course, Pamela had gained the power to live wherever she wished. Perhaps she had moved into the Inkwelo palace. What were her plans for him? And, more importantly, for Tina – who had only ever sought to do good?

It was possible to reach the beach in front of the main building of the Home, although the perimeter fences continued onto the shingle on both sides, cutting off the chance of escape along the beach. Perhaps you might get away by swimming, Julian thought, but you would need to be strong and fit for that. He was not aware of Pamela's Guard patrolling the wire, which on stormy days hummed and moaned in the wind, with trailing seaweed, grass stalks and last year's dead leaves caught up on its barbs.

He had seen Tina praying here, had seen the anguish with which she argued with her God. It was no good trying to talk with her then; she had withdrawn into herself in a way he had not known before. She was grieving for her father, but she seemed to be fighting for her faith as well.

He had always been able to rely on Tina before, her help for him springing out of her Christian teaching but also, he was sure, out of her own very personal love for him – not a sexual love but one far purer than that, of companionship and dangers faced and overcome, and shared values too, and an overriding belief in the world's worth and of the life dwelling upon it, that it should be treated with respect and dignity, and with love – that true love, which as a poet wrote long ago, may be all that will survive of us.

He came up to her on the beach that day, her sharp knees pressed painfully into the hard shingle, and he was relieved to see her turn her head to him and smile – the first such smile she had given him since they had returned here – and he prayed that the worst of her inner torment was now over.

He did pray. His own beliefs had come and gone, at one time angry with a God that allowed such misery to exist, such evil to be done, such subterfuge to prevail in the name of power and greed, for killing to be accomplished as if it were a mere item to be ticked off on a list of jobs to do. And he prayed with Tina now. He sank to his knees beside her and pressed his hands together before his lips.

"Dear Lord," he prayed. "Thank you for the help you have given my friend, Tina, and thank you for sparing her life and mine too. And, please help us further to do your work, so that when we leave this place, we shall be without fear. For you are our comfort and our belief."

He had not known he could pray like this. He was astonished by his own words, and suddenly absurdly embarrassed, looking across at Tina to see if she would be laughing at him; but, no, wonderfully what he saw was joy on her face and her eyes moist, as if filled with spray from the sea.

The breakers thundered, the wind swept the straggling grasses where they knelt, the seabirds wheeled and cried in the sky. The sunlight seemed diffused, as if coming to them through mist – but, no, the sky was clear with small white clouds scudding high.

Tina said, "I told you – do you remember? – that God will let you know when you are ready. It will be at a time when you call upon Him. I think that time has come."

Her eyes that had been so tired were bright again now, her sunken cheeks plumped out once more, so that she looked like the old Tina whom he had known and loved, and whose words he had heard, entering his soul, despite his many efforts to deny them. What errors he had made, what foolish desires, what gross lusts; yet evils had been conquered too by the many good deeds that had been done for him – he thought of Peter, of Sandra, who had given her life for him, and Tina herself – and there were others too, now half-hidden in darkness, but they would come to the light as well. His mind was full of sound and thought, it was hard to sort it out, but he knew he was with Tina and that this was the only place he wished to be in the whole world.

"I have sinned often," he said. "I have lusted and I have killed. Am I worth saving?"

"Every soul has value to God, for your soul has come from God and will be returned to Him. If you truly repent, your sins will be washed away in God's love."

"I do repent."

"Then, come with me now," said Tina, and she took his hand.

They crossed the narrow strip of sloping shingle and came to the water's edge where the sea waves were breaking, sending out whispering rivulets of white foam. Here they halted.

"Kneel," she said, and he bent his legs so that he knelt in the white-laced water facing the open sea, its grey-green moving surface shining with a light that seemed to encompass him – above him and around him, and beneath him too, where the waves were surging as high as his hips.

She stood beside him, the water bursting about her legs, so that for one moment he was concerned for her, but she stood as steady as a rock. She took his right hand into her own palm.

"With the authority given to me, Lord, I receive this man for you into your Church." She turned her face to Julian.

"Do you accept baptism into God's most holy house, to live there in the company of all the saints?"

"I do."

"Then I baptise you in the Name of the Father, and of the Son, and of the Holy Ghost. Amen."

"Amen," he repeated.

She dipped her finger in the sea water swirling at the hem of her smock and with it made the mark of the cross upon his forehead.

They turned and scrambled back to the dry shingle. She kissed him on the cheek. "And so it is done," she said.

"I feel new power in me," Julian said; and he did too. The horizon seemed further and clearer, his arms hung looser, his legs felt stronger, his mind seemed to leap forward like a bird's beak: all that he saw was blissful and in conformity and controlled by God. Why had it taken him so long to realise this?

"Let's say the Lord's prayer," said Tina, and they stood by the pine trees at the edge of the beach and recited together, "Our Father, which art in heaven, Hallowed be thy Name..." He stumbled at one or two points but Tina set him right.

"You're going to have to practice that now," she said when they had finished. "It's all you need to know God. The rest will come to you out of your own spirit. Now we must get inside before we catch cold."

A wind had risen, tugging at the tree tops and sweeping the grass.

"I expect I will be shouted at by our keepers," she called over her shoulder, as they ran for the front door of the Home "But what does that matter?"

"Nothing matters now," Julian yelled back.

Yet, despite his new blessed state, he knew it did, and that things would grow very much worse. His baptism, however, gave him new purpose and new strength. It also gave great joy to Tina – a much better human being than he would ever be.

There was still much he did not understand. Evil, though, was clear to Julian, as was love. If he kept these two well apart in his mind, he thought, there was yet a chance for him – and for Tina too.

For God clearly had His own plans for them all – the sinners and the sinned against, the believers and the disbelievers, those who served Him and those who did not. They were all like ants really in a big white bowl, running this way and that.

A few days later, the new Superintendent of the Convalescent Home called Julian and Tina to her office. She was a hard-faced woman with grey hair, and she wore a long black dress with a white collar.

"I have orders for you two," she said, her face expressionless. "If you are both fit enough – *and I have said you are...*" – she spoke these words with apparent relish, her lips closing on them as if they were tasty morsels – "... you are to be sent to the Ramsgate SupaPod where I understand both of you were once lucky residents. You were on the staff, I believe?"

The last was clearly a question and required conformation.

"Yes," said Tina placidly. "We both worked in Education, although I was later personal assistant to one of the Commanders."

"And your father, I understand, at that time was the High Director, now deceased?" The Superintendent said the words without any tone of respect, let alone sympathy.

"That's correct." Tina stood in her blue smock, her hands together over her belly. Through the barred window behind her, Julian could see a patrol of girl soldiers from the barracks passing by. They were sauntering along without weapons, chatting amongst themselves, one even applying something or other to her face. Presumably the security danger level was now low.

"Well, the new High Director – Lady Lascelles, whom we know so well at this establishment – has personally ordered your return there. You will travel together, leaving this afternoon, so get your things together and be ready outside at 2.00. That's all."

Outside in the passageway, permeated with the ever-present smell of institutional cooking, Julian said to Tina, "Well, it's happening again. We haven't escaped. I don't think there is any escape. It would have been best, I think, to have remained in the OuterWorld." His hands were shaking and he held them close to his body so that Tina would not see his weakness. To return to SupaPodia, he felt sure, would mean his death. They would never forgive or forget what he had done.

"You have your faith now," Tina said quietly. She was attuned to his fears. "And you have me for as long as we are allowed to stay together."

"Will they let us pray in the SupaPod?" he asked. They don't seem to have minded here, but there it may now be different. Pamela's rule, I suspect, is more atheistic than ever."

"If you can't pray outwardly," she replied, then you can do so in your own head. Up to the very moment your body is destroyed, you can utter prayer. It will give you strength. And afterwards your soul will be free and all earthly concerns irrelevant."

"Yet the evil will go on. I should have liked to have fought it further."

"Perhaps you will. We cannot know God's purpose for us. I do believe His love will triumph in the end."

"I believe too, but I do not have the depth of your faith," he said.

"We will pray together, whatever happens, even if we cannot say the words out loud."

"Julian," she said.

"Yes?"

"I love you. You are my rock.

"And I love you too, Tina, as my daughter, with all my soul."

Her eyes filled with tears. Julian knew he now had the honour of standing in her father's place. Although he faced imminent extinction, he could not abandon her, not even to save his own life.

The transport was by an old petrol-driven van with one female driver and two male guards. The guards were not from Pamela's own force but had come with the van. They were dressed casually in tee shirts and jeans, but they carried the latest laser weapons. One guard was locked with Julian and Tina inside the van's windowless interior, all uncomfortable on hard bench seats; the other sat with the driver. They made two stops to stretch and relieve themselves. The last was in an area of dereliction where once houses had stood, now just an expanse of broken concrete and piled rubbish. Black smoke, swirling horizontally with the ground in a strong breeze, hid much of the wasteland. The only people Julian saw were some youths with dogs in the distance, and an old, toothless crone who was clearly mad, sitting on the ground next to a stinking pond and bathing her legs in its green, rancid waters, crying out, "Beautiful. Oh, I was once so beautiful", over and over again.

The driver was sullenly taciturn in an old sheepskin jacket and ragged skirt, presumably on contract to SupaPodia for this journey. The guards said little either, but watched their prisoners closely, weapons always at the ready. Pamela had clearly given orders that there were to be no more escapes. Even if Tina and Julian had been able to get away, did they wish to do so? Tina clearly saw it as her purpose to go where she was sent – where she felt she could still do good – and Julian most certainly did not want to leave her. So he accepted his fate, convincing himself he too was following God's will – although his faith still trembled in that space between prayer and fearful reality.

He knew he was going to die. SupaPodia would have its revenge on him now, but he hoped not on Tina, who had done the organisation no harm, as he had. What he feared above all was a slow torture of mind and body, by which his reason might be overthrown and his faith lost. He had already seen how SupaPodia could achieve such devilry. He shuddered at the memory of what he had seen on those Lower Levels. If he was taken there, he hoped he would have the resolution, and find the means, to end his suffering by killing himself.

They were met in the SupaPod's staff portal by Stanley. Julian had last seen him on the Lower Levels when his implant surgery was being planned as a punishment for him. This was the Stanley whom he would then have willingly choked to death, but who now just sent a pulsation of nausea through him – disgust that was edged with fear.

Tina, who had good cause to detest Stanley as well, viewed him equitably. "Hello, again," she said, and even took his hand. "How are you prospering?"

"Oh, very well," Stanley said in that smooth, unctuous voice Julian recalled; it brought back his detestation. "I've been promoted to Senior Commander"

"Congratulations," said Tina.

What was she really thinking? Julian wondered.

"It's very good to have you back." Stanley's words were at first directed to Tina, but he then added, in what sounded to the apprehensive Julian a rather grudging tone, "And you too, Julian. I'm in need of good staff."

So Stanley was at least putting on an appearance of friendliness. It was as if nothing had ever happened, not the imprisonment, the escape, or the killings. Such a scenario was inconceivable. Julian did not trust Stanley. Was he acting a part, following someone's orders – perhaps those of Pamela Lascelles, as new High Director? Were he and Tina to be pampered, fed and fattened before being slaughtered?

"So we're to be Lilacs again?" Julian felt he was acting a part in a horror film, which had stilled, and was now starting up again.

"Yes, you will be" Stanley confirmed. "But you'll need to settle in first. Let's see, seven complete colour Sweeps and then I'll reassign you. You'll live on this Upper Level until you take up your duties below. He rang a buzzer on the wall. "Gina will show you to your Pods. See you later perhaps at chow."

Julian remembered Gina from his first entry into the SupaPod. She had been one of those who had given him a welcoming party. However, she showed him not a hint of recognition now. She led them down corridor after corridor until they came to a broader passage, which was faced with glass windows looking out over open decking, with a rail and the wide sea beyond. But isn't this part of the Upper Deck where I used to come and walk before? wondered Julian, although I don't remember that outer decking.

Beyond this area lit by daylight through the large windows, the passageway became enclosed again, and a line of individual Pods began, door after door of them entered directly from a narrow corridor, just like a hotel in the OuterWorld, Julian thought, if any such survived. Tina's Pod was one up from his. He did not want to leave her, fearing it would be the last time he saw her. But he had to.

"I'll see you later," he mumbled, forcing himself to turn from her and enter his Pod. It was much larger than the one high on its stack that had been his before, and from which he had escaped that interminable time ago. None of that dreadful adventure seemed real now. Perhaps it had never happened. Perhaps he had been reborn and moved back in time, and his second experience of SupaPodia would be quite different.

He explored the Pod – its various shoots, its Screen, its ordering panel, just like before, but rather larger and easier to work. He ordered himself a cheese sandwich, and it came zinging out of its shoot; so much more convenient than the OuterWorld, he thought. It would be so easy to fall in love with this system whatever its restrictions on personal freedom. But he wasn't going to fall into that mind-destroying way of thought any longer.

He ordered a full set of clothes – beige canvas trousers, a blue pullover, and a white shirt – but there was no lilac blazer for him available, or lilac shirt or trousers. They were simply not on the ordering list. Perhaps they would be added after he had been inducted by Stanley into his new job.

He was forgetting. *He was forgetting.* Already – and he had only been back here in this place of mirrors for an hour or so, perhaps only a fraction of an Orange segment, or whatever colour it was now – he was beginning to be sucked into the system once more. Oh hell! How he wanted to get out. Where was Tina? He was missing Tina already, the calmness and the strength she gave him. He sat on his couch and he prayed. He prayed in his head, because otherwise he knew they might be monitoring his words. Pamela had probably already strengthened the rules concerning the illegality of religion.

He was frightened that Tina might already have disappeared, taken down to a much lower Level. Stanley's aim would surely be to split them up, knowing how they had schemed and planned together. So he was vastly relieved a little later when she answered to his buzz on the door of her Pod. She was wearing a white tee-shirt and slacks, her hair brushed out and shining.

They found the staff restaurant on this Upper Level. Everything functioned here as he remembered it. They took their food to a table and nodded at Lilacs who came in. No one sat with them, though, and Stanley never appeared. Afterwards, they found their way through a narrow door to that outer deck they had seen, open to the air, with its wooden planking like a ship, and walked along it looking out to sea, seeing the white cliffs on the horizon and the shifting steel-grey waters breaking high. Stretching like a great finger into the ocean was the long Goodwins Bar that the Captain and Boadicea had attacked; even now he could see their figures carrying the explosive satchels running out along it. Where were they now? Were they still in that Work Camp on Hayling, or were they – more likely – dead?

Standing beside Tina, he watched the water breaking against the Bar. The waves in places were crashing right over it, although it seemed there was no wind driving them on. Perhaps there had been an exceptionally full tide, for the sea level seemed higher than it had been before. There must be a full moon dragging at the water.

When the moon waned, the waters would surely fall and deep night return.

36

'And there will be signs in sun and moon and stars, and upon the earth distress of nations in great perplexity at the roaring of the sea and the waves, men fainting with fear and with foreboding of what is coming on the world; for the powers of the heavens will be shaken. And then they will see the Son of Man coming in a cloud with power and great glory.'

St. Luke 21: 25-27

The world was out of balance. Mankind was in disorder. The balance of God's creation had been overturned. The forests had been cut down, the coal mines dug out, the natural gases fracked to exhaustion, the oil lakes jetted to the merest trickle, mostly to provide the fuel and the power for the vast, multi-tiered, underground accommodation silos known as SupaPods. These had been designed to run on their own tidal-generated power, which explained the placement of the great majority at the edges of the oceans of the world, yet they needed vast additional power resources that were bleeding the old OuterWorld dry.

The OuterWorld burnt the wood and peat and the coal that was left, the smoke of which fumed upon the continents in unremitting clouds of carbon-saturated mist. The atmosphere could not absorb this. The effect over many years was to raise the temperature of the planet by several degrees. The ice of the polar caps was melting fast; the great glaciers were breaking up, vast sheets of ice drifting into warmer seas. In consequence, the level of the oceans was rising, the water driven on by powerful storms that broke out in the East and the West, the North and the South. The rain fell in torrents, washing away many of the already ravaged settlements of the OuterWorld, together with the top surface of much of its most valuable agricultural land. Vast tracts of countryside were flooded, and remained flooded, the surface waters penetrating the estates of the ruling Eliti, whose support for the SupaPods had been largely dependent upon the opportunities they provided to divide up the most desirable areas of the world's former nations into huge estates for themselves.

Lady Pamela Lascelles, High Director of SupaPodia International, as with her predecessor, had been unwilling to face up to, or even admit, the dangers caused by the rise in the sea levels. She had moved into the Inkwelo Palace, but maintained her principal office in the Cape, overlooking the great sweep of Mandela Bay. When the sun shone, and the grapes on the vines in the office courtyard, blushed a deeper red, she relaxed and pushed away the various reports presented to her highlighting the potential consequences of a change in global climate. There had been recent flooding in the SupaPods at Copocabana Bay, on the Great Barrier Reef, in the Bay of Bengal, on the shore of the Yellow Sea, at New Orleans, Kiribati, the Cocoa Islands, Beira, and Kolkata. And many other SupaPods, the reports read, could be endangered.

The various floodings had not been too severe, however. Most Podders had been evacuated in time, and moved inland to surface camps where new SupaPods were to be constructed. Pamela thought the problems were being 'managed'. She had been assured by one of her climatology experts that the dangers were not as great as had been forecast, and that the overall threat would gradually recede. A new mini Ice Age was anticipated that would refreeze the polar regions. This expert, a busty woman of middle years, much admired, who made regular appearances on SupaPodia Media, considered that the height of global warming had been reached, and much colder weather, world-wide, was imminent.

In consequence of such reports, High Director Lascelles did nothing other than to release the vast sums needed to pay the initial costs of resettlement and reconstruction, also instructing the affected national SupaPods to increase the contributions (taxation and service in kind) of their supporting OuterWorlds.

In April 2085, the Atlantic jet stream, fuelled by a series of cyclonic low pressure systems originating in the Southern Atlantic, developed into a mighty conveyor belt of storms, sweeping in, one after the other, against the western coastline of the island of Britain. Gales with winds of more than 100mph, accompanied by torrential rains, battered much of the seaboard. A sea surge forced back the waters of the Bristol Channel, flooding the SupaPods at Avonmouth and Weston-super-Mare. Compressed into the narrowing English Channel, another great wind-borne surge wreaked havoc on the South Coast, overwhelming the harbours of Southampton and Portsmouth, flooding Hayling Island and Romney Marsh, then, before breaking out into the North Sea, flung its mountainous waves against Sandwich and Pegwell Bays, where SupaPod No.16 Ramsgate was directly in their path.

37

Two days later (two complete Sweeps of the coloured SupaPod time recorder), Senior Commander Stanley Gaylord, an Assistant Director of Ramsgate SupaPod No. 16, appeared in the staff restaurant as Tina and Julian were having breakfast. The more reasonable, yet still inscrutable, Stanley had been replaced by one who looked tired and strained and bit at his lips. It seemed he had reverted to being that most unpleasant, vicious Stanley whom Julian – and Tina now also – recognised well. On looking at him, Julian's heart began racing and he felt the familiar tremor of fear in his fingertips. This was it, wasn't it? He was going to be separated from Tina and taken off to his punishment. He tried to summon up the thoughts and beliefs that calmed him, but they were hard to find. Oh well, what will be will be, he said to himself, and put his hand out to touch Tina's on the table top, so that she turned to him and gave him a quick smile of reassurance, while looking up at Stanley enquiringly.

"I need to get you two back into jobs rather sooner than I had thought," said Stanley. He seated himself at their table. He was wearing his lilac blazer with the SP logo on the front pocket over a plain lilac tunic. His legs were unpleasantly thin and white, Julian noted.

"Christine, I want you to work with Gina on Lilacs Reception. She'll train you up. I'm sorry it's not higher grade work, but I need someone there with Gina straightaway."

"That's alright," said Tina softly.

"You'll keep your present Pod, but you..." – he turned to Julian – "... you'll be going below. I've got a nice job for you in Medicine."

"But I'm trained as a teacher," Julian protested.

"I *don't want* fucking teachers, I *want* fucking medical orderlies." Stanley's voice was suddenly high-pitched and alarmingly out of control.

"Where will I work?"

"Oh, deep below. Level 02, in fact. Almost at the bottom." Stanley pushed his pasty face close to Julian's: there was dribble at the corner of his mouth. "Did you think you'd get away with it, you arse hole? That we'd forgive and forget? You're a rebel and a killer. SupaPodia will get even with you!"

Julian knew then his death sentence had come. Level 02 was one where the true horrors of SupaPodia dwelt on its many floors. He remembered the rows of beds he had seen with the Podders awaiting the removal of their 'spare parts', the obscene cat's cradles of wires and tubes that took the movement directly from their hearts to keep the perpetual pendulum of power in motion.

"The next Green, first segment, will be when you'll both start. Oh, and Christine, none of that religious babbling of yours now, or I'll move you into a much less pleasant job. That's all for the moment. Go back to your Pods and stay there. "

He left them. They sat stunned, aware of the eyes of the other Lilacs in the restaurant on them.

"Come to my Pod and pray with me," said Tina, taking Julian by the hand and leading him into the corridor outside.

They came to the part of the broader passageway that was fronted with glass panels facing the sea. Julian was aware for the first time of a deep thudding sound here, interspersed with many sharper shudderings and creakings, as if they were, in fact, on board a ship at sea facing a storm. Looking through the windows, he realised this metaphor was apt, for he could see the ocean was foaming high and white, waves even cascading over the decking beyond the windows where he had so recently walked with Tina. The thudding sound, he realised, must be the wind buffeting the exposed upper works of the SupaPod. Looking out along the Bar, and then back towards the shore, he could make out nothing but a great mist of driven water, the waves now crashing against the very window he was looking through, so all vision beyond the lashing, swirling water was lost.

He shivered and placed his arm around Tina's shoulders. Stanley's instructions to him just now were pushed out of his mind. This new situation was even more serious. Would the SupaPod withstand this onslaught of nature? It had probably never faced a storm of such intensity. What would happen if the sea broke in? He realised with mounting alarm that the water could flood into the entry portals and pour down the many shafts. Everyone below would be trapped. Thousands, no, tens of thousands, were likely to die. The elevators would stop. The power would go out.

"My God!" he cried out. "Please don't let this happen."

Tina looked equally alarmed, her usual composure shaken by Julian's cries. They came to the row of accommodation Pods, and, reaching the door of Tina's Pod, she pushed him inside.

"It's the storm you fear, isn't it? Not Stanley's posting."

"Yes, the storm! It's going to overwhelm us. Can't you hear it tearing at us, even here?"

It was true. Although there was no window to the Pod, the force of the wind could be clearly heard around them, a booming noise that sounded like a giant drummer beating out a wild tattoo on steel and concrete and glass.

"Pray with me," she said, her calm restored.

There was just room for the two of them side by side on the Pod's couch.

"Lord, hear me," she asked. "Keep your people safe this day. Let the storm abate at your command, let the waves be stilled. In your name. Amen".

"Amen," mumbled Julian. He knew something dreadful, something unthinkable was about to happen.

The Pod lurched. It seemed to move bodily to one side, then spring back. Tina fell to her side on the couch, then looked up, her hand to her mouth.

"Let's get outside," said Julian urgently. "We don't want to be trapped here."

They came out into the passage. A number of others in Lilac uniforms were scurrying by. No one stopped. No one spoke. Julian and Tina followed them along the twisting corridors until they reached an open hall with its moving stairways rising from below and its block of elevators. Surely, Julian thought, this is where I used to be when I came up to the Upper Deck from my Pod on Level 19. A shock awaited him. The carpeted floor was running with water, a trickle here, a steady flow there, some parts still dry. Water had begun to seep down the stairways, which had already stopped. The elevators were pinging, though, and Lilacs tumbling out. There was much shouting, some screaming.

"What about the Podders?" Julian yelled at a passing Lilac in overalls. "Are they being got out through the portals? The sea could break in at any moment."

There was no answer. The man disappeared through the double doors to the Outer Deck, which, on being opened, brought in a great mass of water from outside. There must be a breach somewhere in the glass walling, Julian thought. No one seemed to be in control. Confusion was everywhere. A swirling mass of Lilac bodies, some in groups, were preparing to run for it through the doors, hoping to wade through the incoming water to the Outside. Julian saw Stanley suddenly appear. He had managed to put on high boots and was wearing a lilac rain cape. He looked tearful and frightened, certainly not in command as he should have been. He grabbed at one Lilac, a large bearded man who had a group about him, and seemed to plead with him, but the man pushed him away.

"I'm going to warn them below and see if I can help!" Julian yelled to Tina above the din.

She clutched at him for a moment, then released him. "God be with you, Julian. Come back to me. We may be able to ride this out. Perhaps it's not as bad as it looks."

"Take care, then." He knew how inadequate the words were. He was leaving her to help others when she might have need of him.

He went to the elevator station and pressed the button to go down. Water was running at his feet. As the elevator arrived, he was pushed back by a mass of frightened Lilacs scrambling to get out. He turned and saw Tina bending over a girl in a lilac dress who had fallen, trying to raise her up. He heard her calling out, telling people to stay calm. He entered the now empty elevator, the doors closed and he was on his own, descending fast into the bowels of the SupaPod.

* * *

Julian had selected Level 3 for the elevator, almost as a random thought, but considering that those highest up in the SupaPod had the best chance of getting up to the surface, should the worst happen. That meant, of course, abandoning any attempt to warn all those further below, but at least he would have tried to help some Podders. Perhaps Tina's prayer that the SupaPod could ride out the storm without too much damage or loss of life would be answered. All was in doubt. He was acting now on adrenaline, and his fear had gone.

He did not really know his purpose, other than to warn Podders and Lilacs alike that they should get out through whatever portals were available to them until the current emergency was over. But how to find those portals? Podders did not use the main elevators; indeed they had no access to them. They usually only moved between Levels as part of some organised group managed by Lilacs. Could they be motivated to save themselves? Would they even understand the danger they were in? At all costs, he must not start a panic. It would be far better perhaps to liaise with their Lilacs. But where would he find those? He had seen that Lilacs, who had intimations of impending disaster, were already leaving their charges and fleeing to the uppermost areas.

The lift doors pinged upon at Level 3. A rush of Lilacs, and indeed some orange-clad Podders, pushed him back, but, swearing, he was able to force himself through them out into the corridor. The doors shut with a whooshing sound. He was on his own in the panel-lined corridor. Some of the panels were covered with pictures of happy smiling faces beneath the words, 'Your SupaPodia. Use it. Love it.'

The lights in the corridor dimmed suddenly, then reinstated themselves. His heart missed a beat. God, no! The lights must not go out. In sealed blackness nothing could be done. It would be like being buried alive. He did not know of any emergency lighting, not even a torch.

He reached a doorway and found he was in a large recreation room. There were groups of Podders seated gazing at the various Screens. The nearest turned to look at him curiously as he entered – he knew he must appear dishevelled, wearing casual slacks and a crumpled jacket, his hair wild, his eyes staring – but they soon looked back at the Screen, which clearly held more interest for them than his sudden arrival. Horses were racing across the Screen, a man fell off and was dragged along, his head smashing against rocks. The audience tittered.

A patrolling Lilac, a short, spotty-faced man in a short, shiny tunic, came up to Julian. "Who are you?"

"I'm a Lilac, like you. I've just come down from the outer staff portal. There's a bit of an emergency, I'm afraid. A big storm's hit us and some water's coming in." He saw the fear come into the Lilac's eyes. "Now, keep calm, it may not prove too bad. But you should evacuate, I think. Do you have evacuation procedures?"

"No," he said dumbly. "I'm new. I've never received any training on that?"

"Are there any other Lilacs here?"

"There're all on rest break. I can make a call."

"Do that, please." Julian realised how rigid with tension his body was, the sweat soaking his back and dripping under his arms.

The Lilac spoke into a small device taken from his pocket. He stood listening, with his head cocked to one side. He spoke again, "Hello. Hello…"

"No one's answering," he said. "That's weird."

A red light on the wall above him started flashing. The lights suddenly dipped almost to blackness, then recovered. The Podders' faces were all turning towards them, their Screens frozen, not restarting.

"It's an alarm," said the Lilac, scared. "What do I do?"

Julian, terrified of a total blackout, could only think, I must get these people to the elevators. I'd never find any other portal, even if there is one from this Level.

To his horror, seeping into the recreation room, Julian could see dark rivulets of water from the corridor outside. He pushed open the doors. Yes, there was a flow of water already in the corridor, running like black lava under the dimming lights. Was he too late? The sea water must be crashing into the SupaPod, cascading down its many shafts, its elevators, pipes, and ventilation channels.

"Get your Podders together," Julian commanded the Lilac. "Tell them it's only an exercise. "Bring them in line out of this room into the corridor. I'm going to find a route out."

He hoped he sounded confident. "Oh, Lord, help me," he spoke out, and at once his fear seemed to drop away. God had allowed him to live for this purpose, when so many times he might have been destroyed.

He went a way up the corridor back towards the elevator. Looking behind him, he could see the Lilac bringing the first of his Podders out of the recreation room. There was a chorus of dismay at the sight of the running water. A woman's scream pierced his ears.

"Keep calm, keep calm," the Lilac was saying. "Everything's alright. This is only a test. We have to go to the mustering area and then you'll be back in your Pods."

Julian thought, one day I'll praise that young man. Recommend him for promotion. And then he realised, there would be no promotion, for there would be no SupaPodia. The old order was finishing here in storm and disaster; all that mattered was survival.

Some Lilacs were running in the passage, pushing past his line of Podders, splashing in the water, seeking the elevator. How far was it? Ah, there it was at last, with a crowd around it, Lilacs and Podders together. Fists were thumping the elevator door. Coming closer, he saw with a sinking heart there was no light on now in the control panel. Water was trickling around the edges of the door, dribbling out into the passage where it ran now as high as the instep of his shoe.

The passage lights dimmed to further screams, coming too from the line of Podders now stationary behind Julian, where his fellow Lilac was trying to quieten them. "It's alright. Alright. They're just testing the lights. Just keep in your place until I tell you."

"There *are* stairs," a Lilac shouted out as the lights strengthened again. "They're in a narrow inspection shaft. I climbed it once with an engineer when I was training. Two hundred and eighty feet it is up to the top from this landing."

"Worth a try!" a chorus of voices shouted out.

"This way, I think," said the Lilac, pushing himself out of the crowd, and heading away down an adjoining passage. Julian, with others, hastened after him, splashing through the water. Turning, he signalled to the recreation room Lilac to follow with his long line of Podders.

The lead Lilac had stopped at a low metal door, set into a plinth at the junction of passages. The light was very dim here. The Lilac was tugging at the door, which would not open. "Shit and fuck!" he yelled, pulling, pushing, kicking. A young Podder girl beside him began to cry. "We're going to die... We're going to die..."

Someone slapped her face, knocking her over into the water. "You bitch!" yelled Julian at the offender, a fat female Lilac with a red face. He helped the Podder up, water running from her orange suit. "Keep by me," he said. "What's your name?"

"Avril," she trembled.

"Well, Avril. You're *not* going to die."

He seized the handle of the door and pulled with all his might. To his vast relief, he felt movement. The door then was not locked as he had feared, its hinges probably just stiff from lack of use. He tugged again, and he gained more movement, then more. There was a cheer behind him.

The Lilac took over from him, and the door at last was fully open. He poked his head inside. "There's no light at all," the Lilac said. "We carried torches when I was here before. We'll have to climb in total blackness."

"What's the stair like?" asked Julian.

"It's a spiral stair around a central concrete column."

"You can't fall?"

"No, there's no side to fall off, only back down the stair."

"You go first," said Julian. Other Lilacs, and a few Podders, were bunching around, not waiting for orders, desperate to get through the door. Julian let them go.

Julian turned back to his own Lilac, who was still dutifully in place at the head of his Podder line. "Send some through, then you go up. I'll follow with Avril here. The end of the line will have to take its chance. The trouble will be if anyone falls. And we can only pray that the top is open." And, he thought – not wishing to speak out more of his fears – I pray that it is not flooded there either. If the door at the top is submerged, the water will cascade down like a waterfall and sweep us all into oblivion.

Numbers of Podders and Lilacs were now ducking through the entry door and disappearing into blackness. Some rushed at the door, pushing others aside, but most patiently awaited their turn. The lights began flickering and dipping again. At least there is an escape now, Julian thought, an escape perhaps by feel alone up towards light – the darkened daylight of the storm. He recalled the waves he had seen surging over the Bar and beating against the windows of the Upper Deck. Would everything be swept away in this apocalypse – this Armaggedon?

When Julian judged it his turn to go through the door, he pushed Avril ahead of him and, doubling himself up behind her much shorter body, found the first of the steps. In the faint light through the door, now half-blocked by the person behind, he could see that the stairs went down as well as up. Perhaps others were climbing up from the Level below, and even the one below that, although he could see no one in the blackness. He could hear the sounds of feet above him, however, as he stepped into solid blackness.

He brushed against Avril's back. He could hear her whimpering. He called out to her, "Take each step as it comes, keep your hand on the curve of the wall. Don't think about anything else. I won't leave you."

"I'm frightened. My legs won't work," her thin, terrified voice came back to him.

"Here, let me get by you." He could feel his body sliding past hers. He stumbled on a step, but steadied himself. He held out a hand until he touched her. "Take my hand. Don't let it go. I will pull you up. One step at a time."

It seemed to work. They even developed a type of rhythm. He could hear people ahead, and perhaps below, but no one came into contact with them. At least, he thought, the air is good. And there is no water running down. Not yet, at least. Dear Lord, please keep us safe. His body was wet with sweat.

After a further period, during which he had talked and hummed and sung and tried to chat with Avril, but her answers were brief and few, he suddenly stumbled against something soft on the stair. He called a warning out to Avril, and making sure her grip was firm in his, picked his way over the obstacle. It must have been a body lying on the stair.

There was another body a little higher, and then another, this one giving out groans; getting round them was proving increasingly difficult. There was nothing he could do to help, only a murmured, "Don't give up. Help is coming", knowing the fearsome inadequacy of these words.

Slowly, he became aware of the very faintest glimmer of light ahead, so faint at first he thought it might be coming from within the black compass of his brain rather than from a source outside; but it grew a little stronger, then stronger still, and suddenly he was right upon it – another entry to the stairs, a metal door pushed open, probably on Level No. 2.

Here, a Lilac, half undressed, bare-chested, entered just ahead bearing a torch, the light stabbing a thin beam at the blackness, making out little but the circling rough-cast concrete walls, and the endless circling steps. Julian tried to keep up with him, but he could not do so. Avril's hand was still in his, but she was obviously tiring, as he had to pull harder and harder at her arm, hearing her distressed gasps and cries and able to do nothing else to help her.

A sudden horror – drops of water on his skin and clothing, and a feeling that the steps were now wet and slippery, the water drops more frequent, pattering on his upturned face. Avril groaned and he could pull at her no more: she must have sunk to her knees on the stairs. He sought her with his hands, and found her hair, which he stroked. "Come, my love. Only a little further now."

"I can't go on," she gasped. "I need to rest."

"You can't rest here!" he said, suddenly angry. "Here, let me see if I can carry you."

He tried to raise her, but it was impossible. He could hear others now at their heels. "What's up there?" a man's voice called. "Get on with yer, whoever you are."

"Avril, love, hold my hand. Come!"

He got her up some more steps, perhaps twenty of them. The water seemed to be running onto them much more strongly now. Perhaps they were near the top. Was the top then at Level 1? Had those at the front opened an upper exit door? Was the water running in there? He didn't know any of these things.

He pulled at Avril's arm, and her fingers slid through his. No cry, soundless. She was gone. "Avril! he cried out.

"She's fallen, mate," said the voice behind. "On 'er back, I think. Get on, yer can't stop or we're all lost."

"Avril. You *must* keep climbing!" He was shouting out into a blackness without sense or form, where all things ended, where only breath hissed and water slid on skin, these things happening in another world entirely.

Julian had promised Avril she would not die. He had been sure of God's mercy, but he had been wrong. He was angry with God and punched the concrete wall. He would get even with God. The resolution gave him new strength. He stumbled on.

There was another light ahead, dim and blurry at first, clearer with each twist of the stair, the water now dropping on him like rain – heavy rain; it must be pouring onto the steps, as he could hear it gurgling away below. He could now see the square of light taking form, and some figures balanced against it, and then he was up to it, and stepping out over a metal ledge into water as deep as his knees, gasping, his limbs shaking, doubled up retching, his head almost in the water. He looked up and searched with his eyes the space he was in, seen through a grey, dim light that he realised, with a surge of hope, was natural daylight coming from a source somewhere above. He appeared to be in an open hall, with several stairways coming down into it, moving walkways, they looked like, only they were now frozen still, yet at the same time alive with cascading water, running like waterfalls.

People – Lilacs mainly, but some Orange Podders as well – stood in the water, feeling their way along the sides of the hall, seeking to haul themselves up the stairways against the rushing water, holding onto the rails. As Julian, watched, most succeeded, but two were swept back, tumbling down like logs to the flooded hall. He could not see if they rose again. No one moved to help. A man and woman, naked except for their underwear, began to force themselves up from stair to stair, the woman with one hand on the rail and the other about her companion's waist. They reached it to the top, and disappeared from view.

Looking back at the hatch by which he had escaped the spiral stairs, Julian saw that the water was up to the level of its lip, and already pouring over. Soon those blackened stairs would be impassable. Anyone attempting them would be swept away. Others had exited the hatch after him, Podders mainly, perhaps from the line the brave young Lilac had formed. There was no sign of him, however. There was no sign either of Avril, although Julian, hoping against hope, looked for her to emerge, praying someone else might have been able to bring her up those few last desperate steps to the light.

He knew he could not stay in the hall where the water was becoming deeper by the minute. The only way was to go up the stairways where the others had gone. Perhaps the water would be even deeper up there, but the only chance of escape, he felt sure, was by continuing upwards. He thought of Tina. It was odd – and he felt guilty – but he had forgotten about her until now. Had she escaped? He was still angry with God, but he prayed for her.

He sloshed through the water towards the upper stairs. The level was now over his knees. He stumbled at the foot of one of the stairways, but righted himself and searched with his feet for the steps through the water. There was a Lilac behind him. It was the chubby, florid-faced one who had slapped Avril. She did not seem to recognise him now, and said something to him. He did not answer. He was able to hold onto the stairway rail despite the rushing cold water, tasting of salt, which soaked him entirely: his blue woollen pullover was sodden and heavy. Despite the cold, he would perhaps have been better off naked in the water, like those others he had seen, but he knew he needed his clothes. If he escaped from this present hell, further hells would be sure to follow. Clothes were vital for survival.

At the top of the stairway, he clung onto a post that projected from a wall. The fat Lilac was clinging to it as well. The water level was lower here, up to his calves, but flowing fast through open doors half-broken from their hinges, which flapped in the rushing water like the struggling wings of some dying bird. The Lilac was shaking as if her body was in spasm. She had on only a thin lilac dress, which was now diaphanous. She is cold and she is terrified, he thought. She can't last long like that and I cannot help her. She tried to say something to him through chattering teeth, but she couldn't get the words out.

He pushed himself away from her through the water, facing the current directly to lessen the chances of being swept to one side, then turning to reach what looked like a desk or podium made of yellow wood. It must be anchored to the floor, he thought, for the water swept round it and it didn't move. He wedged his body against it and tried to take stock of what to do.

Some others were clinging to struts and ledges around this same area. He realised that he must be within the hall that led to the Upper Deck, which he had known well. In the murky light, and with the swirling water, it was hard to tell for sure, but he thought he recognised the elevator block, and the broken doors were probably those which opened to the Upper Deck itself. If so, it was here that he had parted from Tina. He looked around desperately, trying to penetrate the darkest corners. Was she still here? He couldn't see her. He had left her helping others. Had she been able to escape before the seas broke in?

When Julian looked again at the tubby Lilac, he saw that she had left the post she had been clinging to and was deep in the water, her head only just above the surface. "Help!" he heard her cry above the continuous rush of the waters. There was nothing he could do to assist her without imperilling himself. He saw her head duck under, and then it did not rise again. He thought the trauma and the cold must have sapped the life from her, like a battery failing, then dead.

If I'm right and the Upper Deck is through the doorway, Julian considered, his own body shaking with the cold…(he knew he had to move – move anywhere – to warm himself)… and it's not totally destroyed, then I know there is a door from it at its far end into that long tunnel which leads through to the hillside terrace where the Guard drilled. That is the route I followed back into the SupaPod after I had been shown around the Control Station. The tunnel rises into the cliff from the Upper Deck and should be dry. I remember it had a moving walkway at one point.

He was excited now. He was developing a plan. Far better than waiting to die, even if the plan proved fruitless. He looked across at the remains of the outer doors from the hall, half-torn from their hinges. The wind and rain were still beating against the building, and might yet tear it apart. The water seemed to be entering in stronger surges, so the waves must still be breaking high over the sea walls, flooding everywhere around. If he could only get through the doorway onto the Outer Deck, away from the point where it was breached, then he might have a chance.

He waded through the water, which swirled at times to his thighs, then seemed to drain away so it was only at calf height. Away from its strongest flows towards the walkways and the elevator boxes, the current was perhaps less dangerous. He found more people propped along the sides here. Most seemed resigned to their fate, many clearly in the last stages of hypothermia, their faces blue, their limbs shaking. They just watched him apathetically and did not attempt to follow. He did not seek to rouse them. They must look to themselves. He had done what he could to help. God had betrayed his efforts with Avril. So he left God to save or abandon his flock as He willed. Julian was intent only on saving himself now, to be reunited with Tina, whom he prayed had escaped while she still could.

He positioned himself as close to the rushing outer doorway as he could reach, clinging desperately to its smashed uprights, and steeled himself to force his body against the powerful flow there. His feet were almost lifted from the ground by the force of the water, but he managed to pull himself forward, hand over hand, clutching at the twisted pillars of one door and then some wall fittings beyond, his body all the time battling the flood surge which rose at times as high as his waist, until at last he was able to pass through the wrecked doorway to find what he had hoped for – that the Upper Deck was still standing to his left, but, to his right, the glass panels had gone and there was only wreckage here foamed over by the crashing sea waves.

Dragging his body away from the breach out of the strongest current, he was eventually able to gain that part of the Upper Deck which was still enclosed. Breathless and gasping, he recognised its broad window panes against which the waves beat fiercely, but had yet to shatter. The passageway shuddered each time a wave struck; soon it too might be broken open like a shell. The flooding, though, was less deep here. He splashed through the swirling waters as fast as he could.

He turned a right-angled corner, and there he spotted him – Stanley, still in his pixy-like rain cape, perched on top of a concrete buttress like some strange goblin out of a nightmare nursery rhyme.

"Hell, my head aches," was all Stanley said on seeing him. "It's Dr. Foster, isn't it? Give my head a rub, would you, there's a good chap."

"Give your head a rub? You mad bastard! I'll throw you down in the water and stamp on it."

"Now, don't be like that. I never wished you harm. I wanted to promote you, but I had to obey orders."

Julian had waded past him. Stanley would meet his fate without any assistance from him.

"Where are you going?" The plaintive voice called out behind him.

"What's it matter to you?"

"You won't get through the door at the end. It's locked."

"Then I'll break it down."

"Ah, that's the sort of talk I want to hear! Here, let me join you."

Julian had turned to look at the grotesque figure, trying to fix Stanley's evil in his mind, so he did not lose that image amidst this forced absurdity. "Why should I want to save you? I'd rather see you drown."

"Because we can probably get through the door together. It needs someone to push at it while I put the code in. The water's made it stick, you see."

"What's the code?"

"Ah," he said. "Now I would be silly to tell you that, wouldn't I? – particularly when you want me dead."

"I'm going to try the door, anyhow," Julian said, and he waded on. A scrape or two and a splashing behind him, heard through the booming waters outside, told him Stanley was following.

He did not look back. The splashing continued at his heels. Another sharp corner of the Upper Deck, and the sliding door he remembered at the far end of the passage was in front of him. Here, the sea seemed at its fiercest close to the cliff edge, flinging itself continuously against the glass.

The exposed structure of the Deck shook and heaved; it was only time surely before the turning, twisting movement destroyed it.

Julian pulled at the handle of the door, but it was locked. He kicked it and swore at it, pushed at it, tried to shove it the other way, then punched in numbers on the adjacent control box, but all to no avail.

"Now, can I try?" said Stanley. His voice had assumed a calm normality.

Julian stood aside reluctantly. He was shivering badly and his nerves were on fire. He must watch Stanley closely. This man was a chameleon. He changed all the time, his mood, his purpose. Do not forget – Julian told himself – what he tried to do to you.

"Push at the door while I put in the code," said Stanley.

Julian braced his feet in the water and leant hard on the door. He saw Stanley punching in the code. There was a loud click and the door slid back a foot or so. Water immediately rushed at the gap, churning through it. Julian pulled the door to as quickly as he could, struggling against the pressure of the water

"Now, you've locked it again," said Stanley. He sounded sulky. He worked the control pad once more, and this time the door opened without Julian having to push at it.

"We'll need to go through in a rush," Julian said, bracing himself.

There was another violent shaking of the glass-fronted Deck, which threw Julian off balance. Suddenly, Stanley made a move, catching Julian off guard. Yanking the door back a foot or so, in one fluid movement he slid his body through. Before Julian could stop him, he had clicked the door to. Filled with rage and panic, Julian pulled at it. It was locked again.

Through the buffeting of the waves and the creaking of the structure about him, Julian could just hear Stanley's maniacal laughter on the far side. "So long, sucker! Have fun!"

A great crashing on the window panes nearest Julian's head, and a long drawn out scream of metal on metal, followed by a gigantic explosion of sound, and Julian was suddenly engulfed with water that washed him forward against the blocked door, which itself had crashed to one side, so that he was flung through its opening, gasping for breath, his body rolling deep under water, then grounding, and being washed on again, raised up and flung back against a stone ledge. The waters receded, then came back at him once more, flinging his body up higher, then leaving him again. By sheer instinct rather than will, he managed to lift himself and crawl further up the ledges which he now saw were metal steps going upwards, with the water frothing and swirling below, covered by a tangle of broken panels and twisted metals. Beyond this terrible vision, there seemed to be just the open, heaving white-topped sea, now beating against the cliffs: the whole Upper Deck of the SupaPod had gone – destroyed, washed away with everyone and everything within it.

Julian, in effect, had been thrown by the sea's destruction into a cave in the chalk cliff – the cave being the tunnel bored for the SupaPod, the tunnel into which Stanley had just escaped ahead of him. Realising the miracle of his survival, Julian managed to raise his soaked, bruised and battered body and crawl on hands and knees up the steps, looking into the darkness ahead to find Stanley. Then, in the half-light he saw him, higher up, standing stock still in apparent shock, his hands spread over his face.

Stanley came back to life as he watched the saturated, dripping figure of Julian, bent-double, coming up the steps towards him. He reached out for Julian, even going down a couple of steps to meet him. "Hell, what a disaster! Here, let me help you, old chap. What a survivor you are. Who would have thought….?"

He aimed a kick at Julian's head, but Julian, finding the strength of sheer desperation, managed to avoid it and seize hold of the leg instead, pulling Stanley to the ground with him, both rolling together down the steps towards the pounding water's edge. Stanley had his hands on Julian's throat, but Julian was able to counter by stabbing at his eyes with his stiffened fingers – a technique taught him by the Beast.

"Ow! You bastard!" Stanley howled, flailing about half-blinded.

Julian, now on his feet, kicked him in the groin with the full force of his right leg, sending himself tumbling backwards, but putting Stanley straight down on his face, screaming, his head at the very edge of the foaming water. With a strength that he had not been able to find to bear poor Avril up the spiral stairs, but which he now summoned up in one convulsive movement, he rose to his feet holding Stanley's shrieking body and pitched it into the water, where it floated for a brief while before being seized by a retreating wave and smashed against a protruding mass of twisted metal rods.

When the only movement he could detect was the angry sea moving the body's limbs amongst the metal and wire of its new found cage, Julian turned away.

38

Julian stood high on the terrace of the hillside overlooking the sea. He had emerged from the long tunnel that linked the SupaPod with the terrace. After his encounter with Stanley, and its deadly ending, it was as if he no longer cared about anything. His last remaining resilience had been used up in the destruction of Stanley, and for the moment he felt entirely empty of thought and feeling, indifferent to his fate. He had even forgotten about Tina. He had stumbled on through the tunnel, which amazingly had still been lit, if faintly, for some of its length, confident that he would find it blocked, or that some other sort of obstacle would occur, but greatly to his surprise there had been none.

If only there had been leadership at the SupaPod, instead of the sort of vacuous uselessness, fronted by an ever-present viciousness, displayed by Stanley – a so-termed Senior Commander – then very many Lilacs and Podders could have escaped through that tunnel. But there had been no information, no emergency procedures, no command, no leadership at all. In consequence, thousands upon thousands were likely to have been drowned, or otherwise killed. It made an indictment of SupaPodia far greater than any other; and the list of the crimes and the inhumanity of SupaPodia was already a very long one. What system could ever survive such a disaster, which Julian suspected had been replicated in many other places as well.

He looked across the terrace through the driving rain, soaked, chilled and shocked. He saw the Control Station buildings were still in ruins, their wired perimeters hanging to the ground. Had they been rebuilt elsewhere? It was not a matter to trouble him now, nor was the overall fate of the SupaPods. Simple survival was the main thing – survival for all those who had escaped, and there would be some at least, hopefully many.

Before him below, there was nothing but flood – the entire seafront under water as far as the cliff into which the SupaPod was built, its upper works exposed like a skeleton from which the flesh had been torn. Through the mist and the rain, he could see the sea water yet surging in from the bay, enveloping office buildings, warehouses, and sheds. The railway lines rose in places through the water in pyramids of twisted steel, the long Bar beyond, just a line of leaping white foam scarring the grey-black sea.

Julian could make out groups of people hunched together on the roofs of buildings, some wearing Lilac, others Orange. He thought of Tina now, and prayed that she was somewhere among them. Had she got away before those exposed, sea-facing buildings of the SupaPod had been inundated?

The upper structures of the SupaPod appeared as just a series of darker lines against the enveloping grey of the storm, and he could see how the sea waves had broken high over them, carrying most away – that Upper Deck where he had walked and where his last Pod had been, the staff portal and reception hall. The water had poured in flooding these spaces entirely, rushing in great waterfalls down the main elevator shafts, Level by Level, filling them from floor to ceiling, their rooms and corridors – Pods and entertainment halls, auditoriums, storerooms, kitchens, dining rooms, toilets, washrooms, and medical centres – down to the very lowest Levels where the sick had lain and where the grim experiments had taken place. All by now would be drowned, the lights extinguished, blackness absolute, oblivion deeper than eternity, the many, many thousands of dead, tens of thousands, hundreds even – perhaps a few individuals surviving for a while in pockets of air, hopeless, the living dead…It was all going on now, even as he watched. If the great storm had come a day or two later, he too would have been one of them.

Julian could see, immediately below him at the foot of the steep hillside, the freight yard with its portal into the cliff from where he had first escaped the SupaPod: lines of people were descending the walls of buildings there like trails of ants, one line making use of a ladder, others scrambling down from window ledge to window ledge.

The wind and rain were driving into his eyes, making it hard to see more. Yet it was clear some groups had made their escape over the roofs of buildings and were now at the edge of the flood, with the hope of reaching the hillside upon which he was standing. He was exhausted and shaking with cold, unknowing of where he could find shelter himself, but he had to help these people. Was it possible that Tina was among them? He could not think – did not dare to think – that Tina had perished. He hoped that she had been able to get onto those roofs below. It seemed to be the only escape route, except for the one which he had so miraculously found.

He made himself descend the hill to meet the survivors who would be approaching. The rain ran on his face and his soaked clothing slopped against his skin. This is the same route, he thought, as I crossed to bring Captain Bradwell out of danger. Why does fate cause us to repeat our deeds in ways like this, or am I just locked in a time loop that will never change and end?

Further down the slope, squatting by a clump of bushes and wiping the water from his eyes, he could see the bottom of the hillside much more clearly. There were large spreads of watery mud here, with the edge of the flood only yards away, probably still rising. The survivors – whether Lilacs or Podders, he did not know: it scarcely mattered – were floundering through the mud, trying to reach the higher ground. Some fell, to be picked up and pulled along by others; one or two lay facedown and did not move again. He thought, they must be very weak, soaked through and covered in mud, and there is no real succour for them even if they reach the slopes on which I stand. How will we cope? Many may die from shock, exhaustion, and exposure. Will OuterWorlders be able to help? They will also have been hit badly by the storm.

The first of the survivors were now approaching him over the tussocks of grass. He called out to them and waved his arms, but they did not seem to notice, only trudged on heads down. He came up closer to them and shouted, indicating they should follow him up the hillside – but to where? Everyone was white of face, many shaking, their bodies running with water, some dressed for the outdoors, most though only in light clothing, one or two semi-naked, some even with bare feet. Those will die first, was Julian's grim thought. Yet, no one now was falling or stopping; all were intent on climbing the hill: they did not look behind them.

Leading these first columns of survivors higher, Julian came to a level area near the ridge top, which he thought was close to the place from which the Nemesis attack had been launched. There were some ruined buildings here and an asphalt surface that might have been a road, and much coiled barbed wire. A number of the buildings, a bungalow amongst them, were still roofed. Julian tried a door: it was locked. He kicked it open, then walked on, turning to see one line of survivors was still close behind him while another was going towards the bungalow.

Further along the ridge to his left stood a stand of pine trees, dark against the grey sky, their tops bending in the gusting wind. Going in amongst the trees, climbing over fallen branches, Julian found a paved area at the centre of the wood, with a low concrete building that was fronted by an up-and-over metal door; it must once have been a garage. The door was unlocked. He pushed it up; one pivot at the top was broken and the door hung down crookedly at one side. Inside, though, it was dry. There were some old cans beside the walls, and piles of mouldering cardboard boxes.

Julian's intention was to shelter some of the survivors here. At least, they would be out of the rain, if little else. The people who had followed him in their mud-smeared lilac and orange clothing were already coming through the trees. With scarcely a word, they entered the garage and stood there shivering, then one by one collapsed onto the floor.

Julian thought, I must help these people and try to lead them. So he took some of the cardboard boxes, and began opening them up, distributing the flattened cardboard as mats to lie on or as covers for warmth. They were snatched from him and soon gone. Other survivors were now coming in, and Julian realised he would have to exert some control otherwise there might be a crush that could be dangerous. He stood at the door and let in a number more, then signalled to others that the shelter was full. Perhaps surprisingly, they obeyed him and stumbled on. Julian continued to stand guard, shivering with his whole body, his soaked clothing stuck to his flesh. Like this, he knew it was unlikely he would survive for long either. And still the rain came down.

After a while, there were no further people coming through the trees to this place. He stepped inside the garage. Everyone seemed to have found a space on the floor and was sitting or lying. No one spoke, no one sighed or wailed or shouted out. Julian found the silence uncanny. They are quiet now, he thought, but they will need to be fed; they will need dry clothes or they will catch cold and die. I will catch cold and die. I must pray. I must pray. I must remember God and say my prayers.

He went outside again. A concrete track led away from the garage between the trees. In the distance, he saw smoke rising, Someone had been able to light a fire. Fire and warmth were needed. He must gather up some of those branches stripped by the wind from the trees. Once he got a fire started, they should dry quickly enough and burn well.

As he stood at the hanging garage door, two women from inside rose and pushed past him. They squatted amongst the trees to urinate. Some men came out also and did the same. Life was coming back, bodies were reasserting themselves. There was even conversation now. He heard a trail of it, "Where were you mate? I was in the loading sheds. The water swept most away, but I got up into the roof girders, then through the fuckin' roof itself…Christ, what's going to happen next?"

It was odd, Julian thought, how people spoke now of their Saviour, who had been denied to them, and by them, for so many years.

He caught sight of more people coming through the trees, trudging slowly in line, picking their way through the bramble undergrowth. At their head was a woman with a lilac shawl wrapped about her head and shoulders, its ends held up against her face. Beneath the shawl, she wore a thin mud-streaked top and trousers. Her feet were bare, but it seemed she walked without pain. As she came up to him, she raised her eyes to him, above the small hand that grasped the shawl. The eyes were clear and blue. He knew those eyes.

"Tina! Oh my God, by all that's wonderful! You are safe!"

"Julian!" She let the shawl fall. Her face was pinched white with exhaustion. There were splashes of mud on her cheeks and about her jaw. But it was Tina. She had survived. Oh, thank the Lord! Thank the Lord!

Her eyes shone in his eyes. The air shone too, trembling all about him. Is she real, he thought, or am I dreaming? They embraced.

"I thought you were lost," he said. He rejoiced at the solid feel of her. Her flesh was cold. "Come inside. I am sure there is space for you and your people."

"I prayed for you. My prayers have been answered. Oh, Julian, we have such work to do."

"After you have rested."

"No, before. Or many more will die this night."

She was right, of course. He had thought the same. But what could he do?

Tina and he, with a number of others – men and women, Orange and Lilac – from the garage shelter, went towards the distant smoke, from which in time they brought back a stick of flame. And they gathered as many dry pine combs as they could find from the innermost places of the wood, and fallen sticks, and then larger branches, and they made a fire in front of their garage shelter. The cardboard from inside, they fed into the flames as well. And the people now had warmth. They stripped themselves of their clothes to dry them. Some, retreating into the depths of the shelter, curled up together so the heat of their bodies would not be lost, and managed to sleep an hour or two.

In the night the rain ceased. The next day, the sun returned. It was a new dawning, a new world. The old had passed forever.

39

"How did you escape?" Julian asked Tina. He had not been able to put that question to her before now. There had been so much to do. Some days had passed; how many, Julian had lost count of. Camps had been set up. Shelters built. Clothes and food had come in from OuterWorlders, as shocked by what had happened as anyone else. To help relieve disaster and suffering, whoever the individual, whatever their status, brought forth humanity at its very best. Tina had no need to teach her gospel here; the goodness flowed in sweetly, the desire to help.

Yet there were tensions as well, almost immediately. Lilacs tended to group with Lilacs, Podders with Podders: there were some fights, in particular for fuel, but the food was distributed as evenly as possible. Tina, herself saw to that. A kitchen had been set up on the cliff top beyond the pines where a ruined house stood: its fireplace and cooking range were still in place. Julian had cleared it out with the help of others, both Lilac and Orange. Tina took charge of the food collected from the old coal-driven lorries that wheezed here from inland, driven in the main by farmers who had animals they could kill and root crops they could dig up. She paid them with scraps of paper as promises, but most waved these away.

She was in the kitchen now, slicing vegetables to add to a great pot, with others helping her, mainly women, their hair bundled up under scarves. The men went out foraging. Julian led them. They collected what they could that was helpful, and were careful not to steal from OuterWorlders. Some OuterWorlders willingly gave, others closed their gates with a snarl and watched from behind shutters. It was ever the way with human kind.

"You know, I find it hard to remember," Tina said, answering Julian's question, leaning against the paddle, brought from a wrecked boat, with which she stirred her pot – a metal drum from a warehouse Julian had found on the shore. "I got out with others over that outer decking you and I had walked on. We were lucky, it was before the main sea surges came, but later the waves caught us. I was in the water at one point being washed out to sea, but by God's mercy I was able to grab hold of something floating – a wooden railway truck, it was – and it surged in on a wave, with me clinging to it like a limpet. Someone – I wish I knew whom – must have grabbed me and pulled me off, and hauled me up onto the roof of a building. I must have blacked out for a while"

Tina was tearful now, in a way Julian had not seen her before, thinking back on how she had been saved, Most of her emotions were usually directed to God. He was pleased to see her tears, though. They might provide her with some release from the burden of suffering she had taken on. Was her escape any less miraculous than his own?

"Whoever saved me, then left me – perhaps I was given up for dead – as when I came to I was all alone. My clothes were all but washed from me. I had to take a shawl for warmth from a dead Lilac I came upon in a room. I was lucky in finding other survivors on the roofs as well, and we managed to scramble from one roof to another until eventually we reached the edge of the flood. It was a dreadful thing climbing down into the water, seeking a place where we could cross those swamps and reach dry land. Then I found you. I speak honestly when I say, I always knew I would. I felt sure you would have survived. It was God's will."

She had not yet asked him about his own escape; how very perilous it had been; of the miracle that had swept him into the tunnel when the Upper Deck gave way. And Stanley? He had not told her about Stanley. He never would. He knew he had to answer to God alone for Stanley's death, for he could have left him at the sea's edge and not watch him drown.

"Was it God's will also that so many people – so many good, innocent people – should meet such a terrible fate, allowing us to survive." Julian could not yet reconcile his new faith with what had happened.

Tina was silent for a while. The stew went unstirred. "Many others escaped, not only us, and we are helping them now. We are all doing our best for each other, here and elsewhere, where there will have been similar disasters – Podders, Lilacs, OuterWorlders alike."

"What about the Eliti?"

Tina did not answer directly. "In time, justice will come to everyone. Every inequality will be smoothed away, for we are all children of God, each one the same in His eyes. Men and women learn from the evil that is done to them, and from the wrongs they may commit in return. God will show when He is displeased, and, yes it is true, at times the innocent will suffer as well as the guilty."

395

"I cannot accept that," Julian said angrily, thinking of Avril dying at his feet, and turned away.

Later, he walked by the shore with Tina. Like the storm itself, his mind was much calmer now, knowing the truth which Tina had spoken. The sea surges had retreated leaving a broad expanse of white sand below the cliffs. The shingle beaches had been stripped clean exposing the sand. The sea looked further out now than it had ever been. The great black Bar of the SupaPod, split in two by the storm, stood high above the sand, its turbines wrenched from their former positions, scattered like broken toys at its base. The sea will come back, thought Julian. The sea will rise again, much higher than it was before. This white beach will be covered and lost forever. Nature – or is that God? – has sucked in the sea and is holding its breath; soon it will spew out the water again.

No one will be safe any more close to the sea, not even on the cliffs, for in time they will erode and crumble away. Julian looked across at the ruins of the SupaPod, with its broken entry portals and concrete facades, the tumbled wreckage strewn with seaweed. The SupaPods will never be rebuilt, certainly not at the sea's edge. He hoped they would never be rebuilt anywhere. They had been an experiment, perhaps at first with good intent, but founded on the fallacious theory that all human beings wished for was security and entertainment, a roof over their head, food, clothing, and things to play with. If you gave them that, then it left the rest of the world for those better fitted to enjoy it – the Eliti, the clever ones, also, the decadent ones, the oppressors.

Through how many eras of history had the same grotesque cycle worked out? The bulk of humanity should not be shoved to one side by shutting it away, even if the intention is beneficent, and it should not be exploited as a resource for the few, even if such exploitation brings greater security to the many. All society – of whatever race, class, and status – has a right to the freedom of the earth.

Holding Tina by the hand, Julian looked out along the great sweep of the beach, seeing, far off, how its whiteness merged with the whiteness of the great cliffs behind. That whiteness, seen with half-closed eyes, was a generality only – a mere sense of space and distance. Closer up, the purity of the white was revealed as illusion: the reality of the beach was obscenity. All about were scattered the bodies of the dead, lying alone or in groups or amongst the other debris of the disaster, the twisting cables, the broken wagons and boxes and upturned boats, the swirls of plastic waste, the heaps of shattered wood and metal, dead animals, branches of trees, whole trunks also, and clumps of earth and vegetation, leaving dark trails on the sand.

Along the shore, coils of smoke were rising, white and grey smoke, smoke as black as jet. The survivors occupied the heights beyond the beach, where camps were dug into the cliff slopes, their pits covered with plastic sheeting or torn tarpaulins pulled from the beach wreckage. Parties scavenged the beach, piling up their gathered treasures at its head. The bodies, stripped of their clothing that might be worn again when dried, were pushed back into the water, hoping that the current would bear them away, although often it simply brought them back. Seabirds squawked over the bodies, zooming, and pecking in flurries of white wings. Survivors tried to scare them away, but they came back as soon as the waving arms and flying stones had ceased. The scent of corruption filled the air, swept away by a keen wind, but then creeping back to taint the nostrils, particularly at night.

Boats began to appear offshore. Were these the vessels of SupaPodia inspecting the damage? If so, no parties were sent ashore. No official aid came. Organisation, if any, was in the hands of the survivors. And here, Tina and Julian began to take charge, at first within their own area closest to the beach front, but then further along the coast, until in time every survivor of the SupaPod who had taken refuge on the shore had heard of them, and came to them for help. Aid too from the inland OuterWorlders was brought in and distributed by them. They were helped by many volunteers, men and women, some ex-Lilacs, others Podders who still retained the native ability for self-help, despite the many years of SupaPodia dependency.

The great relief to Julian – and he had only recalled this additional horror when thinking back on what Stanley had once told him: he wondered how many others knew of it and feared it too – was that the implanted chip within each survivor, including Tina, would begin to act against them, poisoning their bodies, bringing their lives to an end in agony. That, at least, was what Stanley had decreed, that time spent out of the SupaPod would be the cause of such a death.

Yet, as the days went by, there was no evidence of this at all – not even of the buzzings and screamings in the head to be expected from a chip's displaced Guidance function, as poor Sandra had experienced and feared would get worse, making her do what she did for him. It was possible, therefore, that the total destruction of the control system of the SupaPod had served to wipe clean each individual chip, de-activating the whole ghastly business, together with all the other evils of SupaPodia connected with it. As Julian had already suspected, it was likely as well that Stanley, and other SupaPod Commanders, had exaggerated these matters simply to create a climate of fear.

A big help, and a joy for Julian in particular, was the sudden appearance one day of the one-armed Boadicea and Jill Bradwell, whom he had last heard of in the Hayling Correction Camp, where he had thought them lost. They came ashore in a small rowing boat, having been dropped off further out to sea by a larger vessel.

Their story made mournful listening. Hayling Island had been flooded by the same Channel surge as had destroyed the Ramsgate SupaPod. Most of the Island had been inundated and cut off entirely from the mainland. Thousands had drowned. Boadicea and Bradwell had only survived, together with a handful of others, by the lucky chance of having been ordered for duties at Lady Lascelles' mansion that day, and climbing its tower. Much of the building had been washed away around them, but marvellously the tower had stood. They had held out there for days with little food and water until eventually rescued by an OuterWorld fishing boat.

There was no organisation of survival at all at Hayling, but they had heard rumours of such organisation further along the coast. Not wishing to be taken out to sea to some other uncertain destination, they had asked to be put onto the beach, where they could see fires burning and shelters built, to see if they could help. Jill Bradwell's military experience, in particular in the organisation of work parties for food and other supplies, was to prove invaluable. Both were overjoyed to find Julian present, and to learn of the work Tina was doing. So their groups now had leaders, both spiritual and temporal, and, once their survival was assured, the great work of recovery and rebuilding began.

At the head of the beach, upon which the sea was gradually encroaching once more, a great cross, made of salvaged timbers, was erected, and around this cross each day hundreds of people from the new communities prayed. Julian came here often with Tina and they would kneel beside the cross together. Julian prayed in particular for Peter and Sandra, without whose sacrifices he could not have lived to begin this present work of renewal.

Much later, within our own memories, the cross was still standing, although it had twice been taken down and re-erected further inland, away from the advancing sea. As the chronicler of the Augustine Abbey at Canterbury set down in his account of those times –

'The Lord stretched out his hand and stilled the tempest, and the people found the evil they had dwelt within had passed, and they learnt once more how to live of the fullness of the earth and share their blessing, giving greeting to each other and thanking God for their deliverance from Satan.'

'St. Christine and St. Julian saw God's purpose and brought His truth to the people so that they understood. And they set up His Cross on the shore of their deliverance and founded His church again, where it had long been neglected, and the people had great joy in the sight of the Lord. And all were fed and clothed and went forth offering up their praise.'

* * *

High Director, Lady Pamela Lascelles, sat alone in her office on the top floor of the glass-plated SupaPodia Tower, which rose in the hot sunlight like a diamond spire. Far below, she could see the wrinkled ocean stretching away to the far horizon, green and blue and pooled with gold; so beautiful it was, such distances to travel, such promises – which would never be hers now, on account of what the sea had done. The Tower was rooted in the chaos the sea had created; still the water ran in the streets below, the rising floods had covered the city, and the people – her people – had drowned; thousands of them, tens of thousands, hundreds of thousands, millions perhaps, not just here but all over the globe, everywhere that SupaPodia had ruled.

The cause was God's – she saw that now: there was indeed a greater force than SupaPodia, and she had not heeded the warnings, so then she must share the fault with God. Certainly, they all blamed her more than God, the Eliti most of all; out of every quarter of SupaPodia, their complaints had come: why had they not been warned? Many had lost their lands and their fine houses. Some had lost everything. She too. She had learnt her Hayling mansion and all its lands had gone, and her land also by the Corcovado in Rio and at Sydney Harbour, and the flat lands of Suffolk where she had loved to ride – all under the sea now; great Neptune had prevailed, or had it been by the power of that most persistent God of Israel?

She did not know. She was very tired.

She did not see him at first. He was just a shadow deep within the sun's rays. Then he moved forward and she knew he was there.

"Is it time?"

"For you, yes," said the man in black.

"Oh Beast, I would like to live yet."

"Lady you have had your fill of vice."

"But I have loved too."

The Beast laughed. "What is love? You'll be asking me next, 'What is truth?'"

He became impatient. "Let us get this done now," he said.

Taking the diamond sun in his hand, he scored across the glass of the window and took out a great pane, which he leant against the High Director's desk.

"There you are. There is a small ledge outside where you can have a few moments to say goodbye."

"And you. What will you do?"

"I have a journey to make to the far side of the world, where they still think they can do without me."

"Beast, don't leave me."

"Lady, I shall be with you until the end."

And so she jumped and the Beast fell with her, down, down to the streets below that shimmered with water, and she is falling still.

But the Beast swooped into a cushion of black night, out of which we may watch for him – perhaps very soon.

For each age must be fulfilled and the old struggles re-fought.

And the cleverer we think we are, the more we forget.

Time over time,

And time again.